To the Bone

Robert S Ely

DEDICATION

To my beloved sons
John and Chris

With thanks to my friends:
Stephen, Jenny, Pat and Lyn

Dr Peter Harvey
Brisbane

Contents

To His Coy Mistress
By
Andrew Marvell
1621-1678

Had we but world enough and time,
This coyness, lady, were no crime.
We would sit down, and think which way
To walk, and pass our long love's day.
Thou by the Indian Ganges' side
Shouldst rubies find; I by the tide
Of Humber would complain. I would
Love you ten years before the flood,
And you should, if you please, refuse
Till the conversion of the Jews.

My vegetable love should grow
Vaster than empires and more slow;
An hundred years should go to praise
Thine eyes, and on thy forehead gaze;
Two hundred to adore each breast,
But thirty thousand to the rest;
An age at least to every part,
And the last age should show your heart.

For, lady, you deserve this state,
Nor would I love at lower rate.
But at my back I always hear
Time's wingèd chariot hurrying near;
And yonder all before us lie
Deserts of vast eternity.

Thy beauty shall no more be found;
Nor, in thy marble vault, shall sound
My echoing song; then worms shall try
That long-preserved virginity,
And your quaint honour turn to dust,
And into ashes all my lust;
The grave's a fine and private place,
But none, I think, do there embrace.

Now therefore, while the youthful hue
Sits on thy skin like morning dew,
And while thy willing soul transpires
At every pore with instant fires,
Now let us sport us while we may,
And now, like amorous birds of prey,
Rather at once our time devour
Than languish in his slow-chapped power.

Let us roll all our strength and all
Our sweetness up into one ball,
And tear our pleasures with rough strife
Through the iron gates of life:
Thus, though we cannot make our sun
Stand still, yet we will make him run.

1

Bird of Prey

Dark.

Night

Landing...

The wheels thumped the cracked and frosted concrete with an alarming crash before bouncing back into the crystal air and punching down once more, to the sudden roar of reverse thrust. The pilot struggled to keep the Boeing from twisting and turning on the short, partially cleared, runway, as the tyres wrestled to grip the slippery slabs. In the under-wing landing lights, Fisher could see the heavy snow, like so many frozen comets or cotton balls rushing past the wings.

In the distance, he could just make out a few blue tungsten arc lights. The dark, menacing building floated on an island of ice, like a gulag asleep with itself, at once a blended and yet stranger shed. It was hard enough for Fisher to accept that this decrepit tin structure with a plume of steam rising like a geyser was the international arrivals terminal at Pulkova, and recipient of the prestigious *Order of the October Revolution*.

But that soviet award was given in December 1971.

That was Leningrad.

Now, twenty years later, in December 1991, everything had changed. Nobody cared. Even the once great city, the Vienna of the North, the cradle of the Great Bolshevik Revolution, had turned its back to the biting wind of change and with it, its name, back to the old order: St Petersburg.

What's in a name? Fisher asked himself, as the plane came to a grinding, sliding stop as close to the hangar building as it dare go. He hated airports anyway. The less time he spent in one, the better. In truth, he hated crowds. But, on this flight there was no need for such concerns.

The British Airways 737 from Manchester carried only eight people; and five of those were flight and cabin crew. Apart from Fisher, two well-soused smoked soviet shrimps: over laden with, scotch, duty free cigarettes, denims, toilet rolls and plugs for their kitchen sinks. Together with Fisher, they made up the small passenger list. As the crew donned heavy navy blue overcoats and black leather gloves, the three passengers clustered with them, at the still closed exit door, waiting for a set of steps to be positioned.

"It's minus twenty-six out there!" announced one of crew; without the need of a public address system; and, in any case, only Fisher understood English, and to the other two passengers, with the hastily cocked fur hats, minus twenty-six was mild. The crew member was already shivering in her nervous anticipation of what lay outside, and stomping her feet.

"Where are you staying?" queried Fisher, trying, unusually for him, to make some polite small talk.

"Oh…*we're* not getting off! *We're* flying straight back out. We're not allowed to stop here," she said, as if Fisher should know. "It's far too dangerous out there! You must be crazy! How long are you here for?"

"I'm not quite sure…perhaps a few days…a week… maybe more. It could be worse!"

It could be worse! What was he thinking? Ordinarily, he was a man who kept himself to himself, and who was frugal with platitudes. Those trite, meaningless, or prosaic statements, generally directed at quelling social, emotional, or cognitive unease. He hated sayings like: *everything happens for a reason...* to which he would think: *including suffering and early death?* Or, *I hear what you're saying.* He despised people who filled the silence with vacuous nonsense. So, why was he blathering now?

"Where *are* you staying?" she continued, having heard what he said. He, meanwhile, momentarily seduced by her ice blue eyes and flattered by the attention, replied with a smile.

"The Moskva Hotel."

"Really? Why?"

"Why?" he queried, dropping the smile. It had sounded impressive enough. What did she know that he didn't?

There was a desperate knock on the door, as if someone was tring to get in, and then it was opened with a rubber slurp, as the hermetic seals slipped their warm sides to let in a rush of air that cut through the legs like a frozen Cossack sabre.

Places had smells.

Barbados, he recalled, was scented with coconut juice and Aloe Vera. In Malta it was citrus mingled with the fumes of scooters and mopeds. In Thailand, where he had honeymooned, the air was perfumed with papaya and lime juice, mixed with raw sewage and shrimp paste. All these places, and more, Fisher had been with his Jane. His first wife...although Fisher preferred the term, *trial partner*, had been averse to travel: cigarette smoke made her vomit; large objects terrified her; and confined spaces made her psychotic. So, they never left home.

Here, the air had an stale industrial stench, as if hot iron bars had been plunged into cold oil. Hotel rooms were notoriously small, he knew that; monuments were ginormous and cigarette smoke was more common than oxygen. His trial partner would have hated it, whereas Jane would have already decided not to get off the plane.

"Well…good luck!" she said, as Fisher stepped onto the top of the icy steps, that wobbled like a nervous plank; his face nipped by the wind. *What was it that was so bad about his hotel?* He wondered. After all, it was the largest hotel in the world. What could possibly be wrong with that?

Good luck…. he repeated to himself, as her wishes echoed into the empty night air and were swallowed by the wind. It was the sort that sucked the air from your lungs and then caught on the back of your throat as you gasped for breath.

Fisher had heard rumours of the chaos in the city; but, little hard news had been coming out through the wall of pride. The real wall had gone, but the ideological one remained.

The *perestroika* reforms had started the process leading to the dismantling of the Soviet-era command economy and its replacement with a vibrant, if more Darwinian, market economy. However, the transition arguably exacerbated already existing social and economic tensions within the crumbling Soviet Union, and no doubt helped to further nationalist tendencies among the constituent republics, as well as social fragmentation. Fisher was thinking too much and wasn't sure what to expect; with the news being so scant and unreliable. Media attention, instead, was focussed on *Desert Storm,* the start of the operation to liberate Kuwait from the Iraqi invaders. Nobody cared about the old, cold, enemy.

The economic chaos, Fisher knew, had helped both to empower organised crime and allow businessmen, with the right connections, to rapidly amass great personal fortunes, as Russia's new oligarchs. Central Committee members, secretaries of regional committees and generals were rapidly becoming multi-millionaires. Meanwhile, the people starved; and the very fabric of society was breaking down just as the buildings did, crumbling with neglect.

The wheel had come full circle.

The revolution was complete.

This was particularly evident from the welcome Fisher received when entering the colourless immigration hall, which was every shade of grim, grimy, grey. It might have once been used for processing captured Germans after the *Siege of Leningrad* in 1942. Nothing, it seemed, had changed since then.

An elevated man, in a filthy glass booth, examined Fisher's passport under a flickering fluorescent tube that buzzed and clicked. His reddened, crossed eyes, struggled to focus a bit further than the end of his nose, as his unshaven top lip perspired with alcohol. Fisher presumed that breathing fumes of vodka onto the pages helped the unkempt man check for invisible ink, and verify the authenticity of the document and the accompanying visa, which he poised to thump with a rubber stamp.

"What is your business?" he snarled, looking in two directions at once. Fisher instinctively looked around to see if he was gazing at somebody else.

"I'm here at the invitation of...."

"What is your business?" growling louder as he replaced the stamp and reached for the telephone.

"Tourism."

However incredible that might be, it was a lot simpler than explaining the truth to an inebriate half-wit with a penchant for calling Internal Security at the first sign of abnormality.

Fisher took his bruised passport into the luggage retrieval area.

Tourism? Really? Was that his best suggestion? Who in their right mind would come here for a holiday? Maybe Cubans? He supposed.

In the spirit of *glasnost*, and in an effort to introduce the notion of customer service, a hole had been freshly knocked through a concrete wall, into which, a small luggage carousel snaked its way and disappeared into the night. There was a corresponding hole a little further down to allow the infinite loop to be completed, except it wasn't moving.

A horizontal blast of freezing air was coming through both holes, in a seeming physical impossibility.

But no luggage.

Given the number of people hanging around from earlier internal flights, it seemed fair to assume that the pervading sense of hopelessness was governed by entropy, poor probability and the Law of Diminishing Returns. But, the weary soviets had grown accustomed to the threadbare fabric of society, unravelling before their eyes.

The luggage carousel remained frozen for almost an hour, whilst Fisher hopped from foot to foot and pondered the potential consequences of telling lies to a government official about the purpose of his visit, and the prospect of spending the rest of the night in an old cold aircraft hangar. But, by now, a mob of angry Russians, from earlier and subsequent domestic flights were threatening counter-revolution.

Finally, a generator coughed plegmatically and the carousel lurched into life, to a cheer from the triumphant crowd, praising the free market, democracy and the global supremacy of Soviet engineering. After all, they had invented the luggage conveyor....hadn't they? So the shabby sign claimed, although Fisher knew it to be a French company called, *Teleflex*.

Then it stopped.

Then it started again.

Then it belched, and stopped.

Followed by a short announcement, first in Russian, then, presumably for Fisher's exclusive benefit, in English:

"Comrades, in October, on the anniversary of the glorious revolution, the Central Committee Plenum instructed the Congress of People's Deputies to replace pre-perestroika machinery with new western-style state-of-the-market product, in order to improve service and customer satisfaction. This luggage carousel is to be decommissioned. We apologise for any inconvenience."

With that, the first item of luggage was tossed, without care or prejudice, through the hole in the wall. The suitcase, distinctive in its steel shell, belonged to Fisher, and clunked onto the stone floor, before sliding towards him. Had somebody been standing in the way, they might now be in need of urgent medical attention. Inevitably, there were no luggage trolleys, so it was very much a matter of dragging the case through a small doorway covered by a thick sheet of yellow-aged plastic cut into vertical strips. Presumably to keep the draft out...or in. It was difficult to say.

Although Fisher had been warned by a colleague, that the airport terminal had been closed for *renovations*, and temporarily relocated to an old aircraft hangar, he was, nevertheless surprised by the lack of finesse in the temporary arrangements. In the outer lobby, the improvised Arrival Hall, there was a single unadorned light bulb dancing on the end of a frayed wire, lighting a yellow sea of pale miserable faces randomly poking out from a grey, moth-eaten motley collection of coats and fur hats, all jostling and pushing to be seen, as they cried out in Russian. Some held bits of corrugated cardboard on which the name of their passenger was variously written in Latin or Cyrillic script.

There was much shouting and movement in the scrum, above which, a cumuli nimbus of cigarette smoke was suspended in toxic animation.

Fisher immediately noticed two separate people at almost opposite ends of the arc of faces, holding damp cardboard signs with his name on. On the right, a stocky, muscular looking man, with a tatty coat, and a fur hat suffering from the mange, he gestured to Fisher to come forward:

"Come, come, my friend…this way…quickly!"

Fisher was going nowhere quickly, not least to a stranger with a hat of many winters; and, in any case, weighed down, as he was, by his metallic suitcase, that might as well be the ball and chain of rationalism attached to his ankle.

By contrast, the smarter looking, taller man, on the left, had let his card fall to the floor. A lofty, wiry looking man, in a uniform of some sort; dark and somewhat menacing. *Never judge a man by his hat*, thought Fisher. And yet, he couldn't help but notice his neat bonnet of black fur and the well-groomed salt and peppered head it protected. From the corner of his mouth, dangled a cheap cigarette, a *Prima*, Fisher thought. It glowed in the poor light, as he drew the pungent smoke into his lungs and let it cloud out of his nostrils. Whether it was the toxic fog rolling up his face, or his obvious disdain, was difficult to tell; but Fisher felt the narrowing pale eyes burning into the side of his skull, as he pushed on through the crowd. All their gaunt looking eyes were focussed on the exit behind him as they waited eagerly for whomever might follow Fisher.

"Come, come…." said the eager man, grabbing Fisher's heavy case.

Fisher hesitated to let go. Perhaps he had not chosen wisely? Compared to the man with the *Prima*, this man looked like a thief. But who should he trust? The man that looked like an unsuccessful robber; or the more competent one?

"My name is Vasyli Kulnikov," he said.

"Oh yes, Vasyli…. I wasn't expecting anyone to be at the airport."

"Dr Constable…Mark…your friend…my friend…he said you would be here."

The walk and talk had taken them to the exit door.

"This is my driver, Anton."

"Hello, Anton!" offered Fisher holding out his cold hand.

Nothing; not even a grunt. Clearly, Anton didn't want to be here; or, he was a man of great verbal efficiency.

A very small stick of a person with a flat woollen cap and an ill-fitting overcoat, he perched on the compacted snow, like an unwanted traffic cone, next to an old, battered, Volga GAZ 21. It was a three-tone model: white and brown rust from the mid-line up; and pistachio and rust from the line down. It was probably an old East German police car. Also very popular with the KGB in its day. It was the sort of car that if it pulled outside your home at four in the morning, your neighbours could be sure that this was the last time they might see you.

Anton struggled, not only to lift the case, but to figure out a way of squeezing it into the boot. He tried various configurations, only to give in to a worn piece of string from his pocket, to tie the lid to the rear bumper.

Or possibly, to prevent the bumper from falling off? It was difficult to tell.

Vasyli continued:

"I will sit in the rear, you can ride in the front with Anton."

As Fisher complied, he caught sight of the tall man with the *Prima* glowing as it lit up his face, just a short distance away. His back to the wind, with the snow swirling over his shoulders, observing their every move, like some great bird of prey…waiting…watching. There was, already, no escaping the powerful feeling of wariness; the feeling of being watched. But Fisher had been expecting this, together with the silences, the changes of subject, the oblique ways in which people might convey information. All that was to come. But so soon?

"There's no seatbelt!" Fisher, said, aware as always, that his grasp of the obvious, was at times, monumental.

"Seatbelt?" echoed Vasyli, as he proceeded to say something to Anton in Russian. They both laughed.

"We Russians like our rivers. They go on forever. There is little else in the landscape; and so we name things after them; like a car or a sneaky radar system. This is a Volga," explained Vasyli, "…which has an engine that, if we are lucky, produces ninety-five horses. Most of them are, these days…how would you say?… lame. If we are heading for a brick wall, you will have time to get out and walk away and light a cigarette. And, this is the Deluxe model; built like Russian tank. It has three gears and a heater that can melt lead."

Before attempting to start the old KGB clanger, Anton, produced a tatty cigarette packet from his overcoat pocket and placed a cardboard tube in his little grubby mouth. Perhaps it was a starting ritual? His thin lips grasping it tightly, as if to steel himself for what was to come. Fisher recognised it immediately, as an unfiltered, or, as the Russians call it, a *papirosa* cigarette. Quite different from the usual type; composed of a hollow tube extended by a thin cigarette paper filled with strong tobacco. The cardboard tube plays the role of a disposable cigarette holder. While smoking, the hollow part of the tube is usually compressed to make two separate perpendicular flat surfaces, for the sake of convenience.

Fisher, was something of an expert on cigarettes, although he had never smoked one himself. He had acquired his specialist knowledge through one of his many childhood obsessions: collecting cigarette packets. This, he knew to be a *Belomorkanal* brand, made by the *Uritsky Tobacco Factory* in Leningrad since 1932. The brand was named after, not a river, but a canal, built between the White Sea and the Baltic.

It seemed odd, even to Fisher, that a cigarette should be named after a canal. But then, he supposed to himself, that a Manchester canal, known as the *Bridgewater* might be a good brand-name for something, if not a cigarette.

As the engine turned and spluttered into life, Fisher knew there was little point in attempting to open the filthy window. Out there it was freezing, and the smoke from the engine was thicker than the smoke from the *papirosa*.

Anton moved his hands from side-to side as if he was playing at driving a car rather than actually steering it. For a moment, Fisher wondered if he was in a film with an actor who had never driven a car in his life.; or at the very least, that they were being followed. Why else would Anton be driving like a lunatic, albeit in a slow car? And, looking intently in the heavily tarnished rear view mirror, which offered a better prospect than looking forward through a filthy windreen with a single tired wiper. The other, a rubberless edition, constantly provided the driver with an outline of the curvature of the earth and an audible warning screech indicating imminent death.

Cornering was a particular thrill, as Anton practised the art of driving the car sideways as it skimmed over the ice-compacted roads.

"Does he always drive like this?" queried Fisher, nervously.

"Oh no…I told him to take it easy, so as not to alarm you, unnecessarily. As you can see, the roads and sidewalks are not cleared of snow anymore. In the old days, an army of workers would sweep the snow off the ground, all night if necessary, before it had a chance to stick. These days, nobody gives a kopeck, nobody gets paid, so nobody bothers. "

"Nobody gets paid?"

"No…not me…not Anton…nobody….Yeltsin maybe?"

The streets were largely deserted, save for a few drunks wandering here and there; and an emaciated dog or two. A make-shift fire in a brazier glowed on the corner of one street; and on another, a woman was sitting on the pavement as the snow gathered on her hat. The street lighting was blunt, to say the least. It produced vertical cones of harsh white light, creating shadow and plenty of doubt in between.

Anton grunted and Vasyli translated:

"We have arrived at your hotel. Are you sure you want to stay here, at the Hotel Moskva?"

"Why would I not want to stay here?"

"Well…it's a little…how would you say?.. wild."

"Wild!"

"You can stay at my place if you prefer? I can call Lyudmila and ask her to move Pasha out of his bed."

"Pasha?"

"Her baby, the giant poodle, Pasha."

"I'll be fine here…but thank you."

"Anton and I will accompany you to your room," Vasyli insisted, as Anton opened the door of the Volga to a blast of cold arctic air that caught on the back of Fisher's throat.

"Really, there's no…."

"We insist."

Anton looked at the string, now frozen stiff, holding the boot lid to the rusted bumper. Producing what looked like a soviet standard issue throat cutting pocket knife, he plied open the blade, and cut the tight string with the lightest touch, flicking the blade and knife back into his pocket with considerable dexterity.

"Anton was in the air force…a *spets unit*…that knife is his prized possession…after the Volga, of course….and then there is his wife. She comes third… or fourth, depending on whether you include his cap."

As Fisher turned to follow the struggling Anton, shuffling along the ice, dragging the heavy case behind him, gouging tramlines in the compacted snow, he noticed the tall dark man again. Standing a little distance away, in the shadows. Somehow, he had arrived before Anton. Somehow, he knew where they were heading. If, indeed, it was the same man? It was too dark, and there was too much snow blowing about to see his face clearly. But, if not him, why would anyone just be standing there?

Vasyli had stopped at the hotel entrance, to speak to a Soviet Soldier in a grey uniform; he was sporting a Kalashnikov. Fisher watched as Vasyli handed him something, and the grey soldier stepped aside.

"There are many entrances to this hotel, my friend," Vasyli said, under his steaming breath. "Each is controlled by a different criminal gang. They pay these soldiers to keep guard….over their assets."

Whatever else Vasyli was saying, was lost, as he disappeared into the revolving doors of the vast Moskva.

Fisher was greeted by a damp dog smell and a black and white chequered floor, wet and filthy from so many slushed boots, leading to a long wooden desk, more like a bar, partially hidden by a crowd of shouting Russians trying to check in or out or complain about something. In the old order, Russians were renowned for their patient queuing. They queued in shops to buy anything… were given a ticket to join a queue to pay, only to receive a ticket as proof of payment, before queuing at the collection point for the selected goods. Fisher wondered if some of the women hanging around offered a similar system for their illicit services.

Perhaps so; any sense of queuing was gone; now, it was everyone for themselves.

On the right, was a set of frosted glass doors leading to a restaurant or bar, Fisher couldn't quite make it out, in the dim interior lights. Except it was as crowded and noisy and roudy as a wild west Weaverville saloon during the Gold Rush of 1848. Fisher half-expected a discarded unconscious body to be tossed through the glass to land at his feet.

Vasyli, simply pushed his way to the front the desk, and handed something to the harassed man behind the desk and came away with a room key. He then called to a thin man in worn blue overalls, something in Russian, and pointed to the suitcase.

"We'll take the stairs!" insisted Vasyli, "…the lifts are an unnecessary risk."

Although the Moskva was a sprawling semi-circular concrete block, it was, at least not a sky scraper.

Vasyli led the way to the sixth floor, leaving the luggage engineer in the overalls to drag the case up each step with a heavy clunk that echoed in the stairwell. Despite his sense of foreboding, Fisher had little choice but to stay at the Moskva. This had been arranged for him; this, is where he would be contacted in due course.

The corridor was very poorly lit and had a sour smell. It stank of nicotine and stale beer, with a punguent whiff of urine. It followed the curve of the building with a dark brown carpet, adorned with a collection of questionable stains. Fisher thought it to be quite menacing; it gave him the creeps. Not least, he could only see a few yards in front and a few yards behind, due to the curvature of the walls. It was impossible, therefore, to see if anyone was waiting to pounce, or if anyone was following. Except, of course, for the distant clunk, clunk of the hapless man in the stairwell.

"Here we are! *Home Sweet Home!*" exclaimed Vasyli, with an ironic tone, as he prised open the thin brown door. "It is, without doubt, a palace of soviet hospitality."

And, indeed it was….even Vasyli seemed stunned by the austerity.

It seemed crowded, with the three of them standing there. The brown carpet; the grey concrete walls, punctuated by a small square window caked in frozen mud. A table, a phone, a narrow single bed, with what looked like a lumpy horse-hair mattress; and a grey unwelcoming pillow. There was, at least a toilet; but no paper; a small sink, but no plug; and a shower with no shower head, just a pipe protruding from the wall in anticipation of one. It dripped, mercilessly, onto the cracked orange tiles of the mouldy foot tray.

Vasyli began to mouth something, whilst pointing at the phone. He seemed to be performing a charade about a deaf and dumb *Spy Who Came in from the Cold*. Fisher took it to mean…never use the phone…someone is listening.

"There are no more dezhurnavas."

"No more what?" Queried Fisher.

"Stationed at a desk on each floor of a hotel, the dezhurnaya, who was always female, kept an eye on guests, maintained order and was the person you had to speak to get soap, toilet paper, a bath plug, or book an international call. Somehow, she was always icy to begin with and then cracked to show an unexpected warmth that made you wonder what this whole Cold War was all about, anyway."

Clearly, Vasyli was deliberately filling a suspicious silence with idle chatter.

"Let's go to the Rouble Bar!" he said, somewhat animated.

"Rouble Bar?" queried Fisher.

"Yes, there is a Rouble Bar and a Dollar Bar. The Dollar Bar, downstairs, takes dollars, and has lots to offer, but is three or four times as expensive as the Rouble Bar. By tomorrow it could be five or six!"

"So, let me guess..." added Fisher, "...the Rouble bar takes roubles, has nothing much to offer, but is cheap."

Vasyli grinned, "precisely!"

Fisher opened the door to find the man in the blue overalls panting in the doorway, with beads of cold sweat decorating his forehead. Anton dragged the case into the room, as Fisher opened his wallet for a tip. Lacking anything smaller, he gave the man a ten-dollar bill for his efforts. The man looked at it for a moment; and then raised his watery eyes, but said nothing.

"Spacibo! Thank you," Fisher said, as he, followed Vasyli and Anton back to the stairwell.

As he climbed one more flight of stairs, Vasyli said, "You do realise, my foriegn friend, that you have just given that man the equivalent of three month's pay? Except, of course, that in three months his pay will be worth even less, as we are in the grip of hyper-inflation."

"Ah..." retorted Fisher, "it's all that I had."

"It's now everything he has!"

Vasyli continued his excited babble:

"Which soccer team do you support?"

"I don't, really...but, when I was a boy, my father used to take me to see Manchester United."

"Yay!" cried Vasyli. Even Anton, tried, but failed, to smile. "It is my dream…" he continued, "…to see United play at Old Trafford. Perhaps one day, we can do this together?"

"Perhaps…one day."

"Last season, in October, all eleven United players and ten Arsenal players were involved in a brawl in the First Division clash at Old Trafford. Arsenal won but United were docked a league point for this, while Arsenal, who, by this stage, were the biggest threat to leaders Liverpool in the title race were docked two points and both clubs were fined fifty-thousand pounds. You were there, to see this?"

"Well, no… the last time I was at a match was in 1967."

Vasyli seemed confused. Obviously, he was thinking that if you live in Manchester, why would you not go to Old Trafford to every match?

"Sixty-seven? You were there? George Best, Bobby Charlton, Denis Law?"

"Yes." Replied Fisher as they entered the bar.

"These men are the gods of our time. This is the bar where they also serve a sort of breakfast."

"A sort of breakfast?"

"Pasha and I have porridge for breakfast.. it's not too late to change your mind."

"I'll manage, thanks."

The aforementioned Rouble Bar was somewhat basic. It looked more like an old school dining than a bar. A few plastic topped tables and wooden chairs overseen by a longer trestle-table adorned with bottles of beer and a platter of sliced sausage meat, of undoubted questionable origins. *Tomorrow Never Knows* by The Beatles was struggling to escape from a corner of the room.

"Zhigulyovskoe?" asked Vasyli.

"Is that the beer or the sausage?"

"The beer, of course! Nobody knows the name of the sausage! But, they go hand in hand. Come, sit...Anton will bring the beer."

Vasyli took the opportunity, alone with Fisher, to slide a small scrap of cigarette paper, pressed to the table with one finger, over towards Fisher. He looked around, conspiratorially.

"Take it....and eat it," he said, leaning forward as if something heavy was on top of his head. "This is my private phone number. Use only in an emergency. Do not, under any circumstances give it to anybody. Do you understand?"

Fisher nodded, and took the paper. He pretended to memorise it.

"Eat, please!"

Clearly, Vasyli was quite serious.

It tasted of tobacco.

This was all rather strange and unexpected. Why was he in danger? What emergency might he find himself in? Who, exactly, was Vasyli? And, more significantly perhaps, who was the tall man in the dark uniformed coat and black fur hat, that had been lurking outside?

"How do you know our mutual friend, Dr Constable?" asked Vasyli, tentatively.

"We work in the same university," explained Fisher. "He works in the International Office, these days, building partnerships with other universities and recruiting students from overseas."

"Overseas? What is... overseas?"

"Oh... other countries. The UK is an island, surrounded by seas. So, we say, *overseas*."

"And you?" continued Vasyli, "You are a Professor? Yes? You seem too young to be a Professor. Here they are always old men."

"Well, yes...maybe."

"I see. And you are a Professor of... what?"

"Oh…. a few different things…. What about you Vasyli? What do you do?"

"I am a nuclear physicist."

It was a conversation stopper, as Fisher was somewhat taken aback. What was he doing in a Rouble Bar with a nuclear scientist of the collapsing Soviet Union?

Anton came over, balancing three large brown bottles of Zhigulyovskoe, with three small plates of lurid pink sausage meat perched, one on each bottle. Carefully sliding the bottles on the table, he removed the plates to each place. Behind him, Fisher could see the room filling up with people. All of them men; all of them smoking heavily pungent cigarettes.

Instead of sitting down, Anton returned to the top table to collect three small glasses and a bottle of vodka. The lethal drink was now so cheap due to over production, that consumption had quadrupled in less than a year. Russians were, literally, drinking themselves to death.

Fisher's eyes darted about the room, returning to meet Vasyli's just enough to convince Vasyli that he had his full attention. But, Fisher had an unusual skill: he could listen to a conversation, whilst observing a room and write his next academic paper in his head, all at the same time. On a table by the door, he noted a man sitting alone. Nose rosy, face unshaven, a bottle of vodka firmly grasped in his hands. By his side, he had, a half-empty jar of pickles and a loaf of rye bread to help the devilish liquid go down. The man was singing, quite happily, from alcohol-induced jubilation and appeared to be the disc jockey. His world may not be perfect, but the inebriation makes it seem that way, for a while, at least.

So too, the imperfect music distorted by the speaker from a portable record player, as the worn-out needle scratched along the black vinyl of *The Beatles: Revolver*, blasting out a distortion of *Good Day Sunshine*.

It all seemed surreal, as Vasyli continued to expand on his scientific credentials, as if this was some kind of job interview. Was there some particular reason why he should be trying to impress Fisher?

As Anton returned, Vasyli quickly changed the subject, as if he had been answering a question, or in mid-conversation:

"I returned here from Novosibirsk, just last year, to set up my Karate School. There isn't much call for a man with my background these days. We all have to...*improvise*...as you might say. Here is my business card."

Vasyli produced a small white card with no contact details, and with a blue silhouette of a man that looked like he had just cocked his leg to pee on a lamppost.

"What I found in Leningrad was a truly sad and poor place. I remember arriving and seeing long bread lines stretching around the corner and people starving to death on Nevsky Prospect, I was trying to check into the Moskva Hotel where the front desk attendants were unwilling to help unless you gave them something to eat."

"It's hard to believe that people were really starving."

"Yes...starving. The children are thin, there ribs sticking out. My wife taught ballet at the Palace of Creativity to the children of the soviet elite. She said that some were so weak, they could barely stand. Human interaction at its core was dysfunctional. Every male who approached me, did so in order to try to mug me; and every female... how do you say?... *proposed* herself as a prostitute. Is that how you say it? Proposed?"

"Propositioned."

"Every woman...*propositioned*...herself to offer a wide range of satisfactions for a few dollars. I also vividly remember an old man waiting to cross the street in the pouring rain, keeling over from a heart attack, only to see people come out from every corner, not to help, but to steal everything he had and leave him to die. I remember being followed by the security services, although at that time, maybe it wasn't the KGB, or maybe it was. In fact, nothing was what it seemed, and everyone appeared resigned to the fact that there was some fool in Moscow, somehow in control, or maybe he wasn't."

"За здоровье!" called Anton, raising his bottle in one hand and a disk of rubbery meat in the other.

"Za ta-jó da-ró-ye!" echoed Fisher, as if he knew what he was saying.

"That means you fancy his dead grandmother!" said Vasyli, laughing.

For a moment, Fisher thought he had indeed said something wrong, as a seeming altercation developed at a nearby table. But, it was all in Russian... which, to the foreign ear, always sounds aggressive. In fact, they could have been exchanging their mothers' favourite recipes for beetroot soup. Until one stood up, picked up a chair and proceeded to beat the other over the head with it.

Vasyli and Anton seemed unmoved and unconcerned, as a third man began to punch the man left holding what was left of the chair. A table was tipped over and a broken bottle was picked up by the chair wielding man.

Suddenly, all was quiet and still. A man lay unconscious and bleeding on the floor.

"Think..." said Vasyli sincerely, "...think how much better off this country would be, if people like us were running it! Don't *they* see how they're taking us to the brink of ruin and collapse? And these criminals...these violent gangs."

"How do you know these men are criminals, Vasyli? Are they not just drunks, fighting in a bar?"

"There are signs and symbols, gestures. In time, you will learn to read them. It could save your life."

"Really? Signs?"

"Yes. What just happened started with an unspoken gesture by one man to the other… a flick of the finger under the jaw. Like so…"

Vasyli illustrated, by brushing the nail of his index finger off centre up the neck, as if brushing away a pesky fly.

"The other man responded with the same sign. And, they both took their seats, eyeball to eyeball, nose to nose, to talk…as you English might say…as *gentlemen*. Unfortunately, that last part, seemed to have got lost in the gesture."

"And?" said Fisher, "What does this mean?" copying the flick.

"Once, the story goes, there was a drunken carpenter, or maybe shipbuilder. In any case, he somehow rendered a service for Peter the Great…. nobody can remember what the service was…but, no matter. Peter was so grateful that he granted the man a certificate of entitlement to free vodka for life, anywhere in the empire. Such a certificate can but easily be lost on a drunken spree, and so soon enough the tsar, presumably on a tea-break from his wars of conquest, or torturing and murdering his own family, replaced the carpenter's coupon. After a few more copies were lost, Peter finally had his seal tattooed directly onto the carpenter's neck. From then on, the man could simply enter a tavern, tap at his neck, and be served. And so, to this day Russians…and those who drink with Russians… tap their necks to indicate that they are drunk, or someone else is drunk, or that drinking is about to happen; or, more importantly, that two criminals from opposing gangs, would like to sit down and talk, unarmed."

Fisher started to understand just how much danger he was in.

Could he be attacked just for looking at someone in the wrong way? Stabbed or gored with a broken bottle for a careless word?

Clearly, he was immersed in a violent world, where tempers were frayed and fuses were short; people were hungry and others were greedy; where societal moral norms were distorted; where life was as cheap as vodka; and vodka was both life and death: winter fuel and a silent killer.

Two Soviet soldiers appeared in the doorway, armed for combat and prepared to use their weapons. Each took, a long look around, then a trouser leg each of the unconscious man lying on the floor, and dragged him out of the bar, leaving a red trail from the back of his head, like the single stroke of a Rothko paintbrush.

2

Sun Stand Still

Winter.

Morning.

Winter nights in St Petersburg are dark and cold and seemingly eternal.

Of course, the light will come; but it glows slowly, first as a dull grey twilight which then leaves before it has arrived. The pale sun, hangs low on the horizon like a ball in mid-air, and then comes down.

For Fisher, the darkness in his small room was total and it unsettled him. What little silences there were, were splintered by a disturbing array of noises off. Voices; he could hear voices; and the sounds of sex; a woman having the orgasm of her life, or death, or both; and, splitting the night once, a blood curdling scream; the crack of wood as a door is battered in and a man is seemingly dragged from his bed and beaten and taken away by who knows who, to who knows where? Was he dreaming? Perhaps? It didn't seem like a dream; but then, real dreams don't.

In his overtired vodka infused delirium, he may have imagined things. Fisher was well aware of the effects of sleep deprivation and, even, of sleep paralysis; and of their link to stress. The former is a common occurrence; the second, quite rare. And yet during the night, he was convinced he had experienced some form of paralysis. Or, was that a dream, also? Or, was it the beer...the vodka? The sausage? Two things had gripped him with an inexplicable fear: he felt he couldn't move…at all; and he had a strong sense that he was not alone.

Both seemed to have happened to him during the long dark night.

Fisher, knew enough not to worry over this experience, but regretted his rebuff of an offer of a night spent with Pasha the poodle. Which, of course, may have ended up sitting on his chest anyway. But this thing, he had felt in the night…this dark, amorphous shape in his room, he had imagined, had been, despite his rational explanation, quite terrifying. When finally, he was able to get up and away from the excuse for a bed, he s plashed cold water on his face and lay down once more. The small room was extraordinarily hot.

Of course, in the midst of all this real or imagined mayhem, there was no way that Fisher would venture from his concrete oven, no matter what was going on, or who was crying for help. So, he just lay there, in the dark.

Fisher was as much troubled by his evening with Vasyli, a former nuclear physicist and karate expert, as by his disturbed sleep. So, he decided to get up and get out into the morning air without searching out some breakfast. As he walked towards the stairwell, turning the curve of the corridor, he came across a splintered door and a room, identical to his own, but hastily deserted.

Fisher's purpose would begin the next day, on Monday. The whole point of arriving a day or so early was to acclimatise; to get a feel for the place. It was important to his work that he understood the context, the environment, the social and psychological issues. He thought of it like the surface tension of a liquid in a glass; the head on a pint of his favourite beer; or, sometimes as a bowl of molten metal… a crucible, in which a thin skin of impurities coalesce on the surface. The hotter it gets, the thicker the skin. But, scrape it away and you see the true metal beneath the surface.

Outside, in what little daylight was forming, he turned and considered the imposing seven storey building of the hotel, constructed of grey concrete in 1977 at the site in front of Alexander Nevsky Lavra, exactly at the place where the main street of St. Petersburg, the Nevsky Prospect, meets the Neva river. The Prospect ends at the Square named after Alexander Nevsky. But Fisher had already forgotten who this Nevsky geezer was or had been. His warm breath clouded into a thought bubble, but there was nothing in it. Somehow, for some reason, he felt more safe out in the open. People were going about what little business they had on a Sunday morning in a city, frozen, both literally and metaphorically.

The snow had stopped for the time being, at least, leaving a fresh but treacherous dusting over the compact of flakes beneath; but the increasingly leaden sky was holding more in reserve.

Across the street, and within careful walking distance was the Alexander Nevsky Monastery complex, home to some of the oldest buildings in the city, as well as to the cemeteries which contained the graves of some of the giants of Russian culture. The monastery was founded in July 1710.

Fisher had done his homework and revised his knowledge of Russian literature, just to be here with the dead poets.

Like many centres of orthodoxy, the monastery suffered at the hands of the Revolution. In January 1918, the Bolsheviks attempted to seize its valuables, but were driven off by determined church-goers, summoned by the ringing of the monastery's bells. However, it was closed shortly after, and robbed and looted of its valuables anyway.

From 1931-36 all of the churches and cathedrals within the monastery complex were closed. The remaining space was turned over to the city government, which soon distributed it to various different institutes, offices and warehouses. On June 3, 1989, the remains of

Alexander Nevsky were moved back to the Cathedral from the *Museum of Atheism* which had been opened in Kazan Cathedral. The Tikhvin Cemetery across the way, contained many of the most famous graves. Fisher could see to the far right-hand corner from the gate, an impressive bust of Tchaikovsky over his grave, while close by was Rubinshtein, Mussorgsky, Rimsky-Korsakov and Glinka. Dostoevsky lay further back along the wall, towards the gate. The other main cemetery, the Lazarus Cemetery, is the resting place of several of the great architects, who left their indelible mark on the city, including Starov, Quarenghi and Rossi.

Any mention of religion, or recognition of its resurgent popularity, would send the communist party into paroxysms of rage. The so-called opiate of the people, from Fisher's perspective, it was, at least, relatively honest. In England, where church and state existed in an arranged marriage, the weakness of one had strengthened the other. Here, the churches were full; there was a black market in icons and a frenzy of restorations with zealots being thrown in gaol or sent to the gulags.

It was a Sunday morning; the church bells were calling the faithful to worship. Fisher walked along the glassy pavements, that used to be cleared of snow in the *old days*; now neglected and dangerous. He crossed what seemed like a bridge over a moat or small canal, now obscured by snow.

And that was when he came across the dead body.

She was lying frozen on the ground where she had fallen. An old lady, probably on her way to church, the week before perhaps; she may have slipped and broken her hip bone. Just like everybody else, Fisher stepped over her; only to find another, more recent corpse, a little further on.

This time, lying face down in the frozen gutter.

What on earth was going on?

The second body, another older woman, had been stripped of her coat and hat. Her boots lay a little further; discarded, once the thief had seen that they were full of holes.

Fisher felt helpless. What could he do? Both were dead, and nobody seemed to care. Presumably, this was someone's mother? Or sister? Or grandmother?

Fisher's legs felt leaden as if he should crouch for a moment; and so he turned the body over, whether from respect or curiosity, he wasn't sure. He was both shocked and disturbed by the peace on the woman's blue face. Who were these woman? They were old enough to have seen two wars. Fisher imagined...

Vera Golubeva, who spent six years in a Stalinist labour camp for telling a joke. In 1951 she was labelled an enemy of the people and sent to Siberia. "It sounds ridiculous," the former history teacher might have said to him. "But that's the only *evidence* they had on me."

Now almost 98, Vera had walked slowly to the church, leaning on a stick. But this same woman was once forced to lay railway sleepers made of cement in temperatures that plunged to minus fifty-six degrees Celsius.

"Everyone was exhausted and got sick," the other woman, Luba, recalls to Fisher in his head. "The hardest part for me was chopping wood. I was a city girl and not very good at it. So my food ration was cut to three hundred grams."

"That's nothing!" says Vera. "It was psychologically tough, too. Many people went mental... out of their minds. They couldn't cope," she says.

Vera Golubeva survived that brutality, but at huge cost. She says to Fisher her youth was stolen in the Gulag. Her husband was sent to the camps too, and her parents. Vera herself was eight months pregnant when she was taken. She lost her baby and says after that, life became pointless.

"What happened needs to be exposed, so it's never repeated," Vera says, her voice strong and firm despite her age.

"We say here that things go in spirals. But that was a black spiral. It was a frightening time," Luba adds.

But these are only voices in Fisher's head. The reality is lay there on the ground. Stiff, lifeless, cold and neglected. After so much life…just to die like this…on a glassy frozen pavement.

Everything seemed black and white and in between, like the old film of the Siege of Leningrad during the Great Patriotic War: bodies in the streets, starving citizens, eating each other, shuffling about under a threatening sky. The typical Leningrad cannibal, though, was not a bestial lowlife, but a housewife seeking protein to save her children. In the agonised hunt for food, sustenance of sorts could be got from the bodies like these that lay unwept-for and disregarded in the snow. Contrary to the official Soviet narrative, the siege did not sanctify its victims. Disastrously, Stalin failed to evacuate Leningrad before the siege ring closed and made little attempt to stockpile extra food when it was still possible. As starvation set in, the inhabitants began to boil calf skins for hoped-for nutrition or ate joiner's glue made from the bones and hooves of slaughtered livestock.

Orthodox Christians convinced themselves that the siege was sent as a test for mankind… an intolerable but manifest mystery of *His Will*. No matter; it had made no difference.

Reluctantly, Fisher left the women and moved on to the church. And in complete contrast, the inside of the church was warmed by a thousand candles; there was colour; there was music; and there were clusters of women worshipping around an triptych of the Holy Trinity. Above all, there seemed to be hope, false hope perhaps. But to the worshippers, any hope, however frail, was worth holding on to. The men, notable by their absence had taken to the bottle; the women to the opiate of the church. Fisher was certainly no worshipper himself, and yet felt uncomfortable watching those that were. After all, they were sincere in their beliefs, in a context in which, for many, it was all they had left. The collapse of one belief system ruled by a Soviet demagogue, had been replaced by what? *Nothing*, thought Fisher. *Nothing at all*. For some, this was their only point of reference; for others, the altar of capitalism beckoned, and provided succour to the greedy, but not the needy.

With a heavy heart and with careful footsteps, Fisher made his way back over the pavements towards the Moskva. At last, he thought, he blended in more than he had the night before, in his warm waxed trench coat and his Siberian Red Fox fur hat. Or so he believed. To the Russian eye, he was still a western dick! An obvious foreigner, an interloper, a traveller or possibly one of the emerging class of fledgling oligarchs. His coat was too well made to be of soviet origin; his boots were waterproof; and his hat, whilst of soviet origins was from a rare beast, hunted to near extinction, and worn only by those who could afford the very best. Fisher was blissfully unaware of this. As such, he was probably at considerable risk of being robbed or killed for a prestigious hat worth hundreds of dollars. As he approached the revolving door of the hotel, a young man, probably in his early thirties, approached, carrying what looked like a shoe box under his left arm. Fisher noted his heavy eyelids, his long thin nose and full lips; the top being slightly larger than the bottom. He had one of those inscrutable gazes. Blue, impenetrable eyes. Cold, like a dead fish.

"Dr Fisher?" he said, removing a sleek leather glove and holding his warm hand out in greeting.

"Yes?"

Fisher had already grown wary; and looked around for the tall dark man of the night before. But he was nowhere to be noticed.

"Sprichst du Deutsch?"

Fisher looked nonplussed.

"No...er...nine."

"Forgive me...my English is not as good as my German. Please allow me to introduce myself."

"Vladimir.... from the university?" Fisher ventured.

"Exactly, yes. I am the Assistant to the Rector of Leningrad State University...responsible for International Relations. I am here to look after you during your stay, you are welcome to be based in my office. Although I am sure your work will take you out most of the time."

"Yes... Yes. But, I wasn't expecting you until tomorrow morning."

For a moment, Fisher was confused. It *was* Sunday? Wasn't it?

"Tomorrow, yes. This is true. But, I know this hotel is not a...pleasant place, I thought we could get more acquainted. I have a car...so, we could drive out to a special place... some friends will join us there, and we can stay until tomorrow morning, if you would like?"

Although Fisher was a little suspicious of such a generous offer from a virtual stranger, it seemed he had little choice but to accept it. In any case, wherever it was, it couldn't worse than the night before. Could it?

"Yes, yes, please...can I collect one or two things?"

"Please...I will wait for you here, by the car." He said, pointing to a relatively large black car, which seemed a little too luxurious for a university administrator.

"It belongs to a friend of mine," added Vladimir, detecting some movement in Fisher's eyebrows. "It's a Tatra-613, a rear-engine sedan built in Czechoslovakia. These days, you can't get much better than this. Unless, of course, you can get hold of a *Mercedes*, smuggled over the frozen Gulf of Finland."

"Do people do that?"

"Of course, who wouldn't want a *Porsche* or a *Mercedes*...? But it has some drawbacks. Essentially, it advertises your criminality."

Fisher climbed the stairs to his lofty bunker and retrieved a few necessary items, tossing them into a satchel, and made his wheezing way back to the car, where Vladimir was waiting in the crystal air to open the passenger door. It closed with a heavy satisfying clunk.

"Where are we going?" queried Fisher, as the Tatra breathed, quietly and smoothly into life, and Vladimir reversed out of the parking bay.

"Barely an hour and a half north of the city. The location, on the Karelian Isthmus between the Gulf of Finland and Lake Ladoga...it's only an hour and twenty minutes' drive on to the Finnish border from there, in an area that has variously been part of the Swedish Empire, the tsarist Russian empire, independent Finland, the Soviet Union, and now....well, who knows?"

"It sounds...remote."

"It is.... that's what is good about it."

"And, the border? Is it difficult to cross?"

"It is double fenced, with mines scattered in between. Not to mention the wolves and bears. What crossings there are, are guarded by towers. But, in any case, who would want to go to Finland? It's a miserable place! It has more drunks than we do; and, the highest suicide rate on earth!"

"Might they want to come here?"

"For willing whores and cheap vodka, yes. But, they can now make the short journey by ferry from Helsinki to Estonia, and help themselves in Tallinn. Sometimes, in the Winter, for a few weeks, the sea freezes, and they can drive there, get drunk and drive back.

Towards the end of the season, they dare each other to be the last one to cross, as the sea ice thins. Men die each year. But, they need their thrills as much as their play. As we say in Russia: *Без отдыха, даже лошадь не галопом*: *without rest, even the horse doesn't gallop.*"

Fisher had no idea what that meant in the context of a drunken Fin falling through the ice to his death. No matter.... most Russian proverbs were as mysterious as their origins. Nonetheless, a flicker of doubt crossed Fisher's mind as to his personal safety. But then, why would a university administrator intend any harm to him? And, what was in the shoebox?

Stockholm Syndrome, Fisher thought, might be relevant in this context. He pulled it from his on-board encyclopaedia of psychology: when men and women are placed in a situation where they no longer have any control over their fate, feel intense fear of physical harm and believe all control is in the hands of their tormentor, a strategy for survival can result, which can develop into a psychological response that can include sympathy and support for their captor's plight. So, then, as Fisher knew, the best tactic was to get to know your abductor.

As bridges were crossed by the Tatra and imperial architecture gave way to urban utility:

"So, Vladimir...are you from St Petersburg?"

"Yes. I come from an ordinary family. I'm just a normal person. We lived simply...cabbage soup, cutlets, pancakes, but on Sundays and holidays my mother would bake very delicious stuffed buns, called, *piroshky* with cabbage, meat and rice, and curd tarts known as *vatrushki*. After the war, my family moved into a room in a communal apartment, a *kommunalka*, in a typical St Petersburg dwelling, on Baskov Lane. It was a building with a well-liked yard. Fifth floor. No elevator…. or lift, as you say… Before the war my parents occupied half of a house in Peterhof and were very proud of the living standards they had achieved then. It wasn't really much, but it seemed like an ultimate dream to them. What about you, Dr Fisher?"

The Stockholm tactic appeared to be going quite well. Although it seemed that the more Vladimir talked, the more he resembled Spencer Tracy in his driving habits, by paying no attention to the road ahead.

"Stephen…please call me Stephen. Oh, I grew up in a very poor district of Manchester in a small terraced house with no bathroom and a toilet outside in the back yard. These days, I still live in Manchester, but in a nicer house with my wife and two sons. Do you have a family, Vladimir?"

"Yes, after I had finished my Law degree at Leningrad University, I met my wife through a mutual friend. She worked for *Aeroflot*, as a flight attendant on domestic flights and came to Leningrad for a few days with a friend. I was already working, and a friend of mine called and invited me to the Arkady Raikin theatre. He said he already had the tickets, and mentioned there would be two young ladies joining us. So, we went to the performance and the young ladies did join us. The next day, we went to the theatre again, but it was now my turn to buy the tickets. And the same thing happened on the third day. I then began dating one of the girls… three years later, we were married. We have two daughters…they are my joy. One was born here…the other in Dresden."

"East Germany?"

"Yes, the GDR. I have only been back here for a few months now. I took the job at the university hoping at the same time to write my PhD thesis and, perhaps, to stay on and work here afterwards. But, already, I am far too busy… and, it seems, doing two or three jobs at once."

"I'm sorry if I am adding to your work."

"No…not at all, it will be very interesting to assist you in any way I can. You come highly recommended."

"Do I? By who?"

"Stephen…I know why you are hear. And, I know who sent you."

"The university."

"Come now, Stephen…let us be honest with each other, you and I."

A wave of guilt ran over Fisher's shoulders and shivered down his spine. And so he relented:

"The Foreign Office of Her Majesty's Government."

"Exactly. But that is tomorrow…today…we relax. We are going to my most favourite place."

The urban sprawl of endless *kommunalka*, soon gave way to the flat, blasted and starched wastes to the north. Already the light was fading, as the first fir trees began to creep up to the side of the road and form a dark embrace through which even the snow was unable to fall, Vladimir had become quieter, preferring, it seemed, to concentrate on the driving.

Nevertheless, in spite of the initial pleasantries, Fisher felt there was something unusual about Vladimir. Diffident, distant, uncanny perhaps? What Freud might have called, the *other,* or rather: *unheimlich.* It concerns the revelation of what is private and concealed, of what is hidden; hidden not only from others, but also from the self. And that was the point. Fisher didn't think for a moment that Vladimir was deliberately hiding something; or lying about his past. It was more a case of not revealing everything about himself, because Vladimir didn't really know what it was he was hiding.

In other words, he wasn't being deliberately obtuse or mysterious. Far from it, he had spoken openly about his recent history and his relationships. Vladimir was, therefore, strangely familiar; and yet not, Fisher thought there was more about Vladimir than perhaps Vladimir knew about himself.

"You seem to be deep in thought, Stephen. No doubt you are analysing me? Is that what you do when you meet people for the first time."

"I'm a Criminal Psychologist operating in a narrow specialist field. I only need to unravel the insanely criminal mind. I leave the minds of honest folk to others."

"Is it not possible to be an honest criminal?"

"It's an interesting question, that depends on your definition of honesty; and what is deemed by society to be a crime. In some ways, a criminal can be considered honest, in that, they can behave honestly according to their own sense of self. They can, in other words, be *true to themselves*."

"I see... In English, there is a word...hood...or hoodlum. I have seen this in American movies, yes?"

"Yes...a gangster...both are common in American English."

"And in your history books there is a man, a revolutionary, called Robin Hood. Was he not a criminal *and* an honest man, robbing the rich to give to the poor?"

"Well, he is still breaking the law and is only honest in the sense that he acted on a set of self-determined principles, that many people might argue as *the end justifying the means*. If you understand my meaning?"

"Yes, of course. And so, history has made a judgement that he was a good man."

"Unfortunately, it's not that simple: there seem to be several Robin Hoods. Robert and Robin are names often interchanged. Hood was a common name in the fourteenth century. And so, whilst four or five such characters are mentioned in literature, they are mostly mythical, or rather, there is no evidence that they robbed anyone. And so, there is little to support the idea that Robin Hood existed and therefore, is not really part of *history*. More that he is part of a mythology of rebellion against an oppressive State. A symbol of resistance; not evidence of resistance."

"But, isn't *history merely the lies we tell each other about the past*?"

"Yes… Bradbury… interesting… that's exactly right."

"It is something we, in the Soviet Union, have been very good at since the revolution."

Fisher could see that Vladimir was erudite; and, he was no fool. He argued cogently and calmly and without fear of upsetting his opponent. Perhaps too cogently, for a man who claimed his grasp of English was much less than perfect than it is. Modesty? Or, a clever tactic to disarm his foreign visitor? Not many people in Fisher's social milieu would have read Bradbury's, *To the Hermitage*. A complex novel exploring the residence of French philosopher Denis Diderot at the Court of Catherine the Great. Fisher wondered, therefore, what Vladimir's role was, at the university. Yes…Assistant to the Rector. But what exactly did that mean? Assisting in what?

Was he one of those political officers assigned to institutions to ensure that academic freedom only meant the freedom to be academic about the party line, and little else. Fisher had seen such figures before. Once, when a party had visited Manchester from China, for example: there was always someone in a meeting that never said a word, but to whom all eyes would fix for approval. It didn't seem likely that this type of role would persist. Not now. Not with the imminent collapse of the Soviet Union. Being a hard-line communist might soon be a thing of a dark past. Was Vladimir a hard line communist? But this idea made little sense to Fisher. For Vladimir to be such a man, he would be an insider. Fisher was convinced by his *other* theory, that Vladimir was an *other*, an outsider.

He decided to reserve his judgement and to change tack, preferring to get Vladimir talking. The more he talked, the more he revealed his otherness:

"Tell me about this *special place*?"

"It is a tradition, and a dream to own a dacha...a summer house...or second house, you might say, for weekends, for hunting, fishing and comradeship. It is small. The size of a dacha is determined by the State, as is the size of the plot. Accordingly, ingenious ways are devised to expand the space without breaking the rules. The peculiarity of the dacha stemmed from the fact that we were trying to create as much habitable space as possible while complying with the standard. The size of the residential area could not exceed sixty-five square meters. However, the house itself is more than twice the size. That's why we have a house with a spacious, bright corridor, leading from the centre of the front porch to the hallway. There are no rules about corridors. You will see...we are nearly there. Although most of the decor is modern, it was carefully selected by my wife with the history of old dachas in mind. Muted paint colours, antique furniture, embroidered curtains and delicate tablecloths all help to create an atmosphere of the old days."

"You mean the *old days* before the Bolshevik Revolution?"

"Yes, why not? It's a form of escape. It is the difference that matters."

"I don't know. I just got the impression that you believed in the Soviet System."

"What is the point of belief in a system, if the system is ruled by fools in Moscow. As the poet once said: *things fall apart the centre cannot hold.*"

"W.B. Yeats?"

"Exactly. Prophetic words, written by the Irish poet in his poem *The Second Coming*. They have never seemed more appropriate considering what we are facing today and for the immediate future. If the centre is Yeltsin, then he cannot continue to hold together an increasingly erratic and confused administration. It is no longer a question of political loyalty, it has become a matter of saving of the country from a sad, delusional drunk who has lost touch with reality. Make no mistake, if given the option of resignation or being declared incompetent to be President, Yeltsin will choose resignation. No doubt he will make the most outrageous excuses for doing so, but at that point no one will care."

Fisher wasn't sure if it was wise to enter into a political discussion; and so, he said nothing. Whilst Vladimir was astute, even he had no way of knowing which way the dice would fall.

"I should warn you Stephen…you will be asked many questions as to why you are here in St Petersburg. My friends are inquisitive as to what those in the West think about our situation. You will be asked for your opinion on many things. You should be prepared to answer them most carefully."

"Clearly, then, you know the true purpose of my visit?"

"I know enough to know that I don't need to know any more than I do."

Pierced only by the long beams of light from the Tatra, the still night air seemed filled with suspended crystals as the car floated through a sea of diamond dust and followed the beams turning into a clearing.

The air was crisp, without a whisper of wind or a cloud in the visible sky. Just the tendrils of branches and the pines pointing into the black emptiness. As his eyes adjusted, Fisher was amazed by the number of visible stars and smear of the Milky Way sprayed onto the inky canvas of the night. For a moment, he was alone with himself. Aghast. He felt the tranquil splendour above him; unrooted, unfettered and floating in a vast dark ocean, until a voice brought him back from infinity.

"This is my dacha." Vladimir said with pride. "I built it with my friends. It's a weekend house, as I said. There are eight of us in our group; and each is to have his own house here in the forest. But, for now, we use this one in turns with our families, or as in this case, we gather as friends. We call ourselves *Ozero*. It means *lake*. Come inside, not everyone could make it this weekend, but those that are here are looking forward to meeting you."

Vladimir's voice faded into the silence of the snow and into darkness as he walked towards his pride.

Lake? Thought Fisher. Did that mean they were an indistinguishable amorphous whole? An entity? An inseparable mass? A brotherhood. If so, to what purpose? To *merely, gather as friends*? It seemed unlikely to be as simple as that.

3

Instant Fires

Fire.

Ice.

There is an eerie silence in a Winter forest, especially at night, and especially covered, as it was, in a blanket of crisp white snow. There is a dead sound, if there is such a thing? A dead sound? Muffled? Sitting atop this seasonal cake, was a warm wooden house with a roof like Dutch Barn. An orange glow escaped from every window and made a sorbet of the grounded snow, peppered with black current boot steps. As they approached the porch: on the left, a low wall of neatly cut logs, absurdly well-proportioned in an orderly array, stacked like a tight fitting jigsaw, as if for show rather than the practicality of keeping the fire going. It smacked of the obsessive-compulsive.

The interior was as warm and well-proportioned as it could be, with the corridor or hallway, of Vladimir's description, leading directly to the rear of the dacha, passing by what Fisher imagined to be closed bedroom doors.

Fisher couldn't stop himself from looking at the display of framed objects on each wall: six on the left and six on the right. They looked identical, until closer inspection revealed subtle differences in the ridges and crinkles, mounted against a black velvet background.

"Angel's Wings," said Vladimir. "You like them, Stephen?"

"Angel's Wings?"

"Philadidae or Piddocks, shells known as Angel's Wings. I collect them."

"You collect them?" Fisher was beginning to sound like an echo chamber.

"Yes. Piddocks are unique in that each side of their shells is divided into two or three separate sections. One of the shells has a set of ridges or teeth, which they use to grind away at clay or soft rock and create tubular burrows. There...you see?" He said, pointing at the leading edge of a pure white shell.

"Fascinating."

"The Angel Wing species *Cyrtopleura costata* has approximately twenty-six radiating ribs; and are quite rare."

"Beautiful," said Fisher, mesmerised.

"I'm glad you like them. Come, let me take your hat and boots."

The hall expanded into a space dominated by a large open fire that flicked and licked the walls with every hue of yellow and red. Armchairs and two sofas draped with ornate tapestry throws, woven in rich burgundy and amber designs. It had a feel that it belonged to, or was characteristic of, the, so-called middle class, typically with reference to its perceived materialistic values or conventional attitudes. The word *bourgeois* came to Fisher's mind; not that he would dare to utter such profanity. But, it was simple, homely and relatively uncluttered.

"What do you think?" asked Vladimir.

But before Fisher could frame an appropriately polite response, a deep American voice came from behind:

"Has he been entertaining you with his precious, but empty sea shells? Or, bragging about his quaint little doll's house all the way from Petrograd? Wait until we build mine. It will be a Winter Palace and a Summer Chateau."

"Stephen, this is Sergey... Sergey... Stephen," said Vladimir, somewhat deflated. They shook hands warmly.

"Let's get that coat off…come and sit by the fire and we'll start as we mean to go on, with a bottle of Stolichnaya," Sergey insisted.

"Where is Viktor? And Yuri?" Vladimir queried.

"They are out on the lake, fishing for Sturgeon. We should be so lucky!" said Sergey. "I mean…I just don't get it! Where's the fun in sitting on your arse on a frozen lake staring at a small hole in the ice and waiting for hours for a possible passing fish? When you can buy a plump one on the black market."

Sergey was already gathering three small glasses with an empty clink, and a fresh bottle of vodka, as Fisher took his place alongside Vladimir on one of the sofas.

"We are all businessmen here, Stephen," Sergey continued, "all except one, of course, who is a…how do you say it? …a civil servant… a mandarin… a small thin-skinned bitter-sweet fruit with pips!"

Fisher presumed he meant Vladimir, who failed to rise to the bait.

"Vladimir…you'll never make any money being stuck in a university. You should get out, cast your line into the plentiful waters; there is a load of money to be made. Everything is changing."

"Everything *is* changing; but money *is not* everything," retorted Vladimir with restraint. "Power is everything…money comes, money goes. We yearn for the future. Why? When we haven't understood the past. Since the tumult of revolution, we've had stability. What was so wrong with stability? Now, we have developed a talent for insatiability. Some might say, chaos!"

"You see what I mean?" Sergey taunted, trying to entangle Fisher in the discussion. "Money *is* power. We, in the Ozero group…. We intend to encourage insatiability; we will change the course of history and make a fortune at the same time."

"That's a bold ambition." Fisher retorted.

"We don't see things the way that others do," Sergey continued. "We see opportunity where others see chaos. We all spent periods of time outside Russia and the USSR, where we were able to detach ourselves from on-going events...this chaos...and form a more dispassionate analysis of the current state of affairs. Unlike men from the provinces...*glubinka* we called them in old Russia..., *St. Petersburgers* don't really accept the role of being *glubinka* or second-class citizens. The city's downgrade from imperial capital in 1917 to provincial city in the Soviet period, and then the Bolshevik decision to rename it Leningrad, created a sense of deep resentment, a grudge against Moscow. St. Petersburg was supposed to be important....and it will be again! It had been built as the capital and as the centre of high culture for Peter the Great's new Russian Empire. But its citizens were abruptly designated second rank. We have something to prove; power to regain. And, in any case..." Sergey consciously decided to return to a lighter note, "...what is more attractive to women? Money or power?"

"Power," said Fisher.

"Stephen! Who's side are you on? Don't encourage him!"

Fisher sensed that Vladimir felt that Sergey had said too much, too soon.

Finally, Vladimir responded, at first in Russian:

"Я не уверен, что мы должны это сказать. Мы почти не знаем его. For my part," he continued in English, "I haven't had as much international contamination as you, my friend, Sergey, with your Harvard education..."

"Contamination!" Sergey cried, raising his glass, "Here's to *contamination!*"

The glasses clinked and caught in the firelight.

"What line of business are you in, Sergey?" Fisher queried.

"Exports and imports, of course. Russia may be poor, but it is rich in minerals. I buy rare minerals from mining companies in the East. They will give stuff away for a few dollars. Then I sell them to production companies in the United States in return for dollars, food and clothing. I then sell these on to the black marketeers. If I could print money in dollars, I couldn't print it fast enough to keep up with what I make on these markets."

Fisher wasn't quite sure how to respond. What Sergey was doing, wasn't illegal. But something told him it wasn't quite right, either. Nevertheless, there was food at the end of the process; for those that could afford it. The scheme smacked of exploitation; but, wasn't that the basis of capitalism anyway?

Another clink of short glasses, "to the free market!" toasted Sergey.

"I only spent a few years in Dresden" Vladimir explained, "...the exact opposite of America. They were more hard-line soviets than we were here. When you come home with nine months between two trips you don't have time to get back into our life. And when you have returned from abroad it's hard at the beginning to get used to reality, seeing what's been done at home...or not done. And we, the younger guys, would talk to our older colleagues. I am not talking here about the elderly who had gone through the Stalinist period, but about the people with experience on the job, let's say. They were already a completely different generation, with different views, assessments, and attitudes....After conversations like that, you start to think and rethink things...at that time, we permitted ourselves to think differently and to say things that few others could permit themselves to think."

The front door of the dacha opened and a cold blast of air rushed down the hallway with a flurry of powdery snow.

"Любая рыба? Did you get a bite?" Sergey called out.

"Two.. medium. It was like they came to visit!" came a deep voice from the darkened hallway.

"Two fish? Is that all? Did you bring the five loaves with you?" retorted Sergey. "We can have a biblical feast!"

"I think it is enough to feed a few thousand, so it should be enough for the four of us."

"…пять….there are five of us!" added Vladimir.

"Да неужели!"

The two men came into the light: a thick set man with a beard and a thinner one with sallow skin. They set about discarding their coats; one laid two large frozen fish on the table; the other took a packet from his pocket and lit a *Marlboro* cigarette.

"Anyone?" he said, proffering the packet to the room, "American? No?"

There was a moment of reflection as the light smoke was blown purposely towards the central light fitting.

"And you must be… Dr Fish, I presume?"

"Fish*er*…" said Vladimir, before Fisher could reply.

"I prefer, Fish. For there is something slippery about him."

"Back off, Viktor!" said the other, presumably Yuri, "Don't be so damn rude! We haven't even been introduced."

"I don't need an introduction to be rude. But Yuri is correct…I am rude and I'm Russian!"

"Stephen, this is Viktor…and Yuri" said Vladimir.

"Stephen eh? So, we are on first name terms already!" replied Viktor.

"Pay no attention to him Stephen…he's an angry man," offered Yuri.

"Nobody is quite sure what he is angry about. Even Viktor isn't sure any more. But we think it is because he has a big mouth and a small cock!"

"Говорующий язык к добру не принесет.. As we say in Russian: *the tongue will bring the chatterer no good*," added Sergey. "You have this saying in English, Stephen?"

"Not really. We might say…*a fool's tongue runs before his feet*."

There was silence.

Perhaps *fool* was a bit harsh?

Then Viktor began to laugh through his dark beard.

"Sergey, is the banya ready?" he asked, earnestly.

"It should be hot by now."

"Well, then…let's go and see who has the smallest cock. Yuri, take care the birds don't get yours!"

They were on the move.

Vladimir showed Fisher to his small bedroom, and said:

"I should have warned you about Viktor. He means no harm. Hard words break no bones."

"What's a banya?" queried Fisher with a tone of dread.

"It's a traditional Russian bath…a steam room…or sauna."

"Really?" Fisher tried, but failed, not to sound too alarmed.

"Yes…it's what we do."

"Naked?"

"Of course. There is a towel over there, a mat for sitting on, and a small hat to protect your head from the heat. After the first good sweat is induced, it is customary to cool off in the breeze outdoors or splash around in cold water or in a lake or river. In the Winter, people may roll in the snow with no clothes on or dip in lakes where holes have been cut into the ice."

"Like the one they have just been fishing in?"

"Exactly!" Vladimir laughed, his eyes narrowing as he did. "Then the banya is re-entered and small amounts of water are splashed on the rocks. If too much water is used at once, the steam will be cool, with a clammy feel." Vladimir was carried away by his own enthusiasm. "A small amount of water on sufficiently hot rocks will evaporate quickly, producing a steam consisting of small vapour particles. Waving the venik causes convective heat. The second sweat is commonly the first time the venik is used, but some people wait until the third session."

"A venik? Third session!"

"You'll see."

"I'm happy to give it a miss, Vladimir…"

"And what will Viktor say? I think you have little choice, my friend. You should take all your clothes off and leave them here. I will return in a few moments."

Fisher knew there was no escape. Well.. not with any dignity. On the bed lay a grey mat and a small felt cap. The so-called towel was white, and was hardly a towel at all; more of a large face flannel.

Within moments, Vladimir had returned to the doorway, sporting a silly looking pointed hat and a short towel over his left shoulder.

"Come!" he ordered, disappearing into the darkness of the hall, with his bits bobbing like a tangled Newton's Cradle.

On first sight, it is nigh impossible to look at a naked body without the eyes being drawn to the genitals. No matter how hard he tried, Fisher was no different. It follows, therefore, that other people will look at his genitals. And, therein lies the perceived problem: judgement follows. Fisher was aware that this anxiety is culturally specific, particular, but not exclusive to the British.

The others were gathered in a line near the back door that punctuated the kitchen area. There was no sense of modesty. Only Fisher seemed to be holding his flannel in a strategic way. It all reminded him of the school showers. He had hated that, almost as much as lining up in the school corridor to see the nit nurse, in nothing more than his underpants. At least the nurse could purposely check his testicular development with a warm hand, cupped, and with a request to cough; and any non-compliant or over-excited boys were made to stand in the corner of shame. Right now, Fisher felt he had no balls at all and wished there was a corner to stand in. His balls had disappeared in a general retreat in anticipation of the blast of freezing air that was about to hit them.

But, there was no apparent purpose for this queuing by the back door.

"So, Stephen...there is a short walk through the snow to get to the banya..."

"Outside?" asked Fisher, with a mild tone of trepidation and constructed denial.

"Yes, outside...it will be very cold. The banya is a simple wooden cabin, there's an entrance room where you will pick up your banny venik from a basket on the right. This is a branch of white birch." Vladimir explained.

"Come on you two...stop blabbing...it's cold near the back door!" cried Yuri.

"Well... don't bend over so much Yuri!" quipped Viktor. "He's always showing his back door!"

Viktor turned the handle, and rushed out into the night, carrying a bottle of vodka, crying:

"Urah!" the battle cry of the Red Army. "Last one out closes the door! Last one in...frozen balls!"

Fisher felt the cold before he moved a foot. This was madness; and yet he rushed out of the door barefoot and naked, with the others, leaving Vladimir to close the door behind him.

It was something of an embarrassing crush in the small entrance room; but at least it was warmer. The run from the dacha was like running over a bed of hot coals, as the less time the feet were on the ground the better. Fisher could barely feel his feet; as lemmings, they all picked up their banny veniks.

The branch, of course, was no fig leaf. Its purpose was not hide anything, but to beat each other and each self with the leaves in a frenzy of whipping. It did, at least warm things up a bit, but Fisher received a welcome beating and was left with whelps all over him.

"This is the *prebannik*, as we call it. Now we shall enter the washing room, where there is a hot tap. It uses water, heated from the steam room stove and mixed in a vessel with cold water… just for washing."

The others were already in there, splashing water on themselves as the air was filled with the scent of birch leaves and smoke from burning birch wood. The wash, it has to be said, was somewhat cursory; more of a ritual than a thorough cleanse. But it was, at least, a relief to get inside the third room, furnished with wooden benches at varying heights. Mats were placed on the wood to prevent burning the skin, and all but Yuri took positions calmly and quietly. The heat was already intense, as Yuri poured water from a wooden bucket onto the hot clay boulders next to the stove. There was a loud hiss and a reverberating sizzle, as the steam rose to fill the room and afford what little privacy there could be between four naked garelous men and one self-conscious stranger. Some sat more modestly than others, one lay down. Viktor was covered in thick hair, whilst Vladimir and Yuri had hardly any at all. But, of course, the established protocol was not to look at your fellow men in silly hats; and certainly not steal a glance at anyone's cock. Fisher, inevitably looked the most awkward. It was as if he was wishing he was somewhere else. Which he was.

The vodka was poured and the sweat was as free-flowing as the conversation. Sometimes in Russian and sometimes not. When it was heated by disagreement, it tended to fall into their own tongue. When politeness prevailed, it was in English. Apart from himself, Fisher noticed that Vladimir was the quieter of the group; preferring, it seemed, to keep himself to himself, and to think about ideas rather than to share them; or to challenge. After all, he was a public servant and not an entrepreneur.

Fisher listened carefully to as much of the conversation as he understood. Close though they seem to have been, Vladimir was an addition to this group. Of the eight founders of Ozero, seven were businessmen and one was a civil servant. Seven had degrees in physics or engineering, and one had a law degree. The odd man out was Vladimir. What they had in common was the archetypical Petersburg mentality, that they were all outsiders to the Russian capital elite. They were the obsessives looking from afar, watching all the mistakes made by the politicians in Moscow, yet, for the time being at least, powerless to change things. This created anger and frustration in all, except, it seemed, Vladimir. He kept a cool head in his hot felt cap.

The group wanted change, that was clear. But they lacked the means to achieve it. Instead, they had embraced opportunity; opportunity fuelled by personal greed. Perhaps they had always been like that.

Now the rules had changed; now it was about accumulating wealth, not power. Power, not money, had been the currency of the Soviet System. The group of outsiders, who watched what the insiders did... and probably begrudged them for their arrogance and incompetence...defined this brotherhood. And yet, Vladimir seemed to Fisher, to be a satellite, doubly or triply removed from the core.

Quietly, Fisher grew to admire him in this context, as someone, like himself to a certain extent, who, despite his current circumstances, kept to his principles and refused to be assimilated into a group by peer pressure or expediency. He fully realised that there was considerable irony in this though. After all, here he was, forced by peer group pressure into removing all his clothes, running naked with four strangers through the snow, beating himself with a twig whilst wearing nothing but a stupid felt cap.

"….food production has completely broken down, store shelves are empty, rationing is in effect, and there are legitimate fears of widespread hunger in the city, where memories of the Nazi blockade of this city are still strongly felt." Explained Sergey with some passion and conviction.

"I fear we are boring our guest…" offered Yuri.

"Well, then Dr Fish," started Viktor, with some sarcasm, "tell us what *you* think *we* should do."

"I don't know…I've only arrived yesterday. I'm an academic. That means I know a lot about very little. I'm not an economist or a political scientist. And, in any case, I'm not here to solve such problems."

"Then tell us why you are here, Doctor or Professor or whatever you are?"

A cold pause filled the room like a waft of new steam that hissed onto the hot stones and then fell slowly silent.

"Are you all married?" Fisher tried to change tack.

"You want to talk about women in the banya? That's asking for trouble!" said Viktor.

"Yuri and Vladimir are all settled," retorted Sergey. "Viktor and I are still fishing for the perfect catch. Someone like Michelle Pfeiffer or Julia Roberts would suit me. Whereas Vladimir still dreams of Claudia Schiffer!"

"Oh yes! Now we're talking!" cried Viktor. "What about you Stephen? Who's your ideal woman to keep you warm in bed at night? Margaret Thatcher?"

"Are there no beautiful women in Russia?" asked Fisher.

"Of course!" insisted Viktor. "They start off beautiful and one day you wake up next to a warty old toad!"

They laughed, and clinked glasses and then refuelled.

"What Viktor means to say..." offered Sergey, "...is that values are changing towards western ideals. Here, in the forties and fifties the only pin-ups were women that emphasised strength, skills and motherhood... muscles and child-bearing hips like the back-end of a tractor. Poster girls were fully clothed engineers, welders and farm girls, usually depicted holding a blow-torch or a pitch-fork. Not exactly Madonna is it?"

"Although, as I recall, the engineer had pointy tits!" offered Viktor. "Russian women are all look and don't touch... cock teasers, the lot of them. They treat you like a dog...tempting you with a bone, held just out of reach."

"I'm beginning to sweat vodka. Perhaps we should move on?" offered Vladimir. "Now Stephen," he continued, "now we have the final ritual."

Fisher was dreading what might be next.

"But this evening we have been lazy and the night is moving on. So," he said, poised at the outer door, "it is time to cool off in the snow!"

It was as if Vladimir had fired a starting pistol. Like schoolboys, pushing and shoving to be the first to get out into the cold night air.

There was a full moon; and Fisher glimpsed it briefly before being pushed down into the snow. It was a night when lunatics might be abroad, but it seemed to Fisher that lunacy could be the only explanation for the scene before him, as four naked men in silly hats rolled and rubbed each other in frozen snow. Not the soft fluffy kind, that would be bad enough; but the coarse gritted kind that comes from repeated frozen nights. It was hard to tell if the others were laughing or crying; and, of course, it was Viktor that would roll the most and be the last to rise from his icy bed. Fisher, being the most controlled of the lunatics, had simply left a snow angel, impressed in the blanket, whilst around him four ice bombs had gone off.

At least the dacha was warm, and the dry clothes stuck to Fisher, as he emerged to some semblance of normality and sat by the fire once more. As he stared into the flames, he considered his guilt, at all this frivolity. He reminded himself of the gravity of his purpose.

"I'll do the fish," suggested Yuri. "Sergey the potatoes, and Vladimir...."

He stopped in mid-sentence. It was if a chill ran down the back of his neck, and the hairs on his hands had stood to attention, sensing danger.

A tall dark figure had silently appeared in the hallway.

None had heard the door.

As he stepped into the light, a few snowflakes melting on his coat and hat, Fisher recognised him at once. But, for the first time, could clearly see his gaunt face and his cold grey eyes.

"Aren't you going to introduce me to your new friend, Comrade Ivanov?"

Vladimir stepped forward, cautiously, almost standing to attention. But before he could say anything, the figure spoke once more:

"Не волнуйтесь ... it's too late for that. Dr Fisher, come with me. There has been a development."

4

A Fine and Private Place

Silent night.

Quiet car.

Frozen snow crunching under the tyres of the Zil-41041.

"You said there had been a development."

"That is what I said, Dr Fisher." In perfectly clipped English.

"Can you tell me about it?"

"Now? In the car? No, I cannot. Your question is premature."

"Where are we going?"

"St Petersburg...where else?"

"Anywhere in particular?"

"Yes, of course. For someone of reputed intelligence, Dr Fisher, you do seem to ask a lot of stupid questions."

"I'm just trying to ascertain where we are going."

"Why do you need to know where we are going? Is it not enough that I know? I am taking you there. You have no choice but to come with me. So, what is the point in knowing the precise destination? What will you do with this information? If this is your idea of small talk, it is too small for me to be bothered with."

Fisher took that to mean that silence was the preferred mode during transportation. Staring at the white road in the headlamps, and the darkness around it, Fisher saw little point in diverting attention from the fact that he was going somewhere in particular, and that, perhaps, it made no difference where it was, because, as his captor had explained, there was nothing he could do to change that.

"Do you mind if I smoke Dr Fisher?"

"Will it make any difference if I do?"

"No."

"You were at the airport and at the Moskva? Following me?"

"Airport? Moskva? Don't be absurd, Dr Fisher. Your paranoia is of no interest to me, whatsoever! Are we crude savages here? Is that what you think?"

Clearly this wasn't going to be warm relationship.

Fisher, had no idea who this man was.

Why he was at the airport; nor why it seemed, he had followed him to the Moskva? Interestingly, the man had known where Fisher was this evening...at a dacha in the middle of a forest. Neither Vladimir, nor his friends had challenged this man. Not even Viktor. Why was that? None had said: hey, hang on a minute...what's this all about? He simply entered unchallenged and demanded that Fisher leave with him; right there and then. Even Fisher had failed to raise objections. It was as if this man and his powerful presence were enough to command obedience. Who was he? And why did they fear him? Until, these and other questions... he daren't press directly, were answered, it seemed sensible to give into the silence.

Once again, Fisher had that uneasy feeling that he was in a film. It was a series of pictures in his head. This was the part where our hero is taken into a remote forest just outside Leningrad. The villain pulls a gun on him and orders him out of the car. He is forced to walk into the woods until he has no sense of direction. The villain tells him to kneel, points the gun at his head. A wolf howls nearby; there is a scuffle, a loose shot is fired injuring the villain; and our hero escapes through the trees....only to find himself lost in the failing light...in a forest of swaying, identical trees...dripping with melt water. He is lost in every sense, as he succumbs to hypothermia and slumps under a tree to die in the night. He wakes with a fever to a flickering fire in a log cabin; he is somehow naked under the crisp white sheets; a beautiful young woman is mopping his brow...her deaf and blind father is rocking in a chair...and...

The worse thing about being in a film, thought Fisher, was the script. It is a world of predetermined fate. What will be will be, as it is written, and there's nothing you can do to change it. Here, in the real world, Fisher had the anxiety of the unknown; but, at least, what happens next is not a foregone conclusion. He is, to a certain extent, in control of his own destiny.

But, somehow, it didn't feel like that.

He could, for example, push open the door of the Zil, and roll out onto the snow, piled at the side of the road. Then, he could make his escape. But, chances are, he would sprain his ankle and just look stupid. And moments later, that option was lost as the Zil entered the suburbs of the city. Rather than break his fall, escaping from the moving car, he was more likely to break his neck or be impaled on a lamppost.

The car proceeded over the Obukhov Bridge and pulled off Moskovsky Avenue towards the Government Offices on the Fontanka River Embankment. It was late into the night, the streets eerily quiet, except for two clusters of cars haphazardly parked, on either side of the frozen river. One group still displaying flashing lights; the other, merely headlamps. Fisher was on the side opposite the commotion of blue and red lights.

As he stepped out of the car, his abductor, took another *Prima* from its packet, placed it calmly in his mouth and struck a match, tossing the stick over the embankment. He looked over the wall to the iced river, scanning the scene like a predator sizing up his prey. There was an island of lights on large tripods, and Fisher could hear the sound of a groaning generator, somewhere out of sight.

Two black Volgas pulled up next to Fisher and a group of men in plain clothes emerged. One of them, a thin wiry man with a gaunt face approached:

"Comrade General Volkov," he said to the man with the *Prima*, and then continued in Russian, "милиция прибыла первой на сцене."

There was a pause, while some smoke emerged from the nostrils of Fisher's captor. The other men began to stamp their feet for warmth, their breath clouding in the night air. The tall man took another breath of smoke, which drifted aimlessly from his mouth.

"Почему я не удивлен, Козлов? Вы знаете, что ваше имя происходит от слова коза!"

"Да, товарищ генерал"

"Но это не значит, что вы должны вести себя как один."

"Да ... Я имею в виду, нет ... Товарищ генерал."

As usual, the exchange sounded less than affable, like two men in a rouble bar arguing about maternal recipes for cabbage soup.

"This man..." Volkov said to Fisher, "...is, as his name suggests, a stupid goat! Shall we take a stroll onto the ice Dr Fisher."

"...onto the ice?"

"How else are we to take control of this chaos?"

"Chaos?"

The party trudged down some icy steps and stepped onto the solid river. It was coated in several inches of crystalized snow, making the footing crisp and as firm as it could be.

The Comrade General flicked his *Prima* to one side and marched towards the light with the rest of his flock, following behind in a vee formation.

There are all kinds of security authorities and other forces that take care of police and military duties in Russia. Their responsibilities often overlap. Many police are poorly trained. They often don't have guns, handcuffs, vehicles or computers. They direct traffic and pick up corpses. In some places, they don't even have enough money for uniforms. Russia's civilian police force, the *militia*, falls under the Ministry of Internal Affairs. Divided into public security units and criminal police, the militia is administered at federal, regional, and local levels. Security units, which are financed by local and regional funds, are responsible for the routine maintenance of public order. The criminal police are divided into specialised units by type of crime; they rely on interrogations and confessions to solve most crimes. A short fat warty toad wearing his black *Ushanka* hat, jauntily tipped to one side, stepped forward as if to bar the way. He called out:

"Отвали, Волков! У вас нет бизнеса здесь" which Fisher took to be: *fuck off and mind your own business!* Well, it didn't sound as if Mr Toad was greeting an old friend and ascertaining the health of his mother. But, he could be wrong.

The Comrade General, Volkov, was stopping for no such man; especially as he had just greeted him by telling him to procreate elsewhere. Least of all a thick, cold turd from the MVD. He brushed the squat man to one side and stopped at a small crater of snow, cleared to reveal the glassy ice. It glowed green in the intense spotlights.

"Кто этот иностранец"

"Специальный следователь из Англии, доктор Фишер."

Volkov turned to Fisher:

"I was just telling this moron that you are a special investigator from England."

"Am I?"

The fat man called somebody by shouting over to the embankment and a slender man came running towards Fisher.

Breathless; his speech clouding in the cold night air:

"I will translate for my boss."

The fat man and Volkov continued to trade insults, with the thin man relaying every word, competently and without prejudice.

"This is MVD jurisdiction, Volkov, not KGB."

"I'll decide whose jurisdiction it is, Egorov. Now, tell me who was involved, and how this was found?"

Egorov paused, then relented:

"Earlier...late this afternoon..."

"Was it earlier or later?"

"A local...he came out here to fish and brushed away the snow."

"You've been drinking, if you hadn't you might have noticed that the ice is too thick for fishing."

"Yes, but he was starving, and thought to try....so he said."

"Under duress, no doubt?"

"Hardly! It's just a fucking fisherman!"

"I see you have mellowed, preferring to ask questions before ripping someone's tongue out. And I took you for a stupid man. Forgive me, Comrade Egorov."

"Fuck you!"

"Where is he now?"

"I let him go."

"What?"

"He was of no further use."

"Really? He didn't confess to anything, before you let him go? How novel. And, did you think to ask yourself that this is a remarkable coincidence that he should pick this spot? Did it occur to your simple mind, that had he not stumbled to this precise location, then whatever we have here would not have been discovered until the Spring?"

"Well...I..."

"Were we meant to find this now? Is your mysterious fisherman part of a conspiracy to ensure that we do? Was he paid to fish here? The truth is, you have no fucking idea, do you? Why? Because that walnut-sized brain inside your thick skull is pickled!"

"This is none of your fucking business, Volkov. Why don't you get on with your own job, chasing spooks, and leave me to mine?"

Fisher, of course, could only guess at the venom in this conversation, which took place entirely in Russian with a literal translation by an embarrassed interpreter that spoke without emotion. But, it wasn't hard to pick the gist and, of course, the nuance, that these two men hated each other. Not least, echoing in Fisher's mind was the acronym, *KGB*. Why was he brought here by a senior officer of the State Security Service?

"Who is this?" Egorov asked, flicking his head upward toward Fisher.

Volkov, turned to Fisher.

"This is Dr Fisher. He is visiting."

"Visiting what?"

"Visiting here, with me."

"What for?"

Ignoring Egorov and his interpreter, Volkov spoke in English; but, with the interpreter still mumbling the translation to his boss:

"Dr Fisher, this my good friend, Ergorov. He is the Chief Investigator of the MVD. It is an institution based on the dynamics of a cess pit... the shit always rises to the top."

"And," replied Fisher, "Egor derives from Georgy, does it not? Which is Greek for pig farmer."

The thin man paused his translation. Volkov laughed; and for the first time, acknowledged some connection with Fisher. He was nodding silently.

"Что вы два говорите?" Turning to his interpreter, "Что он сказал?"

The interpreter's translation was followed by a long list of expletives, insults and threats, mostly directed at Volkov, but also at Fisher, including some reference to him being a slippery eel working his way up the arse of the Comrade General. Ignoring Egorov, Fisher asked:

"Is that what I think it is, encased in the ice?"

"Come closer and take a look." Volkov urged.

Fisher got down on his knees on the lip of the illuminated crater. He could see the shape of a small naked body encased in the ice, well below the surface. The head was bald, or so it seemed; and there was a severe injury to the pelvic area, making it impossible to determine the sex of the Caucasian body.

"It's been there for a while, I think, but not *too* long," Volkov suggested.

"How can you tell?" asked Fisher.

"The body would be closer to the surface if it had been floating in moving water before it was frozen. This has floated under the first freeze, was trapped, and then as the winter progressed, it was encased."

"Что вы два говорите?" Egorov queried.

"What are you doing about removing this body from the ice?" Volkov parried through the voice of the thin man.

"I have ordered some ice cutters and explosives. They will be here soon."

"Explosives! You damn fool! You could destroy evidence; maybe even damage the body, or lose it altogether. And, in any case, the cutters can only go so deep."

"And what does the Comrade General propose instead?"

"I have already ordered a special team to fly in from Novosibirsk. They have everything they need," looking at his watch, "...and are leaving Pulkhova about now."

"But, with no respect whatsoever, Volkov, this is a murder investigation and I am the Chief Investigator of that murder, and you are the KGB…"

"Who says it's a murder? Did I mention murder? It's a body, encased in ice. It could be a child, drowned in the gulf and drifted in… soft organs eaten out by a blue shark."

"How do you explain the head?"

"A cancer victim… could be suicide. The point is, your half-cocked and clumsy methods are redundant here. But, no doubt, you will still be able to extract a confession from a frozen corpse!"

"You are responsible for greater, more mysterious responsibilities. You are in charge of subtlety and subterfuge…combating foreign interference…" Egorov looked at Fisher, "not *colluding* with them. Yours is a world of smugglers, malcontents and wastrels. Not murder… if it is murder… then this is a serious business, Volkov….best left to expert investigators…."

"Egorov…shut the fuck up!" Volkov stood to his feet, towering over the smaller, rounded Chief Investigator, and said:

"This is a matter of State Security. Your men will stand down and leave the ice. You may deploy them to guard the perimeter on both embankments. Watch and learn, Egorov!"

Volkov's men had started to move the militia away from the crater.

Egorov called out:

"Специальный заказ Шесть"

His men turned as they, and Egorov, pulled handguns… all pointed at Volkov. Fisher was paralysed. All were as frozen as the ice on which they stood; their warm breath clouding in the lights, like thoughtless thought bubbles.

"Anatoly…" Volkov said quietly in English, "…*the raven should not peck another raven's eye*. This is pointless, my friend. I am here on the highest authority. Unless you and your comrades wish to spend the next ten years in the gulag...may I suggest, you put the guns away..." Volhov had stepped forward towards Egorov until the Markarov pistol was right in his face. Fisher could sense the anxiety in Egorov's men; one in particular, trembled, causing his gun to wobble from side to side.

Egorov lowered the Markarov slowly.

In one swift and seemingly invisible move, Volkov, like a magician, grabbed the gun and hit Egorov on the side of his head. He fell to the ice with a leaden thud.

"уберите его отсюда!" Volkov ordered to the militia men. "Эта операция теперь под моей командой!"

This wasn't what Fisher had signed up for; nor was it what he was accustomed to. He was used to Slipper of the Yard, a British Detective, and dealing with a bunch of innocuous Bobbies armed with truncheons.

"My apologies, Dr Fisher. But, I'm sure we will see more of the Chief Investigator...he reminds me of an old, scarred Pit Bull Terrier. He knows he's going to lose, but his jaw is locked by years of training, to fix onto any part of his opponent he can snatch hold of."

"This is not what I was expecting, at all. I thought I was..."

"If you're afraid of wolves, Dr Fisher, don't go into the woods."

A distant voice was calling from the nearer embankment.

It was the stupid goat.

Something in Russian, and a man waving and pointing further along the parapet. Two nondescript black vans had arrived.

Volkov gestured to his men to let them through the cordon.

Six new arrivals, men in arctic combat uniforms, white, with light grey and green camouflage, jumped out of the vans and were rushing down the steps, whilst four others began unloading equipment. The six running towards Fisher stopped in a line and saluted Volkov.

"Товарищ генерал!" they said, in near unison.

Volkov merely nodded.

That was enough to trigger a flurry of activity; of equipment being pulled over the ice; pipes, cables, generators and long metal tubes.

"How will they get the body out?" Fisher asked, tentatively.

"These fine Russian Special Forces, know what they are doing, unlike those militia fools. You have heard, Dr Fisher, of the *sherstyanoy mamont*? How do you say…mammoth…woollen mammoth?"

"Yes…in Siberia…in the Tundra."

"How do they extract woollen mammoth, safely and without causing damage?"

"It's not something I've thought about? But, presumably not explosives!"

"I am reliably informed, that provided we only take the temperature of the ice from what it is now…say minus twenty-five Celcius… to no more than zero degrees, the ice will melt and the body will remain frozen, intact and undamaged. The surrounding area will be sterilised, but the body itself will not be interfered with; and so, any evidence in the immediate vicinity could be lost, but not that on the corpse itself."

Behind Volkov, two generators ignited with the sound of precision engineering. There was loud hiss from one of the metal tubes.

"Steam, Dr Fisher. The ice immediately around the body will be left intact to preserve any evidence. We will remove the remaining block to the laboratory at the university, where scientists will cause the ice to melt slowly, in a controlled environment, to minimise tissue damage. So, it will take some time before we can examine this young mammoth."

"I don't understand. Whilst this is fascinating…what has all this to do with me? I came here to assist in the search for a missing person. If this is that person, then my job here is over. So, why bring me to this place?"

"Questions… questions… Dr Fisher. Even your face asks questions when your mouth does not. But you must learn to ask the *right* questions, if you are to catch the killer. As your poet once said: *man was not born criminal, but fell into error through unfortunate circumstances or the influence of negative elements. All crimes great and small could be traced to post-capitalist avarice, egoism, sloth, parasitism, drunkenness, religious prejudices or inherited depravity.*"

"That's quite a quote! Which poet?"

"Martin Cruz Smith, Dr Fisher. Have you not read *Gorky Park*?"

"No, but I've seen the film."

Volkov was so obviously unimpressed, he looked at Fisher with mild disgust.

"A movie is no substitute for a book, Dr Fisher. You surprise me, given your academic credentials. Reading is a personal experience; a movie is a collective one, filtered through the eye of the director. The detail is lost in the transformation; the poetry diluted."

There was a loud hiss, and clouds of steam began rising from the crater.

"That's all very well, General Volkov, but, returning to my original point… I was sent here, not to find a killer, but to find a missing person. The killer, if there is one, is not my business."

"But you have successfully assisted in hunting killers before."

"Yes… *assisted*… nothing more, and at the invitation of the authorities. I don't find killers; but I have advised those that do."

"This is no time for modesty, Dr Fisher."

"Modesty? You can't even agree on who should be leading this investigation. Meanwhile, a killer may be at large and may strike again."

"Or, has already struck, many times… a serial killer. This is your field is it not?"

"Yes, but…"

"It's late now. We are of no use here. I will take you back to the Moskva. Tomorrow, you will return to the schedule that was agreed before your arrival. Tomorrow you will meet the people you came here to meet. You will deal with them as you agreed. You will say nothing… nothing, you understand …of the events of this evening. Until I command otherwise, there isn't a body here…there is, therefore, no missing person found; no murder, or any other investigation, until I say so. Do you understand?"

Fisher nodded, and then:

"I didn't come here to find myself caught between two competing agencies. Nor did I agree to be placed at gunpoint…"

"That drink sodden fool? There is no need to worry about him. In any case, it was surprising that he was sober enough to point his pistol by holding the butt and not the barrel."

"He could have shot both of us!"

"Egorov? His pistol is never loaded; and, even if it was, he couldn't hit the Gates of Kiev if they were falling on top of him!"

None of this was making Fisher feel any better; or any more at ease with the situation. Nor was it the fact that Volkov knew so much about him, his purpose or his schedule.But, despite his protests, he couldn't stop himself from being interested in the case. If, indeed, there was a case or cases.

"Vladimir will pick you up in the morning, five hours from now, at 10am."

"Why Vladimir?"

"That, Dr Fisher, maybe the right question."

5

Long Preserved

Box.

Room.

It was all too easy to feel depressed. Fisher had come here to help; but had found himself embroiled in a blood feud between the KGB and the Ministry of the Interior; a vendetta, beef, clan war, gang war, or private war, a long-running argument or fight, as often between social groups of people, especially families or clans. In this case…two clans, both on the brink of extinction as dinosaurs of the revolution. The comet of capitalism had landed and Fisher had discovered a post-impact nuclear winter, where survival by greed was the norm; and a life, especially his, was all too easily expendable; or simply disappeared.

He thought about calling Vasyli.

Was this the kind of emergency Vasyli had been referring to?

If he were to call, where would he call from? Not here, in his room, not on this leaking telephone.

And what would he say? I need a place to hide? How would he slip through security at the airport? The truth is…he was trapped.

He wanted to go home. He missed Jane, and his children. Particularly, because he felt endangered.

And what of that body…the one that, for now, at least, didn't exist? It was a body that wasn't there… and yet, it was there, even here, in his room…in his head.

Fisher was convinced it was an older child or a young teen.

What horrors had brought that child to be tossed naked into the freezing river?

What tortures had been endured?

The curiously bald head; and the wound to the lower torso that looked as if something had been ripped from within. The body, it seemed, was almost cut in two...and the face... a face he would never forget... angelic... sleeping... and yet, still screaming. A frozen scream; a silent cry, trapped in the ice. Distorted by refraction, almost featureless and yet, macabre.

It was the last thing he saw as his eyes closed and he gave in to a fitful sleep.

If nothing else, Vladimir was prompt. Once again, he waited by the Tatra; and once again he carried a shoe box under his left arm.

"We missed you last night, Stephen."

"Yes, believe me when I say...I missed you."

"The fish was very good....so fresh, plucked from the icy water. Have you eaten?"

"Oh...some black bread and some dreadful sausage meat."

"I know somewhere near the Fontanka, where the coffee is as good as it gets here, and they serve some hot food."

"The Fontanka?"

"Yes...it's only a few minutes from here."

"Yes, I know..."

The Tatra glided over the Obukhov Bridge.

Without being too obvious, Fisher could just see over the barrier, to the area where he had been the night before. There was no sign of any activity. Indeed, there was no sign of anything; not even a hole in the ice. It was all smooth and white, as if he had dreamt the whole thing.

"Do we have time for this, Vladimir?"

"Yes, yes, of course. There has been a slight change of plan."

Fisher's heart sank like a hot brick through cold thin ice.

What now?

He decided it might be better not to ask.

The car drew in to a space outside a small coffee shop. Well, in truth, it could have been a butcher's shop…or anything. There was no sign outside; just a small door with two filthy leaded windows to the right. The dark interior was filled with a grey acerbic fog and a few small round tables. The volume of voices paused as the door opened, and then resumed into a low murmur, a hum of whispers and conspiratorial glances. Vladimir smiled and nodded to a man behind the bar; and, he in turn, nodded back. Obviously, they knew each other.

Aside from them, the space contained a motley collection of unhealthy looking faces. All male, all pale, all with scurvy blotchy skin and hair that had spent too long sweating under a fur hat in cold weather. If they weren't drinking, it seemed that Russians were smoking themselves to death.

"Let's sit here," Vladimir pointed to an empty table by the window. "Now, Stephen, what would you like?"

"Is there a menu?"

Vladimir laughed.

"You can have coffee *or* something to eat; or you can have coffee *and* something to eat."

"What is the *something*?"

"A stew of some sort, I think."

"A stew?"

"Yes."

"Of some sort?"

"Yes, exactly."

"I'll have the coffee and some sort of stew, please."

"Good choice!"

Vladimir called the man over and ordered in Russian. He waited until Vladimir opened his shoe box, removed a wad of roubles and paid accordingly, what looked like a huge amount of money.

Within a remarkably short time, a thick dark coffee appeared in a chipped cup and a bowl of grey stew with some rye bread.

"Eat…enjoy." Vladimir said, pointing to the bowl.

"You're not having any?"

"No…my job is to look after you, not myself."

"And the shoebox?"

"Ah…hyperinflation. Every morning I need to collect cash from the university…enough to see to your needs. But, every day, the number of notes gets larger. Soon, I may need to trade my box for a suitcase."

Fisher was beginning to see a different Vladimir. Not the one with the steely demeanour.

"It's good to see you smile Vladimir."

He stopped smiling.

"If you were to walk the streets St. Petersburg," he said, "you'd notice that no one walks around with a beaming smile. It'll happen in a closed group of family and friends, whether in public or in private, but it's not the public face you show to people you don't know."

Vladimir watched, with his renewed stony face, as Fisher spooned the stew into his hungry mouth. It wasn't all that bad; it just looked terrible. And there was some meat in there…it could have been anything… a bit of gristly knuckle or cartilage. The odd carrot and a clump of limp cabbage. The coffee, on the other hand, tasted like gritty gravy browning, but a single cup was strong enough to wake a dead elephant. Fisher, at least, was grateful for that.

"So," Fisher asserted, "I am due to meet the British couple today?"

"Yes, given the address, I believe they are British, yes."

"Where are we meeting them?"

"You mean...where are *you* meeting them...my job is to take you there...and wait outside."

"And the change of plan?"

"Oh, nothing really. The meeting was put back an hour...I don't know the reason...and the place of the meeting has changed slightly."

"It's no longer at the British High Commission?"

"It's now at the private residence of...," Vladimir pulled a piece of paper from his pocket, "Her Majesty's Consul General...at this address."

"Why?"

"I have no idea. I was simply told to take you there. It is on..." He glanced again at the paper, "Di Proletarskoy Diktatury Street in the Trentralny District."

"Quite a mouthful!"

"A mouthful? Ah...I see your meaning. Which is why I write it down. We should probably leave now."

As the car purred away, Fisher was confused. He had been asked by his Vice Chancellor at the university, to assist Leningrad University with an investigation. He had agreed, somewhat reluctantly to assist them, together with the local police, in a case they were involved in, concerning a British couple living and working in St Petersburg. But, he had not met a single police officer, or anybody at the university, apart from Vladimir. Only the KGB seemed aware and involved, whilst the militia of the MVD didn't know anything about him. And now he was arriving at the Consul General's residence, presumably to be briefed and introduced to the couple concerned.

But, why the residence?

It was part of a beautiful seventeenth century mansion.

Outside, two uniformed officers of the militia, stood guard. A western looking man in a smart, black, overcoat, hat and gloves stood on the steps, gently stomping his black brogues. The shoes stepped forward to greet Fisher as he got out of the car:

"Dr Fisher, I presume?"

"Yes."

"May I see your passport please? You can ask your driver to wait in the car park around the corner."

"Oh...he's not my..."

It was as if Vladimir was expecting this. Getting back into the car, he said:

"I'll wait around the corner."

Fisher produced his passport.

'Come with me...the Consul General will see you in a few moments. But first, you should follow me."

"And your name is...?"

"You don't need to know my name Dr Fisher. You need to follow me."

Fisher was led inside to be met by and frisked by a cheerless security guard...a young black man with a cockney accent, like a barrow boy from Borough Market.

'He's clean!" the guard proclaimed.

"This way," said the man with no name and the posh, but squeaking brogues.

Fisher entered a small anteroom with a single ornate desk and three chairs.

"Please sit, Dr Fisher."

Fisher complied.

"Before meeting the Consul General, you are required to read and sign this document."

"I'm here to meet the Consul General...? I don't..."

A pen and a folder were pushed across the desk. Fisher opened the folder with some trepidation. He read the heading out loud, quite possibly out of surprise; or perhaps to ensure that he had been handed the correct document:

"Official Secrets Act."

"That is correct, Dr Fisher."

"Why do I...?"

Fisher could see from the stony face of his minder, that there was no point in asking the question; or any questions for that matter. Equally, there was little point in reading it. He knew what it meant. Quite simply, he would be bound not to disclose any information deemed secret or that might threaten the security of the realm. Once signed, he was bound for life; or, if he contravened the act, face up to fourteen years in prison. The stony man was waiting.

After a cursory glance, Fisher signed the document.

"Good. The Consul General will see you now."

Fisher was taken across the hall and handed to the care of a woman, who, at least, smiled.

"I'm Isabelle. May I take your coat Dr Fisher?"

"Yes, thank you, Isabelle."

"The Consul General will usually be taking morning tea at this time. He may offer you a homemade biscuit, baked in-house by his housekeeper, Lyn. It's a good idea to take the biscuit and to comment on the taste and freshness."

This was obviously her usual script.

"Thank you...that's most helpful."

Isabelle tapped on the ornate door, and placed her ear closer to it. A muffled voice came from within, and she opened the door.

"Dr Stephen Fisher," Isabelle announced.

As Fisher stepped forward into a reception room, he heard the door click behind him. The scene wasn't quite what he was expecting. The Consul General got up from a sofa to greet him:

"Dr Fisher...welcome."

"Yes, thank you, sir."

"Please... may I? Stephen? Please call me Alan... this is my wife Jennifer."

Fisher glanced over to the sofa. The woman, Jennifer, eyes fixed before her feet, was still sitting, just as she had been when he walked in. Slumped forward, her head slightly down. She had not looked up at all, and yet Fisher could see, already, the thin, pale face and the red-raw eyes. She was sitting in a defensive posture: arms and legs tucked in, the hands covering her vital organs and a slight rocking on the balls of her feet. Fisher recognised the signs of deep, sustained trauma, anxiety and nervous tension.

"She's deeply upset, Stephen, we both are. What have you been told?"

"Nothing, really. But, given my background and experience, I can guess why I might be here. However, I was expecting you to introduce me to another couple or parent."

"Please....sit down." The Consul General gestured to a nearby armchair.

"Well, it all started over two weeks ago...Jenny and I were at a reception, hosted by the Mayor of St Petersburg. It was the first really cold night of the season. We were gone...perhaps an hour and a half...no more. This house is guarded, Stephen. My personal bodyguard, Gerard, and driver, Petr, were in the car with us. On returning, we passed security at the door and Simon in the hall. Our housekeeper, Lyn, had stayed on late...she was asleep just here on the sofa where we had left her, with...."

"Just tell him!" Jennifer spluttered, her bottom lip trembling. She was trying not to cry, and began to move backwards and forwards, until she lifted up her distraught face and reddened eyes:

"Our daughter... my baby, Eloise, she's been taken!"

Fisher was not well equipped for consolation; he never was. Neither, it seemed was the Consul General. And worse, Fisher knew all too well, that if a missing child was not found within twenty-four hours, then Jennifer was right...she had been taken. If there had been no contact from the abductor after forty-eight hours, then the child was, more than likely, dead. At the shocking forefront of Fisher's mind was the body in the ice. Was this the missing girl? It seemed too much of a coincidence. Nevertheless, Volkov had taken him there for some purpose.

Why?

Of course, even if he could suggest the possibility, he was charged not to mention it at all. But, in any case, how could he be certain? There was little hope of the new DNA tests being available in Russia. Perhaps at the university? But, for now, it could only be done the old-fashioned way, by a visual identification.

"Do you have a recent photograph of Eloise? Something I could take away. I promise to return it."

"Yes... yes...there is one here." Alan walked over to a small grand piano in the corner next to the windows, and brought a silver-framed photo back with him. Fumbling, he attempted to take the back off the frame to remove the photograph.

"There's no need, really..." Fisher offered.

"I can't quite..."

The nervous fingers were painful to watch. Until it slipped from his hand and smashed on to the marble floor. He stared at it for a moment; and then he began to cry.

"Come sit down…" said Fisher, moving to pick up the print from the shattered glass. The girl in the photograph was eleven or twelve; it was hard to tell; fair hair and a pretty face. It looked like a professional photo, in black and white. One of those, a model might have taken for a portfolio; or an actor for their agent to peddle.

"This was taken recently?"

"Yes," Alan replied, "just a month ago, on her birthday."

"The police suggested," offered Jennifer through her tears, "that she had wandered out somewhere and got lost. It's simply absurd. She is a bright young girl. She knows her way around."

"I am sure you're right, Jennifer," said Fisher, "she has, as you said before, most likely been taken by someone; or disappeared with someone. How? By whom? And to what purpose, we will, I am sure, discover in due course. My immediate concern is her safety and wellbeing. But, there is something I don't quite understand. You say, she went missing just over two weeks ago? Is that correct?"

"Yes…. sixteen days and twelve hours ago. " Alan composed himself, and then continued. "But, there has been no progress in the investigation by the police?"

"This has been handled by the militia. But, no… no progress, and little communication," added Jennifer.

"And no publicity either? Isn't that a little odd?" queried Fisher. "Something like this is hard to keep quiet about; and, in any case, if a girl is missing, the public attention may produce some sightings. In the UK, the press would be all over this. This is no ordinary case of abduction, if this is such a thing. This involves the family of a high-profile diplomat, in a country on the brink of collapse. Surely, this is international news?"

They said nothing.

Fisher waited, patiently.

"Tell him!," Jennifer uttered with some contempt. "If you don't, I will."

Alan took a deep breath.

"On the night of the disappearance, I called the British Ambassador in Moscow and he called the Foreign and Commonwealth Office in London. He advised me to contact the MVD, not the police. The police, I was told were incompetent; the militia, were, at least thorough, if their methodology was a bit suspect."

He paused for a moment.

"An hour later, I received a call from the Foreign Secretary, offering his unlimited support. He suggested that some specialist expertise would be sourced, and advised, that for the time being, at least, we should remain calm and quietly focussed on being reunited with our daughter."

"Does he have a daughter!" Jennifer cried, contemptuously.

Alan paused once more.

"The following morning, I received a call from the KGB. A high-ranking official...his name...his name was Wolf."

"Wolf?" queried, Fisher.

"In Russian, it means...wolf. His name was Volkov. He...well...he... didn't exactly threaten me. But, he said that in the interests of my daughter's safety, we should remain quiet about her disappearance. And that was it. He put the phone down."

"That doesn't sound like a threat."

"It was the way he said it...something sinister in his voice. But, then it's KGB, they will always sound sinister, I suppose. When I called KGB Headquarters the following day, I was told that this Volkov fellow had not telephoned; that he had no knowledge of the matter; and not to call again."

"I have met General Volkov," added Fisher. "I know exactly what you mean. But, I don't understanding why he would deny all knowledge. And, I still don't see the need for so much secrecy."

"That's what I said…" added Jennifer.

"You should understand…both of you…I am not a detective. I am a Criminal Psychologist, an academic researcher operating in a narrow, specialist field. Occasionally, I have assisted the authorities in cases of child abduction. In the psychological profiling of those that commit these sometimes heinous crimes. I can only do what I know to be within my field."

"We understand that, Stephen. We do. But, you are our only hope."

"As a parent myself, I can only begin to imagine what you are going through. I can't help with that…I'm not a family councillor. Someone should be here to support and guide you through this."

"They won't send anybody else, Stephen; they are concerned it will draw attention to the disappearance."

In any case, Fisher believed this to be a double-edged sword. On the one edge, the media frenzy could produce new witness information. But, on the other, it all too often, these days, results in a *Bring Her Home* campaign. Celebrities get involved and before you know it, there is inexplicable mass public grief, piles of flowers rotting in the street and candles, vigils, or even a damn pop concert. But here in the Soviet Union it is all very different.

"Well, I need to say a few things to you before we go any further. Sadly, I have been involved in far too many such cases. My advice, based on that experience, may seem cruel and obvious; but it is important that we understand each other."

"Yes, of course."

Jennifer nodded in accord.

"Not knowing where Eloise is or how she is being treated is one of the hardest things you will have to face. One minute you will feel a surge of hope, the next, a depth of despair that will threaten your very sanity. Life will become an emotional roller coaster that won't really stop until you can hold her in your arms again."

They both began to cry, as Fisher continued.

"It will get worse. As you enter more deeply into this nightmare, you should know that you are not alone. Unfortunately, other families have had to travel this same path and have experienced the same emotional drain. Relationships can and do survive and yours will, too, but it will take all the strength, hope, and willpower you can muster."

They both listened, and at last Alan took hold of Jennifer's hand.

"Your ability to be strong and to help in the search for Eloise requires that you attend to your own physical and emotional needs. Although it may be hard right now for you to maintain your daily routine, it is paramount that you both do so. The driving force behind the search effort is you, and therefore you must, for Eloise's sake, be physically and mentally well, in order to handle it. The fact is, the nightmare will continue until Eloise is found, so you need to take as many breaks from this as you can. I'm sorry if this is upsetting you."

"It's just...it's just..." Jennifer was struggling to speak, "...you are the first person to say her name. She has been a missing child...a case... an investigation. Her name is *Eloise*. They've searched her room and rummaged through her clothes; they can take anything they want. But, she has a name!"

Although Fisher had seen many distraught parents, he was moved by Jennifer's plea; by her will to retain her daughter's identity, however futile that might be prove to be.

He spoke quietly and sincerely:

"Looking back, you may feel that there was something you could have done to have prevented Eloise's disappearance. You can literally drive yourself insane asking, *What if...?*

But the fact is, you didn't arrange for the disappearance, you shouldn't hold yourself responsible for not knowing or doing something that may seem obvious in hindsight.

And I remember, at least one child had been abducted out of the safety of her own bedroom while her parents slept in the room next door. As heartless as it may seem, your life must go on.

Although moving on with your life may seem impossible, you must do it, for the good of yourself and your health. You will, of course, find that there is no such thing as *normal* life as you once knew it. Everything has changed, and has changed forever. And whatever the outcome, you will be dealing with this nightmare in some way for the rest of your life. Eloise too, may have to deal with it throughout her life."

"Do you think we will ever see her again, Stephen?"

Fisher paused. He knew this was the hardest question to answer.

"I will do my best to bring her home..."

He knew in his heart, that it would be most extraordinary if he did.

"We must stay positive and hope for that. But, I have to warn you, that you must also be prepared for the worst; for false hopes and dashed wishes; and for the possibility that she may not come home at all."

Fisher halted to let them absorb that.

"By now, we know, from what you have said, she is not lost and unlikely to have run away alone. In this weather, Eloise would need to be with someone. The main concern I have, is that you have had no contact from this person or persons, suggesting this isn't a case of extortion. Is it possible she has run away with someone? A boyfriend? An older man?"

"No!" said Jennifer, naturally outraged by the idea. "She is far too young and has no experience with boys, let alone men! I can't believe it!"

"How can you be so sure?"

"I… I just am. I know my daughter! She has been sheltered all her life in this diplomatic prison; this rarified isolation of security and paranoia. For the first six years of her life, we were stationed in Egypt and then Indonesia….and now this sterile hell hole, where a wrong word here or there can result in a spell at the Kresty Prison or years in a Gulag. Have you read Solzhenitsyn? Do you have any idea how crazy this place is?"

"Jennifer….." interjected Alan.

"This is my point here, we must keep an open mind, until we eliminate all the obvious possibilities; and then move forward. It could be something less obvious and entirely different."

"Then what is it?" stuttered Alan.

He paused once more before the final blow.

"You must come to terms with the possibility that Eloise is being held somewhere, by someone, who wishes her harm, or wishes you or the office you hold, harm. The more they prolong your agony, the more likely you are to cooperate with whatever it is that motivated the abduction. Can you think of any reason, personally or professionally, as to why someone or some body, would wish to put you, or the United Kingdom under pressure?"

"But, Stephen…" interjected Alan, "…you know the Prime Minister's views about negotiating with the enemies of the State."

Fisher nodded.

"We just want her back. We need to know where she has gone and what has happened to her."

"It seems perhaps too obvious to state, but in identifying the 'why' we may uncover the truth. You must also accept the possibility that Eloise may already be dead."

6

Marble Vault

It was enough.

Enough is enough.

Fisher knew he would be back to see them. There were many unanswered questions; but for now, at least, it was time for an even more arduous and gruesome engagement. As Fisher stepped into the car park, Vladimir was sitting in the car; the engine running and the heater on, in an attempt to keep warm. Fisher paused for a moment, reflecting on his last meeting, and the complication of the document he signed.

How should he respond to questions from Vladimir?

What about Volkov? How would Fisher answer his acid questions?

He entered the warm car.

"All finished?"

"For now, yes, thank you for waiting, Vladimir."

"Would you like some lunch? Or shall we go straight to my office at the university?"

"The university, please."

Oddly, there was mostly silence along the way. At no time did Vladimir ask any questions about the meeting, nor did he mention anything about what might be waiting at the university. Instead, he suggested sightseeing. A visit to the Hermitage perhaps? The Kirov Ballet? The St Peter and Paul Fortress? St Isaac's Cathedral, maybe? Or, how about a visit to see Rasputin's enormous penis, suspended, preserved in a glass jar?

None of these delights filled Fisher with immediate joy; the latter made him feel quite sick. In any case, despite his initial lie to the immigration officer, he wasn't a tourist and he wasn't here to enjoy himself; and the last twenty-four hours were a harrowing testament to that fact.

Now that he understood something of his mission, Fisher's mind became gripped by the flow of possibilities. His heart, however, remained behind. From the source to the tumbling stream of details, to the wide river of hope, over wiers and cascading falls in tempo, meandering through the arid plains to the fertile delta of suspicion until he reached the sea of truth.

One sea often looked exactly like another, for the truth is universal: that man is capable of such depths of dark cruelty that are as indistinguishable, one from the other. For here, at the bottom of the ocean resides the terrible beast; a monster that devours childhood and leaves the carcasses of dreams, to be picked at by the scavengers of hope.

The drive, mostly along the embankment of the Neva, passed a number of such sights in any case, including the Winter Palace, or *Hermitage*, as it was known in the West. It all looked rather shabby; just as the façade of the oldest university in Russia looked like the façade of the oldest university in Russia. Many winters of neglect had cracked the stones and stucco of this once great structure. This impressive red-and-white building stretched into the distance and actually consisted of twelve buildings, standing side by side.

It was built between 1722 and 1742, on Vasilievsky Island, and was intended to house the twelve government bodies of Russia. In 1835 the building was given to St. Petersburg University and now serves as its main, if poorly maintained, building.

The inside was no better. It was dark and dingy, with a smell of damp wood, dust and overheated pipes.

The stone steps, were worn into a wavy curve by generations of students, shuffling their shoes up and down them. They took Fisher, following Vladimir, to the Office of the Assistant to the Rector.

Vladimir was immediately handed a note by a rather grim looking secretary, who's face and neck bore a startling constellation of protruding moles, one of which, on her forehead had a long curly hair sticking out of it.

"No time for tea...I think you say in English. I am requested to deliver you to the Faculty of Science, Laboratory Number Three, immediately on arrival. Irina will accompany you most of the way."

"Are you not coming, Vladimir?"

"I must stay here...some things are for you, only, and not for me. Irina will show you the way. She doesn't speak English. In fact, she rarely speaks at all."

Fisher followed Irina as she marched off down the corridor, in a cardigan her mother might have knitted for someone she didn't care much for, and with legs so hairy, she kept them apart for fear of starting a fire. In fact, she had a somewhat military air about her, with a tight, pinched, bottom, and walked with purpose like someone who had taken an overdose of laxatives. Fisher thought she was the kind of secretary his wife Jane might choose for him.

Irina came to an abrupt stop, turned and pointed to a well-worn chair next to a large brown door, and then promptly marched off the way she had come, as if each leg wished to turn opposite corners

Sitting there, it reminded Fisher of his school days, waiting outside the Deputy Headmaster's office, without trial or fair hearing for an unspecified punishment for a minor or major misdemeanour, he had already forgotten. He used to think the wait was worse than the punishment, until, that is, the punishment was meted out in the form of a thick leather strap whipped across the hand at the speed of sound. Not once, but four or six times, depending on the seriousness of the crime. Oddly, never five. That might have been reserved for especially heinous sex crimes, such as, wolf-whistling the Dinner Ladies.

The brown door opened slowly with a long, painful creak and a man in a soiled white coat appeared; more like a butcher at an abattoir than an academic.

"Professor Fisher?" He spoke in a clipped English voice, with only a hint of register.

"Yes."

"Professor Mendeleev...Dimitry, please."

"Stephen...thank you," returned Fisher.

"This way, Stephen," he said, leading him through. "I spent some time in Manchester, at the university."

"Really? When?"

"Oh...it was many years ago. As part of an exchange programme... when things were, shall we say, more amicable. I was part of a delegation accompanying Yuri Gagarin to the city. Did you know that Manchester and Leningrad are twinned cities?"

"No...I wasn't aware of that."

"We are even on the same latitude...more or less. The weather is a little different, of course, due to the Gulf Stream keeping your climate more temperate there. Is it cold outside? Stupid question! I expect it's cold enough to freeze the balls off a shot putter. I've been in here so long, I feel as if my home is but a distant memory."

"It's not as cold as it was yesterday."

These meteorological observations were far too truncated to last all the way to the end of the eternal corridor; and so Mendeleev tacked to the past.

"Did you know, the University was founded in 1819, though some local scholars suggest a much earlier date? One of the most prominent universities in Russia, it has received international recognition thanks to my Great Grandfather, the chemist Dmitry I. Mendeleev, creator of the Periodic Table of Elements, the physicist Alexander S. Popov, who invented the radio simultaneously with Marconi, and many other major scholars. Among the alumni, were many important figures of Russian culture and politics: the writers Nikolai Chernyshevsky and Ivan Turgenev, the poet Alexander Blok, prime minister and reformer Pyotr Stolypin and the head of the 1917 Provisional Government, Alexander Kerensky. Even the great revolutionary Vladimir Lenin attended the university and passed his finals exams in the Law Faculty in 1891."

This was his rehearsed speech. But long enough that they had walked the length of the narrow passage, which Dimitry had reduced with large strides of his long legs until they reached another brown door. This time with a row of variously used coat hooks adjacent to it.

"Please, take off your coat and put on this lab coat and mask. You may as well be comfortable, we could be here for some time....I take it you know why you are here?"

"I'm guessing it has something to do with last night's fishing."

"Quite a catch!"

The room wasn't at all what Fisher was expecting. It was surprisingly sterile and well equipped. For some reason, he had been expecting the laboratory of Dr Frankenstein, with glass tubes, pipes and static electrical discharges from illuminated domes fed by vacuum pumps. Instead, two young female assistants were standing by a surgical table in the centre of the room on a white tiled floor, sloping towards a central drain. They too were wearing masks and also surgical gowns. The table was illuminated by a large cluster of intense spotlights and four infrared lamps, one at each corner. Further away, Volkov was standing without a mask and, absurdly, smoking a *Prima*. He barely nodded to acknowledge Fisher.

"We are almost there, Comrade General."

"Is there no way of speeding this up, Mendeleev?" Volkov barked, impatiently; and probably not for the first time.

"Melting ice involves transferring heat energy to the ice at eighty calories per gram, to be specific. If the pressure stays at one atmosphere, then ice at zero degrees Celsius will turn into water once the heat is transferred. The only way to increase the speed of transfer is to increase the pressure above one atmosphere. This may cause the ice to implode and potentially damage the fragile remains."

Volkov was uninterested and unimpressed, blowing exasperated smoke across the room.

An array of spent bent cigarette ends at his feet indicated he had been there for quite some time, befouling the sterile room.

The ice block lay under a shroud of muslin, that had taken on the shape of the small corpse, indicating that most of the surrounding ice was now gone. Dimitry said something in Russian, and the heat lamps were switched off and taken away to the side of the room. Fisher stepped forward in anticipation, his breath gathering pace as it pulled and puffed in and out of the mask.

Another instruction in Russian.

One woman raised a Zenith camera; as the other began to peel the muslin away.

A smooth depilated head; and a distorted face.

Flash.

Another.

Dimitry pulled an overhead microphone towards him:

"This is the autopsy conducted at the University by myself, Dr Dimitry Mendeleev. Also present, my two assistants Maria and Olga, together with Dr...er...Professor Fisher, visiting from the University of Manchester."

There was no mention of Volkov.

"I will continue to speak in English for your benefit Professor Fisher. The autopsy is begun at 1:30pm on December 18th 1991. The body was presented sixteen hours ago, still frozen and well-preserved in a block of ice. The victim is entirely naked. A prepubescent. The head has been shaved..." said Dimitry gently handling the head, "...the eyebrows remain..."

The terror was still there on the pale blue face; slightly pink on the lips and eyelids. But otherwise, still frozen to the core. A piece of ice, slipped off the neck and onto the floor, startling all but Volkov.

Fisher took the photo from his pocket and held it close to the face. Despite the contortions, there was a distinct similarity between the two: same nose, same mouth; same overall facial structure. No hair for colour comparison; the head shaved completely bald as Dimitry had stated; but the eyebrows indicated fair hair.

Mendeleev was babbling in Russian into the microphone, and then again in English, in slow, soporific, lugubrious tone.

"...the face and head are unmarked...no bruising..."

Flash.

Another.

One more.

And then the thin wet fabric peeled away to reveal the chest. Fisher thought he noticed a slight puffiness in the nipples indicating a barely prepubescent female. But, as yet, Fisher wasn't absolutely sure of the sex.

Flash...and again, until the fabric edge reached the midriff wound.

And the room fell into a stunned, inactive, silence.

One of the young women, the one peeling the muslin, rushed out of the room.

"The body is that of a normally developed white female measuring forty-seven inches and weighing approximately 25 kilograms, and appearing generally consistent with age of twelve years. The body is cold and frozen at the core. Lividity is fixed in the distal portions of the limbs. The eyes are open. The irises are blue and corneas are cloudy. Petechial haemorrhaging is present in the conjunctival surfaces of the eyes. The pupils measure 0.3 cm."

There was no smell. Not yet. It was a purely visual thing, that made Fisher wretch from the pit of his stomach. The pelvic bone had been completely removed. The leg ball joints were exposed, and the lower spine remained.

Mendeleev was the first to speak:

"The hip bone structure, as you may know, Stephen, is formed by three parts: ilium, ischium, and pubis. At birth, these three components are separated by hyaline cartilage. They join each other in a Y-shaped portion of cartilage in the acetabulum. By the end of puberty, the three regions will have fused together, and by the age of twenty-five they will have ossified. The two hip bones join each other at the pubic symphysis. Together with the sacrum and coccyx, the hip bones form the pelvis. It has all been entirely removed. Once thawed, the legs will fall away. There's is nothing but skin and muscle holding the body and legs together."

"How is this possible?" said Fisher, incredulously.

"It is very difficult to achieve; but a surgeon with a modicum of skill could do it, at the level of a butcher, I would suggest, judging from the way the flesh has been cut. As you can see from what remains below the wound, this, as I surmised earlier, is a young girl, about to enter puberty...perhaps eleven or twelve years of age. Caucasian, of course."

Mendeleev switched back to Russian; and then continued in English.

"Closer examination reveals a ligature mark (known throughout this report as *Ligature A*) on the neck below the mandible. Ligature A is approximately two centimetres wide and encircles the neck in the form of a *V* on the anterior of the neck and an inverted *V* on the posterior of the neck, consistent with hanging. Minor abrasions are present in the area of Ligature A. Lack of haemorrhage surrounding Ligature A indicates this injury to be post-mortem. An odour of bleach was detected. Areas of the body will be swabbed and submitted for detection of hypochlorite. Following closer scrutiny, a second ligature mark (known throughout this report as *Ligature B*) was observed on the victim's neck. The mark is a dark red ligature and encircles the neck, crossing the anterior midline of the neck just below the laryngeal prominence. The width of the mark varies between 0.8 and one centimetre and is horizontal in orientation. The skin of the anterior neck above and below the ligature mark shows petechial haemorrhaging. Ligature B is not consistent with whatever caused Ligature A. The absence of abrasions associated with Ligature B, along with the variations in the width of the ligature mark, are consistent with a soft ligature, such as a length of fabric. No trace evidence was recovered from Ligature B that might assist in identification of the ligature used. What remains of the genitalia are that of a young female and there is extensive evidence of injury. Soft pubic hair has been shaved in its entirety within six hours prior to death. Limbs are equal, symmetrically developed and show no evidence of injury, except the wrists where ligature marks (*Ligatures C and D*) indicate restraints being applied prior to death. The fingernails are medium length and fingernail beds are blue. There are no residual scars, markings or tattoos. The oral cavity shows no lesions. Petechial haemorrhaging is present in the mucosa of the lips and the interior of the mouth. Otherwise, the mucosa is intact and there are no injuries to the lips, teeth or gums. The structures are within normal limits. Examination of the pelvic area indicates the victim was still alive during the removal of the hips. There is evidence of recent sexual activity but no indications that the sexual contact was forced. Vaginal fluid samples will be removed for analysis.... *Immediate Cause of Death*: probably cardiac arrest from shock; further tests to confirm. Attempted asphyxia due to ligature strangulation (Ligature B) is, in fact, post mortem. Ligature A is also made post-mortem."

"So, she has she been taken?" Volkov sneered in English.

"If you mean, has she been sexually penetrated, I would say there are signs of penetration, yes. But, this is such a terrible mess! That will need further work before I can confirm. The more important question, is why remove this particular bone structure, especially given the difficulty in achieving it?"

"As a trophy?" said Fisher. "It's not uncommon for the killer to keep a trophy... revolting, though this is. The hips, we associate with femininity...child birth. The pubic bone with sex. The coccyx...I have no idea. Perhaps it's to keep it all in one piece...for display?"

"Display? Once again, Stephen, it's not quite that simple. Once removed, the structure would still be covered in sinews, muscle and loose flesh. To clean it up for display? Well, it could be boiled, to remove most of the tissue. But, that would dissolve the cartilage... so it would fall apart into its constituent parts. The butcher would then have to become a carpenter or engineer, since it would have to be reassembled... bolted or glued together. It's a lot of work!"

"These monsters are often obsessive compulsive detail people. The time and care and skill required, is all part of the pleasure of possession, of power and control."

"Perhaps it's not a monster..?" questioned Volkov, "...perhaps it's not a butcher... perhaps it's a skilled hunter, de-boning his prey."

"Interesting... very interesting," mused Mendeleev. "A hunter? Possibly, yes. A knife, not a scalpel."

"A hunter saves his hunting knife for gutting," added Volkov. "The best knives for butchering are a paring knife with a short blade to cut in to the small places, and a bigger knife blade for general work. A good, sharp pen knife will do it. Army knives are among the best to use for most cutting. For boning out a lot of deer, a boning hook is also a useful tool. It will help safely put tension on the cut as the meat is being sliced from the bone."

"I agree," said Mendeleev, nodding and continuing to examine the massive wound. "Although, in this case, It would be impractical to hang the body like a deer or a hog... the tension would have ripped the body in two, once the bone was detached."

"Is it who I think it is, Dr Fisher?" queried Volkov.

Fisher looked once more at the photograph; and then to the face.

"It could be...there is a likeness. But...I'm really not certain. The shape of the ear looks different but that could be the exposure to water...the freezing...thawing. What about dental records?"

"There is no evidence of any dental work that I can see." Mendeleev offered, peering into the mouth. "DNA..? We are not equipped for that just yet. No distinguishing marks or obvious moles; no scars or blemishes...nothing."

"Then we are left with no choice." Volkov asserted coldly, "We must bring the parents in, for a positive or negative identification. Who knows a child better, than their mother?"

"And let them see her like this? What if it's not her? What will that do to their already terrifying nightmare? It will destroy them, and all hope they may have of finding their daughter alive."

"And, what if it is her?"

Fisher had to acknowledge that the options were equally unpalatable; but, inevitable.

"I will ask Vladimir's office to call them now," Volkov said.

"No…please…let me speak to them first."

Volkov paused in silence, his cold grey eyes staring into Fisher's, as if he was searching for something. His soul, perhaps? If such a thing existed, Fisher was convinced that Volkov could rip it out of him, without lifting a finger. His thin pale lilac lips, squeezed the tip of the Prima, as he drew in a lung full of toxic smoke, and then let it drift, slowly, from his dark nostrils.

"As you wish Dr Fisher. I will have Vladimir drive you there, right away."

"No need, really. I can take a taxi. Perhaps someone could call ahead to alert the Consul General of my arrival? But without giving any reason, please."

"As you wish."

Fisher skipped down the stairs, and out into University Embankment to hail a taxi. He knew they were few and far between these days, but somehow, he got lucky in the first ten minutes. The driver was a short man with a stubble beard, and obviously spoke some rudimentary English. Fisher struggled to recall the address.

"Yes?" said the driver, hopefully.

"Proletarskoy Street."

"You mean, Proletarskoy Diktatury Street?"

"Yes, exactly."

As the taxi moved off, Fisher was already racing ahead of himself.

Who murders children? It was a question he had asked many times; and the answers were always different. But, there were some patterns in the chaos. It is an unusual crime. But despite its rarity, enigmatic patterns were emerging from Fisher's latest research, which, he believed could help track down the perpetrator and help other parents protect their children. It begins by building a profile of the killer or kidnapper by first looking at the age of the victim. If a child older than five goes missing and is feared dead, it is highly likely the perpetrator is someone outside the family.

The contrasting profiles of intra-familial as opposed to that of extra-familial killers are vital clues deployed by the police during a search. His experience confirms the majority of assailants in child murder cases, particularly those below five years of age, are in fact the victim's parents. Most are mothers, often suffering mental illnesses or even post-natal psychosis. Interestingly, almost all the natural fathers who killed their children, followed the act by committing suicide.

Of the extra-familial killers investigated by Fisher, all were males aged nineteen to forty-two and had multiple past convictions. One was termed a *Multi-Criminal-Child-Sex-Abuser* while the remaining four were *Violent-Multi-Criminal-Child-Sex-Abusers*. Fisher believed this high level of previous criminality reflects chaotic backgrounds. Of five extra-familial killers he looked at, four had some known previous contact with their victim, but were not in any type of familial relationship. Often, the child is familiar with their assailant.

Fisher had worked on the idea of two main subsets of offenders. One group having sexually sadistic urges and aroused and gratified by the suffering and the killing of young victims. But this group is distinct from sex murderers, who kill primarily to avoid apprehension and not specifically for sadistic gratification. Clearly, Fisher concluded, that this case fell squarely in the first subset. When the child is between the ages of five and twelve, the suspect is most often male, a close friend or a stranger, sexually compulsive. Killing using means such as strangling.

Fisher's research of hundreds of cases in the United States showed that in forty-four percent of the cases the victim was deceased within one hour after they were abducted. Within three hours, seventy-four percent of victims were dead. Fast action in missing children cases becomes vital because data suggests there is typically a two-hour delay after a child is reported missing. But, perhaps more significantly, Fisher had discovered that in the majority of cases, some seventy-two percent, the radius of the body recovery site to the murder site is less than two hundred feet. But, in this case Fisher had to take account of the body drifting in the water.

How far had it moved before being frozen?

The flow rate would have been slowed by the formation of ice, maybe? So, it may not have travelled very far at all. In a small percentage of cases, the body is placed openly, as if to facilitate discovery. Most murders are opportunistic; in only a small number of cases was the victim picked out because of some physical characteristic. Of course, it was still the case that many children were abducted to be trafficked for sex; and only in a small minority of cases for illegal adoption. Inevitably, the older the child, the less likely this would be. Perhaps...

The taxi pulled up right outside the residence.

As Fisher paid the driver with a few dollars, he said:

"How did you know where to stop? I never told you where to stop?"

The driver said nothing, and moved away as Fisher stepped forward. Once again to be greeted on the steps; and once again to be manhandled in the hall by the cockney barrow-boy security guard.

As Fisher entered the reception room, Alan and Jennifer raised themselves from the sofa and stood, as if to attention. Jennifer was wringing her hands, nervously. They already looked red and raw, as if she had rubbed the skin to breaking point.

"Stephen..." said the Consul General stepping forward to shake hands. But it never happened as Jennifer burst out:

"Have you...have you found Eloise?"

"There has been something of a development, which may or may not relate to Eloise. But, before I explain that, I would like to speak with your housekeeper, please."

"Lyn? Why? Yes of course. She is Polish, but speaks English," Alan said, as he moved to the door to issue his request.

"Shall we leave you alone with her?"

"No." replied Fisher, "I need you to be here. You know her best. She is more likely to be truthful in your presence."

"But why would she not be truthful?" asked Alan with concern. "That woman cannot tell a lie."

"Cannot?"

"She is a good and honest woman, and loves Eloise as if she were her own."

But before Fisher could answer, a small, neat woman entered the room in a plain black dress.

"Lyn?" said Fisher.

She nodded.

"Please sit down. I'm not a policeman, Lyn, or a militiaman. I'm just here to help. This is an informal interview to clarify one or two things about the night that Eloise disappeared. Is that ok?"

Lyn looked at the anxious parents.

"Look at me Lyn, please." Stephen asserted, "..,at me, not at them. The answer is in your mind not in theirs."

"I'm told that Eloise is very special to you, is that correct?"

She looked at Alan and Jennifer once more.

"The answer Lyn is in your heart, not on the eyes of others."

Lyn nodded once more.

"On the night that Eloise disappeared, you were looking after her? Is that correct?"

Lyn began to fill with tears and looked to Jenifer.

"Lyn, I need you to answer yes or no."

"Yes."

"You said you fell asleep on the sofa, and when you woke up she was gone."

Lyn looked up the Consul General, before answering:

"Yes."

"Do you have any idea what might have happened to her? Or, where she went?"

Once again she looked up and to the left where Jenifer was standing.

"Lyn, look at me, and answer please."

"No."

"Was anything missing? Her coat?"

Lyn looked confused.

"Yes," said Jennifer. "Her coat was missing; and a hat and gloves."

"Really?" said Fisher. "Does that not strike you as odd? There is no sign of a forced entry, and her coat is missing?"

"This is why the militia concluded that Eloise had simply run away." Added Jennifer.

"I don't believe that she ran away. Do you, Lyn?"

She said nothing, preferring to remain as still and as quiet as a trembling mouse.

"Lyn..." said Fisher, gently, "...is there something you haven't told anyone? Are you keeping something to yourself?"

She said nothing, but started to cry.

"Lyn, whatever it is...you must tell us. It might help us! I promise you, that no harm will come to you; and even if it upsets the Consul General, neither he, nor Jennifer will be angry with you. We just want the whole truth."

Fisher looked to Alan and Jennifer for support.

"What is it Lyn...? What's the matter?" asked Jennifer.

"She made me promise never to tell...she made me swear on my mother's life...."

"Lyn?" said Fisher, quietly.

Finally, she composed her self sufficiently to speak:

"She wanted to go to the night market...we had been before."

"Oh my God!" cried Jennifer, placing a hand over her mouth.

"We slipped out the kitchen door and over to the park opposite the Metro Station. There was quite a crowd...music playing...lights...She wanted to visit the record stand. We started to search through the boxes of records to find something called...*Shaking the Tree*. I found it, eventually, and picked it out to show her. But, she wasn't there! I looked everywhere! I asked everyone! Eventually, I came back here, thinking that perhaps she had returned without me...but, she wasn't here. I started to feel paralysed...I waited and waited... and then Consul General walked in."

"Why didn't you tell me, Lyn?" asked Alan.

"I was afraid...and, I thought she would just come back. When she didn't, I was even more afraid to tell the truth."

"Alright, Lyn…thank you…that's all for now." said Fisher, quietly, but firmly, as she left the room.

"What…?" said Alan, incredulously.

"It's important to know; but it changes very little. Please, both of you sit down. I have something to explain to you."

"What? Oh no….my baby!" cried Jennifer.

Fisher took a deep breath.

"A body of a young girl has been recovered from the Fontanka River…"

"Oh no…please God no…not Eloise…please…" she began to rock back and fourth.

"She matches a description of Eloise…but we can't be sure. Even the photograph doesn't quite confirm the identity. I need you both to come with me to help with the identification."

Jennifer was shaking, sinking into hysteria and uncontrolled weeping.

"I'll come…Jennifer can stay here with Isabelle." offered Alan.

"No…I need both of you to come….we can go right now."

There was a pause. Then Alan moved to the door and opened it.

"Isabelle…please have the car brought round immediately."

He returned and the door closed with a muffled click.

"I need you to be brave… both of you. It may or may not be Eloise. And, with all due respect to you, Alan, a mother typically knows the body of her child, more than a father might. And, I must warn you that it is quite common to look at a dead body, and see an empty shell. As if it's not that person any more. But, this is different. We are trying to establish identity. In other words, Eloise may be gone…but, is this her body?"

Alan sat in stunned silence…in shock. Jennifer, cried continuously. Neither consoled the other.

"Can I use the phone before we leave, please?"

Nobody replied; but he did anyway, as Alan and Jennifer left the room to collect their coats. Fisher picked up the guest telephone receiver at the front desk:

"Isabelle, could you connect me with the office of Professor Mendeleev at the university, please?... I'll wait…. Hello… oh…" Fisher placed a hand over the receiver. "Do you speak Russian Isabelle?"

"Yes, of course," she replied.

Fisher handed her the telephone.

"Good… then tell her to get a message to Mendeleev right away. Tell him I am about to leave with the Con… our guests…we should be there in fifteen minutes or less."

The black Rover 400 pulled up outside. The glass was dark green and obviously reinforced. The driver and the security guard stood by the heavy car doors, whilst the two armed militia men stayed where they had always been, at the bottom of the steps; but looking around hawkishly.

Fisher sat in the front. The car was barely audible, but for the crushing of ice and snow under the tyres.

Nothing was said….until, finally they pulled up outside:

"Why are we here, at the university?" Alan queried. "I expected the morgue or a police station."

Mendeleev was waiting at the entrance.

He shook their hands and greeted them with calm respect, before leading on, to the staircase and through to the same distant]laboratory. Volkov was nowhere to be seen. Neither was Vladimir. Clearly, someone had decided that this would be a low-key visit despite the importance of the visitors, and the issue at hand.

"I must warn you," said Mendeleev, "…it is not a pretty sight. For reasons, I'm not at liberty to explain, we will be uncovering the head and shoulders only."

Jennifer placed her hand to her mouth, in shock and anticipation; she was visibly trembling. All four went into the stark white room.

The body lay, as before, but covered in a double shroud of fresh white muslin. There was an eerie silence, as Mendeleev positioned the couple on one side, and placed himself on the other. Fisher stood at the feet, where he could clearly observe the reaction.

"Are you ready?" asked Mendeleev, quietly.

They both nodded, but said nothing.

Fisher had seen this kind of scene before...many times. It's not like a film, where the mortician opens a long drawer. A plastic body bag is zipped open to reveal an angelic face. The actor, screams or faints or both, or rushes out to be sick, without saying a word; or cries out...*my baby...my baby*, and then caresses the cold face of the victim.

Usually, there is silence...adrenalin is pumped vigorously through the veins...then anxiety, apprehensiveness, restlessness, tremor, weakness, dizziness, sweating, palpitations, pallor, nausea and... sometimes vomiting, headache, and respiratory difficulties. All brought on by the adrenalin. It is only when that has dissipated that the body goes into shock and there is an outpouring of emotional release.

Even when a death has been traumatic and the body injured, bereaved relatives may have many reasons for wanting to see and touch the body as soon as possible. Some want to confirm there has been no mistake, and that their friend or relative was indeed dead. A few feel an obligation...that they ought to see the body or wanted to care for the body or say goodbye. Those who had made a choice (either to see or not to see) usually said that it had been the right decision for them, even if they had had mixed reactions or felt some initial distress. This underlines the importance of making it clear that there are other ways of identifying the body, offering a choice, recognising that different members of a family may make different decisions, and preparing the relatives for what they might see. The way that relatives refer to the body can be a strong indication for Fisher about whether the person who died retains a social identity for the bereaved.

Some people may see the dead body as an empty shell, but others keep a bond with the social identity of the person, and they may see the body as continuing to harbour a spirit or at least some lingering energy. The language used by people who have been bereaved offers a powerful clue to the nature of their sense of relationship with the dead body.

As a professional, Fisher waited for his clues.

As a parent, he waited for the deluge of emotion.

Mendeleev pulled the muslin back to the shoulders. He had somehow, relaxed the face to a more restful expression; and she lay there, as if sleeping.

"What happened to her hair?" asked Jennifer, quietly and calmly.

"Is this Eloise?" asked Fisher. Alan was hesitating, clearly confused.

"She is so beautiful." whispered Jennifer, quietly to herself.

"Is this Eloise?" asked Fisher, once more, emphatically this time.

"Yes, I think so..." said Alan, with his bottom lip trembling. "What happened to her beautiful hair?"

"We're not sure at the moment," said Fisher.

"Why would anyone do this to our precious daughter?" he continued.

"It's not our daughter!" said Jennifer, assertively.

"But..." started Alan.

"No....it's not her!" Jennifer said, firmly.

"Are you sure?" said Fisher. "Remember what I said before about the state of a body after death, being difficult to see the person rather than an empty shell."

"It's not her! It's not Eloise!"

"But it looks like Eloise?" muttered Alan.

"It's not.... Eloise has pierced ears!"

7

Coyness

Hollow.

Ringing.

It was coming from the end of a long narrow tunnel, or a large sewage pipe half-filled with vigorous flowing water. It was black water. He was wading against the flow...but not really getting very far.

All the time...the incessant ringing of a distant alarm bell.

Fisher had given in to fatigue, he was swimming in his sleep; or in his dream; or in the water; or all three. A body was floating by; followed by another. Still the ringing...closer now. A rat crept slowly on the left, along a ledge nearby. It's soft belly sliding through the slime...it picked at some pale bones, in whispers... hip bones.... gnawing at the sinews and cartilage.

Ringing...always the ringing.

Fisher opened his eyes to the dull grey light.

He had slept in.

On the desk, the black telephone was ringing.

"Dr Fisher?"

"Yes...who is this?"

"It's your old karate teacher!"

"Oh yes...it is good to hear your voice."

"How are you?"

Fisher said nothing.

"Why don't we meet up this morning? ....in about half an hour...usual place...you remember...there was a fight there last time?"

"Yes, it'll be just like old times."

"We can share a bottle?"

"For breakfast?"

"Certainly."

"Or two bottles!"

"That's the spirit. As they say in Russia: *there is good vodka; and there is very good vodka!*"

Fisher got dressed, without bothering to stand under the freezing pipe in his so-called bathroom, and dressed in the same old clothes he had on the day before. He needed to preserve some clean clothes for later. Notwithstanding the fact, that there was no laundry service at this hotel. In fact, there was no service at all, at this hotel.

Unless, of course, you were interested in paying for the smorgasbord of sex on offer in the Dollar Bar.

As there was, when Fisher returned to the lobby last night. He needed a stiff drink; and, he expected to get one in the bar on the right. What he wasn't expecting was the blatant display of sex for sale. The room was littered with young women; most, neatly turned out. They looked around, cocking their heads to one side, like hens. Their gazes and very smiles threatening in their aggressive directness. And Fisher couldn't stop himself from looking back at them. It had been a long time since he had seen such sort skirts on women, and the legs came out from beneath them in barely there thin stockings, brash, high-heeled shoes with their straps attached to the ankle like instruments of restraint. Those walking around teetered on their spiked heels as if on stilts, falling slightly forward whilst their backs arch at the waist, pushing the buttocks out. Some wore lipstick, red, giving a raw look to the dark, damp cavities of their mouths, wanting, waiting. It was hard to look away. Not least, they were everywhere Fisher had set his gaze.

One, drug infused woman who almost sat next to him, narrowly failing to fall off the squeaking bar stool. She engaged Fisher in some polite chit-chat, which began with:

"Want to fuck?"

To Fisher, it seemed an honest approach, if somewhat direct…some might say… blunt. Followed by:

"A hundred and you can fuck me in any hole you like."

Fisher declined this fine, comprehensive offer. And said so…politely, but firmly.

"I've got great tits! You can suck them for fifty…or fuck them for seventy-five!"

Clearly, she wasn't keen to accept his mannerly refusal, without at least, describing today's buffet specials. Fisher let her finish the complete and extensive list…some of which he had never heard of before, and once again, declined, explaining that it was not that she was unattractive, but that he was really *very* tired.

"You mean you can't get it up? Are you a fucking fag or something? Coz I got a friend over there…"

She was bound to have a friend over somewhere, not least one armed with a sub-machine gun or an imported Uzi nine millimetre machine pistol, who might want to shoot him for implying that her proud breasts weren't quite a matching pair.

And, mindful, that someone could be watching, not least, the pimp that looked after her, Fisher wished her a good evening and retreated to his room, by scampering up six flights of stairs so fast as to leave no possibility of being followed.

Perhaps that had been a dream too?

Almost any dream was a welcome dream, so long as it didn't contain the face of the dead girl…who had died…screaming…in almost unimaginable pain.

As he now made his way to the Rouble Bar, to meet Vasyli, Fisher imagined it would be a little quiet at ten-thirty in the morning. He was right about that, and relieved to find Vasyli, sitting at the same table as before, stroking his new toy: a Nokia cell phone.

"It's a marvel." he said, without taking his eyes from the black object, "They used to make shoes; before that it was a paper mill. In 1987, they introduced the first hand-held phone, the Nokia Mobira Cityman, weighing just under two pounds! Gorbachev had one. It gained the nickname...a *Gorby*. Seems funny now. And look at this...the Nokia 1011, not released yet. But I have one! This is the future Stephen. It weighs a fraction of the one before and stores ninety-nine contact details and displays two lines of black and white text. I'm done with karate! I'm going to make nuclear powered mobile phones!"

"Well, that's good Vasyli."

Vasyli raised his eyes from his dark treasure.

"You look like shit! How are things?"

"It's better that I don't say."

"I see. I'm a former nuclear scientist...I understand...completely. There's more... a lot more... that I can't say!"

"I'm sorry."

"It's fine Stephen...really. All in good time...for now...let us live for the moment...in the moment? Whatever it is you English say. You are married Stephen?"

"Yes."

"Is it your wife number one?"

"No."

"I knew it! You and I have much in common. My number one wife was a bitter old sow. My number two wife is an angel. Lyudmila...she is young and very beautiful. She takes her clothes off for money. And why not, I say? If you have it...sell it! Anyway...Lyudmila insists that I bring you to our home for lunch. And, better than that…you get to meet Pasha!"

"I am honoured. Truly honoured."

"Good…let us go then! We will collect her on the way…she is at the studio for…how do you say? A *photo shoot* for a western real estate magazine. It could lead to something big."

"Real estate? A property magazine?"

"Yes! It's called, *Penthouse*. Anton is waiting outside to take us to the studio."

And so he was.

St Petersburg is a city of many bridges, fifty or so; but for some reason Fisher had been across the same bridge many times in just two days. Once again, his eyes were drawn to the spot where the unknown girl was liberated from the ice. It made him angry and sick at the same time. What had happened to that poor girl?

Who was she?

Who and where are her family…her parents?

And, what was the killer doing now?

Did the same man take Eloise? If so, why?

What was the connection between the two girls?

The similarity of appearance was no coincidence, he felt sure of that. But to what purpose?

Imagine the research needed to find two girls of the same age and same appearance, and to be able to successfully abduct both. It seemed implausible, and certainly something Fisher had never encountered before. He thought it might be useful to go to the same night market that Eloise had attended, to get a feel for what might be possible there. Of course, the Night Market was a euphemism for the Black Market; Fisher knew that. Even though there was no real money anymore, there's still a black market. There's always a black market… there's always something that can be exchanged, legally or not. He might ask a few questions of the stall holders. For that he would need a Russian speaker.

Was Eloise chosen for a purpose?

Her looks?

How would the abductor know that she would be there at that time?

Chance?

Unlikely.

This was all very well…asking these questions. But why was *he* doing this? Where were the police, militia or whomever? Why weren't they all over this?

The old Volga sputtered into a parking space outside a nondescript grey soviet apartment building. Squatting between two magnificent, if decrepit, eighteenth century buildings, it must have been the site of a German bomb or an artillery barrage during the Great Patriotic War. It reminded Fisher of his own childhood neighbourhood, where rows of Victorian terraced houses were punctuated at random by bomb sites. These were the playgrounds of his youth. In the fifties and sixties, a cheap modern alternative was shoehorned into place, completely at odds with its surroundings.

Here was a fine example of soviet utilitarian ugliness: stark, monumental simplicity, at its worst!

"Come, Stephen, I want you to meet Lyudmila."

"I can wait here with Anton."

"Absolutely not! Come, come."

The entrance to the apartment block was guarded by a rudimentary intercom. Vasyli pressed the appropriate button; and within a minute there was a loud click releasing the door. The theme of functionality continued up the communal stairwell to the first floor, where the door to the apartment on the left was ajar. Vasyli pushed the door open for

Fisher, who entered a well-furnished, but small living room with a kitchen at one end. Two doors off. From one, a bright light was leaking into the lounge. Vasyli pushed a door open to reveal a white cyclorama screen rolled across the floor and up one wall, to give the illusion of infinity. The eye, therefore, failing to find any horizon, focussed on the foreground. It was lit by diffused light from tissue covered reflectors. All very professional.

Lyudmila was sitting on a stool, peeling an apple into a long single coil of peel that dangled between her legs. The only item of clothing she had on was a white lace collar around her neck, and a brief white underskirt with a lace edge.

She smiled at Fisher, but continued to focus on peeling the apple. Her naked breasts were small with proud puffed nipples. Fisher's eyes were drawn down from her broad angelic face to the apple. The peel dangling between her open legs where a smooth slit was exposed, topped by a wisp of blonde hair.

The photographer was snapping shot after shot with a Hasselblad 500 Classic...an expensive piece of kit... mounted on a tripod. He was mouthing single word instructions in Russian.

Fisher looked away towards Vasyli. He was the proverbial age of her father. Although, Vasyli was well built in the solid sense, there was nevertheless a slouch about him and a roll of blubber forming around his midriff when he leaned forward, as he was now, into the door frame. It might be said, that he was not the stereotypical laboratory nerd to be found in a nuclear research centre. The hair was unkempt; one might expect that from a mad scientist, but Vasyli's merely loitered on his head, like an unwelcome guest; or hanging around on a street corner like a bunch of aimless louts.

Fisher's gaze was once again drawn into the room, transfixed, but deeply embarrassed at the same time. Her wide face and liquid blue eyes, exuded innocence, with a hint of carnal knowledge.

He stepped backward, further away into the lounge.

"It's fine to look," said Vasyli, sensing the unease, "thousands of men will be looking soon enough!"

But Fisher felt uncomfortable.

He was guessing that Lyudmila was around twenty years of age. It was hard to tell, as she looked younger. But presumably that was part of her success; her charm. Fisher preferred the word *charm*, it kept out of his mind the idea that this was exploitation, sexual and/or commercial.

Was it?

Certainly, leaving aside her personal physical characteristics, the photographer was keen to emphasise her apparent youth and innocence within an absurd auto-erotic fantasy. Why, an almost naked girl would be sitting with her legs open, in a room with no furniture, peeling an apple, was a mystery. Perhaps that was part of the... charm? Like a painting by Rubens of plump ladies who all seem to be losing their clothes, simultaneously and for no discernible reason. *But even the most outrageous fantasy has to have some basis in reality*, he thought.

As usual, he was over-thinking it.... probably as a distraction.

The viewer had no interest in apples; unless, of course, they were a green grocer; and there was, as far as Fisher knew, no account of Eve bothering to peel an apple in a long tantalising serpent-like coil, for Adam.

But who knows? Perhaps the whole thing about the snake was a misunderstanding?

The small breasts were unashamedly exposed. The vulva less so. That required the viewer to be drawn into the apple peel, then, behind that, to peek up the skirt into the shadows. It was as if, this innocent fruit maiden was unaware of her titillating display. The voyeur, was free to gaze for as long as he wished. It was going to be a photograph; a frozen moment; his eyes could roam freely, privately. Would he or she be aware that the photograph had a photographer? Not unless she looked at the camera. Was that part of the fantasy, the observer becoming the photographer?

There is a connection after all; the photographer is the first viewer. Oh yes...the first...an important detail. It is through his eyes, thought Fisher, that the image is seen. This detachment and this photographic context fascinated him and revolted him at the same time. He saw it as a metaphor for the fate of the river girl.

To the viewer, the absence of furniture is the absence of everyday context; and this vacuum allows the photographer to take the subject away from everyday life, thereby transforming the subject into an object. *And*, thought Fisher, this was possibly the fate that befell the girl trapped in the ice. By the process of abduction, the killer had removed her from the daily life in which she existed, and as such, she became an object. Unrelated to her surroundings. The perpetrator sees the victim as an object of curiosity; for observation and experimentation, rather than as a human being. Without this detachment, it might be impossible for the killer to indulge in his forbidden pleasure. The longer the victim is with the abductor, the less likely he is to be able to detach. It's an interesting theory. The physical and psychological manipulations become just another opportunity to test the victim's response. Many people, those few, those distorted few, who engage in torture, have various psychological deviations and often they derive sadistic satisfaction from their actions.

Torture may fulfil the emotional needs of perpetrators when they willingly engage in these activities. They lack empathy and their victims agonised painful reactions, screaming and pleading, give them a sense of authority and feelings of superiority. And, of course, the opposite can be true. Sometimes, the tortured victim derives pleasure from the pain and the total helplessness.

It was a sickening thought for Fisher. But the girl in the river is not merely an object; she is someone's daughter. She was a person with a story, with dreams and aspirations and desires.

The beauty is in the story.

No more.

The camera clicked on and the flashes accelerated Fisher's thoughts.

And what of this preoccupation that some men seem to have with the sexualisation of younger girls? Certainly, the media were partly to blame for its *normalisation*... but, here, in this isolated soviet controlled society?

"Shouldn't be much longer, Stephen... but, just look at her! So professional!"

Lyudmila was not a *younger girl* and yet she is represented here as one, albeit for the private sexual gratification of some anonymous men. Detached, they hover in a newsagent, sweating, palpitating, keeping watch on others in their peripheral vision. Before, with apparent nonchalance, they reach to the top shelf, browse a golfing magazine, and then pluck the forbidden object from its moorings and sail into the glorious sunset, for an ecstasy of fumbling. All for a few unnecessary shillings.

Do all men harbour such thoughts and desires? Probably not. But, there are likely to be a lot more out there, than many would like to admit.

Was this internal monologue Fisher's way of suppressing his own desires when confronted with this alluring naked young woman? He thought not. He had seen too much of the darkness in men, and in some women, to be drawn down the path of *ephebephilia*. From the Greek, *to arrive at puberty*. An attraction largely discouraged by social mores. But this was an interest in older teenagers that the photographer was alluding to. And the media were partly to blame, at least in the West, for the open release of these desires. There were notorious cases of *art* or *advertising* disguising such fetishes.

Such as, the paintings by a man who liked to call himself Count Balthazar Klossowski de Rola but was better known as Balthus. A French/Polish artist, celebrated in America, who's work between the 1930s and 1950s focussed entirely on erotic representations of children.

The Guitar Lesson is Balthus's most notorious work. No music is being played in the scene depicted, as the tutorial has turned instead into a sexual initiation rite. Most of Balthus's writer and poet friends have passed over the work in silence. The composition is based on a Pieta, probably the Louvre's mid-15th-century Pieta of Villeneuve-les-Avignons, to judge from the near identical height and comparable sizes of the figures. Balthus depicts a female music teacher, breast exposed, holding a young girl across her thighs in lieu of the toy-like musical instrument abandoned on the floor. The child makes no attempt to struggle. Her body arches in anticipation of pleasure or, perhaps, pain, her posture evoking the *rigor mortis* of its celebrated prototype on the lap of the Virgin Mary. Her female teacher's hands are positioned on the girl as for playing the guitar: one near her exposed crotch, another grasping her hair.

It's a classic Balthus pose. He was nothing if not consistent. He was painting his fantasies in 1938 in *Thérèse Dreaming*, featuring Thérèse

Blanchard, aged 12, in 1941; *The Salon*, Georgette Coslin, aged 13 and in 1944 *The Golden Days*, Odile Bugnon, aged 14 and in that same languid posture, featured throughout his work, as if the girl is an object, unconscious, drugged, or dead.

Somehow, because the medium is paint, it is accepted as art; but should that make it any more acceptable than a photograph? Is this, so-called artist portraying a natural fascination? Or, is he fuelling an unnatural, and profoundly disturbing preoccupation that can, when *in extremis* lead to criminal behaviour?

Was, what Fisher witnessed now, the same process...? Of legitimising the unacceptable? Was there a causal link between this seemingly frivolous image-making and the criminals he spent much of his time investigating?

But, far more sinister and far more relevant to Fisher's current investigation was the much more extreme and rare condition of *hebephilia*: an erotic interest that centres on pre-pubescents. Even more unusual, but not without precedent, was the possibility that Fisher was searching for more than one monster. It could be a group of men; or, a man and a woman. After all, here were two men colluding in the creation of erotic images emphasising the corruption of youth and innocence. And Fisher was standing around witnessing it! But there was nothing illegal going on here; all conducted between consenting adults for the purpose of commercial gain, with no pretensions of art. Well...maybe some?

There was no need for Fisher to be prudish about this; and, it was unlikely to lead directly to criminality. To censor such things, merely pushes them underground. The question was more around whether this was idle titillation, or whether it was the soft crumbling edge of a precipice, that can in certain individuals, lead to more serious deviant behaviours, and they topple over a cliff?

"You seem…how would you say… mesmerised, Stephen. And, I don't blame you. She is beautiful is she not?"

"Yes…yes…very attractive."

The shoot was over, and Lyudmila was getting dressed, Fisher observed the two men garbling extensively and enthusiastically in Russian. A fat brown envelope was handed to Vasyli, and then he and Fisher returned to the car with Lyudmila squashed into the back, alongside Vasyli.

The journey to the suburbs was a relatively quiet one, with the couple in the back exchanging small talk, in Russian; and of course, the ever silent, Anton. Meanwhile, Fisher had decided not to think any more than he already had, and to let the frightened trees along the roadside flash by, they were at such regular intervals that they lulled him into a relaxed stupor. It wasn't difficult, he was tired and this was a welcome break, a glimmer of light, before falling once more into the darkness of human nature and the unspeakable truth about what one human being is capable of doing to another.

The nondescript apartment block, squatted in a sea of nondescript apartment blocks floating in the frozen slurry of so many tracks and treads. Dark, filthy brickwork and grey concrete blocks decorated with rusting metal window frames. All low rise, perhaps five or so floors. Old houses are like old people, and sometimes their eyes: the windows, turn weak with age or go blind. But they absorb the stories of their inhabitants and repeat them for a long time.

Despite outward appearances, Vasyli's flat was warm and relatively spacious inside, with parquet floors throughout; the heating and hot water provided from a communal source. The bathroom and washroom shared with other apartments. This, however, was atypical. In most cases, these buildings have no hot water and residents must go to the public baths to wash.

It had a homeliness and a cosy feel, despite the dull grey light from outside. It was necessary to switch the lights on, just as it was necessary for Fisher to witness the giant grey poodle being pampered and adored by his doting owners. Or was it the other way around...? Was it the dog that lived here and owned the wayward people that kept wandering off somewhere without permission?

Pasha was clipped short, with a mop on the top of his head, and another ball of wool at the tip of his tail. It was hard to tell which end was which. The end with the wet black bobble on it, took a keen interest in Fisher's trousers. Well, he had worn them for a few days now. So, interesting to Pasha, that he wagged his ball of fur at the other end and proceeded to mount Fisher with a vigorous thrusting of the hips.

"He likes you!" Lyudmila announced, just before Vasyli ordered him to sit down. Fisher presumed Vasyli was talking to the dog, but he wasn't sure, so he sat down anyway.

Pasha also obeyed without hesitation, and then proceeded to drag his backside from one end of the rug to the other and circled back again.

"I think he might want to go out," suggested Vasyli. "I'll be back shortly. Lyudmila will look after you."

Discarded of his insulation, Fisher, settled on the sofa. Lyudmila picked up her knitting and sat down in the armchair opposite, a small coffee table between them.

There was a stilted pause.

"Vasyli....is learning me English."

"Vasyli is *teaching* me English." Fisher corrected.

"Oh..." she said, laughing, "he is learning you too?"

"No...he's not teaching *me* English?"

"He is? Or, he isn't?"

"Vasyli is teaching *you* English."

"I just said that. English is so difficult."

Thank God! Thought Fisher when Pasha toddled back into the room dragging Vasyli behind him on the end of a short leash.

"I don't know how that dog can crap so much! And such big turds!" Vasyli said, between gulps of air.

It was probably more detail than Fisher was looking for, just before lunch.

Pasha, with his pink tongue waggling out to the side made a straight line for Fisher and sat between his legs with his big fluffy head resting on Fisher's crotch. The drool was oozing out onto his trousers.

"He likes you." Vasyli said, proudly, as if his specially gifted child had just created an improved version of the Mona Lisa using Lego bricks.

Leaving behind an inappropriate stain on Fisher's trousers, Pasha turned his attention to Lyudmila who was arranging things on a tray in the open kitchen. She tossed something into his waiting mouth, which he swallowed with a silent gulp, as if it never existed.

"She loves that dog." Vasyli said, as if *he* didn't. "She keeps all his hair clippings."

Fisher was afraid to ask why.

But there was no need. Vasyli was holding up the knitting needles attached to a small unfinished bootee sock. It was, uncannily, the same colour as Pasha.

"Are we expecting a baby, perhaps?" Fisher muted, with considerable hesitation. When Vasyli had stopped laughing, he said:

"Does Lyudmila look pregnant? She is so full of Polish pills, she might never get pregnant. The problem with the pills is that there is no way of knowing what the Poles put in them. They hate our guts! So, she takes two a day, to double her chances success! No, Stephen, the socks are for Pasha...to keep his feet warm. He has a jumper too."

The logic seemed a little suspect to Fisher...cutting off the dog's hair to weave it into some clothes to keep him warm until his hair grew back to cut it off again, and then knit him a bobble hat to cover his head in the summer.

Before Fisher could resolve this conundrum...this poodle version of the *Penrose Stairs*, made famous in the drawing by Escher, Lyudmila arrived with a tray supporting a bowl of caviar, warm buttered blinis, a bottle of suspect champagne and three fine crystal glasses.

"Champagne!" exclaimed Stephen, surprised.

"Finest Russian Champagne!" said Vasyli proudly.

Pasha was guarding the blinis without a blink, as if there might be a sausage hidden underneath.

"Stephen... as our guest... you do the honours and pop the cork."

Vasyli and Lyudmila, were poised with a glass each.

Fisher unwrapped the foil and the wire and slowly twisted the cork. There was a low hiss of escaping gas.

"No pop!" said Lyudmila, deflated.

This is how you should open a bottle of champagne," said Fisher. "It should sound like a nun farting."

It was meant to be a moment of light humour. But, their faces looked as if someone had, in fact, farted.

"Here's to health!" Vasyli proclaimed, as he picked his glass and offered a clink. He wasn't disappointed. Lyudmila was still sniffing her glass, suspiciously, to sense whether it had a fart in it.

"Now...eat!" Vasyli said, with gusto.

Fisher needed no further prompt, and proceeded to spoon the caviar onto the small round buttered pancake and then allowed it to melt in his mouth. He had forgotten the taste of rich food. And caviar? A rare treat. So, engrossed in his enjoyment, he had failed to notice that he was the only one eating. The other two, wore a similar expression to Pasha.

"You're not eating?" Fisher said, somewhat guiltily.

"We saved this for a special occasion. This is a very special occasion. It is for you, Stephen."

"No…I can't…I refuse to eat alone."

Pasha gave him a squeak and an adoring glance.

"If you insist." Vasyli conceded and polished off three blinis to Lyudmila's one.

Another glass of bubbles and Fisher began to give in to the languishing mood and the easy, lugubrious, conversation, as Vasyli, and to a certain extent, Lyudmila, asked him idle questions about his life in the West. Fisher felt quite nostalgic and yet distant from his old life.

Pasha said nothing; but listened intently.

He lay spread out on the carpet, until, just as Fisher got to the part where he missed his wife, Pasha rolled over onto his back to display a long, pink penis sticking out like an anteater's tongue looking for a juicy nibble. Nobody pointed it out.

But Fisher's speech began to stumble as his eyes were drawn to the small cerise serpent that might just bite his foot.

Lyudmila, noticed the throbbing penis, went to the freezer compartment of the fridge and came back with a frozen spoon, which she placed, deftly, on Pasha's testicles. His penis shrunk like a snail in salt and left the poor poodle with a look as if dire cruelty had been unfairly inflicted.

"She does the same thing to me in the morning!" Vasyli quipped.

Somehow, Fisher believed him.

"I need to ask a favour, Vasyli. Someone I can trust." Fisher's tone was quiet and serious.

"Yes, of course, Stephen. What is it?"

"I'm involved in something...investigating a criminal case... I can't tell you any more than that... I'm sorry. I need some help this evening. There is a night market...I need to ask a few questions...show a photograph; but, I need someone to translate the questions and the answers. Would you be willing to help me?"

"Of course, where is this market?" Vasyli turned his head from side to side as if searching for it somewhere in the room, on the ceiling or on the rug.

"In the Trentralny District."

Vasyli's face lost all its colour as the blood drained away.

"In the diplomatic quarter?"

"Yes."

Vasyli shook his head in silence, and then said:

"You don't need me, Stephen. You need someone with more experience in such things."

He shook his head once more, and Fisher understood.

"You're right, Vasyli. It is most important that the translation is perfect. I will ask...someone else."

"Good! Well, it's time for Pasha to take another dump. Why don't you come with me?" Vasyli raised his eyebrows.

"Yes, of course."

Pasha was somewhat confused by this; not to mention Lyudmila. He was no ordinary poodle; he knew the time of day; and, he could read *Pravda*, the *daily truth*. Indeed, he knew it to be blatant propaganda manufactured by the machinery of the State, and that the only truth in it, was that there was none. But he was undeterred by such details. Pasha would usually lay on it, after breakfast, and glance at the stories of interest, occasionally rolling over in disbelief. But this... this was another matter altogether.... *walkies* at an unscheduled hour...

unheard of! So much so, he sat by the open door and refused to move. After all, it was cold enough out there, to freeze the proverbial off a brass monkey. His quaffed bum seemed glued to the parquet. No coaxing, no ordering, would make him budge.

"We'll leave him here." Vasyli said, quietly defeated, his cover blown.

The sky was clear, with a hint of blue, with some thin pink clouds of floss suspended between the apartment blocks. Fisher's feet crunched through the snow of the night before, and of the night before that, before Vasyli broke the renewed silence:

"Stephen, I would help, but I can't. There is no way I can go to the Trentralny District; not right now, and especially to that market. It is in the park, I know the place, close to the house of the British Consul General."

Vasyli stopped and looked around, and then continued:

"There is something you should know. But first, you must swear on your life never to speak of this, unless, of course, your life is threatened. If you do…my life is finished. Do you understand?"

Fisher nodded, uncertain of the logic… but, he thought he understood.

"No, I need to hear you say it…do you understand and swear as I said?"

Fisher wanted to swear on his grandmother's life. She was dead anyway.

"Yes." he said, solemnly, "I swear."

"I was working at a facility in a secret location outside… it doesn't matter. I was leading a program designed to respond to the, so called, *Star Wars* project. Reagan, that old fool of an actor, had marked his place in history by starting the Strategic Defence Initiative in eighty-three; an arms race like we'd never seen before. It was intended to defend the United States from attack by Soviet ICBMs by intercepting the missiles at various phases of their flight. For the interception, the new system would require extremely advanced technological innovations, yet to be researched and developed. This system would tip the nuclear balance toward the United States. We feared that this would enable the Americans to launch a first-strike against us."

"Yes, I realise you could see it that way."

"In truth, we had fallen far behind, and the Politburo responded to this by ordering unprecedented expenditure on weapons development. Even now, the Americans have no idea what is going on. And, look, look at who is in charge here. The lunatics are running the asylum; and the drunk, the corrupt, and the greedy few, are fuelling the madness."

"Perhaps you should stop there Vasyli?"

"Why? I've already gone too far. In any case, things are not quite going according to plan."

"Things? Plan?"

"I was leading a project called…how would you say it in English? *Red Arrow*…yes…that's it. A hypersonic missile, capable of speeds exceeding Mach six. So, fast, that the Americans wouldn't know it was coming until it had arrived. No missile defence shield would stop it. The missile employs revolutionary scramjet technology to reach its hypersonic speeds whereby propulsion is created by forcing air from the atmosphere into its combustor where it mixes with on-board fuel, rather than carry both fuel and oxidiser like traditional rockets. This makes it lighter, and therefore much faster."

This was more than Fisher felt he needed, understood, or wanted to know.

"It uses no fans, rotating turbines or moving parts: just an inlet where air is compressed and a combustor where the air is mixed with fuel. Fewer moving parts also means less chance of mechanical failure.

Red Arrow would be capable of destroying the world's most advanced warships and aircraft carriers. The *Red Arrow* is now to be armed with a radar target seeker and an optical-electronic complex that can trace and detect targets, also at hypersonic speed. It is designed to carry a new weapon…a fissile…tactical neutron bomb. Production and testing of such bombs was halted ten years ago in 1981. Well, that's the official story."

"I don't understand. Another type of hydrogen bomb? A bigger bomb?"

"Not quite…it's a massive enhanced radiation weapon. We call it … the *capitalist bomb*."

"Why?"

"It's an air burst bomb, producing no shock wave. Just an intense plasma of high dose radiation…off the scale, in fact. Instead of destroying everything in its…*wake*…I think you say? …just one of these weapons would vaporise all living things in New York or London."

"But leave everything else?"

Vasyli paused, and then:

"You may remember the first to enter the ruins of Hiroshima? They found strange shadows on the walls of buildings and on the ground. These were the silhouettes of those that disappeared in the first flash, before the shock wave. They, simply vanished. *Red Arrow*, makes people disappear; but leaves the buildings intact. Hence the nickname, the *capitalist bomb*: it leaves all assets in place, but removes the enemy. It is, the ultimate first strike weapon; a weapon of conquest."

"Who knows about this?"

"A group of twelve honest men and women…. some are still there. In recent weeks, others have disappeared and have been replaced. Two, I know have encountered fatal *accidents*, shall we say."

"And now, you, Stephen…you know about it. But, no one knows that you know. Not yet, anyway."

"But, I still don't understand why you can't go the night market. Am I missing something?"

"It is well known in certain circles, that if you have a secret to tell. The worst thing you can do is approach the Americans. They leak like a fart in a colander, as we say in Russia. And, it's too obvious. Better to go through their strongest ally: the British. Are you following me Stephen?"

"Yes."

"And so, four weeks ago, I made my approach to the MI6 operative at the High Commission. We met at the night market, as in a black and white film. I was given assurances about my safety and security, and that of Lyudmila. I was given an indication of payment, and of a fresh start…a new life…an opportunity to escape this lunacy. But…my contact has not appeared since. All lines of communication are dead. I am sure the KGB is watching…listening…waiting for me to move. But, they know that I know too much. They may think the details of the weapon are hidden somewhere, held by another *traitor*. But, each of us carries a piece of it in our head; and only I hold all the pieces, and the key to put it all together. I may sound like an opportunist. But this world is teetering on a precipice. It's toes are tingling as it leans forward before the…chasm. The balance that kept the peace since the 1950s has gone." Vasyli laughed sarcastically. "We called it, *Mutually Assured Destruction*, or MAD. Now we need to rebalance the equilibrium. But this, this new weapon, will create a quantum shift of power to the Russian military, in a context in which there is no control, no safeguards, and moral…what is the expression?"

"Moral impediment?"

"Yes! Precisely….impediment."

"Why don't they just shoot you? Or *disappear* you?"

"These days, the State Security is like a wounded animal... dangerous... unpredictable, fragile and vulnerable. It waits in hiding, like a wolf, for its enemies to come out into the open, in this new freedom we are supposed to have. They know what happened in the GDR when the wall came down: all the *Staatssicherheit* files were released, and the retributions began. The KGB will not make the same mistake as the Stasi. They will wait until the traitor is evidently a traitor, openly and without ambiguity. They will only act these days, when they have no choice. That way they ensure that all opposition is crushed with the support of loyal Russians. Who would believe a confession at the hands of such people anymore? No one. It is much more credible, if they catch all the...protagonists...in one sweep. Then the wolf can lick its wounds and grow stronger."

"But with all that is going on... and not going on... surely the government will halt this program until they get their economic and social priorities sorted out?"

"They are like children, dressed in borrowed robes...playing *grown-ups*. Free, without responsibility. They can wear their freedom like cheap perfume and play as they wish. Nobody is watching over them; and nobody is going to tell them that they can't do this or that."

"It is a good, analogy...a comparison, I mean..." replied Fisher.

"There is a book I have read in English, many times. It speaks to me of these nightmares. Rereading it, I recognised that this book, whose chipper, bluff, breezy beginnings career quickly into a nightmarish, lawless, irrational power struggle, was *the* book for now. In its contours, mood and message, it perfectly enfolds our country's ...how do you say? ...entropy."

"*Lord of the Flies*?"

"Exactly! The lost boys do eventually get rescued, or most of them do. As for those in Russia, who are reading, watching, listening and straining their ears, hoping to hear the buzz of the engines of rationality approaching? The signal fires are lit, but the question is: can they be kept going long enough to get us back to a civilization we recognise?"

"Vasyli, you are now in great danger. Is this why you think the apartment is bugged?"

"It was probably bugged anyway. It's like a game of chess. We have reached an impasse. If I do nothing, then they will do nothing."

"But, that might not last long… and presumably the project has stalled?"

"Stalled, yes; but not stopped. They will regroup and find some ambitious young physicist to take over. Most of the plans are still there and the prototypes. It's only a matter of time before someone puts it all together again."

"I have no idea if the boys in Moscow… our current government fools, have even caught up with a project that is so secret. They may have no idea of its existence."

"No technology can be kept monopolised forever, Vasyli, but, if the government do know of it, they have every reason to try slowing the rate of seepage of militarily useful technology…but, in truth, it will always leak out sooner or later."

"I was a passionate believer in the revolution; in a vision for a better world… a communist world… a world without war. I was convinced that the way to achieve that was through strength. The defeat of capitalism would see the rise of communism. Which is why I started on *Red Arrow*. But, I was wrong. An invention can never be *un-invented*. And whatever the system of government… however good its intentions… there will always be people. People are people. Some are good, and some a bad; and a few are just animals....goats and wolves! Russians will come to view the Soviet era as a time of social cohesion and economic stability, with steady employment, adequate wages and reasonable access to broad social services; economic inequality and political corruption exist, of course, but were held in check. Russians also recall that the Soviet Union enjoyed international prestige and leverage as one of only two superpowers. The Soviet propaganda of catching up and surpassing the West was accepted to at least some extent by much of the Soviet population. But look at the state we are in now. We are truly lost...like children in a twighlight forest. Freedom, like a trail of promising breadcrumbs, will lead us deeper into the woods, not out and into the sunshine. We are facing an existential threat and we are deeply afraid. In fear, we may do something terrible; in desperation we may lash out; in the end we will care little about ourselves and even less about the disappointing West."

"There must be hope?"

"There are only two kinds of hope: no hope and Bob Hope! A friend told me this truth as a joke. Truths are thin on the ground here, Stephen...secrets are rife; they are like weeds in an unkept garden."

"I see...," Fisher hesitated, "I too have some secrets, Vasyli. We are have secrets and we all tell lies."

"And, what is the worst kind of lie you can tell? The ones you tell to yourself."

"Yes, but..."

"Don't tell me, Stephen...my days may be numbered... if they bring me in and threaten Lyudmila, I will talk. Or, Pasha, for that matter!"

"It's not as secret as your secrets, Vasyli."

"I have enough secrets ...enough for ten people. Now, all I want is to unburden myself."

They both smiled at each other.

There was a pause.

And then, they threw their arms about each other, as only men in dire circumstances do, who might love each, as brothers, unreservedly.

8

Every Part

Night.

Cold lights.

While exceptions can be made, in general, one does not smile or laugh as much when speaking Russian. Popular wisdom holds that smiling is for idiots. This was the gift of advice, echoing Vladimir, given to Fisher on leaving Vasyli's apartment. The other gift was Lyudmila. She was to be his interpreter this evening, for the trip to the night market in the Trentralny District.

Anton was the driver.

It was surprisingly close to the Consulate, sitting out of sight in an island of light in a dark corner of what was seasonally a verdant green park, but, for now just seemed a flat sheet of forgetful snow.

Anton remained skulking on the street corner, loitering without intent under an arc street lamp, in silhouette, like a poster boy for a spy thriller, with clouds of warm cigarette smoke hanging in the cold still air… like cloudy thoughtless bubbles; but who knows what might be in there, as Anton never said a word.

Above, the night sky was heavy with expectation. There was a stillness; a mild pregnant pause, suggesting snow.

Fisher wasn't at all confident that this foray into the unknown to gain new knowledge and insight into the disappearance of Eloise, would clarify anything. But he felt compelled to try; even if it proved futile. This, he felt, was a matter for the police to investigate, not an academic criminal psychologist.

This pessimism was based, in part, on his experience of Lyudmila's febrile grasp, or otherwise, of English. But once she heard that he was leaving to go the night market, there was no deterring her. The devotion to go with him, and to be of service was without doubt. But, she also wanted to see if there was anything on sale to feed her obsession with the West.

"So.." Fisher said to Lyudmilla, "...you have the questions on that piece of paper."

"Yes."

"If you aren't sure of what they say in English, then tell me you are not sure."

"They will say things in English?"

"No.. I mean, if you are not sure how to say in English what they say in Russian."

"I can ask you how to say it in English."

"No, I won't know what they are saying in Russian."

"I will tell you."

"What do you want from the market?" she said, as they approached.

"Information!"

"I want shoes...stilted shoes. I love high heels."

"Stilettos."

"What's a stiletto?"

 "High heel shoes."

"You want stilettos too?"

"They are named after an Italian dagger."

"He invented high heels?"

There were only thirty or so stalls...makeshift... and swiftly constructed from bits of wood, trestle-tables, plastic sheets and tarpaulin. None really sold anything much; well, nothing worth buying.

Carefully and systematically, they went from stall to stall to converse with the well-wrapped stall holders. The snow had returned, floating to the ground in large wads of white floss, arriving, as if from nowhere, from a heavy ink soaked sky.

As Fisher looked up beyond the lights, he could see the under clouds dotted with pools of reflected street light. In the empty darkness, the snow seemed black as it fell in slow motion into the light.

Like the weather itself, the questioning soon settled into a pattern of melting disappointment: Lyudmila would speak politely to the budding entrepreneurs; he or she displayed momentary interest, until it was clear that nobody was buying...especially, the wealthy looking foreigner with the grim expression and an extinct Siberian fox on his head.

Fisher showed the black and white portrait, whilst trying to protect it from clumps of damp snow. His inclination was to smile a little, if only to indicate a modicum of sincerity without teetering towards idiocy. He felt he was failing miserably, on both counts, conveying instead, a modicum of insincerity, deftly combined with a remarkable degree of stupidity.

Finally, at the music stall, he paused to finger through the covers of old Beatle LPs mingled with Stravinsky, Prokofiev and Rimsky Korsakov. *Why not?* He thought to himself. Then he overheard a young woman give the same answer to Lyudmila as everyone else: *the girl in the photograph she had never seen.*

And, why would she remember a face, however pretty, from three weeks ago? As Fisher walked away, she called after him, in near perfect English:

"May I take another look?"

She looked intently at the picture, tipping it towards the lightbulb swinging on a nearby wire covered from the snow with a makeshift polythene shade.

"A British girl?"

"Yes!" Fisher exclaimed and almost smiled, blowing his cover of gruff sophistication.

"I think it's her. I've seen her here more than once. Perhaps two or three times. Always buys something...the latest illegal imports. She was here two or three weeks ago. I remember because, this time she bought nothing. One minute she was there; the next she was gone."

"Did you see anyone with her?"

"Yes, she arrived, as before, with an older woman. But the woman was still rummaging after the girl had gone."

"Anyone else?"

She hesitated, her voice faltering a little.

"Not really...well, there was a man...standing a few feet behind her. He was looking around. I thought maybe he was her bodyguard or something."

"Did they speak to each other?"

"Yes...briefly. She turned around to find him there...right in her face....she seemed to step back in surprise. He said something...I couldn't really hear...almost a whisper...and, I thought I heard him say her name...Elsa...or Helen?"

"Eloise?"

"Could be? I don't know for sure. They turned and walked away together."

"Willingly?"

"Yes...it seemed as if they might have known each other...I'm not sure. It was dark and I..."

"Can you describe the man?"

She looked up and to the left, as if searching for the truth in the falling snow.

"Maybe, late thirties, early forties...dark overcoat... I don't know, I wasn't really paying much attention. Why? Has something happened to her?"

"We don't know, yet. Thank you very much; you've been most helpful. If you think of anything else...my name is Fisher, I'm staying at the Hotel Moskva."

"The Moskva? Are you crazy? My name is Anna..."

"Thank you, Anna."

Fisher and Lyudmila began to walk towards the empty street, satisfied, at least, that someone had seen something, however frail the fabric of information. There weren't many people about. Slim pickings you might say...even less to buy than there were people looking; and, not a shoe in sight, apart from some rubber-soled Chinese galoshes.

"Mr Fisher!" a voice came from behind. It was Anna, walking into a pool of light; and then stepping backward into the penumbra.

"One more thing..."

"Yes?"

She paused, rather nervously, Fisher thought.

"There was another man."

"Another...a second man?"

"Two days later...after that night...another man...he asked me about the same girl. But he had no photograph."

"Did you tell him the same thing?"

"No....he seemed...how shall I say... official."

"Militia? KGB?"

Her sharp eyes darted about into the shadows.

"I've said too much already."

"Anna...her life may be in danger. Did he say anything else?"

Anna looked around nervously. As if someone might be watching or listening.

"I don't think he believed me when I said I hadn't seen the girl, the one he described. He looked at me...with these... pale eyes...and said, that if I had seen such a girl, and I was questioned about her, that what I had said was the right answer."

Intriguing, thought Fisher.

"I should go...I have to pack up...the snow is getting heavy."

Lyudmila was as confused as when she had arrived, and said very little. A few English platitudes about the weather: *it never rains but it snows*. Likewise, Anton drove the old banger in silence, dropping Fisher at his favourite hotel. He thanked them both and said goodnight.

Admittedly, he too had been rather quiet, preoccupied as he was, by the appearance of the second man; never mind the first. Could the second man... have been... you know who? If so, why would he want Anna to say, that she had never seen the girl, that was undoubtedly Eloise?

It made no sense.

Fisher nodded to the freezing soldier at the Moskva's revolving door, who nodded back, recognising the well-dressed, but rare fox. On the other side of the door, the reception lobby was displaying more chequered floor than Fisher had ever seen before. It was uncannily empty; except that is, for a thin ferret of a man still dressed in his outer clothes of the MVD militia.

Fisher's heart sank.

"Dr Fisher," said the man, sombrely...obviously no fool, "the Chief Investigator requests the pleasure of your company for a drink in the adjacent bar."

His left eyebrow seemed to indicate the door on Fisher's right. It was unusually quiet in there.

"I'm rather tired this evening," muttered Fisher, entirely unconvincingly, "please give the Chief Investigator my sincere apologies."

Having spoken near perfect English, the same man from the night on the frozen river said nothing, his left eyebrow twitched once more, but the face remained unchanged. A cold stare descended on Fisher, leaving him with no choice but to accept.

"It would be my pleasure!" Fisher recanted.

The thin man opened the glass door into the Dollar Bar.

Save for one or two honest drinkers and a barman polishing a glass like a cliché, the room was empty. Egorov, was sitting like a cane toad with a headache, brooding, squat, behind the edge of a table. He was holding a glass of crushed ice, infused with clear liquid, undoubtedly vodka, close to the side of his head, as if it was glued to his temple. His cheeks were red as a slapped backside, with the thin strands of a greasy, pointless comb-over, sticking to his clammy head.

"Comrade Fisher!" Egorov slurred.

Fisher did as he was bid, by Egorov's outstretched arm, waving, vaguely towards an adjacent empty stool.

"The Chief Investigator welcomes you Dr Fisher." Announced the thin ferret as he sat down opposite. He seemed to have a remarkable level of skill as an interpreter; able, as he was, to make a sentence from a barely visible gesture. Egorov, removed the glass from the side of his head to reveal a multi-coloured bruise of blues and greens with a hint of yellow ochre. He gulped from the glass and stared at Fisher, narrowing his eyes as if to focus on a receding target. His short fat index finger, pointed, somewhat cursorily towards a similar glass to his own, as if Fisher should drink from it.

It's true, he needed such a drink. But, more than that, he needed his wits to be sharper than a serpent's tooth, in case he needed to bite back. In any case, Fisher had no idea, what else might be lurking in the glass.

And so, he offered to break the stare with an astute observation, once again mastering the art of grasping the obvious.

"A little quiet in here tonight!" he offered.

The thin man knew exactly how his boss would answer. Indeed, he knew the Chief Investigator's every thought, before even the Chief had it himself; and sometimes the absence of a thought. The man with no name replied, without bothering one way or the other, to translate:

"Everybody has been taken in for a period of reflection and self-determination in a quiet cell."

"Arrested?"

"Precisely, Dr Fisher. It's easy, you see. Nobody cares. Nobody knows where they are; and if they disappeared, nobody would know that either. It happens all the time, people come, people go. They are the *Twilight People*. They exist in the shadows between the light and the dark; between the past and the future. Their light gleams for an instant and then, they are no more. "

Fisher had got the message: life was cheap; his included. Even that of an innocent young girl. The parents might weep and cry out; but nobody is really listening; not even the media. They are all too self-concerned, preoccupied with their own immediate day-to-day survival to worry about a missing child; or, for that matter, a missing foreign academic.

Egorov began to babble in Russian….the thin man simultaneously, and seemingly without pause, translated, as if he wasn't really listening; or didn't need to; as if he could listen and speak at the same time. A skill similar to Fisher's own capacity for multiple thinking, speaking and listening to nearby conversations. But, not like this...not involving two languages simultaneously. That was impressive, he decided.

"Comrade Fisher...I can call you that now, because you are almost one of us. You are a man of considerable knowledge, integrity and honesty. A rare commodity in this wild northern town. We know all about you; your successes and your failures; and all about your lovely family. For these are difficult times."

"Are you threatening my family?"

"Comrade...there's no need to be so dramatic. Are we in a play by Comrade Chekhov? If I were to threaten you, there would be no need to be so subtle. Why would I threaten your family, when you are here, and I can twist off your thumbs if I so wish."

"You are threatening me."

"Quite simply, I am offering to be your guide and mentor. I can see that you are confused; that you need... guidance....in this complicated situation. Your association with the KGB is most unfortunate. You should desist, immediately, all communication with Comrade General Volkov. He is not known as the *Grey Wolf* for nothing. He will stalk you, Comrade, goad you on and ultimately, when he has you exactly where he wants you, he will consume you. If you want to see your family again...I suggest you listen to what I have to say."

Fisher said nothing.

"This case, is *my* case. I have been working on it for some years now."

"Years?" echoed Fisher.

"Surely, Comrade Fisher, in your vast experience, you don't believe for a moment, that this mutilated corpse…this pretty, filleted fish…is the first of such victims? You surprise me, Comrade."

"Someone has to be the first."

"The girl in the Winter ice, is not the first to have incurred this mutilation. We are hunting a man for all seasons. For at least three years now, there has been a fresh cadaver with the hip bone hacked out, roughly, every three months. There is a gap here and there, in his gruesome record, where the killer offers a tease, perhaps. Or maybe he takes a holiday? Or, there is more than one killer? A copy-cat? Who knows? But, the fact remains, that, there will be another carved up cadaver before the year is out."

Egorov made a vague gesture to his spokesperson, the thin man, who opened an old leather document case and produced a thick cardboard folder, of the light brown anonymous type, and placed it, reverently, on the table. He turned it to face Fisher, who reached to open it; but, Egorov's fist, came down on the cover and pushed forward his ruddy, sodden, face with a thick vein pulsing on his damp forehead.

"It's all in Russian," explained the thin man, "and contains graphic photographs. This file is a copy. You may keep it, for the time being, as a gesture of good will… if… and only if… you agree not to share it with the KGB, *and* if you answer the Chief Investigator's questions."

Fisher felt he had little choice. The contents of the file could prove invaluable; and if Egorov *was* right; and if Eloise *is* the next victim, then time was running out.

Already, a crucial piece of information had been, albeit inadvertently, given to him. That there was a regular pattern. That perhaps the killer kept his prize alive somewhere, before eventually hacking them to death.

"I agree…and, I will try my best to answer the questions." offered Fisher.

"Why is Volkov, all of a sudden, interested in this case? He has shown no interest in the others?"

"I don't know." replied Fisher.

The file was withdrawn across the table.

"I *really* don't know! But, I don't think he is interested in the case, generally. I believe he is only interested in the missing girl."

The file was pushed a little closer.

"Why would that be? Of what interest is this English girl to the KGB?"

"Perhaps, it's a matter of principle, perhaps it's because she is the daughter of a diplomat. It may be embarrassing for the government?"

The file nudged forward, as Egorov muttered, incomprehensibly. The thin man continued:

"That may not be the whole story. Time, is Volkov's most precious commodity; he wouldn't waste it on futile diplomacy. To a man like him, no principle, however glorious, can justify wasting his time. Nor, is he sentimental. The girl's life means nothing. It's what the girl is worth that matters to him. Why is she such a precious little angel? That is an interesting question."

"You could just ask him?" offered Fisher.

Egorov moved the glass away from his head once more, as if to say… *you want me to ask him?*

"I will kill that fucking cunt, before I ask him."

Even the thin man's eyebrow could see that there might be a gap in logic here. But, he said it anyway.

"What did you discover at the Black Market this evening?"

Fisher thought about Anna.

"How did you know I was at the market?"

It was a futile question, to which there was no answer.

"Nothing."

"Nothing at all?"

"Let me ask you a question." Fisher asserted, as a diversionary tactic. He pushed the file away from him, as if disinterested. It was a risk, but he calculated that he was of more use to the Chief Investigator than vice versa.

"If you have been working on this case, all this time, why haven't you found the killer?"

"Не нарисуйте свой лук, пока ваша стрелка не будет зафиксирована, доктор Фишер." Egorov smiled like the proverbial idiot, as he spoke very slowly. The thin man translated:

"*Maybe and somehow won't make any good...*" he hesitated, then, again: "...draw not your bow till your arrow is fixed."

Egorov moved on:

"We have so far found three killers."

"What?"

"All confessed to their crimes and were executed. But the butchered girls kept appearing. Too bad, I say. There may be some as yet undiscovered."

"And these men...they were all innocent?"

"They confessed....so, they are guilty; but, perhaps they were just trying to help. Many people might confess...when persuaded to do so... in the best interests of the Party or the State. But, such men are getting harder to find, these days. The party is over...shall we say?"

There was an uncomfortable pause.

"You may take the file on one condition..." uttered Egorov, echoed in translation.

"What condition?"

"That you align yourself to me...that you tell me whatever you find out...first... and, that you distance yourself from the Wolf."

"I don't think I can do that. He will be suspicious if I ignore him."

"True."

Egorov was weighing this subtlety heavily on his aching head.

"But, I will keep you informed if I can," offered Fisher. "And if...or when...the killer is caught. I will say it was down to your insight into the complex criminal mind."

"Don't fuck with me Fisher! Do you understand?"

Fisher nodded. Obviously, he had gone too far.

"And...don't trust that cold, fish-eyed bastard! He is up to something; and, whatever it is, he will swat you like a Siberian fly if you get too close to his real interest. He will keep you to him by feeding you honey. But, as we say on the banks of Lake Baikal...*keep a fly busy and he won't see the smile that splats him.*"

Somewhat confused, though Fisher was, by how a smile could swat a fly, he took the advice to heart. It might be like translating Shakespeare into Russian, he thought; some subtlety is bound to get lost. The poetry might be more like the verse in a Christmas Card than the consummate insight it was intended to be.

Fisher didn't know anybody from Siberia, apart from Egorov, on which to judge the lethal nature of their smile. He knew few soviets; he had seen Olga Korbut, and she seemed ok, including her initials.

These, and other polished gems sat alongside a few diamonds in the rough of his mind, as Fisher, climbed the familiar, yet threatening, stairwell, the six floors to his cave of dreams, his dead animal hat in his hand.

The file, tucked under his other arm, would provide some bedtime reading. Well, not quite, as the typed notes and penned scribbles were all in Russian. But, at least there would be a late-night buffet of gruesome pictures and a cocktail of the worst that a man can do to a child. At least, the stairs afforded him some pause for thought.

Through his research, Fisher was aware of an odd preponderance in this vast country for serial killers and cannibals. Was it because they were bored? Or, quite simply because they could get away with it? For a while, at least.

Like the very recent case of Andrei Chikatilo. In silence, he went about satisfying his yearnings in a twelve-year spree of rape, murder and cannibalism. At least fifty-three people, and some believe more, died directly at his hands. Another man died indirectly, wrongly convicted, and executed, after 'confessing' to a killing later claimed by Chikatilo. Three more suspects killed themselves.

So, quiet was he about his grisly pastime that even his wife didn't suspect what the father of her two children had been up to. On the surface, he seemed an average Soviet man: educated, hardworking, and a life-long member of the Communist Party.

Behind this facade, though, was a man whose troubles started the day he was born, on October 16th 1936, in a little village in the Ukraine, ravaged by Stalinist-era famines. Andrei grew up seeing the carnage of war up close and hearing horror stories of cannibalism, including one about his own brother, who had vanished one day and, the tale went, was killed and eaten by starving neighbours.

Chikatilo worked hard in school and by his mid-thirties, he had landed a position as a teacher in the town of Novoshakhtinsk. Also, in spite of a personal history of impotence; something Fisher had seen, in such men, a number of times before, he somehow managed to marry and become a father.

His troubles started in the 1970s, when he was fired for groping students. Chikatilo got another teaching job in Shakhty, but soon after he arrived, on December 22nd 1978, a little girl from that town, Lena Zakotnova, nine years old, vanished.

Police fished her mutilated corpse from a river two days later. Chikatilo was questioned, but another man, a convicted sex offender, confessed after a brutal interrogation and was executed.

Fisher's thoughts had travelled around the curved corridor and reached the door to his room. He opened it, peering inside, cautiously. He half expected to find Volkov standing in the corner by the tiny window, smoking a *Prima* and asking him to hand over the file. But, the room was empty. Discarding his Winter covers, he continued to search the Chikatilo case in his archival head, grasping for any similarities or constellations in the void.

In the years following Zakotnova's murder, Chikatilo lost his second teaching position, again for molesting students, and got a job as a supply clerk in a factory, work that had him traveling a lot.

In September 1981, a seventeen-year-old prostitute disappeared, and then, in June 1982, a thirteen-year-old schoolgirl went out to buy some food and never came home.

One after another, women, girls and then young boys in the region disappeared. Some would be found later, their bodies bearing the horrific signature marks of the murderer: boys were castrated, women's sexual organs were crudely sliced out. Tongue tips and organs of several victims appeared to have been bitten off.

The murderer was dubbed the *Forest Strip Killer*. We, in the West, never got to hear about this *deviant* behaviour in an otherwise compliant State. Only in the last few months had information become available for research purposes.

Fisher sat down at the small table, wishing he had a coffee or a cup of tea. What he wouldn't give right now for a cuppa and a dark chocolate coated digestive biscuit.

Police, possibly the militia, questioned nearly half a million people, with methods so brutal they drove at least three men to suicide. The

Rostov investigation solved over a thousand cases, including several murders, while looking for the *Forest Strip* monster.

In 1983, investigators became convinced that the killings were the work of a band of unbalanced young men, petty criminals and troublemakers. Interrogations yielded confessions, and for a time it seemed as if the case was closed.

But the murders continued.

MDV investigators turned their attention to public places that attracted large groups of people.

It was in early September 1984, at a bus station, that detective Alexander Zanosovsky noticed a middle-aged man, carrying a briefcase, who was trying to start conversations with young girls passing by. After two weeks observing the man chatting up one young person after another, the detective approached him. At that moment, Zanosovsky recalled later, *drops of sweat the size of raindrops appeared on his forehead.*

It was Chikatilo.

Zanosovsky arrested him; in the briefcase, there was a knife, rope, a jar of Vaseline and a towel. In his gut, Zanosovsky was certain this ordinary-looking man was the monster, but his theory was undermined by science. Chikatilo's blood type was A, and it did not match the AB semen found on the victims' bodies. Scientists had not yet discovered that in some rare individuals, blood and semen can have different profiles. Chikatilo was one of them. He went free. Women and children continued to disappear, and mutilated corpses, some without heads, continued to pop up in the forests around the Rostov region.

Then, just recently, according to Fisher's sources, a detective noticed a tall man walking out of the woods, his finger bandaged and his ear scratched. He asked the stranger for his name. The answer: Andrei

Chikatilo. There was no reason to detain him, but luckily, the officer remembered that name when a body turned up nearby a few days later.

Shortly after his arrest, the killer broke his silence, blabbing about his murder spree. Sexual gratification was the motive; without terror, pain, and blood, he was impotent, and had been all his life. Promises of food and drink rendered him irresistible to hungry prostitutes, and the children, he said, followed him because of his personal *magnetism*.

Fisher knew Chikatilo was now awaiting trial. Would he learn anything from meeting him? Would he be allowed to meet him? It was the kind of thing Volkov or Egorov could arrange.

At the small table, he turned the pages of indecipherable Cyrillic typed text, until he could consider a diagram or two. Which told him nothing of interest. And at the end of each victim's story, was a collection of black and white photographs of the face and body of a naked girl and the terrible gape in her torso.

Fisher felt quite sick, and was grateful for the lack of colour in the images, if not in his face. He noted, however, that the photographs seemed to have an uncanny, inexplicable quality about them. And, the girls were of a type; not identical by any measure. But there was a pattern; a similarity of features, assisted by the shaved heads, in effect, removing the difference in hair style and texture.

More art than documentary; the photographs seemed beautifully composed with lighting that could not have been achieved merely from a camera mounted flash. Perhaps it was different here?

The crime scene is usually photographed to minimise the risk of conflicting statements and, as in these cases, where there is a corpse at the scene, it too will be photographed post mortem so that a record of how the body was found, what position it was found in, and the nature of its mortal injuries are documented for later inspection.

In many cases photographic evidence is very important for both the prosecution and defence. *But here?* Thought Fisher. It is also used as a means of displaying the nature of a crime scene to officers of an investigative team who were not able to attend.

The means in which crime scenes are photographed are such that the most intricate of details can be recorded for future reference. But, something... some... ...*thing*... Fisher couldn't quite put his finger on... was disarming about these pictures. All, it would seem, taken in the same style...but, by the same photographer? Hardly likely. It was as if they were photographed to be displayed, exhibited or published in *True Detective*, or something. Not merely as a factual record for the authorities, or as potential evidence in court.

It didn't make any sense. Crime scene photographs are also used, not only as a means of evidence; but also as a blueprint for reconstructing a scene or event at a later stage. These reconstructive events can be used as a means of jogging the memories of passers-by who may have been witness to an event or saw a perpetrator without realising they had. Did they ever do such reconstructions here? Fisher didn't know. But, these photographs, although graphic, were more *illustrative*. Perhaps that's not the right word? They looked like stills from a film set.

And, then, all of a sudden, buried in between two shocking close-ups of a wound, each showing a particular cut into the flesh... a photograph of a knife. Not an actual knife, found at the scene of a discovery; but more a file photo, of a type of suggested knife; of the sort used to cut the bone from the flesh. It was a standard issue pen-knife of the Soviet Spets, or rather: *spetsnaz* or special unit. The knife in the photograph, was of the exact same type as the one possessed by Anton.

9

Time

Entropy.

Crumbling.

Ultimately, everything in motion, slows to infinite rest; even a clock.

Especially a clock.

Despite Fisher's sense of time running out, and everything around him accelerating in *Brownian Motion*: that erratic random movement of microscopic particles in a medium, as a result of continuous bombardment from molecules of the same surrounding medium, he wanted to get on. But Vladimir had different ideas. He preferred to go to a place where little changed, that wasn't already planned or expected. He insisted, therefore, when he called Fisher in his room that morning, that they should take a few hours from the chaos of cases, and bathe in the still waters of the established art at the Tsar's former *Winter Palace*. He had already made all the arrangements. There was, therefore, no way for Fisher to avoid or escape that, without raising suspicions as to what else he was getting up to.

In any case, what was he getting up to?

If he knew, he would be getting on with it.

But he felt in something of a cul-de-sac. The file had been illustrative, but told him nothing. The market had been interesting, but not interesting enough. It had established that Eloise had gone willingly with a man; nothing more.

And, this excursion, this waste of time, was to be a great honour: the Director of the Hermitage would take both of them on a personal tour of the museum, and his driver would collect them both in his official car.

Was this some diversionary ploy on the part of Vladimir, or on behalf of some other agency, to knock Fisher out of kilter?

For the sake of *expediency*, and on the Director's instruction, the pick-up point for the driver would be Vladimir's apartment. If not expediency, then it might be because the Director didn't want his car to be seen at the Moskva. And so, it was necessary for Vladimir to collect Fisher *immediately*.

He was already waiting inside the lobby.

The problem Fisher faced, was what to do with the fat file that the fat Chief Investigator had given him, on pain of death, not to give to the KGB. And, therefore...if he left it in his room, then...?

Also, Fisher was unclear as to the connection, if any, between Vladimir and all of this.

Was it possible that Vladimir was in fact KGB? Or, if there was such a thing: ex KGB?

It might be best, he concluded, to hide the file in full sight... so to speak.

And so, if he took the file with him, was he at risk of exposing it, somehow, to Vladimir? It was the option of least risk, he thought; and so, he gathered the papers together, returned them to the folder and stuffed the entire thing into his small satchel.

This, he would keep by his side at all times, as if he were carrying the nuclear codes for Armageddon.

Once in the car, Vladimir, provided cheerfully, but without smiling, the context for the visit:

"Mikhail Piotrovsky is the new Director. His father was an institution, having been there as Director for twenty-six years, until his death just a few weeks ago. He died of a cerebral haemorrhage at the age of 82.

Boris Piotrovsky won fame in 1939 for his discovery of the ancient civilization of Urartu, in Armenia. He won dozens of Soviet awards, Tass said, he was an honorary member of the British, French and other foreign academies of science."

Fisher was listening to all this, filing it away in his mental desktop, as material for the shredder.

"He took part in analysing the remains of King Tutankhamen's tomb and helped decipher dozens of rock drawings in Egypt. During his tenure at the Hermitage, cultural freedom in the Soviet Union expanded and contracted, and recently expanded again under Gorbachev. The Hermitage, always a focal point of world artistic attention, has taken some advantage of the openness by agreeing to show some works long hidden and letting others travel to foreign countries for exhibit."

"And his son, Mikhail?"

"Much more unpredictable...for the time being at least. He will feed from the breast of his father's reputation for a while. We shall see. He may want to make his own mark, in time. You can judge him for yourself, Stephen."

Feed from the breast of his father...? Fisher had no intention of judging him, or anybody else, for that matter. Except, of course, the killer or killers lurking in his heavy document case. Fisher was aware that his driver had noticed the bag, weighted with authority, but, as yet, had said nothing.

Vladimir had a surprisingly ornate clock in his otherwise cool and restrained St Petersburg apartment. Fisher recognised it immediately: a *Pavel Buhre* pocket watch set as a clock in Russian silver and enamel guilloche presentation mounting. The watch had a white enamel face with black Roman numerals and notches. Black hour, minute and sub-second hands. The mounting was raised in a floral ribbon design throughout the chase work base. It had a hand painted enamelled scene depicting mother and child in a countryside landscape setting.

"An incredible timepiece, Vladimir."

"Yes…a gift."

It chimed, beautifully, as Fisher studied a photograph on the wall of Vladimir with Erich Honecker, First Secretary of the Central Committee of East Germany. They looked fraternal. Why would Vladimir be photographed with the leader of the German Democratic Republic? Underneath the photograph… was an upright piano.

"Do you play?" asked Fisher.

Without replying, Vladimir sat down, played a few notes and started to sing:

I found my thrill on Blueberry Hill
On Blueberry Hill when I found you
The moon stood still on Blueberry Hill
And lingered until my dreams came true
The wind in the willow played
Love's sweet melody
But all of those vows we made
Were never to be…

…and then, suddenly, he stopped.

"Fats Domino," said Fisher, clapping his hands politely, whilst being acutely aware of how surreal all this was becoming.

"The greatest! Like an overwhelming majority of people, I can neither sing nor play well, but I very much like doing it," he humbly told the still slowly applauding Fisher.

"You obviously read a great deal too, judging by the bookshelves?"

They showed an impressive array of Western literature.

"I have always loved and avidly read the novels of Jack London, Jules Verne and Ernest Hemingway, I like their thematic approaches to nature. I'm more of *The Old Man and the Sea* and *A Farewell to Arms* kind of guy. What about you Stephen?"

"I still like to read when I can. But as an undergraduate I read literature as well as psychology. Writers of fiction can offer incredible insights into the human psyche. And, I did Soviet Studies in my second year, reading Sholokhov."

"*Violence can only be concealed by a lie, and the lie can only be maintained by violence.*"

"Solzhenitsyn?"

"Yes. And, if you read Gogol, Dostoyevsky, Turgenev, Pushkin, Lermontov, Tolstoy, and, yes, even Solzhenitsyn. That's where you'll really find out how Russians think. Russians correctly view themselves as inheritors of something bigger than just another a huge country, they see Mother Russia as the repository of deep and powerful life philosophies through a vibrant literature. They are unbelievably tough under pressure and take a perverse pleasure in demonstrating they can outlast anyone. It's all there in the novels. If the CIA or the SIS wanted to understand the Russian psyche, there is no need to infiltrate with spies. They can just read a few long novels!"

Interesting, thought Fisher...*how many people would know that acronym?* The Secret Intelligence Service is the overarching body that contains MI5 and MI6.

"But, firstly.." argued Fisher, "..it is hard to know which creative works are timeless expressions of cultural values and which ones are reflective of an important, but passing, moment in the life of a country. Secondly, national literary canons get constructed in particular ways for particular reasons. They are not a natural outgrowth of a set of cultural values unique to a given language, region or way of life. They are shaped by global markets, ideologies of purity and nationalism, conceptions of what it means to be an educated individual and often simple accident. The canon also changes over time, and what's left out of lists of great works of literature can be more telling than what's put in."

The apartment intercom buzzer interrupted the intellectual flow; but Vladimir had the last word:

"Literature, like all art, tells us more about the human condition than it tells us about the artist."

The beautiful clock chimed once more, and seemed at odds with the well-read man, albeit in a city of beautiful clocks.

Given what Fisher already knew of the Winter Palace, he knew it would be the first of many chiming clocks that day.

The next marker of time was the cannon that fired at noon, clearly audible as Fisher was sitting in a hushed reception room behind the scenes at the Hermitage, waiting to meet the museum's Director. Of the Peacock Clock inside the Small Hermitage, an ornate contraption constructed in the 1760s by the English jeweller James Coxe in the form of a tree, upon which a gilded clockwork peacock perches and spreads its tail. And of the clock in the small dining room of the Winter Palace, frozen at 2.10am, the time the provisional government was arrested in that room on the night of November 7th 1917, when the Bolsheviks stormed the building in the decisive act of the Russian Revolution.

At that moment, a whole history ceased. The history of eighteenth and nineteenth century Russia, was encapsulated by the *Hermitage*; from Peter the Great's foundation of his new capital in 1703 to the excesses of the nineteenth century Tsars...all came to an end, just as the history of St Petersburg as a capital came to an end. The Soviets transferred the seat of government to Moscow.

And all the clocks stopped.

Or perhaps not all?

"Time never stops," Vladimir said. "The epoch of Peter the Great hasn't stopped yet. You can always imagine you are in this time because the branch of this time is still growing. The world, in my imagination, is like a tree. We Russians, are all...how do you say... cells in that tree and are moving along it. We are much closer to our past than Englishmen are to Victorian times. Our past hasn't become the past yet; the main problem in this country is that we don't know when it will become the past."

Vladimir was filling the time, with all this. Why? When there was no need to fill it, at all. For Fisher, time was already an overflowing cup. No matter how much he drank from the grail, it always filled again, to dribble down the side. Here was an example of Fisher's acute sense of the visual. He often thought in metaphors, in symbols or signs. He was, you might say, a semiotician. An enigma, even by his own admission, and to others, something of a polymath...a renaissance man...out of his time.

This, in part, explained his rather lonely childhood. It never seemed lonely at the time; just now, when he thought about. He spent most of his time alone, in his makeshift bedroom: drawing, painting and collecting things; making things, especially clocks.

A prodigy in mathematics and a junior chess champion. Later...as late as seven years old, he finally cracked the code of reading and writing. Not Dostoyevsky, of course. At first, he studied comics: *Superman*, *Batman* and many other superheroes. He read the pictures...the words came later. The story was in the pictures. The speaking and thinking was in the bubbles. And this was how he saw people in those days, with bubbles coming out of their mouths and clouds over their heads.

Despite his teens being preoccupied with writing poetry, he never lost his visual code. Even now, as he sat in the *Hermitage*, he was envious of those that could express the inexpressible through art. As Jean Anouilh once put it: *life is very nice, but it lacks form. It's the aim of art to give it some...*or something like that.

Fisher had once wanted to be that artist, giving shape to the cosmos.

The light is low in the study; where the acclaimed Director Piotrovsky, described his father's legacy as the *Russian Ark*, as he called it, the depository for the survival of counter revolutionary culture. Above his own thoughts, Fisher could hear the voice of the narrator: Piotrovsky's voice, speaking in a bubble:

"My father," he explained, "with another deceased director, Iosef Orbeli, was responsible for saving the museum's treasures during the three-year siege of Leningrad."

Fascinating, thought Fisher, somewhat sarcastically, all too conscious that this tour was taking too much time before it had even started. He had a young girl to find, even if he was unsure of where to focus his search.

The tour began behind the scenes, in the theatre designed for Catherine the Great by her neoclassical architect Giacomo Quarenghi and modelled on Palladio's Teatro Olimpico in Vicenza in Italy.

"We have had some bad experiences with feature films, says Piotrovsky, as he burst out of the theatre into the museum proper, out of subdued light into a bright, sunlit public space, where it seems the entire unemployed population of St Petersburg has come to spend the morning. It was warm, at least.

Never having visited the museum before, Fisher, accompanied by Vladimir, followed Piotrovsky past old and young, so many faces, through rooms with gilded mouldings, mosaics, balconies, vistas.

Bad experiences with feature films? Fisher knew what he was alluding to. Some extraordinary ones, too. Long before Piotrovsky's time, and before his father's, Sergei Eisenstein shot the storming of the Winter Palace, part of the Hermitage complex, on location, his dramatized account of the revolution, commissioned for the tenth anniversary of the Bolshevik seizure of power.

In Eisenstein's later film, the *Peacock Clock*, the same one made by a brilliant English designer in the eighteenth century, bought by Catherine the Great's intimate Grigori Potemkin, and today still proudly in working order...appears in the film as an historical capitalist absurdity.

"Objects that were once considered symbols of decadence have now rapidly become national treasures," explained the Director, proudly.

In the Hall of St George, Mikhail shows Fisher the newly restored twin-headed eagle, symbol of Tsarist Russia, from the top of the Winter Palace. It is reverently displayed and enraptures the museum's Russian visitors. How different from its representation by the revolutionary *Avant garde* eighty-odd years ago.

> *Death to the two-headed eagle!*
> *Sever its long-necked head*
> *With a single stroke!*

Wrote the poet Mayakovsky.

"Today," explains Mikhail, "people come to the Hermitage to see and celebrate the lost world of past Russia. Today, there is some sympathy for the doomed royal family. It's a far cry from Eisenstein, let alone his more politically orthodox rival, Pudovkin, whose own film restaging the revolution is called, with consummate brutality, *The End of St Petersburg*." He paused, and then:

"Ah...here is someone, I should like you to meet..."

A rather dishevelled looking man, in the modern bohemian sense, tall and cadaverous with a shaved head, was walking towards them. He stopped to shake Vladimir's hand, followed by Fisher's.

"Gentleman, meet the future... my new acquisition...my secret weapon in our war with ignorance... Yuri Molodkovets, who has been the Hermitage Museum photographer for...?"

"Three weeks, Comrade General Director."

"Yuri is our first resident photographer...an artist in his own right. I was just speaking of the great Pudovkin, perhaps you might continue, Yuri?"

It seemed a little unfair, but Yuri was confident and knowledgeable:

"Editing, is what the Russian *Avant Garde Cinema* of the 1920s is famous for, what Eisenstein, Pudovkin and their contemporaries contributed to world cinema; not just the haphazard scissors-and-paste techniques cobbled together by Hollywood custom, but something altogether more systematic: montage, the dazzling juxtaposition of images to convey meaning; in Eisenstein's hands a great modernist aesthetic, but also a mode of manipulation and propaganda. With editing, whether in the films of the Soviet Movement or in the fictive patchwork of today's mainstream cinema, reality is remade in the cutting room; film bends time, routinely distorts experience."

Fisher was deeply impressed, whilst Vladimir, he could see, was glazing over, as they walked through room after room.

"All great old museums are places where time stretches" he continued, "floats, accumulates dust, even has an odour... some people sniff paintings. You lose yourself, cut free from linear time into something more oceanic. The Hermitage has the same historical thickness that all museums have, but to an infinitely more fermented degree."

Yuri was indeed, the future. If he was selling the museum, Fisher was buying. Not to be outshone, Mikhail started to walk into the next great room, with Yuri still in tow. But, it is his turn to impress:

"The location of the Hermitage is peculiarly disassociated from the everyday. The Winter Palace, built by the eighteenth century Baroque genius Bartolomeo Francesco Rastrelli and restored extravagantly to his designs after the fire of 1837, together with the Small Hermitage that Catherine the Great created as her personal retreat, the Large Hermitage that she built to house her art collection, and the nineteenth century New Hermitage that is the only purpose-designed public gallery within the complex, standing along the banks of the river...."

"Speaking of rivers..." interrupted Vladimir, "I need to take a piss."

Clearly, Vladimir's hold on the English language hadn't extended to euphemisms, many of which alluded to a piss without actually saying the word.

"That's fine. Yuri, I will accompany Comrade Ivanov. Please look after Dr Fisher. We will catch up."

Fisher got the impression Mikhail might want to discuss something in private with Vladimir, and so went with the flow, in the opposite direction.

"Yuri, your knowledge and visual literacy is very considerable. I get the impression you are excited to be here?"

"So," he replies, obliquely, "you find yourself in a drawing room, staggering beneath green malachite pilasters and a gilded ceiling, and looking out at a sea of ice, the frozen river; and on the ice, people are walking, skating, fishing. This is a charming fantasy of Russia, like the enormous sled carved in the shape of St George and the Dragon that you came across in some room in the museum, you can't remember which."

"It is quite incredible, even without the art."

"It destroys your mind," Yuri continues enthusiastically. "Working here", he says, "disfigures your sense of reality, alienates you from the life outside. If the Hermitage seems to the casual visitor to inhabit a different time, it is an even more intense for the people who work here. They love it, and become part of it."

Fisher thought it quite refreshing to discover such optimism in a city with so little hope.

"The Hermitage has its own school where children can learn archaeology and art history from the age of five, preselected for curatorial lives like gymnasts or violinists; many, after university, come back to work here. Some start as cleaners and then by steps become curators. Two Vice-Directors began here as labourers, moving things from one place to another."

The rooms were as dizzying and as lofty as Yuri's descriptions of them. Fisher thought, a man like this might one day, become the Director. He was as passionate in his style and delivery, as he was in his content. A rare combination; as rare as hen's teeth in a politician. And, that was the point: the old corrupt order would, he hoped, be replaced by this kind of refreshing visionary leadership.

They continued to walk and talk.

"You can go on for days like this. Everyone makes their own path through this immeasurable museum. The paintings in the Hermitage are so fundamental, it is beyond any discussion," says Yuri. "When you say you prefer this one, it is a little bit shameful; but in fact, I like Rembrandt very sincerely with all my heart and I love El Greco since my school years. I am a provincial man, Dr Fisher, and my first meeting with real paintings was in the Hermitage. Before that I saw lots of paintings by Rembrandt and El Greco, only in books."

Fisher was so taken by Yuri's optimism, he almost forgot the heavy bag he was lugging around; and the, even heavier, guilty feeling that he was wasting time here, when he should be searching for Eloise.

"As well as sniffing the paintings, people go so close as almost to touch them, and a blind visitor, a gymnast called Tamara who lost her sight when she was twelve, came here last week. I watched her explain Van Dyck's *Rest on the Flight into Egypt*. Her feel suggested that art is not only, or necessarily, visual; and Rembrandt, is the painter who exemplifies this most profoundly."

Time again, time that wells up, time we drown in, pleasurably, thought Fisher. Yuri is an unapologetic defender of the idea of the museum in its most, superficially, conservative sense. Museums make culture stable. Museums make the chaos of art into an atrophied structure. Museums also remind modern artists that there was art before them, so they should be modest and humble.

"You are a photographer, documenting this incredible place?"

"Yes, it's better than doing weddings! But, I do a lot more than document, I hope. My current project is, shall we say, unusual. But the Director has supported me one hundred percent."

"So, what else are you working on?"

"Cats."

"Cats?"

A piece of highly irritating musical theatre popped into Fisher's head.

"The idea of the project belongs to Maria Khaltunen, the Director's assistant, who is also in charge of the Hermitage cats. We wanted to show the museum's grand halls from the point of view of a cat and at the same time create portraits of those loyal and honest defenders of the museum against mice and rats. Before shooting, we had to talk to each of the cats, to discuss their behaviour on camera, facial expressions, etc. When we were just starting, we were not sure that we would cope with the task. The shooting was done on Mondays, when the museum is closed to visitors. We had a whole crew, assisted by the Hermitage security service."

"Are there many photographers in St Petersburg."

"Anyone can call themselves a photographer; and, so, yes, there are many. Some try to make a living; but most can only dream."

"Do you know many of them, personally?"

Fisher was moving towards taking a terrible risk, the possible consequences of which were incalculable.

"Well, some, yes. There are clubs and collectives; but, I don't bother with those. I was closer to the underground culture. I was friends with some and published a newspaper and books together with the St. Petersburg art group *Mitki*. And then suddenly I was invited to join the Hermitage."

"Would you be willing to look at some photographs I have in my bag? Forensic photographs? Quite shocking."

"Is that what you do? Forensic work?"

"I'm an academic, of sorts. My specialist area or field is Criminal Psychology."

"And you are working on a case here? Or, doing some research?"

"Both. I can't really discuss the details...but..."

"Yes, of course. Shall we go to my office?"

"That might be better, thank you, Yuri. I must ask you, however, not to discuss these images with anyone....understand? No one."

"Everything in this country is a secret; and nothing is secret. But, I will agree to do my best."

Yuri's long strides made short work of the back-stage corridor to his office...more of a studio, with an adjoining dark room. It was peppered with photographs of cats, taken from ground level in the vast halls of the museum.

"This is a country of secrets and subterfuge: of disguise and duplicity. Above all, we specialise in knowing when to shut up. In the West, a life can depend on knowing something. Here, a life can depend on not knowing something. You work on the basis of truth and lies. To me, in my world, there are only lies."

"Still, your discretion is much appreciated."

"Here, we can use this table."

Fisher took the file from his bag, in the hope that Vladimir would not think to find him there. He placed the photographs in piles on the left, this allowed Yuri to spread them out towards to the right, thereby, he was able to view the images in a cluster by victim. He placed his hand over his mouth, and swallowed, trying to find some moisture.

He said nothing... Nothing at all, as his eyes roamed, scanning back and fourth as if he were reading a wall of hieroglyphs etched in stone.

"What do you think?" asked Fisher, gently.

Yuri thought a little more.

"Some of the different groups are by the same photographer. I'm sure of that. But this...this is more like a montage with a message."

"What kind of a message?"

"Well...firstly, it's a homage...as if she or he likes the subject matter! How...? But, there is more. The position of the camera is different in each case, but there seem to be... And, yet, there is consistency of lighting. He or she may have cropped them in developing the prints, in order to enhance the similarity. It's as if he/she wants the viewer to see the same thing...the same message in each example."

"But this is a forensic photographer employed by the militia."

"Yes, but paid by the police under a specific contract. It's just a photographer...probably does babies in his spare time. There is no such thing as an official forensic photographer in Russia. It's possible they has a normal day job, and this is just an occasional paid hobby.

But, I would say not. This is a man, and I now think it is a man, who knows his craft…his art, even. His photographs are trying to make the unpalatable palatable…to find a…beauty, and a pattern in the shocking confusion."

"What kind of a pattern?"

Yuri was concentrating. And yet, he handed all the photographs back to Fisher, except the images of the faces. As he spreads them out on the table like skilled croupier with a wicked pack of cards. He pauses, and then re-arranges them.

"What is it?"

"It's… no, it can't be…it's a silly idea…but…"

"No idea is too silly."

"Well, if you arrange them in date order, like so…"

Yuri created an unfinished, circle of portraits.

"The angle of the photographs…the first is vertical; the next tipped to the right, and so on….a few degrees each time…together, they form the numerals… the face of a clock….."

Fisher was seriously impressed, but puzzled.

"Why would he or she do that?"

"It's as if he is highlighting the sense of time…of lost potential. That these pretty girls will never reach womanhood. Look at the way the light catches on their lips. Despite the horrified expression on some, he sees something else….something captured…something frozen in time. You know it's there, but you can't quite see it. Like a clock stopping in the dark."

"What does he see Yuri?"

"A terrible beauty."

"But, all of these ideas are predicated on the notion that a single photographer has taken all of the photographs."

"Yes…but, as I said: there are similarities of style. It's possible that it is the same photographer; but, also possible that it isn't."

"If it's not, then how would you explain the similarity?"

"It could be that they were trained together; or, that they have copied a style from each other."

"Which is it?"

"I don't know."

"But then the pattern?"

"Yes, that is difficult to reconcile with multiple photographers. On the other hand, it could be that I've been talking bullshit. Maybe I'm over thinking it."

"You mean the interpretation was not the artist's intention?"

"Exactly…that, in fact, there is no conscious art…just images. But, I am more inclined to the first theory."

"Does the style fit with anyone you know?"

"There are one or two that are inclined towards the macabre. Others who think that the more shocking the image, the closer it is to art. But, no…this is someone who may feel his art is unrecognised; and there are plenty of those out there. Perhaps he makes his living with wedding photographs, or something equally innocuous? Or, maybe, he isn't a photographer? Perhaps he works in a tractor factory and does this on the side? And, I presume you had already noted the similarity of the victims?And the shaved heads? What's that about? It suggests an assault on purity, sanctity; or, just a perverse kink….or, possibly ritualistic?"

"You seem convinced that the photographer is male."

"Undoubtedly."

"Why? Why not a woman?"

"First, this is the collapsing Soviet Union, Dr Fisher. For all our claims to comradeship and egalitarianism, women were allowed to labour in fields and factories, but none, or very few were permitted to express the themselves. How many female soviet writers can you name?"

"Svetlana Alexievich."

"Very good, Dr Fisher."

"But that's it, I'm afraid."

Secondly," continued Yuri, "I doubt a woman would display such a fascination with this. The images are almost auto-érotique. It is as if, the subject is being objectified for the purpose of titillation."

That was insight that Fisher had lacked. Not the motive, He had seen every possible motive in men for self gratification. What he had missed, quite possibly, was the game the photographer was playing. He knew there was something odd in the images; something disjointed. But was it relevant? Merely a distraction? A false clue? Or, it could be a signature; the very thing that identifies the killer as the genuine killer and not a copy...a fake. Copying a serial killer would hardly be taken as a compliment. More likely, it would enrage. The very idea that someone had stolen his method...his identity. For it is often the case, that a killer with weak or damaged personality traits, will seek to establish a new, and terrifying, persona based on their actions. The more shocking the action; the more attention it gets; the greater the fear; the more gratifying it is, reinforcing the new identity. And, the more it is repeated, the greater the notoriety. Oddly, the serial killer rarely seeks anonymity. More common, is the desire to be caught, to be identified, vilified; and to hear people say: *he was such a quiet man...kept himself to himself*. But, ultimately, in being identified and convicted, he enters a Hall of Fame and is recorded as having fooled all around him, including the authorities and more especially, those closest to him.

Yuri collected the photographs with some reverence. He turned to Fisher and looked him in the eyes, as he moved to hand him the images. Fisher, held on to them, as did Yuri.

"Are you thinking what I'm thinking, Dr Fisher?"

"That this is just a style the photographer adopts...a signature?" suggested Fisher.

"Or, that the photographer admires the killer?"

"Or that he is turned on by the same terrible things?"

"Or...?"

"...that he *is* the killer?"

"Ah..." said Vladimir, in the doorway, "there you are! *They are in here, Mikhail...*" shouting off.

Frozen.

Silence.

Vladimir stared at the two men clutching a set of black and white photographs. He said nothing, and made no attempt to step forward for a closer look.

"Please keep the photographs, Dr Fisher...as a memento of your visit. My personal gift to you."

"Thank you, Yuri. I, really, am, most grateful. It's been fascinating and informative....and a totally different perspective on things. It's a significant project and will prove hugely influential. I can see why the Director has such confidence in you."

As he spoke, Fisher placed the pictures in his bag.

"I was just showing Dr Fisher my first major photography project," said Yuri, to Vladimir, leading him away from Fisher to the wall of images.

"Cats?" asked Vladimir.

"Cats!" echoed Mikhail. "They will become an international brand for the museum!"

"Really?" said Vladimir barely concealing his disbelief.

"One day," continued Mikhail, "one day, one day soon, we will publish these images...tee shirts...posters...a book, and a café that sells *cattuccinos!*"

10

World Enough

Proximity.

Distance.

So near and yet so far.

The driver pulled up outside Vladimir's apartment, and they walked immediately to transfer to the Tatra.

"I was planning to take you to the Neva for something to eat." explained Vladimir, getting into the familiar black car, "I even have my treasure chest of cash in the trunk."

"Boot." offered Fisher, "We say *boot* not *trunk*. Trunk is American for boot."

"Really? Isn't that a long shoe...for riding horses?"

"Isn't a trunk the nose of an elephant?"

"Why is that? How are we to know if it's a shoe or the back end of the car?"

"How do we know there isn't an elephant sitting on the back end of the car?"

"Because we are moving!"

"Very good, Vladimir. You're English sense of humour is coming along very nicely. Around 1600, I believe, *boote*, with an *e* on the end, began to be used for an uncovered projecting seat outside the doors on each side of a coach, in which passengers sat facing sideways to the direction of travel. It's often said that these seats were for servants, but this, to me, seems unlikely. It was, according to a colleague of mine, something to do with sitting sideways, having two legs in one boot; like a woman riding a horse sideways."

"Women ride horses sideways?"

Fisher could see a chasm of cultural confusion opening up. But, that was just fine for now, given that he would rather fill the car with kernels of useless knowledge for Vladimir to chew on, rather than talk about the gristle of the case. Should Volkov ask, Vladimir can tell him they spoke about the culturally specific etymology for the rear compartment of a car. And so, he continued:

"Women in England used to ride horses without opening their legs. But, in America, not so much."

Vladimir was trying to visualise, a woman riding a horse with her legs *closed* with two legs in one boot.

Moving on.

"By the beginning of the nineteenth century, the boots had been moved to the ends of coaches and had turned into storage areas. One was under the coachman's seat at the front, the other under that of the guard at the back. Eventually the boot at the front became a bonnet."

"A bonnet? Like a hat?"

"Exactly. But in America a bonnet is a hood."

"A bonnet is a criminal?"

"A hood can be placed over the head."

"Like a bonnet?"

"I see….and what about…the trunk?"

"A *trunk* was a case, strapped to the rear of a motor car….Where are we going, Vladimir?"

"I don't know…I don't know where this going. Oh…I see your meaning…I was about to explain that, in any case, there is not enough time for lunch. Mikhail handed me a message when I'd finished my piss."

Fisher felt compelled to explain the French origin of piss, and the many useful euphemisms applied in polite conversation, but was curious as to the message. Vladimir illuminated:

"I am to take you to the Office of the Consul General at the British High Commission."

"Why?"

"I wasn't given a reason. I'm just doing as instructed."

"By Volkov?"

The car turned two sharp corners away from the river onto Shpalermaya Ulitsa and passed the Tauride Palace before Vladimir answered.

"There is something, I think you should understand, Stephen."

The car turned right onto the street Fisher recognised, as quite close to the night market. And, then Vladimir pulled over. The sky was dull, and the light was already beginning to fade into the murk if eternal winter.

"Are we here?"

"Not quite." Vladimir switched the engine off.

"Until just a few weeks ago…how should I begin? The KGB has formed the bulk of my professional experience. I worked there from the day I graduated in 1974. And, what is more, the KGB was not just a company, but a university. At the Higher School of the KGB, in Moscow, which I attended, young agents took university-level classes. It was important, the KGB hierarchy believed, that the cadres understand the world they were being trained to subvert and manipulate. I was then sent to the GDR. Technically, I am still a Lieutenant Colonel in the KGB."

Whilst not entirely surprised by his admission, Fisher was, nonetheless, stunned by his level of seniority.

"I have already tendered…I think you say…my resignation in August. For reasons, I don't wish to go into. Besides you can't quit. As we say, *it costs a rouble to join the KGB and two roubles to leave.* Shortly, I am to be transferred out of the university into the City Administration, as head of the International Committee at the St. Petersburg Mayor's Office. My task in the new position involves attracting foreign investments to the city economy, establishing and maintaining co-operation with foreign partners and supervising the creation and opening of joint ventures."

"That's… well… quite incredible, Vladimir… quite incredible."

"But, truthfully, Stephen, nobody ever leaves the KGB; and so, within certain parameters, I am willing to assist…with you, for example. But this will diminish over time. I have larger fish to cook. I wish to focus on the future, not the past. All the ideals and aims I had when I went to work for the KGB collapsed in the days of the putsch last summer when Yeltsin called the Red Army to defend parliament.

The putschists' aim," said Vladimir, sincerely, "was *noble*, as they believed in preserving the Soviet Union from disintegration, but the means and the methods they chose only hastened this. This decision is probably the hardest of my life. I was from the democrats' milieu. But it got worrying. Look at the situation the organs of security are in. The democrats want to destroy, to break, to lacerate them, they call for the agency's lists to be opened up, for the secrets to be revealed," Vladimir complains, obviously bitter to the bone.

"When I was based in Dresden…when the Berlin Wall came down in eighty-nine, I helped destroy KGB files. I personally burned a huge quantity of material. We were burning so much stuff that the stove broke down!"

Vladimir paused for a moment, and then, reflecting:

"I was born to hardship and suffering, Stephen, at the end of the Stalinist era in a city that bore the brunt of Stalin's spite. I was born five months before he died, an only child. My father was a war veteran, Communist Party member, and foreman in a factory making subway trains. My mother had survived the nine hundred day Nazi siege of Leningrad, and did a variety of odd jobs as a laboratory cleaner, bakery worker, and janitor. She, meanwhile, was starving in the siege, sustained by her brother, a navy officer. He fed her his rations," Vladimir recounted all this with a rare degree of observable passion. Fisher thought it best to let him finish.

"Then my uncle was ordered away somewhere and she was on the brink of death. That's no exaggeration. Mama passed out from hunger. They thought she was dead and they even put her with the deceased. She was lucky she came-to just in time and groaned. It was a miracle she stayed alive, only later, to die from leukaemia. What I see around me now, could be the start of something far worse; far more dangerous, with far-reaching consequences. The KGB may have splintered into competing factions."

Vladimir turned to face Fisher.

"But, let me be *absolutely* clear, Stephen: I am not here to spy on you...to subvert your mission in any way...even if I was asked to do so...which...I have not. I am not involved in any of this...case. I know nothing of this of this missing girl; and I have no information that can help you find her, or those that may have taken her."

Fisher appreciated the candour. He said so, as the car moved off for the short distance along the same road. But while he accepted Vladimir's confession and statement of distancing himself from the KGB in a carefully planned exit strategy, there was one word that played on Fisher's mind. It was like a worm...a maggot...eating into his troubled mind: *those*. He said...*those that may have taken her*.

Not *the man that may have taken her*. Nor did he suggest that she was already dead.

Why would he say that? A fault in his imperfect English, perhaps? Did he mean exactly what he said? Literally? If so, to what purpose? Fisher had not encountered this possibility before. Of course, there were infamous cases of couples, of husband and wife, even. But, there were driven by sexual gratification between the pair. Often, the female being the most vilified by the media and wider society.

Why would a splinter group of the KGB involve themselves in the capture, torture and murder of young girls with no possible political motivation. And in any case, this splintering of the KGB was very recent, not years ago, when this menace began.

It made no sense.

Fisher concluded, therefore, that this plural must have been a mistake. Should he ask for clarification? No. Fisher had insufficient traction on this notion to press Vladimir further. Notwithstanding this, it may be nothing to do with the KGB at all. It could be that they know more of this case than they care to admit. If so, why would they not act to stop it? And, Fisher accepted that when Vladimir said he knew nothing about it, he was being genuine. But, why was he still driving him around when he had embarked on a new, political career?

As the car, pulled up to the barrier at the consulate security gate, Fisher recoiled from asking that vital question. More than likely, Vladimir, as he said, knew nothing more. A man like him, the outsider, the father of two daughters he obviously adores…Even if he did know more, would Vladimir answer? He had stated his position and that was that.

The Tatra pulled up outside the vehicle entrance to the Consulate.

"Fisher?" said the guard looking into the car. And then:

"Ivanov?"

The cursory examination of identity documents triggered the barrier to arc to the vertical as the car moved forward.

"I will wait for you here, Stephen, in the car park."

"Really, there's no need."

"I will wait for you here, in the car park." Vladimir repeated.

"I'll be fine…thank you."

"Are you sure, Stephen?"

"Yes…I'm deeply grateful to you, Vladimir. But given all that you have said, it might be best for both of us, if we part here, on good terms."

Vladimir nodded:

"You should take great care, Stephen. As we say in Russian: Жить с волками, вы должны вопить, как волк …to live with wolves, you have to howl like a wolf."

They shook hands firmly.

As Fisher watched Vladimir turn the car around and back through the control point and out into the street, he couldn't help thinking that this might not be the last time he would see or hear of him.

On entering the building and being screened, Fisher was taken up a long flight of stairs that split to the left and right, coming back around on the themselves to land on the same upper landing with a rich terracotta coloured marble floor. *Italian*…Fisher thought. The receptionist had a slow, methodical, feline walk…up the stairs and along the corridor. Awkwardly slow, it seemed to Fisher, as he walked behind her in silence, her high heels clicking on the marble and the tight grey skirt, that fitted where it touched, forcing her to place one foot, almost directly in front of the other. But, at least, it afforded a little bit of time to process what had just happened.

Half an hour before, he was convinced, he had a credible *type* of suspect: the photographer. It was a lead, at least…something to follow. It may or may not be the kidnapper or killer. The photographs could be a red herring; or, as Hitchcock might have said...a *MacGuffin*. One of his favourite devices for driving the plots of his films and creating suspense. Many of his suspense films used this device: a detail which, by inciting curiosity and desire, drives the plot and motivates the actions of characters within the story. However, the specific identity of the item is actually unimportant to the plot.

It could be an object or collection of objects. Or, as in so many spy thrillers, a State Secret. Hitchcock has stated that the best MacGuffin, or as he put it, *the emptiest*, was the one used in *North by Northwest*, which was referred to as *government secrets*. But, even though it felt to the contrary, Fisher had to remind himself, that this was not a film; and that, in the space of thirty minutes, he had gone from having a potential type of *suspect*, to a suggestion of *suspects*. Could the photographs be an unnecessary distraction? Possibly faked? Or even a deliberate diversion?

The tick ticking, and it's retarded echo: click-clacking, had stopped by a large door and was replaced by a silence, and then a knock. The door swept open and Fisher was announced.

"Stephen, please come in," said Alan in gentle tones, "Sarah, would you have Patrick join us, please...and bring something for this poor man to eat."

Sarah was about to click-off before Fisher could intervene, but hesitated just in case.

"Stephen, sit. You look terrible, if I may say so? Thin...gaunt...are you...?"

"I'm fine, really...just busy...and, yes, quite hungry...if I'm honest."

"Sarah will bring you a sandwich from next door...and, I'm sure some tea...biscuits, perhaps?"

"Thank you, yes."

She disappeared.

"I called the university. Have you made any progress?"

"Yes, I think so…a witness who saw Eloise leaving the market with a man.

"A man?"

"It appeared as if she might have known him….but the witness was unsure and couldn't really describe the man in detail. More cases have emerged, many more in fact, similar to the one you saw at the university. But, I have no way of verifying these cases as genuine. And, a link to a forensic…."

The door opened, preceded by a light tap.

"Ah, Sarah…yes, set them down on the table. Perfect, thank you."

Sarah placed the tray on a nearby table, just close enough for Fisher to reach the fresh ham and cheese sandwiches…laced with *Branston Pickle*… some British biscuits: *Jammie Dodgers*… strawberry by the looks…and as Fisher knew, named after *Roger the Dodger* from the *Beano Comic*. But, his keen eye was taken beyond that to the Consul General's desk, where another portrait of Eloise stood in a silver frame. Again, in black and white. Not a copy of the one in Fisher's pocket, but, clearly taken at the same time, by the same photographer.

"Patrick is outside, sir. Shall I send him in?" Suggested Sarah.

"Yes, of course…."

"Alan," interrupted Fisher, "could I have the name of the photographer who took that portrait of Eloise?"

"Yes, of course. Sarah, I believe you have the details? Could you let Dr Fisher have the name and address."

"Yes, sir."

"Is it of some significance, Stephen?"

"I'm not sure."

Sarah had left the door frame, and was replaced by a man who filled the space squarely, like a sixteen-point stag. He looked serious and sombre in a dark suit.

"Stephen, this is Commander Briggs…Patrick Briggs. He is our new head of security here at the Consulate."

Fisher stood up to shake his hand. It was a firm, crushing grip, of the sort that leaves the hand, grateful to be alive.

"Please, make yourselves comfortable. And Stephen, please…a sandwich."

As Fisher attempted to pick up a sandwich with his now limp, numbed hand, Alan continued his introduction:

"Patrick…who, incidentally, prefers to be called, *Briggs*…used to be with the SAS before he joined MI6…and they sent him here. How long have you been here now, Patrick?"

"Three days, sir!" He replied, without taking his eyes off Fisher, who, by now had a mouthful of sandwich and an unruly piece of tinned ham dangling from the side of his mouth. Fisher tucked it in with his free hand.

"Is that good, Stephen?" asked Alan.

"Yes, sir."

"You enjoy, whilst we explain recent…how shall I say…developments. Which, I hope don't mean that you have wasted any of your time or expertise."

Fisher couldn't speak even if he wanted to.

The Consul General seemed uncannily calm and optimistic, he noted. Overly so, considering his daughter was still missing after almost three weeks.

"Patrick… er…Briggs, perhaps you should explain?"

His eyes were still fixed…firmly on Fisher's eyes. They had a dead, intimidating, look.

"Dr Fisher," said Briggs, "there has been a development which, you will not be aware of...and, before I proceed any further, may I remind you of your obligations under the Act, which if contravened will result in you being retained at *Her Majesty's Pleasure*."

Fisher nodded, as Briggs continued.

"Not long after, Eloise went missing, a call was intercepted to this office from a man who claimed no identity, except he said he was calling from the State Security Service. We have since confirmed by voice pattern recognition, that the call came from a General Volkov; as the Consul General had earlier asserted. But it came from an untraceable source outside the KGB network....which is...unusual."

"Why would he do that?" asked Fisher.

"He must know that we can't trace a call accurately from here. So, why bother making the call from a dead source? Since then, there has been no further contact until last night."

"Perhaps, it's nothing?" suggested Fisher.

"You mean, that he went out for a pint of milk and decided to make the call?"

Fisher moved on to the *Dodgers,* with uncouth haste, for fear the meeting might end abruptly.

"The caller last night,...a female...spoke only in Russian...again an untraceable source. She left a message on the general answer phone. There is no point in me playing the recording, as I know you don't speak Russian. So, I will tell you exactly what she said: *if the Consul General wishes to see his daughter alive, he should avoid interfering in matters of State Security.*"

"Was that it?" asked Fisher, pausing with a biscuit poised.

"Yes."

"Strange...what...?"

"There's more to it than that Dr Fisher. A few weeks ago, one of my staff here, was approached…in the street, would you believe, by a man claiming to be the lead scientist on a top-secret project called *Red Arrow*."

"Vasyli Kulnikov."

It just slipped out without thinking.

"How do you know this name, Dr Fisher?"

"He met me at the airport, and took me to his apartment a couple of days later. He is the friend of a colleague at the university, back home."

"Is he now?"

"So, he said."

"And how do you know of his association with *Red Arrow*?"

This was more difficult for Fisher to answer; but answer he must....dead grandmother or not.

"Well, I don't really know anything. After a few vodkas, he mentioned something about his last project, before deciding on a new career as a karate teacher."

Briggs waited for more.

"I think he said something about an *arrow*. To be honest, I wasn't really listening. Anyway, what has all this to do with Eloise?"

"Kulnikov…is a leading nuclear physicist, and a valuable asset to the Russians…. Wait a minute! You said he picked you up from the airport?"

"Yes."

"Don't you think that's a bit odd? Something of a remarkable coincidence? That the man at the centre of an intelligence operation; a man well-known to the KGB, the probable leader of a ring of scientists attempting to defect to the West… turns up at the airport, to greet a specialist brought in to investigate a missing person, the daughter of the Consul General at the consulate he is negotiating with for his escape."

Fisher thought it best to sip a cup of tea.

"If I sent in a report to that effect," he continued, "my boss would tell me to stop drinking and to stop making stuff up! But, Dr Fisher, I don't do either of those things! Drink or make stuff up."

Briggs' tone was rising.

"I presume Dr Fisher, that you know a lot more than you are telling me?"

"I know a little of the project, yes; and, I was told that some of Vasyli's friends had disappeared. Are you suggesting that there is some connection between Vasyli, or this group of scientists, and the abduction of Eloise?"

"What do you think, Dr Fisher?" pressed Briggs.

"It's possible, I suppose. But, why would they do such a thing?"

"Leverage, Dr Fisher, leverage. To ensure that we respond quickly and positively to their defection."

"It seems a little extreme...wouldn't you say?"

"When your friends are being murdered by the KGB, *extreme* is what you do. At least, if we comply, they may not harm the girl...otherwise we are unlikely to welcome them with open arms...give them a job, a new identity and a house in Hampshire."

"I thought I understood Vasyli...he seemed authentic and sincere."

"So did Adolf Eichmann! He was a devout Evangelical Christian until 1937."

"Well, I hardly....think that's a fair comparison."

"There is yet another possibility, Dr Fisher."

"Yes?"

"Eloise's disappearance was staged by the KGB...by Volkov, to blackmail the Consul General, or at least put him under pressure...

distract him…shall we say…in order that he does *not* cooperate with Kulnikov; and, in fact, turns him over to the KGB, who miraculously rescues his daughter."

"Surely, it would be simpler if they shot him?"

"They have no way of knowing how much information he has already handed over."

"Has he? Has he already handed over information?"

"Not everything. But, enough to know that what he is describing is a credible weapon of extreme mass destruction. A new class of weapon."

"Why don't they torture him?"

"I think you would know, Dr Fisher, that torture is designed to inflict sufficient pain to extract information, but not necessarily the truth."

"Why then would the KGB assist me, in investigating a case of multiple murders and mutilations of similar girls to Eloise?"

"As a cover…a distraction, to create fear in her parents…to make us think that they are helping, when in fact they have instigated this terror. They may already know the identity of the killer you are searching for. Perhaps they are protecting him for some reason. It could be a group of men, the new rising oligarchs, so powerful that even the KGB can't touch them. Or, that they have sought his/their assistance in this matter. And, remember, Dr Fisher, the caller last night was a woman."

Another red herring?

"Have you tried to identify her?"

"Voice recognition requires a pre-existing sound file to track against. There is no such file for this voice."

Fisher's head was spinning, reeling; he felt he was on a helter-skelter, that was unable to stop.

"And…" Briggs paused. Fisher thought for dramatic effect. *Was he enjoying this?* "…and there is some new information, arrived this morning, an encrypted message from GCHQ."

Fisher was afraid to ask, but Briggs was going to tell him anyway:

"This is where your security clearance under the Act is vital. In the middle of a Russian swampland, North of here, is a rectangular iron gate. Beyond its rusted bars is a collection of radio towers, abandoned buildings and power lines bordered by a dry-stone wall. This sinister location is the focus of a mystery which stretches back a decade or more. It is thought to be the headquarters of a radio station, *MDZhB*, that no-one has ever claimed to run. Twenty-four hours a day, seven days a week, for the last decade, it's been broadcasting a dull, monotonous tone. Every few seconds it's joined by a second sound, like some ghostly ship sounding its foghorn. Once or twice a week, a man or woman will read out some words or phrases in Russian, such as *dinghy* or *farming specialist*. And that's it. Anyone, anywhere in the world can listen in, simply by tuning a radio to the frequency 4625 kHz. It's so enigmatic, it's as if it was designed with conspiracy theorists in mind. Today the station has quite a following numbering, in the tens of thousands, who know it affectionately as *the Buzzer*. They have absolutely no idea what they are listening to."

"And… what are they listen to?" Fisher queried, What's going on?"

"Nobody knows. The frequency is thought to belong to the Russian military, though they've never actually admitted this. It first began broadcasting at the demise of the Cold War, when communism was in decline. Recently, the activity has accelerated.

There's no shortage of theories to explain what *the Buzzer* might be for… ranging from keeping in touch with submarines to communing with aliens. One such idea is that it's acting as a *Dead Hand* signal; in the event Russia is hit by a nuclear attack, the drone will stop and automatically trigger a retaliation. No questions asked, just total nuclear obliteration on both sides. This may not be as wacky as it sounds. The system was originally pioneered in the late seventies, where it took the form of a computer system which scanned the airwaves for signs of life or nuclear fallout. As it happens, there are clues in the signal itself. Like all international radio, *the Buzzer* operates at a relatively low frequency known as shortwave. This means that, compared to local radio and television signals, fewer waves pass through a single point every second. It also means they can travel a lot further. While you'd be hard pressed to listen to a local station such as BBC Radio London in a neighbouring county, shortwave stations like the World Service are aimed at audiences from Senegal to Singapore. Both stations are broadcast from the same building. It's all thanks to *skywaves*. Higher frequency radio signals can only travel in a straight line, eventually becoming lost as they bump into obstacles or reach the horizon. But shortwave frequencies have an extra trick... they can bounce off charged particles in the upper atmosphere, allowing them to zig-zag between the earth and the sky and travel thousands, rather than tens, of miles. Which brings us back to the *Dead Hand* theory. As you might expect, shortwave signals have proved extremely popular. Today they're used by ships, aircraft and the military to send messages across continents, oceans and mountain ranges. But there's a catch."

"Enlighten me, please."

"The lofty layer isn't so much a flat mirror, but a wave, which undulates like the surface of the ocean. During the day it moves steadily higher, while at night, it creeps down towards the Earth. If you want to absolutely guarantee that your station can be heard on the other side of the planet ... and if you're using it as a cue for nuclear war, you probably do... it's important to change the frequency depending on the time of day, to catch up. The BBC World Service already does this. *The Buzzer* doesn't. Another idea is that the radio station exists to sound out how far away the layer of charged particles is. To get good results from the radar systems the Russians use to spot missiles, you need to know this," says Briggs. "The longer the signal takes to get up into the sky and down again, the higher it must be. This isn't *the Buzzer*. Instead, many believe that the station is a hybrid of two things. The constant drone is just a marker, saying *this frequency is mine, this frequency is mine...* to stop people from using it. It only becomes important in moments of crisis, such as if Russia were invaded. Then it would function as a way to instruct their worldwide spy network and military forces on standby in remote areas. After all, this is a country around seventy times the size of the UK. It seems they've already been practicing. Last week they broadcast a special message, COMMAND 135 ISSUED that was said to be a test message for full combat readiness."

"I don't quite get what this has to do with Eloise."

"Two days ago, the voice broadcast the words... *Broken Arrow*, and then...*Missing Girl*. A broken arrow is a phrase used to say that a nuclear bomb or missile has been lost, stolen or compromised."

"I see.... And you think Eloise is the missing girl they are referring to? If so, why would they be broadcasting this? Surely they know we would be listening?"

"We have credible intelligence, that suggests a girl, fitting the description of Eloise, is being held at the *Red Arrow* research facility near Archangel...or Arkhangelsk, as they call it here. It is largely deserted, but a few loyal scientists remain in a heavily guarded compound where the missiles were constructed and tested. The new warheads are also stored in an adjacent hanger."

"But why would they keep the girl there?"

"Because it is undoubtedly the most secret location in Russia. In this game of chess, even a pawn can bring victory."

"Can we call their bluff? The KGB?"

"And risk losing everything...the intelligence...the Consul General's daughter? No."

"Are you sure about all this? I'm getting close to solving this case...I can feel it in my bones."

"Whatever case you are getting close to solving, Dr Fisher, it is not going to help, since Eloise is not in the hands of a psychotic serial killer with a fetish for hips."

Alan shuffled uncomfortably.

"So, what are you going to do?" asked Fisher apprehensively.

"First, the Consul General and his wife, I have recommended be repatriated to the UK on a flight, this evening. For their own immediate safety. We will say that they need a break to deal with a private matter, and that we expect them to return in a couple of days."

"We won't be going anywhere, Briggs. Not without my daughter!"

"I have orders, sir!"

"And, I'm telling you we are not leaving."

There was a pause...a stand off...and then...

"Kulnikov and his colleagues will be informed that they should expect some action to remove them in the next few days. If they are involved in this disappearance, it will flush them out."

"And, if not?"

"We may yet proceed to protect them from the KGB."

"What about Eloise?"

Briggs hesitated, as if he was searching for a truth that perhaps didn't exist.

"The SAS are gathering across the Finish border, with everything they need to mount a raid on Archangel with three helicopters. *Operation Angel*, will begin…"

Briggs looked at his watch, "…some eight to twelve hours from now, at zero dark thirty."

"Zero what?"

"*Zero Dark Thirty*…it's military slang for an unspecified time in the early hours of the morning, before dawn. Which, as you know, is late in these parts. They will strike when they think best. They know what they are doing Dr Fisher."

"And, precisely… what are they doing?"

"Their primary objective is intelligence gathering and the destruction of the facility…whatever the cost. Our allies believe this is the only facility of its kind. So secret, even the Russian Government might not know of its existence."

"What about Eloise?"

"If she is there, we will get her out."

Alan, put his head down and started to bite his knuckle. And then let his face fall into his hands.

"It sounds dangerous," said Fisher, "…and high risk."

"It is…but these men are the best we have, all Russian speakers… *who dares wins*, Dr Fisher. The plan is for a clean extraction. But, it's possible that Eloise, and, therefore, the facility, may be under the protection of KGB Special Forces. If so, they will not give her up easily; not without a fight. The worse-case scenario is that a stand-off develops. Russian military units, heavily armed will be there within minutes of the raid being known. We can only try to negotiate with her captors. Which is where you come in, Dr Fisher."

"Me!?"

"Your experience could be invaluable. You have negotiated the release of kidnap victims before."

"Yes, but…"

"And, you will be able to identify the victim as Eloise or otherwise."

"I have never met…"

"Second Lieutenant Baker, one of my junior officers… she will come along; but only to assist you, if need be. She will hang back at the drop zone. But, you will know how to handle Eloise in the immediate aftermath; and she can help."

"This is quite diff…"

"You've done it many times…Dr Fisher." Briggs was getting beyond assertive.

"I can't…"

"Stephen…" interrupted the Consul General. He was weeping quietly but copiously, his lip trembling almost as much as his hands, "I need you to do this…please, I beg you…bring my daughter home…."

For a moment, probably the first in all sincerity, Fisher thought about his own children. Those gorgeous, precious little boys. His *little miracles*, as he liked to call them.

What if one of them were abducted?

What would he not do, to get *them* back safely?

But, this was different, this was not *his* daughter. Why should he risk laying down his life for the life of someone else's daughter?

Personally, it made no sense. Ordinarily, he usually avoided such thoughts on a live investigation, as they might cloud his judgement. His judgement was seriously clouded; and his resistance irreversibly compromised.

"What do you need me to do?"

11

Deserts

Tinted.

Dark.

Three black Land Rover Defender vehicles left the compound of the consulate, simultaneously, but casually moved off in different directions, as per plan. One would circle back an hour or so later. The point being, should the KGB, or militia, or anyone else, be aware of some movement, they would have to rapidly deploy enough resources to follow all three, without being detected. Briggs had gambled that this would overstretch them in the available time. They might manage to scramble enough to follow one...but three? It seemed unlikely.

And, which one would they choose?

Of course, the vehicles stuck out like the proverbial throbbing thumbs...three black British off-road vehicles with tinted glass on near empty roads, except for a few decrepit old Volgas smattered here and there. But, given the petrol shortages, there was no way of avoiding that. The key was to move efficiently; not so fast as to draw attention, even in the dark, poorly lit streets. But through all the side streets, no highways or wide, bright boulevards where cameras might lurk. Inevitably, this would take more time; more than they could actually afford.

The two *mission* rovers would leave urban St Petersburg, separately, to the South and to the East, finally meeting up West of the city in the Kirovsky District, before speeding North, along the coast, towards the fortified border with Finland.

The lead car, contained Briggs, driving... Baker and Fisher in the back, followed by the second, a back-up car with three consulate security personnel on board.

It was all very quiet, a silent theme backed by a relentless soundtrack of tyres on compacted snow and the quiet, reliable, hum of the dependable *Defenders*.

No one had spoken, until Fisher broke ranks:

"Stephen...," he held his hand out to Baker.

"Carey..." she replied, briskly, taking his hand.

And that was it.

What was there to talk about?

Are you looking forward to being shot at?

How often do you kill people?

Are you trained in First Aid?

How many necks have you broken this year?

Have you thought about losing a limb to a rocket propelled grenade?

I've never fallen out of a helicopter. How about you? In fact, I've never been in a helicopter.

None of these imaginary questions were likely to put anyone at ease; not least Fisher himself, who felt an involuntary loosening of the bowels.

Briggs was concentrating on the driving, as the roads became narrower, as if they were suffering from frosted arterial sclerosis; and more and more distant and less and less devoid of compacted snow. Much of it was piled either side of the road, as if they were frozen hedgerows, creating a tunnel effect, in the glare of the headlamps.

Briggs was as cool as a cucumber.

Baker was obviously nervous; perhaps even more so than Fisher. Her hand had been a little too damp for confidence. Maybe she too, hadn't signed up for live fire exercises or combat operations? Perhaps, he ought to ask? Better to know who you are teamed up with. He was a liability, he knew that; but was Baker an asset?

What if it turned out she was in the catering division? Deadly with a potato peeler! Trained to blind a man at twenty paces with a carrot! Or, like himself, had never fired any weapon...not even a potato gun? Perhaps she was less like the shrew she appeared to be, and more of a Taekwondo black belt champion, with its emphasis on unarmed combat, head-height kicks, jumping and spinning blows, and fast kicking techniques...for chopping a cabbage. And...he wasn't being sexist here...oh no...he was trained not to be...but, he knew he was sailing close to the wind; but, then, she was rather petite. If anyone could make an oversized khaki British Army uniform look attractive, she could. Not that she was wearing one anyway; just that Fisher imagined that she could....if she had...or was...or ever had been.

Fisher thought it might be best to move his rambling mind onto something else. If the feminist *thought police* ever got hold of him, he was doomed. It was enough to warrant a confession in the church of burning bras: impure thoughts leading to the mortal sin of chauvinism. And his lovely wife was a High Priestess, a *Vestal Virgin of Womanhood*. Well, maybe not a total virgin. For all he knew, his boys might be informants in the youth wing. Whereas, Fisher liked to think of himself as a feminised male above all that extreme feminism. They targeted chauvinist pigs for immediate castration. He regarded himself as a *new man*. Whatever that meant.

Still, no matter how *new* he was, he knew that he would never be accepted by the feminist sorority, since his commitment to their cause was tainted by the dangly thing he kept in his pants, and the notion that all men are considered by them to be potential rapists. Now, that's a depressing thought. That is because, no matter how hard he tried to escape his gender indoctrination or how much he tried to change; or, to change others, he was still an outsider. That his feminist credentials were forever tainted by the stain of chauvinism. It was akin to being a fully committed, paid up member if Black Panther without being black.

When Fisher was a student, at the height of the feminist movement, he had no bra to burn. And, whilst his underpants would, undoubtedly, have benefited from incineration, they had no symbolic resonance. Had he thrown a pair on a brazier of burning bras, he would have be hauled away for an act of contamination via encrusted bodily fluids. He did, however, sign up for an honours course in *Sex-Role Stereotypes*. It seemed like a good idea at the time.

Dr White explained to the class, that although Fisher was a man, he was equally welcome. It seemed an odd thing to highlight; like welcoming a black student in an all-white university, by pointing out the colour of their skin. Inevitably, the rest of the class were not only grungy potato women, but ardent feminists of the extreme order of neophytes. They hated him.

But, to Fisher, it made them an easy target. The more he goaded them into sexist behaviour towards him, the more he pointed out their inherent social and cultural prejudices. Dr Judith White loved him; because every class was a tinder box, heated by a candle; and once he called his female associates chauvinists, the fireworks went off.

In truth, Fisher didn't like *real* men anyway, he preferred real women. As a *new man*, he had tried cooking, cleaning and doing the washing up. Others carried babies on their chest in a pouch, to work, and all but breast fed them. Which he admitted would be a challenge. But then, having failed to be accepted as a feminist, he became an endangered species; a relic of gender history, doomed to extinction because women didn't actually want to sleep with a new man. Despite their principles, they wanted to sleep with a real man.

Leon Trotsky, speculated about such a man:

Man, he said, *will make it his purpose to master his own feelings, to raise his instincts to the heights of consciousness, to make them transparent, to extend the wires of his will into hidden recesses, and thereby to raise himself to a new plane, to create a higher social biologic type, or, if you please, a superman.*

Fisher, the superman, mused on this for a moment, until he realised that Trotsky had been posthumously *disappeared*, erased from history; and died, listening to an ice pick! It seems, Fisher, then, had gotten off lightly with the *feminista*.

The road, if it could be called a road, came to a stop; not an abrupt end, it just seemed to wither away to a pile of snow. Aside from the headlamps, it was pitch black dark, especially to the left, where the snow fell away into the dark void. A light flurry was coming from nowhere and floating aimlessly. Not a street lamp, or a city light in sight; not even a single domestic dwelling, or a dacha.

"Now's the time for a pee, if anyone wants one." said Briggs, getting out of the rover with a pair of night-vision binoculars. Along with the driver of the other vehicle, they stood on a mound of snow, looking out to the north-west, passing the glasses, and discussing something of substance.

Baker went off into the darkness, to squat, presumably, and to do as instructed, whilst Fisher went to read, at nose length, the bark of a tree. He was convinced his pee would freeze as it hit the trunk... there's that word again...trunk. *Was it possible*, he thought, as he tried to relax enough to empty his warm bladder onto a cold tree, *that he might end up with a frozen penis attached to a tree?* How would that go down with Commander Briggs? Not well. No doubt the SAS have a protocol for such a scenario, involving a warm knife and a sticky plaster.

The idea wasn't helping with the flow; or, lack thereof, neither were the other two security people, smoking nearby, and laughing about something or nothing. Obviously not at Fisher; or at the size of his frozen member; but, it was, nevertheless, off-putting.

He couldn't help but think that perhaps this mission was an expression of his failure. He had failed to find the girl. Thus, despite his tenuous connection to the Red Arrow, through Vasyli. Instead, he had gone off on a loose elk trail of artful photographers masking a hideous display of anatomical horrors. Hip bones? Angel's Wings? Empty Shells? Operations? Angels?

"OK, people!" cried Briggs, piercing his uncertainty "Let's move! We are up against the clock!"

As they got back into the car, Fisher closed his door and said:

"Where are we going from here? It looks like a dead end….just piles of old snow."

"It is a dead end." The engines started. "We are going down there!"

"Where's *down there*? It's just a dark ravine!"

"The sea is down there…this is the Gulf of Finland, the eastern Baltic. It's frozen."

"Frozen!"

"Yes…as far as we can see….it should be thick enough to drive on."

"*Should be!*"

"The satellite images were not definitive about a section in the middle. It gets churned up by shipping going in and out of St Pete's….but by now, they will have given up until the Spring."

"How will we know if it's thick enough to drive on?"

"When we get there, we will know. If it cracks, we will know. If it gives way, we will all be dead in less than two minutes!"

It was a bit of a conversation stopper.

Fisher's stomach churned as the Defender's front end tipped upward and over the hump of snow and down a steep slope, eventually to right itself, stopping on a white flat plain that stretched off into the distance in the full beam of the headlamps. The two vehicles lined up next to each other, as if a drag race was about to start, rather than one behind the other, as in a safari, a caravan. That way, if one vehicle weakened the ice, and/or stalled, the other was alongside and not behind, running into the back of it…and into the same sink hole. If one vehicle got stuck, the other might be able to pull it free…and so on.

The headlights reached forward almost to infinity across the starched arid plane, or, at least as far as the falling snowflakes allowed, whilst two spotlights mounted on the front grill, pointed at the ice itself. It looked as though the snowfall was abating, and the stars began to peep through the dark canopy of the night.

Too late, Briggs nodded to the other driver, and they were off.

Briggs was suddenly uncharacteristically chatty.

Perhaps he was nervous for once? Which, in itself was worrying.

"The Baltic Sea has a lot less salt in it than most," he said, "you see… around seven parts per thousand compared with an average of thirty-five parts per thousand. That's largely due to freshwater run-off from the surrounding lumps of Scandinavia and Eastern Europe, combined with sewerage and with its relative shallowness…and some other… complex marine science…I don't quite get. It only needs to be at freezing point to cultivate an icy lid."

"Good to know." said Fisher, wringing his hands, slowly.

"So, what are the consequences of falling in? I hear you say, Dr Fisher."

Briggs didn't wait for a reply, not least because he knew the occupants of the vehicle didn't want to know.

"Assuming you took a ten-second dunk followed by a ten-minute walk to safety, in minus twenty-four degrees centigrade, you would initially start to shiver, then get a bit confused. After which you'd stop being able to use your hands, then turn blue, followed by a huge decrease in pulse and respiration rates, and, of course, organ failure."

Fisher thought this was utter nonsense. He would wander off into the night, of course, to be rescued by the young woman with the log cabin; the one with the small, but heaving bosom, and the deaf and blind father, who had no idea what his desperate daughter was up to.

Still, before that, he wondered if Briggs really knew what was at stake.

"You've done this kind of thing before then, Pat?"

"Briggs if you don't mind. Pat sounds like an insincere accolade slapped on the back. Once, in training, in Norway. Ice roads have their own esoteric speed limits, depending on what sort of ice it is. You can choose between two parameters: ten to fifteen miles per hour; or thirty to sixty miles per hour. The differing margins are all about resonance...rumbling three tons of car across five inches of ice causes quite a lot of vibrations, and between those speeds you're transmitting damaging energy and not moving quickly enough to spread it across an area large enough to soak it up, without the sort of consequences that involve frozen bollocks! Sorry, Baker, you may not have bollocks, but I know you've got balls!"

"Yes, sir! Thank you, sir!" retorted Baker, in an annoying military knee-jerk kind of way.

"Occasionally, what looks like a frozen wave peeps out of the whiteness ...there's one coming up now...they tend to be around a foot tall and have the uncanny effect of launching one side of the Defender clear off the ice. They're usually well camouflaged by the snow, too, so suddenly, before you even have time to swear, much

less enter negotiations, you'll bounce your skull off the headlining....
Like that!"

Fisher thought he might actually throw up. He wasn't sure if it was the idea of the bump or the bump itself. Either way, he wasn't going to tell Briggs he felt a bit queasy.

Clearly, the two vehicles were driving at the top of the range Briggs had mentioned, so any distortion in the ice was a major test of the chassis, and of Fisher's guts. With each mile, the tension mounted, as the ice, presumably, got thinner and thinner, towards the shipping lanes.

The first crack, sounded off into the distance behind them. But the second sounded as if it came from some short way in front. It was so loud, even Briggs jolted rigid, and then glanced into his rear-view mirror where his eyes met Fisher's. There was a third crack, that seemed to cause the back of the car to dip and the rear wheels to slip. Baker was gripping the edge of her seat with her right hand, so tightly, all the blood had drained from it. In the dim light, Fisher reached over, and placed his warm hand on top of hers, as if it was accidental, but he said nothing. He felt, her hand relax a little, even though it was as much for his own comfort.

There were no more cracks; just silence, and the surface tension of the thin ice, like a soft icing skin on a cake, with taut and stretched.

Fisher started to relax into the hum of the Defender as the ice seemed to flatten out into an arid plain and his thoughts turned to his task ahead: to negotiate the release of Eloise from her captors; not least in the wake of an illegal SAS raid on a secret nuclear facility; and then, if all went well, to reassure the captive of their good intentions and take the poor damaged girl home. But what state might she be in?

And what of his still incomplete investigation...and the butchered girl in the river? Whatever might lay ahead this night, it changed nothing.

There was still a killer or killers at large; there was still the very real prospect that there would be other, fresh victims. But, what he couldn't get his head around, was the similarity in appearance of the victims...to each other...and to Eloise. That, surely, was no coincidence? And yet, the crimes were dispersed over a number of years. Fisher, discounted the idea that these were somehow faked. The mutilated bodies were sickeningly real. It's possible, he supposed, that they, the fakers, could have used cadavers.

And so, therein lies the problem.

According to Occam's Razor, when there are two or more conflicting explanations, the one with the least number of assumptions is probably the correct one.

Therefore....

"Fuck!" cried Briggs, "Ferry at two o'clock...it's a fucking ice-breaker!"

Both cars turned their lights off and took a rapid vector-turn slightly to the left, by a few degrees, just off course. It was as if the vehicles were tethered, together, each driver responding intuitively to the movement of the other.

Fisher could see the large vessel out of his window on the right, getting bigger and closer as each second passed. It looked surreal, grounded, with lots of twinkling lights along the side. At the front, sheaths of ice were slowly being ploughed away; and at the back, a trail of open black water.

"Fuck!" said Briggs again, thumping his hands to the wheel. "The ice won't hold us to the West! We have to cross the bow, or we'll be left with open water! Fuck!...fuck!"

With that, he put his foot to the floor; and the other car responded a few seconds later with the same. They were now racing ahead of the icy bow wave of the ship, with Briggs leading and the other car right behind. An unseen bump...like a ramp of white death...and first one car, then the other, took flight with all wheels leaving the surface and then crashing onto the cracking ice.

"Sir!" cried Baker, "We're not going to make it! You have to stop!"

"Too late!" replied Briggs…

"Brace! Brace!" he cried.

Fisher closed his eyes to the sound of metal being stripped from his side of the rover, and the sensation of a vehicle spinning out of control, followed seconds later, by a loud crash and an explosion.

They skidded in a wide arc and came to a stop, sideways on.

A ball of flames rose up from the prow of the ship, lighting up their faces, mushrooming into the black sky to light the underside of the thin clouds, with a deep orange glow…

And a klaxon siren began to wail into the night like a wounded wolf.

12

And Yonder

"Another two to three hours from here, on Route 6, to Möhkö. Where we hook up with the extraction team." Briggs explained, quietly and without any sign of emotion, as talking to a dental team. These were the only words spoken that evening, as the rover sailed through the forests of the Finnish Tundra, giving way to frozen lakes; and stopping only once to refuel and to grab some thick coffees. Baker finally succumbed to sleep, gradually leaning over towards Fisher until her head rested on his left thigh.

Fisher became largely unaware of the time…his watch ticking away, hidden under Baker's head and into her right ear. He wondered if it might be bothering her; but, in reality, he knew from personal experience that she had probably gone into a post-traumatic deep sleep.

This was all very well, thought Fisher. But more immediately, how was he to get out from underneath the ice, of the freezing river he was drowning in. The only way, it seemed, was to swim against the fast-flowing current and break through, so that he could breathe at last. The ice was too thick; he hammered onto it with his fists and as he opened his mouth to let out a scream, all the air was expelled from his lungs, and bubbled on the underside of the ice. The panic subdued into the cold calm of realising he was trapped; and that he was going to die. A soldier's body swept by, in the swirling current, followed by two more…their dead, fish-like eyes staring at him from cold grey faces; one was burned, and the flesh looked raw. Then someone tapped on the ice. It was Briggs. He was wielding a large fire axe….

The rover turned a sharp exit off the main road and down a forest track barely wide enough to take it. Fisher had woken from his dark horses with a start, and Baker, too, sat, bolt upright, as if she had been in that position all the time.

"Almost there!" announced Briggs.

The rover bumped up and down across the rough terrain.

"Are you ok, Carey?" Fisher asked.

She nodded, whilst trying to get the gunk out of her eyes, and feeling the sleep crease in her right cheek, the shape of a Rolex wrist watch.

They pulled up to a horizontal barrier of red and white chevrons, with high chain link fences, topped with barbed wire, running off in both directions until they disappeared into the darkness. Two armed soldiers stepped forward in full arctic camouflage combat gear, shining torches into the rover. Briggs wound his window down, to a rush of extreme cold night air, as he handed over his identity paper.

The soldier snapped to attention, and with a firm salute:

"Commander Briggs! Welcome to *Echo Bravo One*."

With a nod of his head, the barrier was lifted and Briggs drove the Defender slowly into a very large open compound....about the size of a football field. But, instead of a rectangle, the perimeter appeared to closely follow the contours of the tree line. Lights, mounted on low towers pointed downwards, were dimmed to almost an eerie glow, and everything Fisher could see was white with grey and pale green camouflage.

As he got out of the car, putting on his coat and hat, he noticed two domed inflated buildings: hangers, each, roughly the size of a tennis court; three large objects nearby, covered in camouflage netting; and a collection of small, temporary structures: cabins, and a cluster of small white tents. On the far right, over by the trees...a substantial number of oil drums, a fuel dump; again, covered in white netting. A few men were rushing about, carrying things and organising boxes; all were wearing white padded parkas, with face masks and helmets that made them look like puffed-up *Star Wars Stormtroopers*. Everything they wore was white, except the black tinted snow goggles on their helmets.

Two men were already tossing a cold net over the warm Defender to hide its infra-red signature, and pegging it to the ground.

The only man not wearing any headgear, came striding over from the larger hut.

"Commander Briggs!" he said, stopping to salute.

"Mac!" replied Briggs, returning the salute, along with Baker.

Both men smiled, and then gave each other a bear hug.

"Second Lieutenant Baker," Briggs gestured, "and Dr Fisher. This is Major Macintosh of the SAS; he is running this show. I'm just along for the ride, you take it from here, Mac."

"Thank you, sir, Right, well, if you'd like to follow me into the Command Shed, we can have a hot cup of tea, and I can explain where we go from here... Where are the others? We were expecting three more?"

"They didn't make it, Mac."

It was a bad omen.

Nothing was said.

It was warm inside.

A wood-fired stove bristled away in the corner. Some tin mugs, a tin of powdered milk, a large tea pot and a plate of digestive biscuits were set on the table. Almost everywhere else, easels and with the walls covered in maps, photographs and satellite images.

"Wilson!" said Macintosh to a man removing some images from a board, "Just leave that for the moment, and go and see if you can organise some gear for our guests. Rough sizes will do."

"Yes sir!" said the young man, as he marched off to the door. A flurry of snow blew in as he left.

"What's the forecast, Mac?" asked Briggs.

"High pressure moving in. It'll be cold and almost clear. High clouds obscuring a full moon. The snow will stop in about thirty minutes, and lay off until dawn."

"Good." said Briggs, "Good…that's good!"

That was a good omen.

"Alright, listen up, and listen carefully…" started Macintosh, who Fisher could sense was as much a cliche as his gabardine namesake. "This is a live fire search, destroy, and, if necessary, extraction operation. We have orders to engage all resources if and as necessary. We expect light weapons resistance at this defended installation, with some special forces present in small numbers. But, these guys are not regular soldiers; these are crack troops."

"How many?" asked Briggs.

"Regulars…thirty to forty conscripts, with half-tracks. Specials….we don't know, but intelligence suggests as few as six or seven. But even a handful of these guys are a major challenge: hardened, asymmetric battle-experienced troops. These people are seasoned killers; loyal to the revolution; they will fight to the death! Thirty minutes' drive away, however, is a Russian Army Base, with heavy armour and troop carriers; but, no air support. Given the general disarray in the army, and the confused command structures, we don't anticipate they would get organised and respond within an hour of the alarm being raised. We are working on the basis that they don't get that signal; but, if they do, we expect to be out of there well before they arrive. If not, we could be overrun. The primary objective is to search the two laboratories and take whatever we can; but no personnel… we lay charges as a back-up for *Operation Flash*, to destroy the facilities and render the area hot."

"I'm sorry…," said Fisher, nervously, "I don't quite understand…there are *two* labs?"

"Yes, one contains the missile assembly and testing area; and the other building is used for construction and storage of the warheads."

"You're going to blow up a building full of nuclear bombs?" said Fisher, incredulously.

"Well, possibly, these are hardened silos…so laying some charges inside will ensure that some damage is done in the first phase. The warheads…Dr…look, I'm just going to call you Fisher! The warheads will be destroyed without any danger of a nuclear reaction. The fissile material…which, incidentally, Fisher, we still don't know exactly what this is…will be dispersed over a small area. We suspect, the weapons are encased in a shell of Uranium-238. But the core? We have no idea. Our own neutron bombs…."

Macintosh paused and glanced at Briggs.

"Cleared…both of them." Briggs nodded. Our own version is an abject failure. It was supposed to yield 80% but only ever reached 30%. It's a toy by comparison to what we believe these new enhanced radiation weapons are capable of."

"I thought such weapons were banned after mass demonstrations through Europe?" Fisher added.

Macintosh looked at him with combined derision and considerable disgust. Ignoring Fisher, he continued:

By the end of the night, the Russians won't be able to go near this facility for a century or more. Where was I? Oh, yes…"

"But, excuse me…isn't this an Act of War?"

"Technically, yes…but…look, Fisher…I'm not a politician…we are already at war…it's a Cold War, about to get hot. The whole point about sending in the Brits, is that we're not Americans. But, we get the job done. I'm a professional soldier…and, I'm here to carry out orders. The lawyers at the United Nations can argue about the definition or declaration of war…the Russians are too drunk for war! They can organise a piss up in a vodka distillery, but that's about it. And, if you are going to ask any more questions like this, especially as we go in, I'll throw you out of the chopper myself! Is that clear, Fisher? You're an unwanted distraction as far as I'm concerned."

There was an understandable, long and awkward, silence.

"Go easy, Mac…," said Briggs, quietly. "Just one thing, I'm not briefed on…*Operation Flash*?"

"A late addition. HQ wanted to ensure the full neutralisation of the site. I'll come to that in a moment, sir, if I may?"

"Please, continue."

"We are going in with three choppers. All new Merlin prototype MH1er. They are not in service yet. The *er* stands for *extended range*. The target is at the flight limit of the new Merlins. Which is one reason why the ruskies won't be expecting a ground force. So, two will carry a full team each, Alpha and Bravo, and the third, Charlie will mostly carry fuel for the return. During the operation, two Merlins will be refuelled, and charges set to destroy the third on wheels-up. Pilots, a technician, a two teams of eight, plus the three of you. Baker you will stay with the pilots, technician and the choppers. You'll be with Bravo, sir…and I'll be with Alpha. Two men will go to ground and return to the border on foot. They will use lasers to guide in *Flash*….and get out of there as quickly as they can."

"Lasers?" said Briggs.

"Just outside, sir…two hardened field hangers…there's a Harrier AB-8V in each silo…vertical take-off, of course…full kit, including

Brimstone laser-guided missiles and GBU-12/16/27 Paveway laser guided bombs."

Briggs said nothing, but raised his eyebrows and nodded sagely. He recognised that this had become a much a bigger operation; one of the largest for the SAS since D-Day, indicating the seriousness of what they were about. At the same time, Briggs knew that the larger and more varied the force used, the more likely it was, that something would go wrong.

Fisher, undeterred about the warning concerning being hurled from a helicopter, said:

"And what about Eloise?"

"Oh... the girl... she may or may not be there. If she is... we'll get her out. But... my orders are to snatch and destroy... my duty is to get my men out...safely... the girl is...a bonus at best...at worst a distraction."

"A distraction?" said Fisher. "You think she's a distraction? Well, fuck you Mac, and your fucking action man operation. She is the only reason we are here... and we lost three good men getting here! This *distraction* is one of twelve young girls... girls no more that twelve years old... raped and mutilated and murdered by some twisted fuck! Her name is Eloise, and if she is there... if only for the sake of the other girls, their parents, the three good men... we will get her out of there with or without your blessing!"

Macintosh looked at his watch.

"Wheels up in forty minutes! Now, if you'll excuse me."

Macintosh walked to the door, his heavy boots thudding on the wooden floor. As he opened the door to a cold blast, Wilson and two other soldiers came in with sacks and boxes and lay them on the floor, before standing to attention.

"That'll be all, thank you," said Briggs. "We should get kitted up. Baker, you've had basic firearms training?"

"Yes, sir...basic."

"Good. Fisher, you ever fired a weapon?"

"No, but, I don't need..."

"You will carry a weapon, Dr Fisher...and you will know how to use it...and you will be prepared to use it. I want everyone that goes in their to come out alive. It's not just for your defence, carrying a weapon might save someone else's life. Is that clear?"

Fisher nodded. And Briggs relented.

"Stephen...this is a high-risk operation...so many things could go wrong: we have poor intel; too cloudy for clear sat-imagery... a chopper malfunctions? We are heavily outnumbered? The Russian Army might turn up... to name just a few unknowns. You need to be prepared. I go into these operations with a philosophy: if it can go wrong, it will go wrong. If Mac thinks you are holding things up... putting his men at unnecessary risk...or being responsible for an unnecessary death.... believe me... he will take you down. You *will* carry a firearm, and you *will* use it, if necessary!"

"What could possibly go wrong?" Baker quipped.

Briggs gave her a filthy look.

This wasn't putting Fisher at ease.

"Now, let's step outside, while Baker gets changed, and I will show you how to use this pistol...agreed?"

Fisher followed Briggs outside, their warm breath clouding in the cold, dark, air and, the snow squeezed underfoot as they found a space under a dull perimeter light. Fisher's eye was immediately drawn to the hardened silos...doors now open... two Harrier jump jets... incredible, he thought. They seemed so large and imposing on the ground. The ground personnel, like worker ants, scurried about in well rehearsed moves, dragging hydraulic trolleys weighted with missiles, as each wing was armed with fire and brimstone.

"Pay attention, Stephen...this could save your life."

Briggs removed his gloves and was holding a black, squared pistol, with a brown texture handle. He treated it as if it was weighted with authority, balancing and rebalancing the centre of gravity.

"This is a Browning HP, it is a reliable gun...in use and unchanged since the Second World War. It's a nine millimetre handgun with a military designation of L9A. The Browning has a magazine capacity of thirteen rounds, plus one in the chamber. It is a single action pistol which means it must be cocked...hammer pulled back...like so... before firing the first round. For this reason, the SAS carry the Browning cocked, with the safety catch on, to allow for a quicker draw and fire."

Demonstrating as he spoke, Briggs withdrew the magazine, pointed the gun until he pressed the trigger to a click.

"The pistol has a tendency to *bite* the web of the shooter's hand, between the thumb and forefinger. This bite is caused by pressure from the hammer spur, or alternatively, by pinching between the hammer shank and grip tang."

Briggs could see he was losing Fisher. Defending yourself with a gun, only to be bitten by it, seemed too illogical to grasp. Why not choose a toothless gun instead?

"Here, you try...we can't live fire in here...but, you'll get the idea."

Fisher held the weapon at arm's length and, trying not to close his eyes, pressed the trigger until it clicked.

"To place the *safety* in the *on-safe* position, push the safety lever, here, upward into the recess located in the rearward portion of the slide. The safety lever cannot be placed in the *on-safe* position if the hammer is in the dropped position."

"I'm not going to be able to remember all this in the heat of the moment."

Briggs ignored him.

"When ready to fire, move the safety lever down into the *off-safe* position, take aim and squeeze the trigger. Remember, you're not Han Solo and this fires bullets. The recoil is hard to control. Take your time...aim...steady hits the target. One of these bullets can blow a man's head off! Practice this sequence until it feels instinctive. Imagine the worst person, the most heinous killer you have ever encountered...and he or she is who you are about to shoot. If you hesitate, and think for a split second that the target you are aiming at is anything other than that. He will shoot you before you have finished that thought."

Fisher began his ritual sequence.

"What happens if I run out of bullets?"

Briggs retrieved the weapon to demonstrate.

"After the last cartridge in the magazine is fired, the slide stop automatically holds the slide in its open or rearward position, like this. If firing is no longer imminent, close the slide by pushing down on the slide stop, like so... lower the hammer to the dropped position and remove the magazine."

Fisher was more worried about not shooting his toe off, than getting the magazine re-loaded. Magazines were things to read at the dentist. It was hopeless. He managed to remove the magazine and the bullet in the barrel. He preferred to keep it that way. But, he knew it was utterly hopeless.

Briggs slapped his shoulder.

"We'll be ok, Stephen...I've got your back! We're going to bring Eloise home...safe and well."

"Safe and well..." echoed Fisher, nodding like a toy dog on the back shelf of a car. The motion was there, but, it meant nothing.

For obvious reasons, Fisher was the last to complete getting his kit on. He wasn't sure if he felt like an SAS trained killing machine; or one of Santa's more militant Arctic Elves. But, he felt he might grow into the first role, more easily than the second.

The door opened with Macintosh stepping in; in full gear...helmet, with a pair of night-sight lenses attached; but, his face mask, hanging underneath his chin. There was another man filling the doorway....in the background ...a terrific noise, as three helicopters started their engines and began to pick up rotor speed.

"This man," he said, shouting over the din, "could save your life! This is Peeters...he's our field surgeon. He's Belgian, by the way. But that's not his fault! OK, people...on your feet...wheels up!"

Baker's eyes met Fisher's.

"What could possibly go wrong?" she said, under her breath.

The Merlin was accessed through the ramp at the rear. Briggs boarded the one on the right; Macintosh and Peeters on the left; and Baker and Fisher, the one in the middle.

Fisher wasn't sure why they were all running. It's not like they were going to leave without them. But it seemed appropriate...more dramatic. By the time he got to the top of the ramp, Fisher was already out of breath and wheezing in the cold air. Two rows of four seasoned killers looked at him, as if a farting pig had just walked into a beauty bar asking for a Brazilian Wax. Despite the cold, there was an overpowering smell of aviation fuel, sweat and... frankly... fear.

"Strap in!" shouted one of the pilots, as Baker and Fisher walked the steel gauntlet of piercing eyes and identical Stormtrooper face masks. "Low night flying and snow dust landings are a real challenge...so, sit tight," said the pilot.

The two empty dark green seats were at the far end near the opening to the cockpit. Bright yellow straps hanging, waiting for a pair of shoulders.

The Merlin tipped forward as it lifted off in a cloud of powdered snow, the other two did the same, but swept off to the right and left as reflections of each other. They stayed low and tight, the undercarriages skimming just over the bonnet of snow on the treetops, creating a downdraft of frozen snow, which clouded off, in between the trunks.

"Settle down, everybody…" said the pilot, over the speakers, "two hours to ZDT…keep cool… flying low, already approaching Russian airspace and early warning systems. Any radar locked-on, you will hear a loud ping. Any missile approach will trigger a master alarm and you should brace for impact. Counter-measures will be launched… but, frankly, they're fairy lights on a Christmas Tree…fucking useless!"

Some of the troops laughed into their masks…Fisher felt sick; and Baker looked like a bladder evacuation was imminent. Fisher thought to take his mind off the possibility of his testicles being showered in shrapnel, by taking out his pistol for trigger practice.

"What the fuck!" said a trooper opposite.

Another:

"Put that fucking thing away, you stupid git!"

Fisher wasn't really bonding all that well, he thought. But it only needed a bit of time and conversation to find some things in common.

"There aren't any bullets in it…" Fisher's tone wasn't all that convincing.

"If you don't put that fucking toy away, I'll come over there and ram it down your throat, and then pull it out of your slack arse, with my bare hands!"

That was clear.

Fisher put the gun away.

Ping!

All eyes looked to the cockpit.

Ping!

Some looked at each other.

Ping!

Despite the tremendous noise of the rotors overhead, chopping the cold air with a regular incessant thump, Fisher was having some difficulty distinguishing between that and the thumping in his chest.

"Relax fellas! Looks like we got away with those two stations. ZDT one hour and thirty-two minutes."

Baker looked terrified. But, there was nothing Fisher could do, but smile and nod. She was too far away to reach out his hand. He started to think about what sort of state Eloise might be in, physically and emotionally. How had she been kept? Transported? Had she been abused by her captors? Raped? He had seen it all before... everything. Even if the intention had been to feign a connection with a series of horrendous murders, and to keep her merely as a bargaining chip in a game of spies, there was no way of being sure that she had been treated humanely by those in immediate charge of her well-being.

And what of the girl in the ice, and all the other mutilated victims? There was a sadistic murderer out there...still killing...still raping...still torturing and mutilating someone's daughter... someone's sister. Out there, there were mothers and fathers grieving, driven to madness by questions about what had happened and who was making it happen. Questions about what they could have done to prevent this horror. Fisher felt that as soon as he got Eloise home, he should go back to Egorov and help him find this serial monster.

Except, he had promised Jane he would be home by Christmas. And now this madness. He might not get home at all.

And what was Volkov going say about all this? If, as it seemed, he might know something about her abduction, or at least compliant in its execution. How was he going to react to the game being over? Once Eloise was home...once the research installation was destroyed and the intelligence compromised, what would he do with Vasyli and Lyudmilla?

"ZDT twenty-nine minutes!"

One of those most distressing aspects of this, was that Fisher had not been able to contact Jane, or talk to his sons. If he died chasing down a perverse killer, they would learn of his sacrifice, his bravery and hopefully understand why he did it. But this? To die like this? On a secret mission to kill or cripple innocent soldiers, destroy a research facility and rescue a girl who may or may not be there? But worse than that...the very existence of the mission, whether it succeeded or not, would be denied by the government, and his involvement, therefore, never acknowledged. They would probably tell them, that he slipped on the ice coming out of a rouble bar and somehow fell onto a stray land mine, to explain the state of his testicles, eventually being shot to put him out of his...

"Ten minutes to wheels down!"

The troops tensed up, checking their weapons that had already been checked several times. Typically, in the SAS, there were no obvious signs of who was in charge...who was more senior...there were no markings on their uniforms. They were a smoothly honed homogenous whole. Until one calm voice said:

"We've got this lads! Weapons armed! Let's fuck these cunts! No one gets left behind!"

The man's a poet, thought Fisher. Eloquent, sensitive to the needs of others; and emotionally grounded.

There was a sickening thump as the rear ramp fell open and hit the ground, a split second after, the wheels were down and the powdered snow was swirling all around in a white-out blizzard.

"Go! ...go! ...go!"

Fisher was still trying to unbuckle his safety harness...which was so safe, it wouldn't;t let him go...when the others were all gone into the night forest.

Baker unclipped him, "Come on Stephen, you have to keep up! They're not going to wait for you!"

He ran off into the maelstrom and the darkness, swerving to avoid trees...he ran and he ran until the sound of the Merlins was a diminishing hum and there was nothing but that dull dead silence that comes with snow on the ground and the scent of crushed pine needles. The only thing he could hear was his heart thumping and his breath catching at the back of his throat; and, the only thing he could see was his nose in front of him. Tripping up, he fell into a ditch and rolled over onto three frozen corpses.

"Ugh!"

Each was wearing a white lab coat; each killed by a single bullet to the temple. One had a hand missing; roughly hewn to the bone; and another, his face half-eaten away to the skull. None had eyes, just empty sockets of dried blood.

Fisher wanted to cry out. Indeed, he may already have done so.

And then he saw it... vulpine... coming, slowly, stealthily, over the edge of the crater. It's breath clouding in the cold night air, teeth exposed, with a low guttural growl. It's grey-blue eyes fixed on his, it moved without breaking the stare or moving it's head. Fisher began to back out of the pit, pushing his boots into the snow, as if climbing a ladder, backwards, whilst at the same time, removing his Browning pistol, slowly raising it to meet the eyes of the enormous grey wolf.

Someone grabbed the hood behind his helmet and pulled him out of the pit. The wolf relaxed his stance.

"Wanker!" said a voice in a hoarse whisper behind him. "You're making more noise than two skeletons fucking in a biscuit tin. Now, let's back away, nice and slow….and leave him to his dinner."

There was a dull, grey light, as the high cirrus clouds thinned to let the moon shine through, and when he looked back, silently the wolf had gone.

"Those bodies! Did you see those bodies?"

"If you don't shut the fuck up, you'll be joining them!"

Fisher could see a chain link fence up ahead topped by spinning razor wire. Some well-worn vehicle tracks lay to the front, running parallel to the boundary. Behind the fence, there seemed to be some flat undisturbed snow, followed by another similar fence.

"Fuck!" whispered his new friend, "Mines!"

Another made a scissor sign with his fingers, and a third moved forward. Within seconds, there was a hole in the fence, as he held the wire back to let a trooper lean in, tentatively. He was holding a long knife ahead of him…prodding the ground, gently, teasingly, in an arc in front of him. In a few moments, he was inside the fence.

Finding mines with a prodder involves pushing a tool into the ground and relying on tactile feedback to identify an obstruction that may be a mine. Easier in warm sand...but in hard frozen tundra? Many military groups are trained to use their bayonets as a detection and excavation tool, the SAS were legendary in this regard. But it was slow work. Like asking an ice pick to find an ice cube in a glacier. No doubt, Alpha team would be doing something similar somewhere else, off into the darkness.

"That's Fitz," whispered Fisher's new best mate, "he's a dab-hand at this… the best!"

Despite prodding every inch of the ground with his bayonet, Fitz couldn't search the soil deeply enough to reliably locate all the mines. But those he found, were marked with a small black flag taken from his pocket. It was hard because the ground was hard; but he found two likely suspects…both to his left, about seven feet apart. On reaching the second fence, the cutter followed through, carefully retracing the knee and foot prints of his predecessor. All went through, including Fisher, in a snaking line, like processional caterpillars. The last man, replaced the hole in the fence and removed each flag, gently brushing snow over his tracks. Nobody said anything; they moved like a single organism, efficiently and effectively, knowing each other's thoughts and intentions, complimented by a few hand to eye signals. They moved swiftly and smoothly, in between two buildings, and then stopped on a hand signal, dipping into the shadows.

A guard was smoking a cigarette, his Kalashnikov, hanging over his shoulder. With one swift movement from behind…a sickening dull click…like a large knuckle being cracked…his neck was broken and he slumped to the ground; being dragged away next to Fisher.

"Alexie!" a voice called out from the dark, followed by something in Russian, followed by a laugh. Probably something to the effect that Alexie should stop playing with his small cock and get back to his station.

"Alexie?" the voice repeated.

The troopers backed away, further into the shadows, and waited.

The soviet soldier with the voice appeared, looked at the disrupted snow, and raised his Kalashnikov. As he stepped forward, a trooper grabbed him from behind and in one clean swipe slit his throat. As the victim tensed, four or five rounds clacked off in different directions as slumped fell to the floor.

"Fuck!" said the trooper next to Fisher, "Game on!"

A siren went off, howling into the night, as flood lights came on. Alpha and Bravo, poured out from the shadows and ran towards two large aircraft hangers on the far side of the compound. Russian guards appeared on the right from a large guard house. They were partially clothed for the weather but unprepared for the hail of muffled bullets that greeted them. They fell to the ground, one by one, without firing a shot.

"Cover!" cried one voice, which Fisher recognised as Macintosh.

Two troopers lay down flat on the snow and lay down covering fire as the others made their way over open ground. Shots were coming from multiple unknown sources and directions.

"Fire in the hole!" another voice called out, as one, then another explosion came from the direction of the hangar doors. Someone grabbed Fisher by the scruff of the neck and pulled, pushed and dragged him across the open space and into one of the hangars. Moonlight was pouring in from high panelled windows, and skylights casting the shape of the windows on three large and long objects covered in grey dust sheets.

A trooper pulled the sheet from the nearest object.

"Fuck…" he said, "…what the…fuck?"

It was a sleek cruise missile finished in what could be titanium with a square intake and two thrusters to the rear. The others were similar, but only partially assembled.

"Grab as much as you can!" cried Macintosh. "And wire the rest for sound!"

Some were stuffing everything that would fit, into back packs. Another snapping dozens of photographs; and others crouched at the base of the missiles, laying charges.

A door burst open, from the side, as five or six men in vests and long underpants came out with their hands in the air.

Two troopers brought them down with single shots to the chest. Each man fell, one on top of the other...they had radioactive sensitive tags on a chain hanging from their necks.

"Stop!!" shouted Fisher...but it was too late. "What are you doing...? They surrendered! They had their arms in the air!"

"Fisher! Shut the fuck up! Or, I swear...I'll shut you up for good!" It was Macintosh. "Bring him over here! Now look Fisher, from here on in, you will stick to me like shit to a bog wall. Where I go...you go! We will be as tight as a crab's arse, you and me. And, if I hear any more crap like that, I will finish you on the spot..."

"Charges set!"

"Right! Out of here...next door...in case you hadn't noticed, the Russians are coming!"

As they poured out of the door, there was a storm of bullets.

"Man down!" came a voice from outside.

"Cover!" shouted Macintosh, and rushed out, dragging Fisher with him.

There was no need for Fisher to see where he was going; he just kept his eyes shut and waited to be shot, or pulled into the next hanger, or both.

No dramatic objects here...just wooden crates...and shelves behind a cage of impregnable reinforced bars.

"Grab and set!" called the Major.

Fisher saw a trooper on the floor, his arm covered in blood. He was being tended to by another trooper, Fisher assumed it was the Belgian.

"I'm ok..." said the wounded trooper.

"Shattered humorous!" Peeters said.

"There's nothing funny about it! Give me a fucking shot...I'm ok!"

"Right...Alpha, you take all the gear we've gathered back to the choppers...we will cover!"

Bravo took up crouching positions near the door. Behind them, Alpha; each trooper with a white backpack, stuffed with electronics, charts, diagrams and photographs, stripped from the walls.

"Cover!" and rapid fire commenced, as Alpha streamed through the hail of sprayed bullets and into the relief of darkness.

"We need to get out of here! Come on! Come on...with those charges."

"Special forces! At eleven o'clock! RPGs....incoming...incoming!"

There was a hot flash.

Fisher was thrown somewhere against a wall; and became aware of a severe ringing in his ears, his white parka was spattered in blood and lumps of splintered bone and burnt flesh. He couldn't see...he couldn't see if he was wounded...he couldn't see anything much as there was a cloud of dust...someone was shouting at him...no face mask...it looked like Briggs...shouting right in his face... but there was no sound...just the ringing, and his moving jaws...eyes wide... gaping. Briggs pulled him up from the floor, and shook him, as Fisher took in the stark horror of what had just happened. There were four or five bodies and body parts strewn over the concrete floor.

Someone was shouting...*cover fire*! But Fisher could barely hear it; it was as if he was at the end of a long wind tunnel. He felt sick...an unforgettable cocktail filled his lungs...the smell of cordite, fresh blood and burnt flesh. Two troopers were kneeling either side of what was left of the hangar door and firing an automatic spray of covering shots. Fisher was pulled out into the open...a sharp turn down a narrow passage and across a gap between two buildings. He was starting to hear the sound of gunfire, as the ringing began to subside. Briggs was mouthing something at him, whilst trying not to shout:

"I think she's in the grey concrete block over there!"

Then he shrugged his shoulders to indicate a lack of certainty.

Fisher still couldn't quite hear him, but understood, as Briggs pointed at the block. There was heavy gunfire coming from the two ground floor windows, and an open window above, with movement in the shadows.

There was a flash and a whoosh from the window, as another rocket propelled grenade spun through the air towards the same gap in the hangar doors.

A direct hit, just at the entrance.

More hand signals, between the six or seven troopers left, crouched in the shadows. Cover fire; and they all rushed forward towards the grey building to squat behind a low brick wall. More signs and gestures, followed by shots and three troopers springing up to throw hand grenades; two simultaneous and one retarded flash inside the rooms, including the upstairs window. A Russian staggered out the front door and was taken down by a single shot.

The troopers stormed the building, through the door and open windows.

Kill shots.

Fisher could hear them clearly now, and tried to push his hand between his ear and his helmet to make more room for sound. Blood had been streaming from his right ear and had dried on his neck.

"We don't have long, Stephen…regular armoured units will be here soon…maybe…ten or fifteen minutes at the most…and *Operation Flash* in twenty."

"Where's Macintosh?" asked Fisher.

"Dead…shrapnel through the face."

"Two of the troopers will have to go on ahead to tackle the main gate guard towers; there's no way we can go back through that fucking minefield; and another two to take up laser target positions. That leaves, me, you and these two guys. Is your pistol loaded?"

"Yes…If she's here…she'll be in the basement…if there is one?" replied Fisher. Of course, he had no reason for this statement, other than the idea that it seemed logical.

"Over there, behind the stairwell!" Briggs signalled the location of the door to the troopers, with a flick of his fingers. Some raced away purposely into the night and the two remaining, moved cautiously, towards the dark stair well, and the closed door. They took up positions either side of the door, one turning the handle very slowly.

It was unlocked.

He nodded to the other, and pulled the door wide open to reveal a pitch black void as the first trooper rushed in.

Shot.

He fell back, shot through the forehead. A dark thick stream of blood poured from the exit wound at the back of his head.

His partner rushed in and rolled down a staircase, firing his pistol as he went. Briggs rushed forward, with Fisher close behind. The trooper was unharmed, but crouched on one knee, on a half landing, with his pistol out at arm's length…rigid. His eyes were fixed on something out of sight.

Quietly, he said:

"We have a delicate situation down here, sir."

Briggs moved down the first few stairs, followed by Fisher. Both holding their pistols. Crouching, they could partially see into the room. On the right, a small bed...a table and a chair and in the corner, a bucket.

"Opusti pistolet." said the trooper, in a quiet, steady voice.

"I admire your Russian...very good accent...from the Ukraine it sounds, I would say...and, no...I will not be putting my gun down." the voice, belonging to the boots Fisher could see, was a near-perfect English speaker.

"The Red Army Artic Division Four, will be here in a few minutes. We may as well make our acquaintance. Come down, gentlemen and join us...why not?"

The trooper stayed put, while Briggs and Fisher stepped into the room, lit by a single bulb hanging over the head of a Special Forces Officer. In his right hand, a pistol...held down towards a girl, kneeling on the floor. She was wearing a simple grey dress, trembling and shivering, her lank fair hair hanging down over her face to her chin, which rested on her chest.

"Eloise?" said Fisher, quietly.

She urinated...it pooled around her knees.

"We don't have time for this..." muttered Briggs under his breath.

Fisher's hostage training kicked in; although, it was usually deployed over time. There was no time; no time for a word; no word for the time. First, every point following this one will be dependent on remaining calm. Fisher knew that. He also knew he would be incapable of higher thought if his brain seized up in fear. Second, calmness begets calmness. If he panics, he in turn is going to panic Eloise, with a gun close to her head; and the Soviet officer, who obviously feels backed into a corner.

If the officer was determined to murder her, she would already be dead; and every second that passes is usually one passing in her favour when it comes to surviving the situation.

*Telegraph actions before you do them...*Fisher recalled from his training:

"I'm going to put my gun down on the floor, very, very slowly."

He did, as he said it.

"As you please." said the officer.

Try to get them talking about something, especially what they believe in if they have some cause compelling them in the situation, was the advice Fisher used to give to his students. Of course, his classes focussed on the criminally psychotic mind. This was different. *Speak in measured, even tones, and defer to their intelligence and passion. Identifying with them creates a social connection they will have to overcome if they are deciding whether or not to kill you later.*

The officer raised his pistol, slowly, until it was touching the girl's head.

Shot... shot.

The lightbulb smashed into a hundred pieces.

Another shot. And then a forth, flashing in the dark.

Fisher was on the floor. The trooper flicked on a torch.

"I'm sorry!" he said, "I don't know what happened ...Fuck!"

Briggs was holding his left shoulder, he was bleeding profusely.

"Eloise?" he said.

Fisher and the trooper rushed forward....the officer was dead...a bullet straight through the head. He was lying in an expanding pool of sticky blood.

"The torch...over here!"

Fisher fell to his knees.

She had taken an executioner's shot straight through the temple, and was slumped forward, her hands still tied behind her back.

"Closer…" said Fisher, moving her bloodied hair away from her pretty face.

"Is she…?" started Briggs, struggling to his feet.

"She's dead…" replied Fisher, respectfully, "…but, it's not Eloise."

"Are you sure?"

"Sure."

Fisher stared at the poor girl, wondering who she was and why she was being kept here. There was a pause, part disbelief part disappointment, infused heavily with guilt.

"Gentlemen…we can die here… or we can move and live."

"Sir, we should move!" said the trooper.

"I can't leave her like this?" Fisher said, quietly.

"We have to…now come on!" Briggs insisted.

"We should take her with us."

"What for? Now, let's get out of here while we still can! This place will be overrun, then torched in minutes!"

Fisher retrieved his pistol and climbed the stairs two at a time behind Briggs and the trooper. He stopped and looked at the bloody scene for the last time. Who was that girl?

It was quiet outside. A few bodies here and there, but any remaining Russians had either gone to ground or run away. Fisher felt numb, as they ran towards the front gate, following the footsteps left in the snow by the rest of Bravo. It was open…three Russians lay dead, bleeding into the snow. A forth, disturbed by the kerfuffle, tried to sit up with a pistol in his hand, and raised his arm towards Briggs. Fisher took aim, stopped, and shot him in the chest, without thinking, freezing to the spot.

"Keep moving!" cried Briggs. "Move!"

In the distance, there was a rumbling of tracked and armoured vehicles approaching at speed.

"Tanks!" called Briggs.

The unnamed trooper led the way into the forest, following in the footsteps already impressed there, until he stopped at a point where the tracks split off in two directions.

"Those two have gone to higher ground… you can see it rising over there. We need to go right to the choppers," said the trooper.

All three were running as fast as they could…Briggs clearly struggling with his shoulder wound and, no doubt, still losing a lot of blood.

Shot! From somewhere. From the trees.

Multiple shots!

The trooper dropped to his knees, and fell forward, shot in the back of the neck.

Fisher and Briggs hit the deck, and crawled on their bellies, falling into a dip. Briggs reached out to feel the trooper's neck.

"Fuck!" he said, hoarsely. "Dead!"

Through the trees, they could hear the Merlin engines starting up.

The figure of a young Russian soldier stepped forward, nervously, looking over the lip of the ditch, and lightly kicking the trooper's body to see if he was dead. He said:

"Поднимите руки"

What were they to do?

"Поднимите руки"

This time, the Kalashnikov was thrust upwards at the tip.

"I think he wants us to put our hands up. Smile and put your hands up."

Fisher did as instructed by Briggs, grinning like an idiot.

"Поверните в другую сторону! Повернись!"

"I think he wants us to turn around. Clearly, he doesn't like to see your smile. Don't turn...stay right where you are! Once we turn, we're dead."

The soldier, his hands shaking, raised his Kalashnikov to fire, first at Fisher, aware that his grin was the most inane.

Fisher closed his eyes.

Shot... at close range.

Fisher opened his eyes to see the blood pouring from the side of the soldier's head as he fell over on his face, at Fisher's knees. Fisher stared at him for a moment, as the life before him, drained out of the skull. He looked no more that nineteen years old. *Somebody's son*, thought Fisher.

"Come on you two! Wheels up!"

"Baker!" cried Briggs.

There was a terrifying roar, which made all three of them duck instinctively, as two low-level Harriers went over their heads, releasing two missiles each and peeled off, one to the left, the other to the right, arching up into the night sky with afterburners glowing lilac. They were turning for another run.

All three ran towards the direction in which the Merlins had started their engines, as the missiles smashed into their targets and the night forest was illuminated in a deep penetrating crimson light. Moments later, another intense flash of light and the sound of explosions echoing into the night. As the sound abated, the Harriers could be heard roaring overhead in the direction of the Finnish border.

"This way!" cried Baker. "Quickly! We have to move, or we'll be left behind."

Baker moved through the trees like a doe, springing and swerving to avoid all obstacles. One Merlin was leaving the ground; the second was closing the ramp. In the twilight, th pilot spotted Baker running towards him from the trees, with Fisher behind assisting Briggs…now limping badly.

As the ramp scooped them up, the Merlin pulled away, as the third chopper exploded in a ball of orange flames.

13

All Before

Shadow.

Umbra.

Grey light.

The Land Rover Defender pulled up behind the consulate on Proletarskoy Diktatury Street.

Baker was driving.

Between her and Fisher, they had managed. Briggs, sitting in the rear, giving directions and instructions... his arm in a sling, his ankle bandaged.

Nothing much else had been said.

Nothing much had happened.

There was no ferry on the ice; and not even a scar where the vehicle had exploded. All frozen over once more.

Nothing.

It was as if it had never happened.

Even as they had disembarked the Merlin, nothing was said.

Except one trooper, who turned to Fisher and stared at him for an uncomfortably long time:

"Was it worth it? Was it?" he said. "Well, fuck you!"

Fisher had no answer for anger or such questions.

The Consul General, Alan and his wife Jennifer, were waiting in the lobby. Suitcases were stacked and ready to go. They had refused to leave without Eloise. They came out onto the steps

Jennifer looked thin and grey, her eyes straining to see through the tinted glass. A security officer stepped forward to open the rear door as Fisher and Baker emerged from the front. It was a moment they were all dreading.

Briggs, now clearly visible as the only passenger, struggled to get out of back.

"Where is she?" asked Jennifer, anxiously. "Is she in the other car?"

Alan could tell from the three faces that all was not well.

"Where's the other car?"

"It collided with a ferry, exploded and sank through the ice. All were lost."

"Where is she?" Jennifer repeated even more emphatically, as she began to cry.

"It wasn't her," said Fisher, quietly. "It was another girl altogether... not Eloise. We don't know her name or why she was there. She was executed by special forces as we were trying to get her out. But, Eloise wasn't there."

"Anything from the soviets, sir?" asked Briggs, as he hobbled in.

They stepped off the lobby into a small meeting room.

"Not a peep," said Alan, "...nothing."

"The resistance was heavier than we expected. The guards were young conscripts; but the Special Forces must have been troops seasoned in Afghanistan; and they were well armed...determined. The intel failed us on several counts."

"From the Americans?"

"I'm afraid so, sir."

"How many did we lose?"

"Including the three on the river, thirteen."

"Oh my god!" said Jennifer.

"Tragic...might be the biggest single loss the SAS has faced since the Falklands War. But, we got plenty of intel and destroyed a major threat to the West."

"You forgot to mention the civilian deaths." said Fisher.

There was a moment of exchanged glances. Alan looked at Briggs for an explanation. Briggs took a breath:

"A group of scientists and technicians. They appeared in the wrong place at the wrong time. A couple of troopers let rip as a knee-jerk reaction."

"How many?"

"Six, I think. They'll be a report and, no doubt, an investigation…but… I doubt whether any charges will be brought. I'm afraid, they are just collateral damage."

"But, we will still need scientists…?" Alan, asked.

"We had no orders to take them back with us…even if they were willing…which I doubt."

"Hold on…" interrupted Fisher, "…hold on a minute….why do *we* need scientists? Isn't it enough that we murdered the ones we found and rendered this site a death trap for the next twenty thousand years? The project is dead!"

"Steady on, Stephen," said Alan. "This is about the security of the realm. We need as much information as we can gather. If *we* have the weapon, then it doesn't matter whether they do or not. We're not going to use it first, and neither are the Americans"

Fisher tried, but failed, to stifle a guffaw.

"This may not be the only facility." Briggs quipped.

"I don't think so." said Fisher.

"Why? What makes you think this is a one-off?" Briggs, retorted.

"Otherwise, it makes little sense," offered Fisher. "Why were KGB Special Forces there? On the other hand, given the strategic significance of the weapon…why was it developed so close to the border? Why was it guarded by young, inexperienced conscripts? Two chain link fences…and…possibly…but we can't be sure…a few landmines…come on! This is not a government operation…which, would have to have been initiated before the collapse of the Soviet Union. This has to be a splinter operation; or, some rogue elements in the military. The government would at least, have lodged the strongest protest about an incursion…perhaps without referring to the nature of the facility. But, the silence shouts loud and clear: the government doesn't know about this weapon."

"You may be onto something, there, Stephen." said Briggs, thoughtfully acknowledging Fisher's insight.

"And…" Fisher continued, bringing it back to his concerns, "…are we really, seriously, suggesting that the Russian government has sanctioned State agencies to kidnap, mutilate and murder minors in order to facilitate this…cover?"

There was a burst of sobbing.

Fisher realised he'd gone too far.

"Is anyone…" said Jennifer through her restrained tears and clenched jaw, "…going to talk about *the girl*? She is…was…somebody's child! That girl could have been our daughter! I've been sitting here, listening to all this high and mighty strategic bullshit… and, not once… once! …have any of you said any more about that poor girl! That could have been, Eloise! My child has gone! And I want her back! I just want my baby…"

A wave of guilt washed over the room. Baker pushed her chair back and went around the table to sit with Jennifer, and to take her hand.

Fisher took a deep breath. Quietly, he said:

"It could just be a coincidence, that a girl of similar age and appearance was at the facility and got caught up in this madness. We may never know who she was. Perhaps, the daughter or granddaughter of one of the scientists who needed some persuasion to pick up where Vasyli and the others had left off? I came across a pit

246

in the forest, containing three executed scientists. Her minder spoke perfect English. Had there been a connection with Eloise's disappearance and she was merely a decoy, then that means that they knew we were coming. They were ill-prepared and poorly defended if they knew. I also believe, that a man, trapped as he was, in a basement with three guns pointed at him, would have been strongly inclined to let his ego override his duty. Clearly, he didn't know who I was... to him, I was just another foreign invader. I think he would have tried to inflict a sense pride in outsmarting us...in tricking us to go all that way... with all those risks... to be faced with failure. The failure to find and rescue, which was the reason we were there."

"I think you're exactly right, Stephen." said Briggs, nodding.

"In truth," Fisher continued, "there was nothing we could have done that we didn't do to save that poor girl. And, yet, she will stay with me for the rest of my life. I failed to save her life. I failed to convince her captor to put his gun down. Not Briggs, nor Baker or anybody else. It was my failure!"

There was silence.

Briggs was the first to speak:

"Stephen, I think you are being a bit hard on yourself. She had a gun pointed to her head; we had minutes to go before the mechanised units arrived. We were at ground zero just as the site was about to be lit up. I don't know who fired first, but the truth is, that we did all that we could."

"One thing is clear to me though," continued Fisher. More than ever, I am determined to find your daughter. I promise you, I will turn my mind, body and soul to this end, as if she were my own daughter. I will do whatever it takes to bring her home...alive. We still have a case... we still have hope... and, we have the utmost determination to succeed. If we fail...or rather, if I fail... I need to know, as much as you do, that I did *everything* possible. If not, Eloise will haunt our waking dreams for the rest of our lives. And, no Party, no State and no splinter group, however inglorious, can diminish that resolve."

Jennifer and Alan were weeping. Fisher dropped the resonance:

"Jennifer…Alan…, I want to go home…I want to see *my* children, and my wife, Jane…. but, for now I am here for you both. I'm here to bring Eloise home."

Alan tried to compose himself:

"Is there anything we can do…Stephen…anything?"

Fisher took a deep breath.

"After the last twenty-four hours…" he shook his head, "I realise how precarious this whole process is; and how vulnerable we are, as everything collapses around us. In my business, we tend to work alone. We progress an investigation in our heads and in our hearts. It's a lonely, desolate, journey. If anything had happened to me last night, then key elements, crucial connections and investigative leads, might have been lost…and this, this environment is high risk…it's dangerous. I need someone with me; someone I can trust."

Briggs responded, intuitively:

"I am more than happy to work with you Stephen… anytime… anywhere… right here and now."

"Thank you, Briggs," replied Fisher, "but… your shoulder is shot and your ankle badly sprained…you need to get some rest. I want to move on with this."

"I'll do it!" cried Baker. She turned to Briggs, "Commander Briggs, I am formally requesting permission to be seconded, indefinitely, to Dr Fisher, until this investigation is concluded."

"Granted." said Briggs, shaking his head with mild concern.

"I expect you're all very tired, as we are..." said Alan, "I suggest you get some rest, and we can start afresh in the morning. Stephen...a car will take you back to the Moskva."

As they walked into the lobby, Fisher stopped to speak to Baker:

"I can't let you do this, Carey." he said, "I think it's going to get very ugly and complicated."

"More complicated than what we've just been through? I like complicated..." she replied.

"But..."

"There are no *buts*....I'll come by in the morning....about ten. What could possibly go wrong?"

Despite the now familiar, discomfort and discomforting surroundings, Fisher knew, as he entered his grey brick box, back at the Moskva, that the lumps in the mattress would feel like soft clouds and the weird shrieks and other testimony of winter nights would sound like birdsong, because he would fall into a pit of sleep, as deep and dark as any cave of dreams.

And so, he did.

The first indication that a good night's sleep is over, is that lovely feeling of gradually waking up...no alarm clock...just a natural emergence from the comforting cocoon and the absence of context. But, there is no rest for the wicked.

It was a quiet morning.

The low Winter sun was streaming, golden, through narrow horizontal slits in the warm wooden blinds creating a pattern of thin trapezoid blocks that came up the side of the bed and turned to a chevron before curling over the covered contour of Jane's feet. The Venetian was moving slightly, to and fro, as the hot air from the heating radiator below the window, wafted over it.

The amber stripes of light complimented the yellow ochre walls, on which Fisher had painted a flaking, whispered image of a flowering wisteria. Racemes of lilac flowers seemed to stand apart as a sign of summers gone. Fisher had painted one cluster, for every year they had lived in this house. They stood as proud testament to the evenings of garden pleasure; of warm balmy times, with a cool glass of Chardonnay, sitting under the enfolding arms of the Turkish Fig Tree.

A tree they had planted eight years before in a stone circle at the top, in the far corner of *this little piece of heaven*, as Jane used to say. It had grown through a hole in the middle of a round wooden table, where a parasol should be. But, they lived in Manchester, where the word *parasol* was not in the local lexicon. Umbrellas, yes; but parasols were a foreign thing; a thing that lived in a warm dry southern land...Spain or Portugal, perhaps.

Fisher knew of such places, remembered from teenage school holidays. But, he had never found the time or the money to take Jane and the boys away. He convinced himself, that the garden was the thing; and that was all they needed. But, really, it was work that kept him pinned to the ground.

They had created a small pond, in the shade, just behind the table, in the space where the round edge of the stone met the corner of the square garden. The water trickled over the lip and down onto a bed of smooth, round, pebbles in shades of grey and ochre. It struggled over them, tumbling down through two, smaller plunge pools, large enough for a pair of feet to stand in. Through a narrow gap in the stones, it continued past a shingle spar, under an arched wooden bridge, finally falling into a deep pond surrounded by plants, commonly known as hostas, plantain lilies and occasionally by the Japanese name *giboshi*... interspersed with the uncurling fronds of verdant ferns.

Stephen could move a single pebble, and it would change the course of the water; to make it louder as it tumbled; or, to change the ebb and flow of life in the margins. But, of course, it was Winter now, and all the plants would be sleeping beneath the frosted soil; the pond would be frozen and the stream, a dry bed under the bare bones of the fig. The uncovered feet of his boys would, no longer, be standing in those pools, splashing and throwing water at each other. Giggling. For a moment...a still moment... he saw them there...trapped in a memory, like a piece of beautiful music, frozen.

The first inclination Fisher had that he wasn't waking up in his own cosy nest, was the sharp sound of splintering wood and three or four strong hands pulling him from his bed and throwing his shirt and trousers at him. Torches...voices...torches in his face, on the walls... more voices, shouting...Russian. A hood over his head, hands tied behind his back. Being dragged down the corridor, his bare feet burning on the brown carpet. The lift, the unreliable lift, he had never been in...why wasn't it breaking now? Kitchen noises, voices off...the smells of borsch, of stews...of cigarette smoke, pungent, sickening... the cold air...his feet on crushed snow and being thrown onto an icy metal floor. A sharp blow to the head. A vehicle door slams...

Fisher came to, with a shock of iced water tossed over his face and shoulders. Such a cliché. A bright light; a dark room; his vision blurred. Was this another nightmare? Or, was he in a film? Was he unwittingly caught in the middle of an international conspiracy involving stolen diamonds, an exiled Nazi war criminal, and a rogue government agent?

A brutal montage of scenes from *Marathon Man*, flashed through Fisher's mind. Was this his coping mechanism? It was a technique he developed as a child, Fisher's dentist refused to administer anaesthetic. He claimed that only a poorly skilled dentist needed to use the stuff. So, Mr Khan went about his gruesome work whilst Fisher distracted himself with quadratic equations interspersed with scenes from his favourite films. In this case, Laurence Olivier plays the Nazi SS dentist Dr. Christian Szell, known as *Der weisse Engel: The White Angel*. Olivier's character was inspired by Josef Mengele, known as the *Angel of Death*, infamous for leading human experimentations at Auschwitz. Hoffman is a graduate student in History at Columbia and, although he is haunted by his father's persecution and suicide under McCarthyism, he knows nothing about the diamonds that motivate his torture by Szell, an innocence that leads to increased brutality…

The agent, standing before Fisher, was alone, with the typical, clichéd, bright light behind him. He came slowly into focus. It was the Wolf.

"Good evening Dr Fisher…or, is it morning? Yes, it's morning, of course. It's a soviet tradition to drag a traitor from his bed at four in the morning, when he is least expecting it… least aware… more pliable… shall we say? Let us play a game, shouldl we, you and me? I will ask you some questions, and you will answer. It's a simple game. Where were you last night?"

It sounded polite enough: quiet, and yet immensely threatening.

"I went to the British Consulate to ask the Consul General some questions. Vladimir, dropped me off there. If you ask him, he…"

Volkov hit him, hard, across the face with a short piece of black rubber pipe. It turned and shifted in his hand, ready for the next blow.

"This is nothing to do with Ivanov. He knows nothing of this. This is between us Dr Fisher. You will need no verification from anyone, because whatever you tell me is going to be the truth. There's only one truth, and it's inside your head. Now, let's try that again, shall we?

Where were you last night? You were not at the Moskva…so, where were you?"

"The Consul General suggested I stay the night there, so that I could question…"

The black pipe came from the shadows without warning and with a stinging blow, struck Fisher across his left cheekbone. He felt the warm rush of blood.

"Where were you last night?"

"Look, *General* Volkov, I understand this *game*, as you call it. I'm a criminal psychologist and you are a criminal…"

Volkov raised the pipe as if to strike, his face, rigid; his cold, grey eyes sharper than… the wolf in the forest. But, he said nothing.

"You already know where I was last night. The idea is that you beat me into telling you what you already know, not because you need verification or admission, but just because you're angry… just because you are a wounded wolf defending the cancerous heart of the body politic… and just because you want to beat me! Go on! Beat me! It makes you feel, better doesn't it? The truth is, you probably enjoy it!"

Volkov raised his arm higher, his breathing audible through clenched teeth. The anger was palpable. He swung down with all his strength, striking Fisher on the side of his head and he blacked out.

The shock of iced water roused him to the realisation that the nightmare was real, that it wasn't going to stop, and that he might die. Why was he holding back? Something that only happened in films. Was it the Official Secrets Act? No. This seemed to be a matter of principle. Principle! How stupid was that? It was a battle of wills, that if he lost…then, he was lost. His mission would be so compromised, that he might never discover the truth about Eloise. He said he would bring her home. Above all emotional considerations, he wanted to bring closure.

"Let us continue, Dr Fisher."

"In situations of extreme stress and pain, human cognitive processes begin to break down, sometimes irrevocably," continued Fisher, relentlessly bombarding Volkov. "Extreme stress and pain bring about false memories, reduce the ability to remember information, and seriously affect decision-making and memory performance. So, I'm never going to tell you a truth that will satisfy you."

"Fuck you Fisher!"

"If you want the truth, I'll tell you the truth... We must continually question not only what it means to be cruel; a cruel bastard like you, Volkov; but also what it means to receive cruelty, and the ultimate interpretation of power through these mechanisms. If we cannot condone other injustices, like slavery, false imprisonment, and servitude, then we are fully denying that man can take the sacrilegious position of god. Are you a god, Volkov?"

Fisher was deliberately goading him. The risk was, that it merely infused Volkov with more venom, in which case he might be beaten to death. Or, that by remaining rational and critical, Volkov might tire of him telling a truth about himself that he wishes to deny. But, Volkov raised his hand to the zenith for a final maximum blow, perhaps a lethal blow, to Fisher's temple.

"If we cannot be gods, we cannot condone torture. Ownership over another life, in any sense, implies our irreverence and ultimately, the absolute irrelevancy of human life."

Fisher could taste possible victory in his mouth, along with the blood. Victory or death.

"Do you have a life Comrade General Volkov? Do you have sons or daughters, or sisters? Do they have lives? How would you feel if one of your sisters was taken…raped…tortured…mutilated? Are you really any better than the man that tortures your daughter?"

Volkov's face was puce with rage, sweat forming on his brow, and a vein pulsing there, like a ticking clock, his raised hand trembling.

Volkov's arm swung down with great angular force, as Fisher felt the rush of air and the pipe brush over his face. He heard it hit the wall to his right, over in the shadows.

A door slammed.

Fisher was dumped without care on the corner of the Alexander Nevsky Square, hoodless, but still with his hands tied behind his back, as he rolled onto the icy pavement, shivering in shock more than the cold. It was getting light. He lay there for a few moments, his nose bleeding into the ice. He saw the filthy boots of two or three people passing by; and a pair of older feet, with shoes bound in thick rags of hessian sacks. The swollen legs, ankles, covered by heavy black stockings:

"Я могу вам помочь," said a female voice.

Fisher looked up with his only open eye, at the old wrinkled face.

"My hands…" he said, trying to move his arms held behind his back, the cord cutting into his wrists.

She said something to a passing man.

He shook his head and walked on by.

"Жди здесь. Я получу помощь" the old woman mumbled to Fisher, and then walked away.

"No…No…wait!" Fisher said, behind her as she went.

He tried to get up, but it was too slippery and he had insufficient strength.

The old woman returned, with a soldier in grey uniform, with his Kalashnikov strapped over his shoulder. He took a pen knife from a black leather pouch on his belt, and in one flick, released Fisher's hands. They both helped him sit, and then to get up.

"You now ok?" said the soldier.

Fisher nodded and thanked them both, especially the old lady. She shuffled off around the corner, nodding... saying something to herself... and then shaking her head.

"Where you go...where?" said the soldier.

"Moskva." replied Fisher.

The soldier looked puzzled.

"Moskva?"

"No, no...Hotel Moskva."

"Ah!" he said, "You me... we go." And he lifted Fisher under the arms to stand him up.

It was only a short walk to the familiar revolving doors; a short walk, that is, for someone wearing boots. For Fisher, it was difficult, painful; but with each step his feet hurt less and less, as he pressed them into the crisp snow, until, at the entrance he had no feeling in them, whatsoever.

Fisher, turned and thanked the soldier and shook his hand.

"У тебя запястья кровоточат" said the soldier, pointing to Fisher's wrist. He took his watch off and offered it to the soldier.

"No..." he said, "blood...bad.. need doctor."

"Ah... yes... thank you."

Fisher shuffled through the doors into the hotel, dragging his bloodied feet across the floor. Nobody seemed all that surprised, until:

"Stephen!... What...?"

It was Baker, she had been waiting for him in the lobby.

15

Lie

Blue.

Red.

Cracked mirror.

The water from the pipe sticking out of the shower wall, was, for once, a welcome relief for Fisher. Cold though it was, cascading over his head, stinging, and yet numbing is swollen face.

Baker waited in his bedroom.

Fisher emerged with a towel around his waist, stepping carefully over the splintered remains of the door. At least, he was grateful that, as yet, no one had stolen his trunk or his boots.

"Stephen, I think you should come and stay at my place."

"I'll be fine, Carey, really. Nobody is going to beat up a man with an already beaten up face...are they?" Fisher doubted his own logic, "... And, why would the KGB, if Volkov, still is the KGB, arrest me twice and beat the same pulp out of me? But, then, there's still the MVD. Egorov might want to have a go!"

Baker turned the corner on the edge of the bed, to allow Fisher to get dressed in private...albeit, with no door onto the corridor.

"Egorov? Who's Egorov?" she said.

"Anatoly Egorov, the Chief Investigator of the case we are working on. He is a senior officer of the militia, which is the policing arm of the Ministry of the Interior. They focus on extracting confessions to solve crimes via torture, intimidation and blackmail. It's a technique, I'm well qualified in. My credentials are all over one side of my face."

"Charming. But, I suppose some of the so-called suspects might actually be guilty?"

"I think that's the idea. But, from what I've seen so far, a human life has so little value here, that I question whether Egorov is really serious about finding this killer. He has already found two, who confessed to the same crimes. He doesn't get paid by results."

Fisher pulled on his trousers and tucked his shirt in. Every movement of his head and neck was deeply painful.

"There!" he said. "All I need is my coat, hat and a new face!"

"Let's get your bag packed!"

"But...really..."

"Let's get your bag packed!" Baker was already doing it.

In truth, Fisher was relieved to be saying goodbye to the Moskva. Life, he concluded, was complicated enough. However, he did wonder what his wife, Jane, might say... about him sharing an apartment with an attractive, young woman. But, in his defence, he would cite mitigating circumstances and the distinct possibility of torture, disability and premature death. Would that cut the mustard? Probably not. More likely, he would face torture and premature death when he arrived home.

"For once, I think we'll take the lift. I really don't fancy lugging this trunk, clunk, clunk down six flights of stairs..." he said.

"What could possibly go wrong?" she said, as the lift doors closed.

"Car?" asked Fisher.

"Lenny's waiting outside."

"Lenny? The driver?"

"Lenny the land rover. Commander Briggs has given us exclusive use of his favourite girlfriend or boyfriend. And...he gave us both a gift."

Baker removed a Browning from her coat pocket, a magazine and a small box of cartridges. She handed it to Fisher, handle first.

"This is yours."

Ordinarily, Fisher would have refused point blank. But, given his overnight experience, he willingly stuffed the pistol into his right coat pocket and the ammunition in the left.

"What could possibly go wrong?" he said.

Was this going to be their new shared mantra, Fisher wondered.

The trunk loaded in the back… no boot on the Defender.

How confusing is that?

Fisher and Baker climbed into the front seats of the land rover.

"Where to first, boss? The hospital?" said Baker.

It almost made him smile, had it not been for the painful swelling on his face. Hospital?

"The residence of the Consul General, please, driver!"

"Why?"

"Yours is not to reason why; yours is to do and drive."

"Right-oh, chief!" she said, starting the engine.

"Is it chief or boss?" said Fisher, "…let's just keep it to… Stephen, shall we?"

"Yes, boss."

Inevitably, they both failed the frisk by the security guard. At last! He found something! As they handed over their weapons, Jennifer came to meet them in the lobby.

"Oh my god! Stephen…what happened to your face?"

"Let's just say, I fell out of bed."

"Out of a sixth floor window!" added Baker.

Jennifer almost smiled. Turning to Isabelle on reception, she said:

"Call for Dr Harvey, please?"

"Dr Harvey?" queried Fisher.

"Yes. Peter is the doctor for the diplomatic quarter."

"No, really, I…"

"I insist, Stephen. You should at least follow your own advice, that we need to stay healthy during this ordeal."

He admitted defeat. At least to himself.

"Now, whilst we are waiting… what can I do for you? Alan is in a briefing, on a secure line to the Ambassador."

"Actually, it was you I wanted to see. I have a request, but, if it's too difficult or painful for you, then, we can leave it."

"What is it?"

"I would like to see Eloise's room, if I may?"

Jennifer looked quite shocked.

"We…haven't been in there since the day after she went missing. The police looked in there. What are you looking for?"

"I don't know…I just feel we should take a look."

"Alright…come this way."

"Carey…" Fisher said, "…would you go next door to the main reception and ask Sarah for the name and address of the photographer Alan mentioned. She'll know what I mean."

"Of course."

Jennifer went on up the stairs and Stephen followed. He knew this was going to be difficult for her, which is why he sent Baker to do something else. And, so, he said nothing. No point, he thought, in idle distractive chit-chat.

Half way along the landing, Jennifer paused at a door.

"You don't have to come in if you don't want to" said Fisher, gently.

"I don't think I'm quite ready for that, if you don't mind."

Jennifer stepped aside.

"If you could wait here…in case I have any questions?"

"Of course."

Fisher entered, what at first glance was, a typical pre-teen girl's bedroom. The pink phase had ended, it seemed, replaced by a more lilac scheme. Not that he was expert in such matters. But, in the circumstances it felt very uncomfortable, as if he was somewhere he shouldn't be; prying into a personal space. It was almost too sensitive, too private; and he was conscious of the fact that if he touched or disturbed anything, then he was violating a shrine, desecrating a sacred tomb. But, inevitably, he needed to search. This, was not his usual modus operandi. But, how could he begin to profile this killer without the base information?

The wardrobe, the chest of drawers and the bedside table revealed nothing out of the ordinary, except in one regard: the more he searched, the more connected he felt. Increasingly, it was as if he had known her; as if he was rummaging about in her mind.

The bed was wedged into a corner, above which, the wall had been turned into a portrait gallery of photographs and posters featuring a single fashion model. Fisher recognised her as Kate Moss. There must have been twenty or so images....With her incredibly thin, boyish body, Moss had created quite a stir in the fashion world, launching what became known as the *waif* look. Fisher examined the images. They had been carefully chosen by Eloise, he presumed; and so...they mattered.

Fisher tried to *read* the images, in the same way that Yuri Molodkovets might have. After all, it was a montage, chosen, selected, arranged.

Moss started working young, after being discovered at the age of fourteen at JFK airport in New York State. She appeared on the cover of a British magazine the next year. Coincidentally, Fisher had seen a television interview with her, quite recently. It stayed in his mind because he thought that her age played into the psyche of those he studied. He saw it as part of the sexualisation of youth by the media. Why had Eloise focussed so much on Kate Moss, he wondered?

There was nobody else here, just Moss, growing all over the wall.

He was about to turn and leave when he thought he noticed something about the corner of the perfectly made bed. The closest to where he was standing looked slightly higher than the other corners. Judging by the wrinkle free bedding, so called *hospital corners* might explain the slight rise. But, maybe not? And so, Fisher lifted the mattress, to find nothing but an enviably folded corner. But, much further in, there was what looked like a scrap book or photo album. He removed it, and sat down on the bed, to turn the first page.

"Everything fine, Stephen?" said Jennifer from the landing outside.

"Yes...all good...just a few minutes and I'll be done."

There was no point in upsetting her further.

Black cartridge paper pages were occupied with images, set, one per page, with photo corners. Clearly, she had, or someone had, gone to a lot of care to assemble this collection. Each page contained a black and white photograph of Eloise, obviously taken in one professional shoot, against the same plain monochromatic backdrop. One headshot after another, beginning with the same one Fisher kept in his coat pocket and moving on to less formal poses. She seemed relaxed and to be enjoying herself. But as the pages turned and the camera became more distant, to include the top half of her body, Fisher became more concerned.

Firstly, the clothing: she was wearing a loose, white vest displaying her shoulders and glimpses of her underarms. Secondly, the poses, becoming more and more coquettish; and in one image, the vest strap had fallen off the shoulder. It was by no means...pornographic... hardly even suggestive... with a slightly open mouth. Nevertheless, it was, at the very least, inappropriate, Fisher felt; not least in one so young. Even more so, when he looked at the last three images, which were full head to toe shots. Eloise was only wearing her vest and panties. How did this happen? Was she alone with this photographer? Had nobody accompanied her? Security?

As he closed the book and looked up, Fisher noticed similar poses in the gallery over the bed, almost as if they had been copied. And, again, the vest and the slightly open mouth.

Here was a moment when Fisher wished he had access to his acclaimed academic colleague at Manchester. Dr Susan Millett was an expert in this field. A social psychologist, she had studied the *hypersexualising* of young women in the media for more than ten years. The research that she and her colleagues conducted over the last five years found a steep increase in the pervasiveness of images in magazines that show young, even underage looking women, in highly sexual ways.

Whereas Fisher, in part, was relying on his own subjective, albeit male reactions. Millett had studied fashion photography and images in teen magazines. She used a coding systems to rate the images for sexualising traits. Those traits varied from study to study, but included: body parts shown, body pose, facial expression, activity, camera angle and clothing. Some of her other studies, like the analysis of *Rolling Stone* covers, assigned a sliding scale of points for each coded trait in order to get a more accurate rating of images. For example, exposure of body parts is usually coded high for sexualisation, but doesn't always register. In the absence of other traits, a girl wearing a vest might not be coded as a sex object, while a fully clothed girl in a suggestive pose could be considered a sex object.

Fisher had attended Susan's, inaugural professorial lecture; but in truth he felt he had no need to apply her scale of points or coded traits to these images. Eloise was being groomed.

But by whom? And for what, exactly?

He replaced the album to the place where he found it and stepped out, closing the door behind him. Jennifer was looking at him anxiously.

"Well," he said, "she obviously has a bit of an interest in Kate Moss?"

"Yes, Eloise was… is… quite obsessed with Kate. In fact, I would say she has a crush on her. It's a thing some girls go through at a certain age."

"But we shouldn't dismiss it too lightly. It could be very relevant. Consider this: crushes are of two kinds: identity crushes and romantic crushes. In both cases, the teenager feels smitten by a compelling person who captivates their attention for good or ill. A third kind is the celebrity crush that shapes ideals and stirs fantasies, but there is usually no interpersonal contact to play them out. However, this is definitely where Eloise was at… shaping ideals and fantasies around Kate Moss."

"But she's not even a teenager."

"No. But these feelings are often stirred by hormonal changes, which are occurring earlier and earlier. Driven by these urges, she may have been prepared to take risks, if they engaged her infatuation. Is she interested in modelling and fashion, in general?"

"Oh yes… loves clothes! She probably dreams of being a fashion model."

"Does she eat a normal healthy diet?"

"Yes."

"No signs of anorexia?"

"Nothing."

"And one last question, if I may?"

"Of course."

"Did you notice any physical changes related to, so called, precocious puberty? Early onset breast development, for example?"

"Well…yes. But that's the new normal these days, isn't it?"

"It's common.. I wouldn't say, *normal*. Researchers are not quite sure why it's happening. Did you discuss these changes with Eloise?"

"Not yet, no. I was planning on getting to it. But, it's finding the right moment. You know how difficult it is… judging the best time… the right moment."

"I'm just trying to understand why she didn't come home… keeping an open mind."

"You have boys?"

"Yes… one wants to be a palaeontologist; the other once told someone he wanted to be a sabre toothed tiger when he grows up! I'm worried about the dental bills!"

It was a brief moment of near normality; of parent to parent chatter.

They walked down the stairs together.

"Which school did Eloise attend?"

"The Diplomatic International School. It's a five minute walk away. Until now, there have been no security concerns. So, most children walk there. Since word of the disappearance leaked out, however, there is a line of diplomatic cars every day stretching down the road."

"Does she have any particular friends?"

"*Particular*…? That reminds me of my convent school days."

"Why?"

"Oh…the nuns used to say that *particular friendships must be avoided*. In their twisted little minds, everything was about sex. We even had to take the polish off our new shoes with wire wool, in case a man would stare at them and look up our skirts in the reflection!"

It was the first real smile on Jennifer, Fisher had seen. If only a nostalgic one.

"Is there a particular friend we could speak to?"

"Yes, of course. That would be Cami. She's French, but her English is better than mine. I'll speak to her parents, shall I?"

"Thank you….perhaps tomorrow if it's convenient."

Baker was waiting at reception and nodded as he came down the stairs, to indicate that she had the information he required.

"Isabelle?" said Jennifer.

"Dr Harvey is waiting in the ante-room."

"In you go, Stephen. I'm waiting here to make sure you do."

"Jennifer, I'm very grateful, thank you. Oh…one last thing…would it be possible for someone to call Chief Investigator Egorov at the MVD."

"What shall we tell him?"

"To meet me…best not here perhaps…tell him we will come to his office this afternoon…about an hour or so from now."

"What if he's not available?"

"Oh, he will be."

Fisher nodded to Baker, as he went in to the adjacent room.

"Dr Harvey… Stephen Fisher… I'm grateful you could see me."

"It looks like I needed to see you. Come and sit down. You had an argument with a brick wall?"

"Something like that, yes."

He opened his bag of tricks.

"Let's take a look at the face first. I'll need to clean it up… it will sting quite a bit…"

"Not as much as it did getting it!"

"I suppose it would be futile to ask how you came to be so beaten up."

"Best if I don't say."

"I understand. Well, those lacerations on the cheekbone and over the nose and eye, will leave a scar unless we close the wounds."

"Stitches?"

"No, no… nothing so crude. These medipore strips will pull the skin together. Another day, or so, and it would have been too late. There. Now, let's take a look at your brain."

Dr Harvey took a torch to Fisher's eyes.

"You can see my brain through there?"

"I can see whether you have a concussion. And, there has been trauma. Any blurred vision? Vomiting? Nausea? Headaches or dizziness?"

"No."

"Ringing in the ears?"

"No."

"I would say a mild concussion… but, it's very difficult to be sure it's not more serious without X-rays… and you're going say that you don't have time for that. Am I right?"

"Yes… I'm afraid so."

"And, it's pointless telling you to take some rest?"

"Yes."

"The wrists are a mess. Ankles, likewise?"

"Yes."

"Let me cover these with a light bandage. Any other injuries? Any pain?

"Nothing I can't handle."

"Well, then, I think we're all done for today. Any of those symptoms, you call me. Understood?"

"Yes, thank you."

"Good. Well then, I'll be off."

"Dr Harvey, can I ask you an unrelated question?"

"Yes, of course."

"This is going to sound a bit weird…"

"Go on…"

"The pelvis... I'm involved in a case... or cases... where the victims have had their entire pelvis removed."

"Removed? How?"

"Cut out."

"That's very difficult... lots of ligaments. The ischiofemoral ligament is made up of a band of strong fibres that originate on the ischium just behind the acetabulum. These fibres blend with the fibres of the joint capsule of the hip. The acetabulum is a cup-shaped cavity in which the three parts of the coxal bone fuse. It's incredibly hard to remove."

"But, is it possible?"

"Possible, yes. But why would anyone do that? It's a lot of work."

"That's what I was going to ask you. Why? Can you think of any reason to do such a thing... I mean a non-psychological reason?"

He thought for a moment.

"The ilium is the largest and most superior of the three bones that join to form the hipbone, or os coxa. It's a wide, flat bone that provides many attachment points for muscles of the trunk and hip. You can find the crest of your ilium by placing your hands on your hips. The superficial location of the ilium makes it a common site for extracting bone tissue for grafting and bone marrow for transplants."

"Bone marrow? Transplants?"

"Yes, but...there is no need to remove the bone itself, just the marrow."

"And the extracted bone marrow can be used how?"

"To replace damaged bone marrow in leukaemia cases, for example. But, the marrow has to be a match between donor and patient."

"The same blood type?"

"No...it's not that simple. It's not my field, but...the best marrow transplant outcomes happen when a patient's human leukocyte antigen or HLA and the HLA of a registry member or cord blood unit closely match. This is much more complicated than matching blood types."

"I see. Thank you so much Dr Harvey."

Fisher and Baker retrieved their belongings, coats, hats and pistols, and left by the front door.

"Anything interesting?" asked Baker.

"Very possibly…I didn't tell her…a photo album of images of Eloise. Professional studio images, edging towards the vastly inappropriate for a girl of her age…seemingly alone with a man."

"A man?"

"Yes…why?"

"The name I have here is a woman."

"What?"

"*Maria Kutsnova: Photography.* I have the address…it's not far."

"Well, let's go and have a word with Maria and ask her what's she's doing taking pictures of young girls in their underwear."

The land rover's engine was barely warm when they turned into Rabfakovskiy and stopped at a rather grim looking building of four stories of grey brick.

"This is Block Thirteen." said Baker, "…unlucky for everyone that lives there! The Soviets certainly know how to build a *des res* don't they?"

"Yes, but poor architecture is not a skill exclusive to the Russians. It's not unlike a block of flats in Hulme in Manchester."

There was no security lock at the entrance to the apartment block, which, in any case, didn't close properly. The door, swollen with damp, caught on the floor. Fisher pushed it aside.

"What number?"

"4B"

"Yes, it would be, wouldn't it?"

They climbed the stairs to the fourth floor: 4B was opposite 4A

"Are you sure we've got the correct address?" said Fisher, "I can't see the daughter of the Consul-General, being allowed to come here."

"No …it doesn't add up."

Baker knocked on the door; and then again, louder.

The door of 4A opened a couple of inches on a security chain. A wrinkled, half face appeared:

"Moskva!" she said, "Moskva!"

"Damn it!" cried Fisher as the door closed. "We can ask Egorov to come here with his gorillas and search the place. But, I'm not hopeful they would find a banana in a green grocer's display."

"We still have some time to kill. What would you like to do?"

"Let's go and see my good friend Vasyli for a glass of tea. I can't call him, so, we'll take a chance on him being there. He has a new-fangled mobile phone from Finland. But nobody can call him, because he keeps the number to himself, and a few trusted friends, who have to swallow it, once memorised. I can't for the life of me, remember the damn thing! In any case, it's not secure….nothing is! But, at least I can remember where the apartment is…I think."

In a sea of uniform kommunalka akin to a concrete maze, it was easy to get lost. But Fisher recalled an enormous sign along the side of a factory just before the turn into the group of blocks where Vasyli lived:

Советский Союз освободит рабочих всего мира! Да здравствует славная революция!

"Ah! There it is...Long name for a company! They'll need to trim that down into something more snappy if they want to succeed in the West."

"It's a propaganda slogan," explained Baker. "All factories have them as a kind of advertising. This one probably says something about an increase in production and the success of the latest five-year economic plan...probably a bit dated now."

"Turn left here at the end. I wonder what they make in there? Tractors? It looks busy."

"It's a toy factory!"

"How do you know?"

"It's my business to know. They will be flat out, churning out dolls and cars and other things for kids to choke on, in celebration of the first Christmas for seventy years!"

"What! Turn right here, I think."

"Haven't you heard? As part of Yeltsin's ambitious plan to revive the traditions of *Old Russia*, the republic's legislature declared last month that Christmas, long ignored by the Bolsheviks, should be written back into the public calendar. He acknowledged, however, that this year's decision on Christmas came so late that there was little time to prepare, and there was still some confusion about how to celebrate it."

"Over here...down this way! What did they do before that?"

"New Year was Christmas. And so, with the twenty-fifth of December at the weekend..."

"It's Christmas next week! Christ! I need to go home!"

"Better get your skates on then! On the other hand, you're a dead giveaway in a Santa outfit with a face like that!"

The days had tumbled by and Fisher had hardly been counting. It was entirely unacceptable, that he might not get home for Christmas. It was a fundamental rule: *go where the hell you like on business, but be home for Christmas...or else!*

He might as well be dead.

There was an established pattern.

No deviation from the family tradition.

Jane still believed in Father Christmas. Well, so she said. She claimed that when she was a child, she heard the sleigh landing on the roof, and Santa's footsteps crunching on the frosted tiles.

"Pull over here! This is it."

The day began with Jane giving the boys a nice warm bath and a new set of pyjamas, whilst Fisher went downstairs, stopping by the plate on the hall table to drink a glass of scotch, eat a mince pie and nibble the end of a carrot. He hated the raw carrot, and left it, presuming Rudolph might be fed up with carrots. Candles, music, twinkling lights and a log fire, just about to catch with a few flames licking at the bark.

"Well? Are we going to sit here until Christmas, or are we going inside?" said Baker, getting out of the Defender.

Fisher pressed the security buzzer, and Lyudmila answered.

"Lyudmila, it's Stephen Fisher," he said, very slowly and clearly, "I have a friend Care…"

He didn't get to finish his long introduction before the buzzer and the click of the door opened into the lobby.

"Stephen…welcome here!" she said, excited, Vasyli is out something…"

The eager poodle was already mounting Fisher and thrusting his hips against his leg with his pink penis hanging out.

"Pasha is pleasured to see you! His cock is out!"

"Yes…I can see that…this is Carey."

"Yes, very scary… your face is a terrible mess!"

"No…this is Carey!" repeated Fisher, pointing at Baker. To no avail.

"Scary…it's a strange name. Come in. Pasha! Spuskat'sya! Get down! I'm also teaching him to speak English. Please…come…sit your arses down…I will make some tea."

"Vasyli has been teaching her English." explained Stephen, quietly.

Fisher was pinned on the sofa, with Pasha between his legs and his drooling chops firmly in Fisher's crotch. Baker had wandered over to the table, where some two dozen photographs were spread out. She raised her eyebrows to Fisher.

"Interesting!" she said.

"Ah..." called Lyudmila from the kitchen, "they are for my England port...portfolio. I need to choose the best ones, for when I work in UK."

"Are you English, Scary, or American?"

"English."

"You have pretty face...good body...you are model, Scary?"

"No...my name's Carey."

"Yes, I know...I said."

She came in with a small tray carrying three glasses of minted tea, in silver filigree holders, and a plate of three salted biscuits. Baker came to sit and Fisher started to explain why they were there:

"Lyudmila, please, listen carefully to what I have to say..."

"Yes."

"You must tell Vasyli that it is time to take a holiday." Fisher raised his eyebrows.

"Holiday? He is taking holiday?"

It was no use.

"Why is he taking holiday without me?"

"He's not taking a holiday without you."

"You just said he was going holiday."

"I think it's a surprise!"

"Yes, it is surprise."

"I wanted to make some suggestions about the places he should visit. Do you have some paper and a pen?"

"Yes...here...paper...pen."

Fisher wrote on the paper:

Vasyli, you must make your move now! There have been some developments. You MUST leave! Take a few things only, and go to Di Proletarskoy Diktatury Street in the Trentralny District to the place you know. Ask for Briggs. Tell him I sent you. Destroy this note now.

You should bring everything you need with you.

Stephen

Fisher folded the paper three times and handed it to Lyudmila.
"Now…it's a surprise…remember, …don't read it!"
"Yes."
"Just forget about it!"
Lyudmila looked confused.
"So, give it to Vasyli, just as *soon* as he comes in." Fisher emphasised.
"What?"
"The paper, the note I gave you!"
"What note?"
"The one there, on the table!"
She looked at it suspiciously.
"The one you told me to forget about?"
"Yes!"
"So… you want me to remember or forget? English is so difficult."
Fisher's main concern was that she didn't read it aloud. There was no way of knowing if anyone was listening. Paranoid though that may seem to be.

"Remember, yes! We should probably go… thank you for the tea, Lyudmila."

"Oh…before leaving…I need help with choosing photo. You as English man…and Scary as pretty girl. Come, I show."

Lyudmila took them to the table.

"Which one you like? This one, or this one?"

They were equally graphic and left little to the imagination.

Silence.

"You don't like?"

She could see Fisher's eyes were drawn away to another photograph on the far side of the table. He walked around and picked it up.

"You like that one! Boring face shot!"

"These were all taken by the same photographer? The one I met? When you were peeling an apple?"

"Yes…same."

Fisher's eyes were all over the table, picking up one photograph after another. The similarity to the Eloise portrait was quite striking; but, in itself, it was not enough. Many photographers might adopt such a style, reminiscent of Greta Garbo photographs: head to one side, keyhole lighting. But, then he noticed something.

"What is it Stephen?" asked Baker.

"Pass me those two over there!" he said, pointing a couple of apple peeling wide shots.

Fisher looked at them carefully, quite close.

"You like?" said Lyudmila, smiling coyly. "He likes!" she said to Baker, raising her well groomed eyebrows.

"I like." replied Fisher, not really thinking. He had noticed something he saw on the wider shots of Eloise, standing in her underwear. On the bottom left, there was a mark on the print. He thought it could have been something on the lens, or on the photographic paper.

"You can keep if you like…I have negative."

"Can I see the negative, please?"

It looked as if the background paper screen, in the shadow of the stool, had a small blemish just to the edge. These were cropped, possibly altered images. The negative, is the original; and Hasselblad negatives are large and clear.

"Here…this one…" said Lyudmila.

Fisher held it up to the light, squinting his one good eye; the other already half closed. And there it was…the same as before… a small tear in the paper backdrop, just where it curved upwards from the floor to the wall.

"The name of the photographer?"

"Anatoly."

"Anatoly…what?"

"Anatoly Morozov….I can give you card…here."

"Thank you, Lyudmila."

"So…which one you like?"

"This one." said Fisher.

Baker nodded in accord.

"Why?" asked Lyudmila.

"It's a nice apple." said Fisher. "Very nice… well peeled! All in one piece!"

"The English are a strange people!"

He was already walking towards the door, putting his coat back on, followed faithfully by Pasha, who was looking at him as if his pockets were full of biscuits, instead of a Browning pistol, a magazine and a box of cartridges.

"Oh…one more thing…this… Anatoly…he lives at this address?"

"Yes, mostly...but he spends lot of time in forest, taking pictures... that's why he likes my apple. He told me once, his friend have dacha there."

"Do you know where?"

"I don't know, sorry....to the north, I think...near lake, he said. He goes there, nearly every two day...no...he goes one day...but not next day, just for few weeks, then he stays in city to do work."

"He doesn't stay there? At the dacha?"

"Sometimes, I think...but mostly not. I really don't know...men... dacha... hunting, fishing... naked men sweating... who cares? They are all...how do you say...homo sapiens."

"Does he do other kinds of photography?"

"What you mean?"

"Does he work for anybody...? The police? MVD?"

"Police! Why would he work for police?"

"Will you be seeing him again?"

"No... kaput. We are finished here."

"Good."

Fisher kissed Lyudmila on each cheek.

"Now, remember to give Vasyli my suggestions...and look surprised when he tells you! Have a wonderful holiday!"

"Goodbye, Stephen... goodbye Scary!"

Once inside the rover, Fisher explained his discovery to Baker; and they set off.

"What now?" she said.

"Sadovaya Street. Let's go and see Egorov and get the other apartment searched. But, I'm not going to tell him about this just yet. I need to think carefully about how we proceed."

"Is she likely to be in his apartment? Or possible kept at the Kutsnova one?"

"No, I really don't think so. Too many risks…too noisy. The previous victims would have screamed until they lost consciousness. No… I think it has to be remote… the dacha. But, she said he shares it with a friend. It just doesn't make any sense."

"Why not? If they can help each other."

"The problem I have with the idea, is that men who are obsessed with minors, *and* are prepared to act on their obsessions, are usually loners. In one sense, their desires eat away at them, gnawing into their normal sensibilities. And, almost as soon as they are satisfied, they are overwhelmed by guilt. Until they get that feeling again, that pang, rising from within. But two men… or a man and a woman… Maria perhaps? But, let's say two men… acting in concert to satisfy the same urge? I just don't see it here.

Once the victim has been raped and abused… she is soiled. The other party will not want a soiled victim. Purity and innocence corrupted, is all part of the thrill. It's possible, I suppose, that one party, captures the victims and feeds them to the other. But why? What's in it for the first party? Who, after all, is taking most of the risks in the first place? Are we to suppose, that there is some monster waiting in a cage to be fed with virgins? I think not."

"They would have to have a very special bond, like that between a captor and a captive; a lion tamer and his lion."

"Interesting. But, captor-captive relationships are consciously and explicitly for the purpose of harming or hurting subjects. Power is used ruthlessly and inhumanely. Instead of raising the person's self-esteem and strengthening healthy defences, the aim is to break down, to weaken the will, and to make the captive totally subordinate to the captor."

"What if it was just about their own sexual gratification?"

"You mean with each other… two homosexual or bisexual men?"

"Yes."

"Unlikely, but possible. But why the interest in young girls? There is one case, I can recall, involving two men acting in concert. On October 31st 1979, sixteen year-old Shirley Lynette Ledford accepted a lift home from two men outside a petrol station in the suburbs of Los Angeles. Forty-eight hours later, after being bound with construction tape, repeatedly raped, and enduring sexual torture with pliers and a... sledgehammer, she was found dumped on a random lawn."

"Really?"

"Yes. Ledford was the final victim of Lawrence Sigmund Bittaker and Roy Lewis Norris, the serial killers nicknamed the *Tool Box Killers* due to their habit of sexually torturing victims with equipment they picked up from a DIY store. The men murdered five teenage girls over a five-month period in Southern California. Bittaker, first met Norris in 1977 when both men were in prison. The two struck up a friendship, and shared fantasies of sexual violence, including their fantasy of murdering one girl of each teenage year from thirteen through to nineteen after they got out of prison. Ten years ago they were convicted of committing five horrendous murders together and recording the agony of their victims."

"How do you deal with all this, Stephen?"

"It's what I do. But two men? A man and a woman? A couple doesn't make sense in this context, over this length of time, given the nature of the crimes. No, this has to be a rogue beast, a predator...an outsider."

"You didn't really answer my question."

"No, I didn't did I?"

"Is that because you don't deal with it? Or, is it just that you don't want to talk about it?"

Fisher paused for a moment.

"I suppose it's both. You have to deal with it in order to stay focussed. But, that doesn't mean you shut it away and don't want to talk about it. A certain degree of emotion is vital, otherwise you rely purely on logic; and sometimes that's not enough. Instincts play a part, as does some empathy with the victim or the victim's parents. I'd go as far as to say, that in some cases, empathy with the killer can lead to a breakthrough, no matter how shocking or unpalatable that might be."

"And, in this case?"

"It's complicated. Logic dictates that there is a pattern in the photography of the victims. And yet, my instincts tell me it's a red herring. The removal of hip bones from the victims, probably whilst still alive and conscious, seems illogical, repulsive and a pointless mutilation. And so, I ask why? And yet, it's easy to become sickened and angry about it. Too much anger will get in the way; just enough will motivate. All my experience; all my logic, tells me that this girl is already dead. But, I refuse to accept that. Until I find her; and see for myself, I will not believe she is dead. I don't know why I feel that way; but I do."

16

VAST

Red.

Blue.

Under a blood red sky.

It looked as if it might snow or sleet overnight; a warm wet front was rolling in from the South.

It is a myth, universally misconstrued, that Eskimos have more words for snow than any other people. Actually, it's only forty-nine. The winner by a clothier's yard is Scotland, with four hundred and twenty-one. The words are all sorts of things to do with snow; the way that snow moves, the types of snow, types of snowflake, types of thaw, clothing you might wear in snow, the way that snow affects animals; they even have a category for snow and the supernatural. *Feefie*, was one of Fisher's favourites from his grandmother: snow swirling round a corner; and a *Fildrinkin*, was another, meaning a light shower. But in Russia, there is only one word for snow: *fuck!*

Despite its dishevelled facades, and dire circumstances, Fisher thought St Petersburg to be a beautiful city. It was rather like looking at an aged film star: crinkled and cracked on the surface, but the beauty is still there. That is, as far as the original buildings are concerned. The more modern soviet additions, were far from that. They are an acquired taste. They contain a fearful symmetry. Not so much an Elizabeth Taylor; but more of a Boris Karloff.

Fisher always imagined that soviet ministries would be exactly as Orwell might have created them in the novel, *1984*.

But, most of the topography in *1984* turns out to be relatively straightforward and mostly what the author saw from a bus window on his way to work. The Ministry of Truth, where Winston Smith sits falsifying back-numbers of *The Times*, is the University of London's Senate House building in Malet Street. Big Brother's statue in Trafalgar Square, rechristened *Victory Square*, adorns the plinth previously reserved for Nelson, while the waxworks museum on the square's eastern side, where visitors queue to inspect tableaux of military atrocities, is the Church of St Martin-in-the-Fields put to sinister propagandist use.

And so it is the same here. The most terrifying ministry, could be housed in a primrose yellow, neo-classical building, of perfect proportions, belying the function within.

However, the MVD building was an intimidating edifice, an altar to soviet dullness and a maze for the uninitiated. Notwithstanding the confusion, Fisher and Baker eventually found their way to the Office of the Chief Investigator. It was a large room, with three rows of desks, all facing the same way; perhaps fifty or so. The air was heavy and pungent with cigarette smoke, which rose in discarded clouds towards a high arched ceiling, catching the orange glow of the setting sun, in, almost, horizontal beams of incandescent shapes. Each one fell, as if discarded, on the opposite wall, like a window in repose.

At the far end, a glass panelled wall concealed an office beyond, hiding behind broken and bent Venetian blinds. The whole place had a grubbiness about it, and a stale smell: the smell of men, steeped in Russian nicotine and stale vodka.

No doubt, Egorov was in there, somewhere, waiting to gloat at the state of Fisher's face. The rat-a-tat-tat ding of multiple typewriters, punctuated by the occasional phone bell, made it look like a scene from *1984*; in the Ministry of Truth; and it sounded like a room under siege. Perhaps it was, in a way? The Apple computer had launched in 1984.

The cold wind of change was coming, thought Fisher. Ten years from now, this room might house a large computer from IMB, and not much else.

The heat was stifling, from the large pipes running along the walls, down by the floor. As Fisher's eye followed the pipes, he caught sight of the tall thin man from the Dollar Bar, striding his way.

"Dr Fisher and Miss Baker, welcome. Follow me, please."

Of course, it was no longer a surprise that they already knew the name of someone they had not been introduced to.

"The Chief Investigator is keen to hear all about your progress in recent days. He will see you now."

The thin, still nameless, ferret, opened the door for them with disarming valour.

Egorov was squatting behind his desk, lit only by a desk lamp which created a pool of light, through which smoke was swirling. Somewhere, under his fat backside, a chair was trying to escape. There was a photograph in a silver frame, facing, oddly, outwards, towards the visitor. It was a photo of a slimmer version of himself as a toad, shaking hands with another slimy amphibian, Richard Nixon, when he visited Leningrad in 1972.

"Comrade Fisher..." mumbled Egorov, scraping the phlegm from the back of his throat and swallowing again.

"The Chief investigator invites you both to sit."

"Vodka?" Egorov continued.

"He would like you to share an aperitif with him."

"No thank you, it's a little early." said Fisher.

"The Chief Investigator would like you to share an aperitif with him!"

Egorov mumbled something in Russian.

"A man who is tired of vodka, is tired of life…he says."

Three shot glasses of vodka were poured.

"You're not having one?" said Fisher to the thin ferret.

"I'm tired of life."

The three glasses clinked.

"Here's to your face!" …said the Chief, via his minder. "He says it looks like the arse of a baboon bitch in heat!"

"Please thank the Chief Investigator for his good wishes."

Egorov laughed and poured himself another *Stolichnaya*.

"He understands that your injuries may be connected to falling out of a helicopter?"

Fisher smiled, and finished his drink.

"My injuries," tell the Chief, "were the unfortunate consequence of head-butting a very thick rubber pipe. The pipe came off worst!"

Egorov laughed again.

"The Chief Investigator wonders if you are accompanied by such a pretty woman in order to distract him from how ugly you are!"

"The Chief Investigator is entirely correct. A lesson I learned from him."

"What can we do for you, Dr Fisher?"

"I would like to return this excellent file, you kindly let me borrow."

Fisher leaned forward to place the file on the desk.

"Did it help?" translated the ferret.

"Possibly. I have a question about the photographs."

"What about the photographs?"

"Did an MVD officer take the them?"

"No. We hire photographers."

"Were these photographs taken by the same photographer?"

Egorov shrugged his shoulders.

"The Chief Investigator has no idea. He wants to know why you are asking," relayed the ferret.

"There is a similarity in the style of the photographs."

Egorov issued some instruction to the tall man. He receded into the shadows and opened a filing cabinet. Moments later, he returned with a sheet of paper.

"Here is a list of the photographers we used in each case."

"Could you read me the names please?"

The thin man proceeded to read the Russian script one name at a time. Whilst the same name appeared twice, all the others were different; and none of them were Anatoly Morozov, Lyudmilla's photographer or Maria Kutsnova, the photographer seemingly used by the consulate.

Fisher was confused. How could he get this so wrong? How could the museum photographer get this so wrong? Fisher felt a sickness in the pit of his stomach.

"The Chief Investigator would like to know if there is anything else, he can assist with?"

"There is a property I think we should search."

"What are we searching for?"

"I believe the British girl may have been there?"

"Where is the property?"

"Well, it belongs to a Maria Kutsnova, a photographer; we need to search the premises most carefully...a neighbour said that she had gone to Moscow."

"Where is the property?"

Baker handed him the paper with the address from this morning, written on it.

Egorov stood up, his tarnished shirt hanging out at the front, and slouched over to his coat and hat on a stand by the door, whilst the thin man stepped into the larger room and blew a whistle, followed by instructions. Eight or nine men left their desks and rushed out.

"You will follow." The thin weasel ordered.

"But…"

It was too late… they were on their way.

Baker trailed the line of black cars, illuminated by blue flashing lights and sirens: the perfect way to advertise you were on your way to search a property! Being that there was nobody there, it probably didn't matter.

The car doors opened and the keystone cops rushed up the stairs.

By the time Fisher and Baker entered the building, there was no point in joining the rush. Egorov was in any case, blocking the stairs, as he took one step at a time, wheezing and puffing, as he went.

The door was already in several pieces, one piece hanging precariously from a hinge.

Egorov waved his hand at the thin man, and everybody else left.

A narrow passage, or hall, invited the visitor into two main rooms: an empty bedroom on the right; and a larger room…one might say…a lounge on the left. There was no furniture to signify function. The 1950s wallpaper was peeling away from the dank corners and the wooden floor had a few rotten boards, here and there. The air was pervaded by a damp, sweet smell. Moulds give a musty, earthy odour. It smells similar to the smell experienced while walking through a dense forest. Mould odour is quite unpleasant like that of rotten wood or paper. Some feel the smell of mould similar to that of cedar while some compare it to the smell of wet socks. For Fisher, it was the latter.

The so-called lounge presented a stack of boxes, containing *Johnnie Walker Red Label Blended Scotch Whisky*: a centenary blend from the year before. Two rolled Persian rugs and a box of Cadbury's *Fruit and Nut* chocolate bars.

"Nothing in here, then." said the thin man.

"But…" started Fisher.

"This room is empty Dr Fisher," he insisted.

The bedroom was more interesting, in any case.

Baker flicked the light switch. It failed to light.

Fisher noticed two pieces of sticky tape up near the ceiling in each corner of the windowless wall. A third had been in the middle at the same height; and left a mark there. There was an old bentwood café style chair in the middle of the room. The backrest had become detached from the main frame and the raffia seat was torn.

Each of the two windows were covered in a bedsheet, stapled to the wooden frame, and given the time of day, the room was barely lit at all.

"Over here!" cried Baker.

A small, black plastic bag, the sort that might have contained photographic paper, had been pushed into the corner.

Fisher opened it very carefully.

It contained a ball of light blonde hair.

"I'll take that!" said the thin man, snatching.

"Will you be sweeping this place for fingerprints?" asked Fisher, hopefully.

"What for?" replied the man.

"To see if we can identify who has been in here. This is a crime scene!"

"Possibly it is, yes…" he replied, somewhat languorously.

"So, shouldn't we…?"

"There's little point, Dr Fisher," he explained, "there are one hundred and forty-four point one million people in Russia. Assuming most of them have ten fingers…there may be a few missing…that's over a billion fingers. How are we to find a handful of pertinent fingers that might have been in this apartment, surrounded as they will be by prints of no interest whatsoever."

"Isn't there a national database of fingerprints?"

"It's an interesting idea! There is nothing in this room, Dr Fisher. Just a bag of useless old hair."

Fisher snapped, grabbing the man by his coat lapels.

"You fucking shit! You're all useless, fucking turds! That's not a bag of old hair! That's *all* that might be left of a beautiful young girl. Are *you* going to give it to her mother? And tell her, useless old hair? Of course not, you fucking coward!"

Baker was trying to restrain Fisher. Not least because the man who's coat he was spoiling and was calling a turd, was twice his size; and, let's face it, Fisher didn't need beating up more than once in twenty-four hours.

"What exactly is a *fucking* turd?" The ferret said, calmly, brushing the creases from his coat. "I know what a turd is and I know what fucking is…but a *fucking* turd?"

"Scotch?" said Egorov, filling the doorway with a bottle in his hand.

"Go fuck yourself, Egorov!" said Fisher. "Sideways, with a stiff wire brush!"

The thin man moved to translate, then thought better of it.

Fisher pushed both of them out of his way and stormed out. Baker followed in his wake.

They sat in the car for a moment, in silence.

Baker was afraid to speak, but relented:

"Just to be clear," she said, "it was *sideways with a stiff wire brush*? That *is* what you said to the Chief Investigator of the MVD?"

Fisher almost smiled, but it hurt too much.

"I know..." she said, "I know. But, we've had a good day. We're getting closer. We have to believe that we're not wasting our time. Where to next?"

"Back to base...we need to speak to Briggs. We need to handle this ourselves from here on in!"

It was unusual for Fisher to lose his temper like that. He was the one that hunted people with lost tempers. But, he was also losing patience. From what had been said; and from the file Egorov had given him, Fisher knew that the time was almost up. In a few days, the pattern of previous killings would hit the mid-point average of bodies turning up. Meaning, that the killer had decided to discard his current victim and to move on to another.

It was hard to be sure, since a body might lay undiscovered, for days....weeks even, like the one under the ice. That poor nameless girl.

But, roughly, some bodies had turned up sooner than this point in the cycle, by only a few days; and, some later. How much more time did Eloise have left, in the circadian rhythm of serial killings? And what about this hip bone issue? Fisher was no closer to understanding that. Was it fuelling a macabre collection of trophies? Or, providing bone marrow, that fatty jelly substance, to aid someone with cancer? The donor and the subject had to be a close genetic match. True... the girls looked similar, but that's not a genetic match. Even if Fisher could gather all the blood types of the victims, which seemed impossible in this context, what would he gain from doing so? A motive, yes, perhaps. But the shaved heads? And the fact that it appeared the bones were removed without anaesthetic. If the motive was medical, then why torture the victims? It's possible that the missing bones conceal the procedure; the fact that marrow has been removed. It just doesn't make any sense.

"Where's Commander Briggs?" said Baker, whilst she was being frisked.

"In the Comms Room, I fink." replied the security guard.

"Follow me, Stephen." Baker said, leading the way through the back of the building, and down a narrow staircase to the basement. Baker swiped a card, and opened the door. Briggs was sitting at a small desk, his heavy head in his hand, the sling removed, writing with the other. He was surrounded by screens, reel-to-reel tape recorders and all sorts of electronics Fisher had never seen before.

"What the fuck happened to your face?"

"A run-in with Volkov. He knew where we'd been."

"So…why did he need to beat it out of you?"

"He didn't. I just think he wanted to beat someone."

"So, if there's is a splinter group, he eithers knows about it; or is part of it."

"That's not our immediate concern. It's probably a red herring. We need to talk to you, Pat." said Fisher, earnestly. "About something really important."

"Well, I hope it's good news, because I could do with a bit of cheer. I've just spent the last four hours writing letters to next of kin: to fathers, mothers, wives and siblings. It never gets any easier. Every one of these lads had a life, a family…and in most cases, kids. The Service doesn't allow me to explain the circumstances, or the reasons why their son or husband or father has died. So, you end up with vague generalisations about courage and country. And some of them, I hardly knew; they were Mac's men. But, he's not here to write about them. This fucking business! I hate it!"

They didn't know what to say.

"Enough!" Briggs snapped out of it. "What's going on? What have you uncovered? How do we get this girl home?"

"We have a good lead and a suspect: it's a fucking photographer! I think it was him at the night market, as well. Worse…I have actually met him! He takes nude pictures of Kulnikov's wife!"

"No shit!"

"We searched the apartment of a Maria Kutsnova. She was supposedly the person that took the photographs of Eloise. But, either she wasn't really involved…just a cover… or, she doesn't exist. There was some evidence that photographs had been taken there; and a bag containing hair."

"Hair?"

"Yes, the victims have all had their heads shaved."

"What the fuck for?"

"We don't know."

"Was it…?"

"We don't know who's hair it was… In any case, the MVD kept the bag."

"Any blood? Signs of a struggle?"

"No… nothing."

"So, where do we go from here?" asked Briggs, assertively.

"We have a live address for the photographer, not far from here…a ten minute walk, in fact…his studio and apartment. But, we know Eloise isn't there."

"How do we know?"

"I've been there, with Kulnikov. It's a small place…two, three small rooms. There's nowhere there, he could have hidden her."

"Should we get the militia to pull him in?" asked Briggs.

"Those clowns! No!"

"They'll beat it out of him, for sure."

"Or, beat him to death! All the while, she may be out there, somewhere, starving to death."

"We could pull him in here? Extract him to a neutral country…"

"Same difference. He may never talk. He may enjoy being tortured! Who knows?"

"So, what are you thinking?"

"My source…someone that knows him in a professional context, said that he often goes to a dacha, owned by a friend…sometimes, three or four times a week."

"So, you're thinking…she may be there?"

"Yes…he could be going to feed…or… do god knows what to her? But we don't know the location of the dacha."

"We have to follow him." added Baker.

"Where is he now?" asked Briggs.

"We don't know…and, I'm obviously not going to knock on his door!"

"Well, we need to have eyes on the apartment twenty-four-seven. That way we can track him coming or going. We've got a few walkie-talkies, but, they're not secure…limited range…and, they can easily be traced. So, we need to be aware of that. The problem I can see, is that, for reasons all too obvious, we are short staffed in security. I could stretch things here and release two guys to keep an eye on things over there. But they will need to be on standby to get back here, should some unexpected shit go down. Unlikely, but in this context, anything's possible. Between the three of us, we'll have to make up the surveillance shortfall."

"Are you well enough, Briggs?" said Fisher.

"What? Sitting in a freezing car watching an apartment? I think I can handle that. If he does move, we'll need to be ready to follow."

"When can we start?"

"Right now!"

"Great."

"Give me the address and a description of the target."

Fisher handed over the business card.

"Anatoly Morozov. We'll start a search on him, but I suspect he will be grey."

"Grey?"

"No profile."

"So…he's in his late thirties, maybe forty. Dark hair and full eyebrows. Handsome, some might say. Physically fit, I would say. Possibly recent ex-army. Well-dressed …western clothes. He has a small brown mole on his…right cheek, I think. Oh, and I noticed a tiny nick on the top of his left ear. Might be a scar…might be natural? That's about it."

"That's a great start. Is he your typical profile for this kind of thing?"

"No… not at all, but, I have been surprised before. The capacity for one human to perpetrate horrors on others, never ceases to shock and amaze and surprise."

"Hold that thought." said Briggs. He picked up a telephone. "Briggs here…. can you find Brian and get yourselves down to Comms for a briefing? Good, asap please." He return the phone to the receiver and turned back to Fisher, "I need to understand a bit more about this guy…his motivations…what makes him tick… that way, we can nail him. And, I *will* nail that bastard!"

"Well, as I hinted earlier, he has capacity to intentionally harm another person, with a high degree of emotional detachment. Firstly, this man will have a history of that, long before he came to be a serial killer. Second, the perpetrators of such are typically portrayed as enjoying the harm they inflict. Even the Devil is sometimes depicted as a trickster who takes sporting pleasure in bringing misfortune on his hapless victims. The link to reality is tenuous here, but…"

"So, we are dealing with a sadist?"

"Not necessarily. Victim accounts, in my experience, often emphasise that the perpetrators were laughing or smiling, or that in some other way they derived pleasure from what they did. Perpetrators' accounts are far, far less likely to indicate enjoyment. The victims' insistence on perpetrator enjoyment may be to some extent an assimilation of perception to the myth. To perceive the perpetrators as someone who reluctantly and with anguished inner struggles inflicted harm is to make them seem less…evil, in comparison to perpetrators who cheerfully go about their actions and derive pleasure from them."

"So, will he be a miserable bugger? Or a smiling sadistic megalomaniac?"

"He is more likely to be just like the rest of us. We all have the capacity to do harm to others. But, he may appear cold, distant, even. But, the point here is, that there will be nothing obvious; nothing you can point to, and say: *he's a serial killer!* Otherwise, these deviants would be easy to spot; but, they're not. Some go about their ordinary lives, unnoticed and undetected for many years. In this case, we have the added complexity of a collector."

"A collector? You mean, like… stamps?"

"Yes….well, not exactly. Whatever someone collects: stamps, precious stones, coins, shoes, thimbles, watches, photographs of young girls… hip bones. Ordinarily, it's a hobby, teetering on the edge of psychological disorder. Leaving aside what you collect. It helps in the development of normal positive skills and attitudes. Such as: perseverance, order, patience and memory. But, in a few it gets out of control."

"Obsessive?"

"Yes, in some it can result in hoarding. But, the collector, is characterised by perfectionism, meticulousness. He or she is likely to have low self-esteem, poor social skills, and a difficulty in facing up to challenges. When he feels intense personal inefficiency, compulsive collecting will make him feel better.

"Is he likely to be violent, dangerous when confronted?"

"Oh yes...extremely defensive and dangerous... willing to sacrifice himself to protect his collection. If Eloise is still alive, he will defend his power over her. He may even love her."

"Love her!" cried Baker, incredulously.

"What? Really?" added Briggs.

"It's not uncommon. In some documented cases, the captors, abductors, aggressors tend to develop positive feelings towards their hostages, very often letting them free."

"Your world and my world," pondered Briggs, "are not in the same universe! I just don't get that. He's a sick fuck!"

"The final act to execute the victim, might be the result of a perceived or real rejection of the perpetrator. To those of us who have studied these killers, it is wearyingly disappointing to see a stereotypical killer in one film or television show after another, depicted as relentlessly confident and optimistic. In reality, they certainly have high self-esteem. Even when embarking on very risky ventures, they remain convinced of their superiority and of their chances of success. Meanwhile, their lack of self-control is most commonly evident in their proneness to sudden rage and violence. Our man, may even be expecting trouble; he may have made preparations on the assumption that sooner or later, someone will find him."

"So, you think he might be sensitive to being followed?" asked Baker.

"Possibly. He may have already put plans in place to cover his tracks. And, there is on other thing to think about."

"What's that?" asked Briggs, suspiciously.

"It's quite rare...and the jury is still out on this... But, it's possible that he is suffering from *Dissociative Identity Disorder.*"

"What's that?" asked Baker.

"Well… he may not be aware that he is doing any of this."

"How's that?" queried Briggs in disbelief. "How can he not know?"

"Some psychologists think that serial killers have multiple identities or personalities. The idea is that they develop another persona in order to deal with the trauma of what they are doing. And so, they go about their ordinary day-to-day lives unaware of what their *other* self is doing."

"So, if confronted, he might seem confused and genuinely alarmed about why he is being followed, or challenged. In which case, he will be more cooperative and compliant if we handle him carefully."

There was a knock at the door.

"That'll be my guys. You'll be at the Moskva, if I need to get hold of you?"

"Well, no, I left the hotel on the basis that it posed a health risk."

"Ah.. yes…so…?"

"I'm staying with Carey."

Briggs looked at Baker.

"It's not what you think?" she said.

"Did I say I was thinking anything? None of my business. Except, that as Head of Security, I might be concerned that a relationship might impact on performance of duty."

"Relationship?" said Fisher, irritated by the suggestion.

"There's nothing going on, Commander," asserted Baker.

"Nor will there be!" added Fisher.

"I acted out of concern for Stephen's safety, Commander… not out of self-interest."

"Ok, ok… I get it!"

There was an awkward silence.

"I get it, I said!"

There was an insistent knock from outside.

"Come in!" Briggs called to the door.

"Let's get your bag," Baker said, as they left the Comms Room. "We can walk to the apartment...it's just around the corner. It's no palace... and I haven't tidied up... and..."

"It'll be fine...believe me."

"Shower...food...sleep."

"All, three please. Sounds wonderful!"

"And, you're on the two-seat sofa! It's leather... which means that you'll probably slide off and end up on the floor!"

"I don't care...I'll sleep on a window ledge if I have to."

17

Eternity

Deep.

Dark.

Satisfying sleep.

Until the phone rang at eight in the morning, pulling him from his sleepy bower.

"Yes…" said Fisher.

"Briggs. Our friend returned to his apartment last night around six. Interesting…he was on foot. No movement since then. Brian is on his way over there now, to take over."

"Good, thanks. We'll be over as soon as we can."

"Oh, and some French people are turning up here in about half an hour. Something you know about, apparently."

"Yes…all good. Should be there by then. Any other movement, let me know right away, please."

"Of course. How's Baker?"

"I don't know, she's not up yet."

"You better not hurt that girl."

"Firstly, she's not a *girl*. And, secondly, I have no intention of *hurting* her. She's not anybody's property… and she is quite capable of looking after herself!"

"All I'm saying…"

"I know what you're saying. Why aren't you having this conversation with her? Why aren't you telling her… *you better not hurt that boy?*"

"Right…yes! I'm just saying… you understand?"

"Fully. But there's no need for you to worry about either of us. Everything is fine. We all have bigger things to be concerned about."

"Yes…see you soon."

Fisher considered himself in the bathroom mirror.

It was something he did less and less these days. Occasionally, he caught a glimpse of his father in a mirror or a shop window. But, it was only Fisher himself, growing to look like his father. A man now frozen in time; his age and image set by death… unchangeable. To Fisher, his father would always be the age he was; and in time, Fisher might exceed that age. Then, who would he look like in the mirror? A man that never lived that long; and a man that never existed? It was an odd thought.

Right now, he didn't look like anybody in particular; he looked like shit! Although, his face was much less distorted, and had settled into a myriad of hues of blue and brown, like a Dulux swatch card. Particularly around his left eye. But, at least he was able to shave without too much discomfort.

Emerging from his steamy cocoon, he could see Baker was already in the kitchen area…. wearing a long white shirt.

"Scrambled eggs?"

"Yes, please! Where do you get the eggs from?"

"Cornwall, I believe. For the last few months food has been flown in. Tempting to sell it on the black market. A fresh egg can fetch Fabergé prices. In fact, thinking about it, I can claim food for you as well."

"Glad to be of service. Did you sleep well?"

"I think I woke up in exactly the position I fell asleep in. How about you? Sleep ok?"

"Yes, the face is a bit sore on both sides, still; but, I managed to get off, and then…I don't remember a thing."

They sat down at a small table. Of course, it was still pitch dark outside, but in the light from the window shining out, Fisher could see snowflakes falling, like goose down, floating from some great pillow fight in the sky.

"You have no idea how good these eggs taste...and the coffee."

"It's just instant."

"I don't care...it's just that I feel almost normal again."

"That's good. You look less like Quasimodo this morning!"

"*Less like*...? That's encouraging. Oh! We have a meeting...French couple. You just reminded me... at nine."

"What? Why didn't you say? Nine! I need a shower...back in a minute."

Soon enough it was Fisher's turn; and then they wrapped up for the short walk to the consulate.

Fisher felt remarkably refreshed, even with a sore face. The cold air was making it tingle, as they walked across the road towards the Consulate. The snow had abated.

"Does it feel warmer? Or is it my imagination?" asked Fisher.

"Yes, the snow always take the chill out of the air. Odd that. But, in any event, there is a warm front moving in over the next few days. Coming up from the south."

"How you know?"

"It's my business to know. It will only last a few days. People will be complaining like hell!"

"Complaining?"

"They hate warm winters. Countless Russians every year mark religious feasts by plunging into water through holes in the ice and shivering vigorously in the frigid air. Bonkers! If it's too warm or the ice is too thin, they moan about it."

"There's a lot more than that, to moan about around here!"

301

"Have you been able to phone home?"

"No."

"An ordinary line requires an advanced booking twelve hours ahead for an international call. But, Briggs can let you use the secure line."

"I don't think I should. What would I say? I'd end up lying, and I don't want to do that. If I tell the truth, not only would I be flouting the Official Secrets Act, but it would just cause anxiety and upset. Jane isn't expecting me to call. So, If I do, she will know something is wrong."

The eager young man in the lobby doing the frisking was getting to know Fisher quite intimately. Jennifer was on hand to supervise.

Baker had her own special frisky female, for a change.

"They've just arrived, said Jennifer. "I have put them in the reception room. Obviously, given the age of their daughter, Cami, they will be present throughout. Did you want me there?"

"If it's going to upset you, no."

"Then, I won't if you don't mind. Carey will be with you?"

"Yes."

"Good, I'll just come in to introduce you then, shall I?"

"That would be nice."

"Your face is looking… a lot better…but I might explain it with a white lie, if that's alright?" she said, opening the door to the reception room.

"Of course."

They were sitting on the sofa, with the girl between them. All had a dusky southern French look, and the girl looked older than Fisher was expecting. Pretty, with long black hair tied at the back. All three were staring at Fisher's multi-coloured face.

"This is Monsieur and Madame Tricou, and their beautiful daughter, Cami."

"How do you do?" said Fisher, holding out his hand.

"Dr Fisher and Miss Baker…" Jennifer continued, with a gesture.

"C'est un plaisir de vous rencontrer. Merci d'être venus si rapidement." said Baker.

Fisher looked at her as if she had a pineapple on her head.

"Nous sommes là pour vous aider, si nous le pouvons. Cami est profondément attristée par la disparition d'Eloise" replied Monsieur Tricou. "S'il vous plaît ... appelez-nous Albert et Adelene."

"Carey et Stephen," she replied.

Fisher was beginning to feel like a spare cake at a wedding.

"I should explain that Dr Fisher had an unfortunate car accident a few days ago. Not surprising really, given the state of the roads these days. I'll leave you to it, then," said Jennifer, as she left the room.

"Please sit down," said Fisher. "This won't take very long; and I know that school is waiting. I guess there must be lots of things going on, leading up to Christmas?"

They both nodded; the girl looked totally disinterested. Clearly, the platitudes were not going to make them feel at ease. Baker stepped in:

"I will speak in English if that's ok?"

"Of course" replied Madame Tricou. "Please continue."

"Cami," said Baker, "We want to ask you a few questions about Eloise?"

"Her name's not Eloise. Only her parents call her that. She hates it! Her name is Elle. And while we are on the subject of names, she will know me as Cam. Everybody does. Only *they* use Cami. My parents named me after a pair of knickers!"

"Cami, ne soyez pas si grossier! Vous n'avez jamais dit quelque chose comme ça avant. Votre nom est court pour Camilla, qui était la femme de guerre guerrière," said Madame Tricou. She was clearly upset.

"It's ok… Cam… How much time did you and Elle spend together?" asked Fisher.

"As much time as we could… every day, every weekend. When your parents are professional nomads, moving around every five minutes, you can get a bit defensive about friendship."

"How so?"

"Well, because we get moved every few years. At first, when you arrive somewhere new… another new school… you don't know anyone…so, you sort of hang back. It was different with Elle. She and I arrived on the same day…we became instant best friends."

"And you are a little older than Elle?"

"Yes…two years…so?"

"So, you would know about her interest in Kate Moss?"

"Interest? She is crazy about Kate! We both are! The other girls make fun of us… shouting: *kiss me kate*! And some other stuff I can't repeat. We are going into the fashion industry together; that's our dream. I design the clothes and she models them."

"Did you know that she had some photographs taken recently?"

"Yes."

Fisher detected some eye movement: upward and to the right. The pupils were dilated, indicating, in this context, arousal, or at the very least, approval. He continued:

"Did she show them to you?"

"Yes. Why wouldn't sh?"

"Did she show you all of the photographs, Cam?"

The girl shrugged her shoulders. Then:

"Yes… why wouldn't she?"

"Did you have your photograph taken, as well?"

"No!"

That was the truth.

"Did you go with her to have her photograph taken?

"No."

That was a lie.

"What did you think of the photographs?"

"I thought they were beautiful."

"And the woman taking the pictures? Did Elle comment on her? Maria?"

"Maria? Who's Maria? His name was Toni."

"Anatoly?"

"He preferred, Toni."

"Did you meet this, Toni?"

"What if I did?"

"Cessez les questions, cela suffit!" said Madame Tricou, angrily.

"Have you any idea where she might have gone?"

Cami shrugged.

"Did she have a boyfriend? Or someone she might have gone away with?"

"She would have told me if she had."

"And, obviously, you haven't heard from her?"

"Obviously!"

"Did you two part on good terms?"

"What does that mean?"

"Did you have an argument, or, fall out about something?"

"You'll never find her."

"Why do you say that?"

"Because she's gone...she's said nothing...she must be dead!"

"Whatever!" retorted Cam.

This was obviously Cam's final word on the subject; on any subject, in fact.

Fisher thanked them for their patience and support. Neither of which it seemed they had displayed. But, he had garnered all that he felt he could, in the circumstances. If he pushed any further her parents might demand to see the photographs to see what all the fuss was about. Cam was still a minor, and as such, interviewing her, on, technically, British soil, he was bound by English Law. Meaning: that he could not interview a minor without parental consent and the parents or guardians being present, even though Fisher wasn't acting in an official capacity. Nevertheless, was there any more to be gleaned? Probably not, given all that they now know about the photographer.

As they walked out the door, Cam turned and said:

"Find her, and tell her that I love her!" her brown eyes were glassy and dark.

Madam Tricou pulled her by the elbow, as the door closed behind them.

"Wow!" said Baker. "According to her mother she's not named after a pair of loose French knickers, but, a swiftly running amazon warrior! She's got some balls!"

"Indeed!" agreed Fisher, puffing air through his lips. "Frozen balls!"

"Did we gain anything from that?"

"You realise she was lying?"

"Was she?"

"Yes. She went with Eloise to the photo shoot…. and she had seen *all* the photographs."

"Really? How do you know?"

"It's my business to know."

The door opened, and Briggs came in, holding a Nokia mobile phone to his ear, exactly the same model as Vasyli's:

"He's on the move! And is heading in this direction!" he said, listening to the phone.

Fisher moved to stand up.

Briggs gestured for him to stay put.

"He's gone into the Metro Station at Proletarskoy! Great! Keep on to him! We might lose signal…Brian? Fuck! I've lost him…still…it's better than an old radio com."

"Yes" said Fisher, "I've see one before. Where did you get it from?"

"Where else? The black market!" he said. "I have a couple for you two at reception. Here are all the numbers you need. The cellular network only operates in the city and some outer suburbs. But, remember, they are analogue radio transmitters, they are *not* secure."

Briggs handed over two small cards with the typed numbers and names of the four mobile phones.

"What now?" asked Baker.

"We wait. The phone won't work underground. So, at some point… at station, Brian will come up."

They waited.

Finally, Briggs broke the silence:

"How did you get on with Little Miss Tricou?"

"Like a house already burnt down!" said Fisher.

Briggs laughed, "Yes…she's a one! She virtually accused the search officer of being a lesbian! Fourteen going on thirty!"

Silence.

"What will we do when Brian calls?" asked Baker.

"Listen. Brian is solid. He will know what to do. But once he tells us where he is, we should get there asap."

"Should we be making at start?" Fisher was anxious.

"We don't know where he might come out. The line crosses a major interchange at Nevsky Prospekt, so, it's anyone's guess. But, if it's north it could be the end of one of two lines: the uncompleted section of the M2 or the Devyaktino Station, at the end of the completed line. Although, he may routinely cover his tracks by changing line, twice or more. You said, he might be prepared to be discovered."

It was agonising to wait for the phone to ring.

"I'll get our phones" said Baker, walking out to reception. She returned almost immediately and started to unpack the phones.

"They'll need charging!" warned Briggs.

"Alright, let's get to it" she said, plugging them in and picking up the instructions…. Nokia P4000. They're in Finnish!"

"Yes, but it's not rocket science" said Briggs. "Talk-time they say is roughly five hours."

"Wow! That's incredible! And it's so light."

There wasn't much else to talk about; and so they talked about nothing. Fisher considered the silence.

Briggs' phone starting ringing.

"Briggs… right… yes… and…? Fuck! Right… get back here as soon as you can."

"What happened?" asked Fisher.

"Fuck! And fuck! Brian followed him; and as we expected, he changed trains at Nevsky and headed towards Devyatkino. He got out there, and Brian tailed him outside. There, in the car park, he got into a black Mercedes 500E and drove off. Brian had no means of following. Fuck!"

"That's a hell of a car for a wedding photographer!" said Baker.

"And…it's fast. A V8 I think, made by Porsche. That could outrun anything we can get hold of."

"Assuming," added Baker, "he thinks he's being followed. Why would he race off, unless he felt threatened?"

"True. Then we need the most boring unassuming car we can get hold of."

"I think I know someone with such a car" Fisher quipped. "The only threat is the driver."

"Let's get onto that, then. We were close…so damn close. I thought we had him!"

"He's gone to ground. We have to wait for next time. But, we will have to have a car waiting at Devyatkino. We could take a vehicle up there now and leave it there."

"Should we stay with the car?" suggested Baker.

"And freeze to death? No…we have no idea when he might return or when he might go back to Devyatkino. It's a risk, but the only option seems to be that we follow him on the Metro, then take the car. For all we know, he may switch stations from time to time to cover his tracks."

"And if we lose him?" asked Baker.

"We lose him."

"But, I don't think we will. Typically, his expected profile and his record of killing suggests he is OCD."

"What's that?"

"Obsessive Compulsive is an anxiety disorder, characterised by the presence of recurring intrusive and unwanted thoughts, images, or impulses… obsessions and repetitive behavioural and mental rituals… compulsions, such as his collecting behaviours. People with this condition are usually aware that their symptoms are irrational and excessive, but they find the obsessions uncontrollable and the compulsions difficult or impossible to resist. That may be why he is such a *regular* killer."

"So?"

"So… he travels at the same time, every time… unless he has some other compulsion not to."

"So, he may get the same train tomorrow?"

"If he comes back today. And, if he is going there tomorrow."

Briggs looked at his watch.

"Right…so, we could leave here tomorrow at 9.30am, and every day, until he moves."

"What could possibly go wrong?" said Baker.

"I don't think that's a good idea. Acting out of the ordinary might spook him. It's better to be there at the right time, in the right place, with the right car. Has Vasyli Kolnikov been in yet?" asked Fisher.

"No," said Briggs. "Should I be expecting him?"

"Let's try this phone then, shall we?"

Fisher dialled the number barely recalled from his mental rolodex.

"Vasyli? Stephen….No, I'm fine, really. ….No, I'm not staying at the same place anymore. I was wondering if you got my note? ….Good. I was hoping we could meet at the place I suggested? ….I understand how she feels…Pasha is an old friend of mine too. I don't think it's a problem. It isn't a problem! Pasha is always welcome at my house. Can you bring our drinking friend with you, I need to ask him a favour? …Good. Good… well, I'll see you tomorrow morning then! Perfect."

"What's the problem?" said Briggs.

"His wife won't leave without the dog."

"Dog! They can't defect with a dog! They'll have to leave him behind. What kind of a dog is it?"

"A Giant Poodle."

"There's no way they will do that."

"I can't transport a great big poodle… a *chi wah wah* in a handbag, maybe. But not a bloody great poodle! There must be quarantine restrictions…or something!"

"Quarantine!" Fisher laughed sarcastically, "We've illegally raided a Russian nuclear research facility and bombed it to kingdom come! We're about to smuggle a leading nuclear scientist out of the country! And you're worried about quarantine regulations!? You'll just have to find a way! They'll be here at eight in the morning."

18

Before the Flood

Forest.

Twilight.

The first light of the short day stretched its orange fingers through the trees. Carefully, they ran between the sharp needles, touching and caressing the myriad drops of dew. Hanging there, those little worlds, pendulously, like tears, waiting for the slightest vibration to make them fall. Even so, in a forest of tall thin fir trees, it was hard for Fisher to see far enough ahead of him without the vaporous sunbeams groping for the ground, reading the frozen litter like a blind man reads Braille.

A light mist was rolling in, sliding between the trunks, created by a waft of unseasonably warm air making contact with the melting snow. Over to the left, where the ground sloped away, the clouds of mist cascaded, swirled, keeping low, clinging to the damp underbelly of this primordial forest. It crept softly over the leaf mould to the slimy bank of a frozen lake, only to settle over the cool ice in a damp fog.

Fisher saw him before he saw Fisher.

The brown hare stopped right in front of him: standing, stretching, sniffing, grooming, and then sprinting away towards the lake, his tail dancing behind him. Fisher was envious of the hare, in his capacity to move soundlessly, spirited, as if his feet never even touched the snow. With a flick, and just a powdery puff of crystals, he took off.

Icicles, like crystal chandeliers, hundreds of them, perilously hanging from the branches, dangled overhead, and dripped a drip every few seconds. So much so, that it felt like Spring rain. It was dripping onto

Fisher's face as he looked up, allowing a few pure drops to relieve his dry mouth.

Moving forward in a slippery mix of wet snow and leaf mulch, he placed a hand on the bark of a tree to steady himself; first the right hand, then the left, on another. Progress was agonisingly slow, counted out in broken twigs and bogged down in the brackish mulch under his bare feet. Why wasn't he wearing his boots? Had he forgotten them?

Every now and again, he passed a shrub of *red sprite*, bare of leaf, and with frightened yellow branches, but dotted with bright crimson winterberries, like splashes of blood. A Robin Redbreast seemed to be following him, bush to bush; or, was it leading *him* somewhere?

The snow was getting deeper and deeper, making it hard for Fisher to walk, since he was unable to lift his legs high enough to step forward. It was like wading through deep slush, squeezing between his toes.

The robin flew into a clearing up ahead, and settled on the lip of a wooden bucket, It tried to peck at the block of ice, floating, like an island, in the clear meltwater. The pail belonged to a house; the house to the pail, its reflection captured in the water. Fisher made his way to the front porch, up two wooden steps. A clapboard style house, with the paint peeling away from the white wooden walls, like so many flakes of snow. It was almost a camouflage, a motley of greys and greens, which is probably why he hadn't seen the house at all. But the robin knew where it was. Sitting on his regular spot on the window ledge, picking a few breadcrumbs, left there by…? Who?

Fisher twisted the round brass door knob, it was laden with dew, wet and as cold as his hand. Why didn't he bring his gloves? Had he forgotten them? The door was locked, and so he moved around the side of the house, the wall bathed in orange sunlight, to the first sash window. That too was locked. He peered through a pane of frosted glass and lace curtains. He could barely see a black stove in the hearth, with an open door giving the room a warm inviting, flickering glow, as if the furniture itself appeared to be on fire.

He moved on to the next window, where the robin took flight ahead of him.

It was a bedroom. Still not a soul in sight; not a sound. But a bed, an empty bed, with ruffled sheets, and blankets, and a discarded pillow on the floor. Either, somebody had slept uncomfortably, and left in a hurry, or the impressions in the sheets were that of a torrid scene of twisted passions. Nobody to be seen. Not a sound, and the cold morning air was devoid of smells.

Following the skittish robin, Fisher turned the corner and found a rear door and six steps down off the porch, indicating the house was built on a ridge of sloping ground, and therefore, stood on stilts at the back. Two neat piles of logs on either side of a set of rough stone steps disappeared between the rotting stilts, to a dark, dank door. Fisher turned the handle, and the robin flew directly into his face, the wings fluttering and the tiny talons scratching at his skin. He brushed it away with his hand, and pushed the door open.

More steps.

A small landing.

Another door.

It's warm, but dark inside.

Muffled, dank, with a smell like a wet dog.

The windowless space was filled with a low hum, as if a boiler or a generator was running, somewhere inside.

As his eyes grew accustomed to the dim light, Fisher could see that there was a narrow passageway ahead. The walls, ceiling and floor were black, with a series of dim spotlights pointing alternately to recesses to the left and to the right. His eyes darted from side to side.

It was a gallery of objet d'art. A sudden gust of wind from behind…it whispers in his right ear, like a child telling him a long-kept secret: *But at my back I always hear time's wingèd chariot hurrying near*….and then another in the left ear, echoing the first: *…But at my back in a cold blast I hear the rattle of the bones, and chuckle spread from ear to ear.*

Fisher realised, he was in a dream; in a world where nothing quite made sense, but it was real enough to keep his heart racing, thumping in his chest. He stepped forward towards a distant door, ajar, at the end of the passage. His eyes were drawn to the left, to a small recess, where a faceless wooden wig-stand was placed, beautifully hewn from a fir tree. It supported a wig of long dark hair. To the right, and directly opposite, affixed inside the recess to the wall, a pale, small, pelvic bone…the hip bones, spread, like angel's wings, or ears, listening to the chill wind at his back.

Fisher was struck by the symmetry.

As he crept softly forward, passed each opposite recess, he could see a wig, of a different hue or style on one side; and opposite, each pelvic bone on the right, pared from a living soul. They looked stark, white, against the black wall, like a display of dead moths, giants, pinned to a board. By now, Fisher could see more of the room at the end: a tripod leg, a camera, and a sudden bright white light, that blinded him for a moment.

When his eyes came back from the burn, the bones had gone. They must have flapped their wings and turned into strange butterflies. The outer door behind, slammed shut with a hollow ring, that echoed in the chamber and resonated in his ears like an alarm bell.

It was the alarm clock, like a clarion call, from Baker's bedroom.

Fisher lay in a cold sweat. His heart still stumping in his chest. What is the stuff that dreams are made on? Or, rather, from? What substance do they have? They seem real enough, as real as any experience.

Fisher had always dreamt such dreams. Mostly innocuous; but sometimes seemingly poignant; shifting; repeating and reflecting from a tarnished mirror, whatever was troubling him. But this dream, like others of late, had a different feel. More vivid than most; and deeply disturbing. We're he to treat himself as a subject of study, as Freud might a shell shocked wreck, he would dive down into the sunken vessel and struggle to explain the treasures within. There were no Freudian jewels, no Jungian coins, no semiotic chest and no recent traumatic chains or links to anything in experience. It all seemed quite literal.

Soon enough, Carey emerged in her now familiar garb: a man's white shirt and nothing much else.

"Breakfast or shower first?" she said with cheerful tone.

"Breakfast, I think."

"Sleep well?"

"A lot better than at the Moskva" said Fisher pulling some pants on. "But, strange, strange dreams."

"What about?"

"A house…near a lake…very disturbing…and a line from a poem. Well, two poems, I think…being whispered in my ears."

"You know the poems?"

"Yes…both I studied at school. One was by Andrew… somebody? I can't remember…a Restoration poet. The other, *The Wasteland* by TS Eliot. The same line, but different."

"I don't know how you can remember such detail. I don't have dreams."

"Everybody dreams. It's just that some remember them and some don't."

"Not surprising, really. Mine would be very boring. Do you think our man, Anatoli whatsit, has dreams?"

"Even serial killers dream."

"About what?"

"The same things as everybody else."

"Really?"

"Serial killers can be very charming and charismatic. They aren't the psychopath running down the street; they're the man or woman next door. They're so completely ordinary," Fisher said. "That's what gets a lot of victims in trouble. Why would a young girl go somewhere with a relatively unknown man? It's because of that ordinariness. Victims don't even remotely consider the fact that the serial killer can be just that, because the killer seems so ordinary. So, even in their dreams, they are unlikely to be out of the ordinary."

Baker was already cracking eggs and whisking them into a creamy mix.

"They must be different in some way, otherwise, why would they do such terrible things?"

"For now, we're only speculating with what we know about the brain, which is practically nothing," Fisher said. "True you see behaviour, true you see something wrong with the brain, but does that mean they're connected?"

The eggs were tipped into the hot, smoking pan, with a satisfying sizzle.

"The world," Fisher concluded "has become desensitised to serial killers, which makes it difficult to convince governments to allow me to conduct the necessary research."

"But, in a sense," added Baker, "you are doing field research every time you investigate a case. You get to know these killers more and more."

"Yes…but, only after the fact. What we should be able to do, is identify causes in the psychopath, before they go on a killing spree."

"Toast?"

"Yes, please."

"So, why don't they claim insanity in their defence?"

"Because they're not insane."

"I don't get it. How can they not be insane if they are a psychopath?"

"Psychopathic serial killers know right from wrong, and are able to comprehend criminal law. In particular, they know that murder violates the laws and mores of society. They do understand that they are subject to society's rules, but they disregard them to satisfy their own selfish interests and desires. In court, psychopathic serial killers are rarely found not guilty by reason of insanity, simply because psychopathy does not qualify as insanity in the criminal justice system. In any case, I don't think *our man*, if he is *our man*, is going to end up in court. Our objective is simply to get Eloise back, safely, where she belongs."

Fisher felt at odds with his circumstance; as if he should be doing something; or, as if he shouldn't be here at all. He watched Baker move in the kitchen; but felt that he shouldn't. Her dark hair was tied back behind her head. She moved gracefully and yet efficiently, as if she knew she was being watched.

"Shall I make the coffee?" he offered, coming into the kitchen area.

It still felt strange… even guilty, somehow. As if they were sharing breakfast having spent the night in the same bed. And, an old familiar adage came to mind.

And, breakfast after sex? When in doubt, sneak out!

What was Fisher thinking?

He hadn't had sex, and yet the breakfast thing still felt awkward. It created a false sense of intimacy, of togetherness. When single, his instinct had been to enjoy the sex they had had, for what it was; and to skip the forced breakfast. Of course, if he liked her and wanted to see her again, he would hang around. Wouldn't he? Have a coffee and a cuddle, but don't stay after noon. He had never wanted to be the man sitting on the sofa at three in the afternoon, when her mother turns up for tea. Always best to leave her, wanting to see him again. Not thinking that he'd already moved in! He could say he had a morning meeting with a serial killer. Not only does that keep the mystery, but, most importantly, it would give him the opportunity to decide... for both of them to decide...whether or not to spend more time together. But, in marriage, he was done with all that. And yet, it felt as if he wasn't.

The kettle finally boiled.

It was as if they had been intimate in the night, passionate, locked in a warm embrace. Neither intended it to happen; it just did. Except it didn't.

Fisher felt guilty, without the guilty pleasure. He felt he had been unfaithful, even though he hadn't.

Was he being unfaithful, just thinking it through?

Had he already *sinned* by virtue of feeling that he had? Or, that he might?

It wasn't unlike the catholic sin of *impure thoughts*. Whereby, absolution is required and penance meted out on the basis of *thinking* about a sin, before a sin had been committed. *Bless me Father, for I have sinned... well not yet... I might never do it... in fact I won't... is that a sin, Father?* It probably was. Most things were. It was one of the reasons he was no longer part of a religion based entirely on guilt.

It was a morning any couple might have shared, in the bliss of domestic normality, and Baker was also aware of that, as she deftly placed the scrambled eggs on the plates. Turning, she looked at his still bruised face:

"It's looking a lot better" she said, and stroked the side of his face, softly. She didn't mean to.

It just happened.

It felt natural; but then it didn't.

Fisher swallowed, as his heart was visibly beating in his partially bared chest. She raised herself on her toes and moved to kiss him.

"Let's not do this" he said, with gentle persuasion.

Baker moved back onto the flat of her feet, her eyes still locked in a virtual embrace with his. She felt a strange palette, an odd mix of excitement and embarrassment, tinged with a hue of the unprofessional and a foolish blush of pink.

Fisher smiled affectionately.

"Can I at least have a cuddle?" she said, lowering her eyes.

"Of course," he replied, and put his arms around her. She placed her cheek on his chest, where she could hear his beating heart.

"I'm sorry..." she started to say, a little more embarrassed. But Fisher stopped her.

"Ssh!" he said. "There's no need to say anything." But pulled away anyway, gently releasing her to the rapidly cooling eggs and the task in hand.

"I have two slices of bacon!"

"Great! Let's go mad and have them both in one day!"

Despite all the best of intentions, the strained superficiality made the conversation over breakfast somewhat plastic and moulded into a shape that fitted nowhere, and that neither really wanted, but resigned themselves to.

Finally:

"I need to wash my hair," she said, as if he needed to know; and, as if it really did need washing. Was it just that she needed something to do; something normal; something that didn't involve Fisher... a distraction.

Baker went off to shower, first, before Fisher this time. She came back with rosy cheeks and a towel on her head. Meanwhile Fisher, designing his own distraction, had picked up a copy of *Gorky Park* and started to read. Something of a cult success, it wasn't at all like the film; and now, it was hard to get to grips with, even without recalling the actors and the locations. Perhaps he should have read the book, before seeing the film? His mind was impatient with the writer. A film is much more efficient: there is no need for long descriptive passages, or deep narrative insights into character. In a film, what you see is what you get. In a sense, it's a lazy way to read a book. Passive. Someone has already done the hard work. Ultimately, however, it is filtered through the eyes of another. And, seeing the film after reading the book might have disappointed him; he might not have bothered.

And what of the writer's voice?

The one that speaks inside your head?

We've all been there.

Fisher certainly has.

We're watching a film that's based on a novel or a short story, and we're thinking while we watch that it's actually quite good. We haven't read the book but we enjoy the story, the acting, the direction, the music and the cinematography. Perhaps we didn't bother with the book, simply because everybody else did. The credits roll and we nod enthusiastically to our partner or friends, and murmur words of approval.

When we then speak about it to friends, we find that we are in fact, *fools* who will never get to experience the delights of the story as it was originally *written*. This select few who watched the said film, these happy few, this rebellious band who refused to conform and to give in to media pressure, *after* reading the book, seem to take on an air of superiority over us poor ignorant wretches. Is reading literature a form of snobbery? Literature has always been associated with the upper class because traditionally only rich people had access to it. They are also more likely to have the education necessary to appreciate literature. But in this day and age of global communication, when you don't have to be able to read or understand a single word of French to appreciate Proust, is it still snobbish to read *Remembrance of Things Past?*

Ultimately, it's about the reason to read a book. Would anyone read *Ulysses* by James Joyce for pleasure? A few, perhaps. For most it is read for the purpose of bragging, to say that you have.

Fisher, who never managed to read *Gorky Park*, or even knew that the book ever existed, because he was too damn busy chasing psychos, instead of reading about them. Those that have done the reading, will boast how, in their inflated opinion, the film never matched up to the novel and that there are many more elements to the story that we missed, having jumped straight to the ninety-minute abridged celluloid version.

It was nothing like the book.

That actor destroyed his or her character.

They missed that whole scene out.

I hate that actor!

Three young people are seen ice skating in Gorky Park. Three days later, Soviet militia officer Arkady Renko investigates the discovery of their bodies a short distance from the skating rink. All have been shot in the chest and mouth; their faces and fingerprints have been completely removed. Renko is left anxious and paranoid when the KGB refuse to take over the investigation. Renko enlists the help of Professor Andreev to reconstruct their faces.

Somewhere in the background of his thoughts, a hairdryer was humming.

Well that's how Fisher recalled the opening of the film…. But without the hairdryer. Flicking over the pages, there are a hell of a lot of words and pages to get through, before we get to the nub of reconstructing the three faces.

The Nokia phone rings.

"Briggs: the boxes have arrived…three of them. They will be leaving shortly, to be delivered to the other place. The one we visited recently. I didn't know whether you wanted to inspect them before they leave?"

"Yes, I'll be right over. Just need a quick shower."

"Make it snappy, the boxes are going the long way round. Oh, and there's another small parcel, addressed to you, personally. It's in the lobby."

"Fine…I'll be there in a jiffy"

A *jiffy*? Where did that come from?

What would the eavesdropping Russians, if there were any, going to make of a jiffy? *I'll be there in a jiffy*? Sounds like a small Italian car, available only in bright orange or Neapolitan.

Fisher took a cursory shower, concentrating on the essential three *p* components of masculine hygiene: penis, pits and posterior, and was already getting dressed when Baker emerged with her hair still damp.

"Bugger!" she said. "Are we on the move?"

"Yes!"

Wet hair in a cold climate… not a great idea; but, stuffed under a hat, nobody would notice. The trick was to keep the hat on, at all costs.

Two security guards were standing outside. One of them opened the door for Baker:

"Morning Ma'm, he said.

Briggs was standing there, without his sling, but with questionable stains on his crotch.

Vasyli and Lyudmila were already in the lobby, along with Anton.

"Where's Pasha?" asked Fisher, waiting to be pounced on.

"In car, already," said Lyudmila, "sleeping like dog!"

"Like a *log*!" said Fisher.

"Log?" echoed Lyudmila.

"Sleeping like a log."

"Leica? Log? English is so difficult! Why is dog sleeping like log?"

"Manchester United!" Vasyli said, throwing his arms around Fisher.

"Manchester United" repeated Fisher.

Anton looked a little glassy in the eyes.

"Anton will do whatever you need him for. He is a good man!"

Turning to Anton, he said:

"Я буду скучать по тебе, друг мой. Вы будете выглядеть после того, как д-р Фишер, пожалуйста"

"Could you ask him to wait here?" asked Fisher. And then later to drive North with us. He will need a full tank of petrol."

"Он хочет, чтобы вы подождали здесь. Вам понадобится этот бак с бензином."

Anton nodded to Fisher.

"Yes...he has full tank. I gave him one."

"It's time!" said Briggs.

"Thank you Stephen. I hope you find what you are looking for."

"And you, Vasyli...and you."

"A gift for you Stephen. Please keep it, always."

Lyudmilla pulled from her bag, a carved wooden doll, painted garishly in red, with a woman's face, and a mushrooming bright red flower on her apron.

"It is Matryoshka," Vasyli said. "It means *matron*, or *mother*."

"She has baby inside for you," added Lyudmilla. "With flower... here... see. It is..."

"Salvia," completed Vasyli. "Я думаю о тебе. It means: *I think of you*."

"Thank you... I..." began Fisher.

"If anything should happen to us..." added Vasyli, "...it will remind you of our friendship."

"Nothing bad is going to happen to you."

Fisher kissed Lyudmilla on each cheek. And they were gone.

"He might be here for a long time. Shall I get Anton a cup of tea?" offered Baker.

"Yes...no milk... piles of sugar, I suspect, from the state of his teeth, and a plate of *Jammie Dodgers*!"

"Roger that!"

By the time Briggs returned, Anton had two full biscuits in his mouth and was straining his tea through the crumbs, between his teeth.

"Not a bad idea to keep him here for a while, anyway," said Briggs, "as he's likely to be arrested by the KGB as soon as they get wind."

"Can we get him out of here, when all this is over?"

"Tricky. But, we'll see. He may not want to go. Let's go down to the Comms Room and discuss tactics."

This was Briggs' territory, his base, where he felt most comfortable and in control.

"So, here is my suggestion," he said to Fisher and Baker. "We wait for Brian to call. I have told him to ring on the first sign of Morozov leaving the apartment. We need to move rapidly. The metro to Devyatkino doesn't take long, about twenty-seven minutes from

Nevsky interchange. Perhaps, from his apartment, thirty-five in total, plus a few minutes for the change. Brian will follow as far as the Nevsky at this end, to make sure he leaves on a train. But, I've told him not to follow beyond that point."

"Why?" asked Baker. "We might need him at the other end."

"He followed him yesterday. Few people go to the end of the line. Brian said only he and Morozov and one woman got off. It's too risky. If he thinks he's being followed, he will simply go somewhere else. We will have to handle this ourselves."

"You're going?" said Fisher, "What about your shoulder? And, more immediately, your ankle?"

"The ankle is good. I just need to be a bit careful, because it remains weak. But, in a good pair of boots, no problem. The shoulder is stiff, but, I'm working on it."

"I don't expect it to be anything like Archangel, but, it may get a bit hairy."

"Really?"

"We discussed this. He might get violent. He's a killer!"

"Why would he be armed? As far as he is concerned, he's going about his business...gruesome though it is. It's possible, I suppose, that there might be a hunting rifle at the location..."

"But, are you fit enough if there is?"

"Yes...we are all going armed. That's three-to-one! Look... I take it we're not arresting this guy. We just want Eloise. If he puts up a fight, then we take him down. If not, then the MVD can deal with him later. It's not our job to bring him to justice, is it?"

"No... I suppose not. But, he might just go off and do it again."

"That's not our concern."

"In any case, if he has harmed her in some way... in any way... we won't need the MVD."

"Briggs... I'm as angry as you are. More so, maybe. I've seen what this man has done. But, we're are talking about murdering a citizen without trial."

"We may have no choice," added Baker. "This is going to be difficult, and, frankly, we don't have a plan because we don't know what to expect when we get there. What will be, will be."

"I'm fine... really! I'm going, and that's it!" Briggs was obviously sensitive about this, so Fisher decided to back off and change the subject:

"And Vasyli? Lyudmila? Pasha? What's going to happen to them?"

"They should be fine. They're not going to the base, as I said on the phone. I just needed to say something. From here they will leave the city in one of our vehicles. Nobody is interested anymore. But, once they approach the border...that's a different matter. If anything can go wrong...it's at that point. From the city, they are driving West, to Estonia, in an unmarked van. From Tallinn, we can still drive them over to Finland...it will take a couple of days in total. Then a flight from Helsinki. You wouldn't believe the admin associated with that dog! He'll need to see a vet to check for rabies...a whole pile of vaccinations!"

"But, he's worth it!"

"If you say so. Look at the state of my pants!"

The Nokia started to ring.

"Fuck!" said Briggs, as he snatched the phone from the table:

"Briggs...!"

He said nothing else. Just listened. It was few seconds and it was over.

"Move!" he said.

Anton was asleep in the lobby when Briggs picked him up by his coat collar and hustled him out into the carpark. The magnificent two-tone Volga was waiting.

"That's it!" cried Briggs. "Are you serious! We can't chase a Mercedes 500 in that thing!"

"We're not *chasing* anything. We are following with a low profile... remember? Get in!"

"Low? It couldn't get much lower! In fact, it's so low that it draws attention to itself. And, it's going to be a bit of a squeeze in the back. Just as well, Brian's not coming!"

They piled into the Volga. Fisher in the passenger seat; Baker and Briggs in the back.

"Right, Anton! Let's move!"

Anton put his hand in his inside pocket, carefully removed a cigarette packet and pulled a slightly bent *papirosa* from its resting place, putting the end between his thin lips.

"Come on...come on!" cried Briggs!

Fisher gestured to Briggs to relax, in order to let Anton perform the engine starting ritual, which seemed interminable, as he fumbled in his coat for a match, with which to ignite the motor.

Only when the cigarette was aglow, did Anton attempt to start her up. After a short cough, she was up and running. In the back, Briggs was shaking his head as they pulled out of the car park at the break-neck speed of fifteen miles per hour.

19

Rubies

Black.

Mercedes.

Unmistakable, in a car park of dull coloured Lada's, Zil's, Volga's and Moskvich's. *Which sounds a little like a firm of Manhattan lawyers,* thought Fisher.

It was lunch time, and they were starving.

It was something to moan about; to talk about, to pass the time.

Each minute seemed like an hour.

It seemed somewhat absurd, and incredibly suspicious, that they were packed like salted anchovies in a small tin box, waiting in a place where there was nothing to wait for.

Anton, went into his pocket, and instead of a packet of cigarettes named after a canal, he produced a *Jammie Dodger* named after a Roger. One after the other, he doled them out... first to Baker, with a wink; then Fisher, with a smile... pausing for effect, before producing, a third... which he took a bite from. It made Fisher smile. It was like watching a grubby magician at a children's birthday party. Finally, he produced one for Briggs, but not from behind Briggs' ear, as Fisher half expected him to, but from his pocket as before. It was just enough to stave off the pangs.

Although Anton's unappealing fingers were abhorrent to most people, aside from a microbiologist, as they harboured a smorgasbord of filth, tipped by ripe fingernails where only archaean extremofiles could live in the old engine oil.

Fisher was in the front with Anton; and Baker and Briggs still squashed in the rear, with Briggs' head firmly pressed into the filthy roof lining. The windows of the Volga had steamed up without exception.

"This wasn't quite the car I had in mind," Briggs said. "I think we are just ahead of the train. We will see it coming in from here."

Anton was blissfully unaware of the complaints about his beloved car, and of the implied criticism of his driving; or, his hygiene.

"I can't see anything!" said Baker, wiping her window.

"It's not underground then?" asked Fisher.

"No. Devyatkino Station is above ground. The southbound train tracks are on the left side of the station while the northbound tracks are on the right, allowing for easy transfers between the subway and the trains. He should come out just over there."

The seconds ticked by with the Volga engine still running, purring, like an old, grumpy, Tom Cat. It also smelled like one.

Fisher gestured to Anton, to cut the engine by swiping his hand across his throat. It seemed to Fisher, it looked too obvious...all of them sitting in a car with the engine running. Whereas, to Anton, it was a matter of assurance, in that, he had no way of knowing if his mistress, Olga from the Volga, would play ball when the time came. She was something of a wayward whore. His wife was even less predictable, but then, he never cleaned her plugs, changed her oil, or greased her nipples.

"It is the northern terminus of the Kirovsko-Vyborgskaya Line. The name of the station is derived from the name of the nearby suburb, just over there." Briggs added.

"Who knew you were a closet train spotter!" said Fisher, taunting, nervously. They were all on edge. Apart, of course, from Anton. Fisher felt he was close; closer than he had ever been to finding Eloise, but, equally fearful of what he might find instead.

More seconds ticked by.

"Devyatkino was opened on the twenty-ninth of December 1978 as part of the last segment of the line. Until 1982 it was the northernmost metro station in the world, which was surpassed, eventually, by the Helsinki Metro."

"And what date was it *surpassed*?" asked Fisher, sarcastically.

They all laughed, more from stress that humour. Except Anton, of course, who had no idea what was going on or why he was there at all, staring at a near empty car park in the middle of the day in the middle of nowhere in the middle of his life.

He had lost his closest friend, Vasyli. It was a sad day, perhaps the saddest day of his life. And, yet, he was happy for his friend. He had known Vasyli almost all his life; since they played together between the kommunalka as little boys. Vasyli was the smart one; too clever for his own good; and with a mouth to match. It was always getting him into trouble; and Anton was always there to get him out of it. Nothing much had changed, except the degree and complexity of trouble.

They were separated for a few years only: Vasyli went to university in Moscow; and Anton went into the Special Forces. But, the next time they saw each other, the time and space didn't matter. They were just as before. Except in one regard: Anton had married a secretary from his base, who looked like an angel...for about four years... before she turned into a turnip. Vasyli, had been more sensible, in marrying a woman who would always look like the woman he married: a bad-tempered sow. That way, he said, he would never be disappointed if he woke up one morning and there was a pig in his bed.

It had been a special moment when they both realised that; but, at least they had each other. And now, Anton had Olga; and Vasyli had Lyudmila. He was happy for his friend. Not least, he was relieved that Vasyli had escaped with his life, his wife and his faithful hound.

"Here's the train now!" said Baker, wiping the condensation from her window into an oval viewing port.

"I think that's him!" said Fisher, "Going down the subway steps now."

The tension in the car, was like an over stretched guitar string, ready to snap at the slightest vibration.

"Anton..." Fisher pointed to the car dashboard where the key was located, and Anton nodded, poised to start her up.

As the subject emerged from the subway, Fisher could see that the photographer, their man Morozov, was carrying a sports bag of some kind: *Adidas Etrusco Unico* or something like that...It was bright green with red handles and had a soccer ball logo on the side. He walked right in front of the car, without even looking. He was confident, even arrogant, in his self-assurance.

It took all the willpower Fisher had, to stop himself getting out of the Volga right now and beating Morozov to a paste. But that was not their purpose, was it? Their purpose required a more subtle approach: measured, patient; like the hunter to the hunted

With the bag tossed in the boot, he unlocked the door and got inside the cold Mercedes. It was a serious engine that sparked into life without hesitation; not so much as a cough or a stutter, as the pinnacle of German engineering hummed into life. It sat there for a few moments whilst the engine warmed enough to melt the ice from the windscreen. At the rear window, the ice melted in bars like a Venetian blind. Just enough for Fisher to see the outline of the driver.

"Hold back!" said Briggs, putting his hand on Anton's shoulder.

As the Mercedes reversed and turned out of the car park, he let go of Anton's shoulder. They all held their breath. The Volga came to life, and moved off slowly, taking up position way behind the target. There were few cars about on the frozen compacted road. Two passed, travelling in the opposite direction, kicking up the powdered snow in a double vortex.. Their headlamps were on against a dull grey sky, that appeared to be clearing in glimpses of pale blue. A third car, pulled out from the right, in between the target and the Volga. Anton let it stay there, until, ten minutes later it pulled off to the left, down a narrow road.

After thirty minutes or so, a few trees started to appear, gradually increasing in number and proximity to the road.

"I've been here before," said Fisher. "This is near Lake Ozero."

"Ozero!" cried Anton. "Da...Ozero!" he repeated, pointing ahead and to the far left. Almost half an hour further up the road, the Mercedes' brake lights came on and the car turned off and to the left, at a sign.

"Skotnoye!" said Anton. Presumably what it said on the sign.

Anton held well back, for fear the Mercedes might notice him slowing in his rear view mirror. He turned his lights off.

"Ozero!" he said, as the Volga continued to follow the track through the forest, north of the Ozero junction. Increasingly, the terrain became more difficult. The wheels of the Volga were slipping on the mud and melted snow.

"We're losing him!" cried Baker.

Anton shook his head, and stayed his steady progress. He obviously knew the terrain.

"Elizavetinka!" he said, and pulled the car off the track and into a small clearing. He switched the engine off and said something in Russian, whilst gesturing with his hands. He made a tee-shape with his hand on top of his finger, indicating that the road ahead was a dead end.

"Ozero Elizavetinka!" he repeated, pointing to the ground.

"I think that's the name of this place," said Fisher. "The road goes no further…he says we should walk from here."

"Ok then!" said Briggs.

"Anton…" said Fisher, gesturing back. "Stay here! Here!"

Anton nodded and took out his cigarettes, as they got out of the car. Briggs rubbed his stiff shoulder, and then took out his Browning pistol, loaded the magazine and pulled the pin to half-cock the weapon. Fisher and Baker followed suit.

They walked slowly along the track, following the treads of the Mercedes embedded in the slushed tracks it had left behind. Some hundred or so metres ahead, the tracks turned off to the right and disappeared, snaking through the trees.

"Smoke!" said Briggs, as quietly as he could, gesturing with his chin and bottom lip, to the treetops in the distance, as the ground started to rise in that direction. It was eerily quiet.

Not a sound.

Not a bird.

Nothing.

Like the calm before the storm.

Despite the remaining snow, the air was warm, almost muggy.

Briggs made some signals with his hands and eyes.

Fisher shrugged his shoulders.

Baker translated with a low whisper:

"He wants us the spread out… he'll take the right… me on the left… and you go straight ahead."

Fisher nodded, as Briggs moved away through the trees.

Baker to his immediate left, moved down the slope and disappeared into the shrubs. In the distance ahead of Baker, Fisher thought he saw a clearing, or an opening in the trees, and a flat white area. What could only be a frozen lake or a wide open field. It looked vaguely familiar, but strange and unfamiliar, at the same time.

He looked straight ahead, pausing to remind himself of why he was here, and what was at stake. And, then saw it. From the corner of his eye: a robin, sitting on a branch of *red sprite*.

20

Deserve this State

Red.

Feathers.

He knew the place as before.

I know this place! Fisher said to himself and within himself, slowly, as he stepped forward. *How can this be? Did I dream this place? A premonition? But, of what?*

Fisher stepped forward, and the robin fluttered ahead. He thought, perhaps, that thinking about a portent of death was not the best thing to be doing, at this particular moment. On the other hand, if he thought about death, logically and practically, as an inevitable consequence of birth, then it might remove the fear of death. His breath was hastening, his mouth drying out and his heart was thumping in his chest. *We give birth astride of a grave*, he thought, *the light gleams an instant, then it's night once more.*

Fisher moved forward, slowly and quietly… waiting for the hare of his dreams to appear.

After death, there is life, though.

Not in a spiritual way. Fisher was done with that; he had no capacity to reconcile it. But, neither did he have an explanation for this sense of having been here before; even, if only, in his dreams.

He felt quite different. It was a fear unlike the Archangel mission, which all happened so quickly. This stealth; the silence and anticipation was far worse. He couldn't help but think about the worst.

It's difficult to describe the complex smell of death, to those who have never experienced it. Fisher had... all too often. The smell of decomposing human flesh smells sickly sweet.

Some may have heard that the nails and hair keep growing, at least for a while, after we die. This conjures up creepy images of exhumed corpses with an urgent need for barbers or pedicurists. Fisher knew, that the idea probably came from actual observations of hair and nail *growth*, but it's all an illusion. The truth is, that the rest of our body shrinks due to dehydration, making the nails and hair look longer.

Water was dripping on Fisher's face.

He looked up and took some drops into his dry mouth. It tasted soft and fresh with a hint of pine.

A hare pelted across his path, startling him. Not like in the dream; it never stopped; it just ran by, over towards wherever Baker was. It was so fast, just a blur really; and a puff of powder.

Crack!

Crack!

Two shots over on his right!

Fisher was frozen to the spot.

Suddenly, Morozov was running in front of him in the same direction as the hare, over towards Baker. He had a pistol in his left hand. He hadn't see Fisher, who raised his Browning and tracking, followed his target, taking aim...

Click.

Nothing.

It jammed....and Morozov was gone.

"Fuck!"

Where was Briggs?

Fisher moved to follow Morozov, as he disappeared down the slope. Obviously, he was trying to go around to get back to his car.

But where was he?

Ahead, he stopped, and turned towards Fisher.

Crack!

He took a shot at Fisher, which smashed into the tree next to him, sending splinters stinging into the right side of his face, close to his eye. He felt a nip and a warm trickle of blood.

He turned again by ninety degrees down the decline, keeping as low as he could, darting between the trees.

Crack!

And Morozov then started running to the clearing below, Fisher in pursuit, but his gun still jammed.

"Fuck!" Where was Briggs?

As Morozov reached the edge of the frozen lake, he stopped.

Further along the hard shingle some fifty yards distant, blocking his exit, Baker was standing. Her arm out straight from her eye-line to the target, holding the pistol towards Morozov.

"Put the gun down, Anatoly!" she shouted, "It's over!"

Of course, he may not have understood the words, or the cliche, but, he certainly understood his situation. He glanced sideways at Fisher, who was also holding his pistol, at arms-length, useless though it was. Morozov bolted out onto the ice.

Crack!

Baker took a shot and missed. She was running in a diagonal from Fisher directly onto the ice. Fisher followed in a straight line for Morozov, who was already increasing his distance from them both. But, he stopped and turned.

Crack!

Crack!

Once again he missed Fisher with the second shot, but the first seemed to hit Baker in the thigh. She let off a steady shot, in spite of the jolt from the impact.

Crack!

He was down.

But Fisher kept on running. What he was going to do when he got there, he had no idea. But, he wasn't going to let him get away; or die without kicking him a few times.

Baker was also running, as best she could.

Morozov got to his feet and moved off again, a trail of blood staining the ice red.

Crack.

It wasn't a shot.

It was a different sound.

Fisher stopped in his tracks.

He was literally on thin ice.

A long crack had started at his feet and was moving forward like a tree branching out towards Morozov and Baker.

"Stop! Carey! Stop!" he shouted.

They both stopped.

Morozov, turned to look at them both and held his gun directly at Fisher.

Crack!

The ice gave way under his feet.

Baker stepped forward.

"Leave him!" shouted Fisher, as he watched Morozov desperately trying to grip the ice... clawing... grasping... like a man drowning in air, nails scratching into the surface... increasing panic on his face.

Then suddenly, a moment of calm; of realisation that death was upon him. And he slipped into the black water, taken away by the current under the ice. Fisher could see him, but only in his mind... still clawing at the current, as he passed under his feet and sank into the deep dark water, where the crabs would pick his bones in whispers.

Fisher turned to Baker and gently gestured that they should slowly and carefully walk backwards. The ice was still flexing and cracking, having thawed a little in the past day or two.

It was a question of care and no sudden moves. And yet, Baker was bleeding from a thigh wound, leaving a trail in her shuffling steps. Once into the shallows and off the ice, Baker collapsed onto the shingle.

"I need a tourniquet!" she said.

Fisher pulled a thin scarf from under his coat and tied it tightly around Baker's bloody jeans.

"Here," he said, "we'll use this stick to twist it, but you'll have to hold it there, while we walk"

"You should go on! Where's Briggs?"

"I don't' know...but, I'm not leaving you here...come on! Let's go!"

He helped her up.

"I'm completely disorientated...which way?"

"This way... I know this place," he said.

"You do? How?"

"It's my business to know."

It was a struggle, moving up the incline in the mud and melted snow. There was no sign of Briggs anywhere. As the incline flattened out close to where Fisher had seen the hare. Baker, exhausted, said:

"I can't...I can't go any further. Let me sit down here under this tree. You go!"

She sat down and waved the back of her hand.

"I don't want to leave you," he said.

"You have no choice. Go!"

"I won't leave you like this! Let me, at least go and get Anton to help."

"Every second you waste here, is just a moment to us. To Eloise, it might be an eternity. We've come this far…you have to find her!"

"What about Briggs?"

"If he's not here right now, it's because he's been hit."

"I should go and see if he's ok."

What first? Thought Fisher. And then he moved off to where he thought Briggs might have been. There was blood…lots of blood… some bloody footsteps… and, there he was… lying in a ditch on a bed of crimson snow. He had lost a lot of blood.

So much blood.

He had a hand to his throat in an attempt to stem some profuse bleeding, and still, in the other, gripping his pistol. Fisher leapt forward and crouched next to him.

"Briggs…?"

"Nothing to be done!" said Briggs, with blood gurgling from his lips. He struggled to speak.

"You've been hit, twice?"

"Yes."

"Did you get that…fucking bastard?" he said, in more frothing blood… he seemed to be trying to swallow it back down.

"Yes…he's dead."

"Then, what are you waiting for, you sentimental prick?"

"But…"

"I'm done…go and get the girl! She will be there…waiting…I need to know that all this…meant something! It has to mean something!"

"I will…but…let me help you first!"

Briggs shook his head and then took his hand away from his neck and let the blood flow freely.

"No.. no.." cried Fisher.

Fisher stood up and stepped back quietly, as Briggs bled to death, his eyes glazing over to a cold stare.

Briggs was right, of course, she could be waiting...and all this needed to be justified or not, by whatever was waiting. But, there was no way Fisher could know in what condition he might find Eloise. If, indeed, she was here at all. And *if*, she was still alive?

As he moved back to the clearing, Baker was gone. The footsteps seemed to move back in the direction of Anton and to the Volga, *to safety*, he thought...he hoped.

But something else was troubling him, as he moved towards the trees where the smoke had come from. Whatever was smoking, it wasn't smoking any more. But Fisher was more preoccupied with why Morozov had doubled-back with a gun. He must have known they were approaching. But how? Was it by chance that he came across Briggs first? Taking Briggs down by surprise, was the smart thing to do. Briggs being the only seasoned killer. But, how would he know that?

Fisher walked through the fir trees, tear drops of water were falling all around.

Up ahead, he could see the black Mercedes, parked in front of the dacha. There were no other vehicle tracks.

There was no bucket; and there was no robin; and yet, he still knew this place; he knew that house. In his psychological universe, Fisher had no rational explanation as to how he had dreamt this place. But, somehow he had. Was there any point in checking the front door? Looking through the windows? No? It was all deserted. No, he would go around the back to the heart of the matter; to where, Eloise was, or had been, kept....or so he thought. Why else would he dream that? And so he did go to the rear of the house.

Fisher almost felt as if he now depended on it being as much like his dream as possible. As he turned the corner at the rear of the house, it was largely as he remembered. And yet, as before, the details were quite different. The stilts, and the logs either side of the steps. But, there was a tree stump, obviously used for splitting logs; a few lay scattered about, and an axe, leaning on the first pile. It look as if it had been there for months. The head, pushed into the snow and mud, was rusted.

Fisher moved down the steps to the door.

He knew there was no known mechanism for precognition. Precognition violates the principle of antecedence that an effect does not happen before its time. There had been studies, he was aware of those. However, none had offered a shred of rational thought; and, some were, quite simply, flawed. Despite his *premonition*... there was no other word for it... premonition or precognition, he was dreading what he might find inside. Above all, he was terrified of finding Eloise dead. Which was worse? Dead or alive? Or, a child alive... raped... mutilated... destroyed?

His heart hammered in his chest, like a heavy clapper in an empty bell, with such force, he thought he could hear it.

Slowly, he turned the handle of the outer door.

Locked.

"Damn it!' he said, stepping back and kicking it hard, at the weakest point.

The lock splintered the dank, soft wood.

Steps.

Another door.

This one wasn't locked, and introduced a dimly lit narrow passage, with four bare light bulbs hanging from the ceiling by their wires. On the left, a door ajar. Inside...deep porcelain sinks... a dark room? A room for rendering bones? None of which was in his dream.

It was surprisingly warm.

Like one of those basements where a boiler or water heater is located. But he could see nothing of the sort. Just iron pipes running along the skirting board.

Fisher released the buttons on the front of his coat.

Suppose someone can remember ten things from a night's dreaming, at least when prompted by a similar thing or scene occurring during the day. He began to walk slowly along the passage.

Now consider how many incidents happen during a day, including those in the newspaper, on television or hear in conversation. There are a vast number and Fisher knew it was highly probable that from time to time one of them will, at least to some extent, resemble one of those from his dreams. When one or more of these coincidences occur, people are likely to conclude that dreams foretell the future. But, this wasn't quite the future he had seen....or envisioned.

Along the passage, there were no spotlights and no wigs; and, despite his expectations, no pelvic bones. Where were the bones? With Morozov dead, he may never know.

Notwithstanding his concern about these apparent anomalies. There was still, a door ajar, at the end of the passage. It invited him to move forward and open it, fully. Indeed, he felt compelled, even though the vision had ended at this point with the whispering wind, and the words: *but at my back...!*

Fisher felt a sudden and severe blow to the back of his head, which knocked him to the ground. He turned over, severely dazed... his fur hat lying next to him, bloodied.

The wolf was standing over him, holding the rusty axe in both hands.

"If you're afraid of wolves, Dr Fisher, don't go to the woods."

It was Volkov.

He raised the rusted axe over his head, until it touched the ceiling, to bring it down on Fisher's skull. There was a moment in aspic. *But at my back…*he thought.

Volkov opened his mouth, as if to speak or express anger, or to let out a primal roar, as he brought the axe to bear on Fisher and to end his life, here, in this place. A place, in which, his body might never be found.

Volkov paused at the zenith, tipped, and fell forward, as if stiff and hinged at the feet, almost crushing his prey. Fisher struggled to get out from under him. There was a short knife handle protruding from the back of his neck at the base of the skull.

Anton was standing there.

He said nothing, as he placed his foot on Volkov's back and pulled his knife from the spinal cord, wiping it clean on his victim's shoulder.

"Baker?" asked Fisher.

Anton nodded.

"Good?"

He nodded again.

Fisher moved immediately to the door, pushing it aside, to a vision that would populate his future dreams and nightmares. There was a tripod and a Hasselblad camera on the floor, not yet mounted; and the green sports bag next to it.

A small, thin girl with shoulder length red hair, sitting, naked, on the edge of a bed, her head lowered in shame; her hands, resting on her thighs, trembling.

"Eloise?" Fisher said, gently and quietly.

She didn't move.

He removed his coat and wrapped it around her shoulders.

It was as if he had put hot coals on her.

She stiffened.

Fisher moved to his knees, to be less threatening and to search the girl's face for any sign of cognition.

"Elle?" he said, "I'm here to bring you home. Cam told me to tell you that she loves you."

The sad little face looked at him, and pulled the wig from her head, to reveal a smooth pale scalp. She began to cry, most pitifully.

21

But at my Back…

Dark.

A night flight…

The wheels lifted off the cracked and frosted tarmac without a sound, into the crystal air, before the rush, as the gear folded itself behind the cowls. The pilot struggled to keep the Boeing steady against the runway crosswinds. A heavy front, bringing snow, was tearing across his path. An hour later, and the plane would have been grounded. In the navigation lights, Fisher could see the snow, like so many goose feathers rushing past the wings, in a pillow fight with the wind.

The plane banked sharply, turning left towards the West.

In the distance, down below, Fisher could just make out a few tungsten arc lights. The dark building floated on an island of ice, like a gulag at sleep with itself. It was hard enough for Fisher to imagine that this decrepit shed was the international departures terminal at Pulkova, and recipient of the prestigious *Order of the October Revolution*.

As before, the plane carried few passengers.

As before, the same tatty old plane, and the same nervous crew.

Fisher thought of all that had gone before; and all those he had left behind, in the wake of Perestroika. And, for some reason beyond his considerable psychological knowledge and understanding, he broke down and wept, bitterly.

Was it the feeling of relief? Or guilt?

Of escape?

Of the sense that somehow he was already on home turf?

Was it stress?

Whatever it was, he had never reacted this way before. Much of the work of a Criminal Psychologist doesn't necessarily involve such actions as those required in this case, largely because the system of law enforcement and investigation is already in place. But, this had been very different.

A multiple, or serial-murder investigation, forces the psychologist to confront stress, directly related to his or her own projected image of unwavering strength and determination, their ability to respond competently and dispassionately to crises, and, a willingness to place the needs and demands of the victim above his or her personal feelings.

This is magnified in high-profile cases with greater media attention. The sheer magnitude and shock-effect of many mass murder scenes and the violence, mutilation and sadistic brutality associated with many serial killings, especially those involving children like Eloise, often exceeded the defence mechanisms and coping abilities of even the most jaded investigator.

Fisher was, by no means jaded; but he was bruised.

Revulsion may be tinged with rage when innocent victims, or those assisting in the investigation have been killed or injured, and the murderer seems to be mocking attempts to capture and prosecute the killer, or killers. And, in this extraordinary case, one he would never be able to talk about. He would not be able to share his nightmares, and the lessons he had learned, due to his legal and moral obligations to the Realm of the United Kingdom: Her Majesty's Official Secrets Act.

In cases where the investigation drags on, Fisher's inability to solve the crime and close the case, further frustrated and demoralised him and seemed to jeeringly proclaim the hollowness of society's notions of fairness and justice. All the more disturbing were situations where the killer had been identified by Fisher, but the existing evidence was insufficient to support an arrest or conviction. Stress and self-recrimination are further magnified when the failure to apprehend the perpetrator, is caused by human error, as when a police officer's misguided actions or breach of protocol, leads to loss or damage of evidence or suppression of testimony, allowing the perpetrator to get away.

But, in this case, Fisher had taken the tattered law into his own hands. He had witness a murder; or, was it a summary execution? The killer and his accomplice had been dispatched, and the subject rescued. There would be no interviews, no trial, and no punishment.

Was he angry or upset about that for some reason?

There were certainly, many, many unanswered questions, such as:

What happened to the bones of those poor girls?

What was the role of the photographer in all this?

Which of the two was the killer?

Volkov?

Morozov?

Or both?

Where did the photographs end up?

And, who was looking at them right now?

The corrupted innocence of those girls was now in the filthy hands of many thousands of men; perhaps hundreds of thousands?

What would they say, if the context of their self-gratification was exposed to them? Do they have daughters too? Would it matter if they knew?

To the vast majority it would; but to a few, it would not. And, in some cases, it might even turn them on. Only since the nineteen-sixties has material been more openly available, and yet, there was still a considerable stigma attached to admitting exposure to it; and, barriers to getting hold of it. *But, what would happen now*? Fisher thought, as the first *dial-up internet service* had started just a few months ago. Would this internet thing, make such material more readily available? Was Fisher in danger of morphing into Mary Whitehouse? A schoolteacher who began an unlikely second career in the mid-sixties as a self-appointed, and much derided, guardian of British morals. As founder president of what became the *National Viewers and Listeners Association*, she was a unique public personality, who brilliantly used and manipulated the BBC and other media in the very act of castigating them. Her benevolently steely smile, baroque spectacles and ready quotes, made her better known than most government ministers. A raft of, in her eyes, malefactors fell victim to the force of her dedicated, some said blinkered, personality. It really wasn't Fisher's style... well, not the baroque spectacles!

All of these thoughts and reactions were intensified by a cumulatively spiralling, vicious cycle of fatigue and cognitive impairment, as the sustained and exhausting effort to solve a case such as this, could result in sloppy errors, deteriorating work quality, and fraying of home and workplace relationships. Fatigue also exacerbates the wearing down of normal psychological defences, rendering Fisher even more vulnerable to stress and failure. Was that why he was still crying so bitterly?

Even more so than for other types of offenses, sex crimes, especially those like this one, against vulnerable children, evoke a certain special revulsion and corresponding denial in Fisher. And so, the people who would choose to specialise in solving this type of crime may be imbued with a certain air of aloofness that serves to isolate and alienate them from the rest of their colleagues.

Fisher had often been accused of walking along the corridors of the university with his nose in the air; and of deliberately avoiding social niceties. After all, the thought of some people perpetrating violent, loathsome acts on others is so distasteful, that anyone who would willingly immerse himself in this kind of work must be a bit odd? Even so, wearing his nose at an oblique and unsociable angle, seemed an unreasonable accusation.

And, in this case, more than any other in his files, was the powerful sense of paternal protection he felt for Eloise. It was without explanation, cause or precedent; and yet... quite simply... he couldn't get that image out of his mind, of her sitting there: trembling, naked, hollow and dead inside.

It had made him angry.

Was that why he decided to burn the dacha to the ground?

Baker had stood there too and watched as Fisher and Anton splashed kerosene around the patio and torched the place. As the flames turned the snow to orange and lit the shadowy forest with light. A plume of sparks like a thousand fire-flies rose into the night sky, as if to take their place in the starry firmament. Fisher noticed the constellation *Gemini*, as clearly visible as he had ever seen it. The twins, Castor and Pollux hanging there, almost joined at the hip. Pollux's pelvis represented by the star δ *Gem*; and Castor's, represented by the star ε *Gem*.

Whilst the blaze took hold, Fisher and Anton recovered Briggs and placed his body,a as e could, in the boot of the Mercedes... and then Anton took his seat in the same car, leaving Baker and Fisher to join him. Elle was wearing Fisher's hat and holding on to Baker. They gazed at the burning building for one last time.

"We need to get you both to a hospital," said Fisher.

"We're coming into land Dr Fish...er ... are you alright?" asked the crew member.

"Yes, I'm fine...just a little upset about something."

"Can I get you anything?"

"No, really…but, thank you."

"Do you want to talk about it?"

Fisher's instinct was to say no, and so he did so, politely.

He thought about those last few moments in forest, as they watched the fire engulf the dacha.

"It's time to go home," he had said to the girl.

Eloise took hold of his hand, but said nothing, her bottom lip trembling.

I… had an experience… Fisher thought, as he composed himself, *I can't even explain it, but everything that I know as a human being, everything that I am tells me that it was profound. I was witness to something terrible, something that changed me forever…*

Eloise never said a word to him; not then in the forest; not later. It would probably be sometime before she would speak to anyone at all. But, she did squeeze his hand, which meant more than a thousand words.

It was probably about four-thirty in the morning when Fisher emerged from Manchester Ringway Airport into a cold, damp, rainy night. The tacky Christmas decorations inside, however colourful, had not lifted his mood. But, then, why would they? In fact, it was the normality of it all that was so disarming.

The taxi driver complained about the weight of Fisher's bag. But that was only the start of it. He had no doubt that Jane would insist he wash all the filthy whiffy contents himself. And, why not? It was his filth.

"Parkfields Road South, please" said Fisher getting into the black cab.

"Christ!" replied the driver, acknowledging that it was a relatively short distance from the airport.

"My last job of the night mate! I was hoping for the three wise men, a couple of shepherds and a boot load of myrrh. What the fuck is myrrh, anyway?"

"It's a tree sap from Ethiopia."

"How do you know?"

"It's my business to know."

"You a professor or something like that?"

"Something like that."

"Can we drive a bit further... the long way round, to make it worth my while?"

"I'll make it worth your while." said Fisher.

"Double fare tonight mate anyway!" he retorted. "Christmas Eve... well.. Christmas Day now, technically speaking. You been on holiday then? Bit of shoppin' in there? Present for the wife? Kids?"

"No."

"Crickey! You're in big trouble then?"

"Yes."

Of course, Fisher had one gift in his bag. He had kept it safe, close to him, in his satchel. The Matryoshka, given to him by Vasyli. *Salvia*, he had said...*I think of you.* The flower, Salvia, painted on the matron's apron. It commonly comes in blue. Fisher had a clump growing in his own garden. The red variety is known by the shape of the flower head: *Red Arrow*. Fisher had opened the doll as he was packing, by twisting it at the waist. And, not surprisingly, there was another identical, but small doll inside... and so on. Seven dolls in all, with an eighth and final doll to be found in the middle. But it wasn't there. Instead, there was a small roll of negative microfilm.

Fisher had decided to keep it to himself for the time being.

"Bin a quiet night...hardly a whisper... rain you see... nothing like a white fuckin' Christmas is it?"

"No."

"We ought to sue that geezer… Bing whatsit! Nothing worse, is there, than pushing a trolley round the supermarket with thousands of other people buying bloody turkeys… to *Let It Snow, Let it* fuckin' *Snow*! … over the speakers. Outrageous! We all hate bleeding turkey's anyhow. I don't know why people bother with Christmas… waste of time and money. Still, at least no drunken sod has chucked up in my taxi tonight. Got to be a silver lining somewhere, eh?"

"Yes."

Fisher had defaulted into his familiar air of aloofness. He could almost feel his nose turning upwards. But, as the taxi turned into Parkfields Road South, a simple thought brought a smile to his tired face: his vision of Anton, driving around St Petersburg in his nearly new Mercedes 500; the one with the slightly soiled carpet in the boot. But he would replace that, just as soon as he could, from his new business venture in luxury limousine services for the filthy rich oligarchs. Fisher imagined him… polished, clean and suited up. One of a new breed of entrepreneurs.

The long red brick walls of the tree-lined road, paused at the gate to his dark house. And his pulse quickened.

All was quiet.

Fisher thought for a moment about whether all this was worth it. Not the risks; and not the pain; but, the time spent away from Jane and the boys. Little else mattered in life.

It's not as if Criminal Psychologists compete with each other, jostling for who gets the most gruesome psychopath. In truth, many will have a success rate on a par with a clairvoyant, a pendulum dangler or a reader of chicken giblets. Fisher wasn't trying to be better than anyone else; he was just trying to be better than himself.

But, after all, he was still that lonely boy, in his bedroom, drawing and painting the pictures in his head.

He left his thought bubbles, his boots and his trunk, by the front door. He was too tired to bother with either; and if someone stole them... then so be it! They could take away the pain and do the damn washing!

He opened the familiar front door as quietly as he could. On the left, on the hall table, a plate was waiting for Santa. For so many children there is no Father Christmas; he was murdered by some sick bastard! Or, impersonated by an old fool in a department store. Fisher drank the glass of port, nibbled the carrot, munched on the mince pie, and then crept upstairs.

All was quiet. He walked passed the boys, still fast asleep, took all his clothes off, on the landing. The pile, a vertical crumble of clothes, looked as though he'd been vaporised. He stepped into the bedroom. Jane was fast asleep, in a foetal position, with her back to the middle of the bed. He spooned himself up against her warm body, and smoothed down the ruffles of a white cotton vest.

She didn't stir. He stroked her straight red hair down to her shoulders, caressing the back of her neck, and then put his hand around to cup her breast, and promptly closed his eyes.

The day after, is known as Boxing Day.

A young unknown substitute replaced Bryan Robson at half-time and was taunted with donkey noises after losing control of his first touch of the ball. Oldham fans should have known better. It was Ryan Giggs, and he silenced them by waltzing round the Oldham keeper for Manchester United's sixth goal.

"Come on you reds!" was the deafening chorus. Vasyli and Lyudmila roared with the rest of the ecstatic fans, as the final whistle blew. For them, it was a first real Christmas present. The gift of freedom, was a bonus. About the same time, the red flag of the *People's Soviet Socialist Republic* was lowered from the Kremlin for the last time.

As the long Winter gave way to the germinating seeds of Spring, the March roads of the squalid city of St Petersburg returned to brown. Streets spattered with blood and mud, and littered with the shells of crippled cars. The facades of public buildings were still there, suffering from cracked and blistered paint, like an incurable skin disease.

On the first day of April 1992, a small, thin body was discovered near Oseki, in the forest north of the city. It had recently been dumped there. Alexander Petrov, the local man who found her, was out hunting. He believed she had been attacked by wolves, who had eaten into her soft stomach and taken away her pelvic bone.

However, no one could explain how the young girl came to be there and why her head was shaved.

Afterthought

In writing this piece, over a few shorts weeks, memories of that Winter, from 1991 in St Petersburg flooded back, and a fair few have found their way into this gruesome tale.

Some are pleasant, but most relate to what was, undoubtedly, the most terrifying week of my life. I am grateful to the man with the shoe box full of cash, who tried to look after me; to the nuclear scientist who opened his karate school, to his young wife and model, who fed me caviar and blinis, when they had nothing themselves; and, of course, to Pasha the giant hairless poodle. Together, they helped me through that terrible week, to come home safely, to my family.

www.ingramcontent.com/pod-product-compliance
Lightning Source LLC
Chambersburg PA
CBHW030634260626
47157CB00007B/2330